Wolfpack

by
Matthew Clarke Lenton

PublishAmerica
Baltimore

First printing

ISBN: 1-4137-1450-1
PUBLISHED BY PUBLISHAMERICA, LLLP
www.publishamerica.com
Baltimore

Printed in the United States of America

Acknowledgements

To Louise Feary, my best friend. This book is yours; you did the real
work, and you never stopped believing.
Thank you.

Prologue – The Omen

Restlessly he turned once again, throwing his sweat-soaked sheets from the bed. Quickly his breathing came in harsh laboured sobs, his massive chest rose and fell, in time to the rhythmic beating of a tormented dance, a macabre ballet now playing through his frenzied mind. Beads of sweat poured from his skin as the fever burnt uncontrollably, a demonic fire that raged like an inferno within. He began to shake, his limbs uncontrollable, his hands balled into taloned claws that tore frantically at soaking bed sheets. Inside his subconscious mind, Magnus Vandersar found himself lost in a world he had never seen before, a dark desolate pit, a vision of hell itself. Alone, he stood in an expanse of dark wasteland, the ground blackened and unfertile, the sky a dirty and dark mass of clouds that cast impenetrable shadows that harboured a fear he dare not know.

In front of him he saw a hill, reaching up into the clouded murky sky. Movement caught his eye, a dark shadow that seemed to appear from the sky itself, almost an apparition of darkness. Magnus watched as a figure emerged from the gloom, moving with speed, its dark form hidden against the black landscape. It came closer, still unrecognisable in a dirty half light that hid shadows. Magnus strained his eyes, his senses suddenly alive, adrenaline coursing through him like a pulsing living force. With sharpened senses, he saw the shape closing the range at breathtaking speed, a predator that hunted the shadows, stalking him with eyes that burned like the fires of hell. Like an icy hand, a deathly cold wind swept the land, reaching into him, curling its long searching fingers around his heart, closing like a vice.

Magnus felt fear taking its cruel hold, washing through him like a wave. Again he strained his eyes through the shadows. The predatory shape was now at the foot of the hill, moving swiftly forwards, unstoppable, unyielding in its pursuit, heading onwards like a living shadow, a dark entity. Magnus began to back away, desperately searching for a way, a chance to escape the advancing shadow. From up ahead he heard the unmistakable sound of heavy panting, a menacing low sound that sent a deep primal fear within his very soul. With hearing heightened by absolute fear, he tracked the shadow as it closed him down.

Suddenly out of the gloom he saw the eyes of the beast, bright red as if fuelled by hate, burning the fires of hell. Magnus began to back away, never taking his eyes from the demonic shadow that now had his position, that now hunted him like a frightened prey, lost and alone in a world of darkness. Madly he began to back away, but his feet frozen with fear, refused to obey. Clumsily he began to fall, landing on his back with a heavy thud. In an instant the shadow was on him, bursting out of the gloom a picture of pure evil. Magnus froze with fear. He closed his eyes instinctively knowing the thing that stalked him was an incarnate of death itself. A massive roar washed over him, and the foul stench of something evil, something long dead, decaying and lifeless assaulted him. A wave of deep nausea began to spread through the pit of his stomach, growing in intensity as he fought to contain it.

Great waves of pain began to grip him. He thrashed madly, his left arm knocking his bedside table over. It crashed loudly to the carpeted floor, spilling its contents carelessly. His back arched as a convulsion shook him,. Spittle sprayed from his mouth through a deathly smile, lips drawn back over teeth that bit frantically at thin air.

"Please, please" he moaned, as a fresh wave of agony swept through him.

"P-L-E-A-S-E, N-O!" He let out a long, low scream that pierced the silence of the cold night. In the furthest corners of his conscious mind, Magnus Vandersar begged for release, prayed for an end to a turmoil that tore his soul apart, a battle that raged, a conflict he neither understood or knew how to survive.

Silence fell. Only the cold echo of a biting wind caught his ears. Magnus wondered if he was dead. He began to open his eyes, no longer afraid. Instantly he recoiled, eyes wide again with terror. Standing over him, a huge dark menacing shape loomed, fiery red eyes, massive jaws brimming with lethal teeth. He blinked hard, praying this vision would disappear, like a nightmare he longed to escape. The foul smell of rank decaying breath reached him, and he knew the nightmare remained. Towering over him, a wolf of mythical proportions fixed him with a terrifying gaze. A long wet tongue hung lazily over wicked teeth, that glinted even in the darkening half light. Magnus didn't move, he merely waited for death. His heart beat heavily, like a bass drum that reverberated through his body. Intently the wolf regarded him, like a super predator, now toying with its beaten prey. Those eyes, forged from something Magnus didn't care to imagine, watched him, studied him, mocked him.

"What do you want?" Magnus laughed, unable to believe he had just asked the wolf a question.

"You going to eat me? Eat me then, you hairy bastard. Come on!" he screamed loudly, bringing his face up to those massive deadly jaws. Gently the wolf brought his head down, and with a delicate grip, clamped its huge teeth onto his left arm. He expected to feel a blinding pain as his arm shattered under the impact of teeth capable of unimaginable carnage. Instead he felt only a tender pressure, as the massive beast began to back away, pulling him along.

"What the fuck?" Magnus began to scramble to his feet, sliding on the muddy ground as the wolf relentlessly pulled him along.

"You want me to follow you?" he said, staggering wildly. Suddenly, as if the creature had understood, it released his arm. Instinctively Magnus rubbed it, sure there had to be some terrible injury. To his surprise, and deep relief he found only a wet patch, coated in warm saliva. The wolf slowly began to trot away, looking back at him, as if beckoning him to follow. Magnus followed, unsure of what lay ahead, but then he realised that if the wolf had wanted to harm him, he would have been dead already.

"Where are we going?" he said, as he caught up. The wolf threw him a quick glance, before continuing on, across blackened earth, under a dark evil sky.

They had walked for hours, across a great distance, through a landscape Magnus had never seen before. The blackened fields gave way to occasional clumps of trees, unlike anything he had ever seen. Huge dark twisted forms, their branches deformed like mutated limbs, growing obscenely from terrifying angles. The wolf, still leading the way, avoided the trees carefully, always giving them a wide berth, its bright red eyes scanning intently as they passed. As they walked, the wooded areas grew thicker, at times only leaving a narrow pass between. Magnus saw that the wolf slowed almost to a crawl, watching the shadows, its hackles rising at the merest hint of movement. Suddenly the wolf stopped, its body taught like a spring. A long low growl escaped between jaws now displaying a fearsome grin.

"Easy, doggy, easy now." Magnus knelt down, stroking the wolf gently, rubbing his hand through silken fur reassuringly. He carefully scanned the trees on either side, desperately trying to locate the source of the wolf's concern. There, to his left he saw the faintest movement. Again the wolf let out a growl, slightly louder this time, carrying a message of clear and unmistakable intent. Magnus saw it again, a shadow moving through the trees. Now the wolf growled heavily, its massive body readying itself to attack. Magnus pitied whatever it was that hid behind those trees, and yet, a cold unease rippled through him, an odd forbidding feeling he couldn't explain. Through the darkness of the twisted mutilated forest, a figure began to emerge. The cold feeling intensified as Magnus began to make out the form of a man, cloaked from head to foot in a dark shroud, the face hidden beneath a hood. Now the wolf began to inch forward, lowering itself, head slung low, its massive teeth exposed by lips drawn back into a nightmarish smile.

"Easy," he whispered as the wolf moved towards the hooded figure. From the trees more cloaked forms began to appear, emerging from the shadows like haunting spectres. Then terror began to race through him, as one by one the figures began to remove their hoods. Eyes that burnt the fire of hell itself pierced the darkness. Magnus began to tremble as fear suddenly began to overwhelm him. The wolf had now stopped in its tracks, still slung low to the ground, but as if suddenly sensing the fear itself. The wolf began to back away, as more forms appeared from the shadows. Magnus looked on with fascinated terror as from beneath their cloaks, each figure produced a wicked curved dagger, the deadly sharp blades clearly visible to Magnus. They began to approach, like a huge all consuming shadow that swept the land, devouring all before it.

"We gotta go, dog!" Magnus said urgently. The wolf sensed his fear, and began moving away, picking up speed as it went. Magnus broke into a jog, urgently trying to keep pace. He looked round, expecting to see a wicked deadly dagger bearing down on him, but to his relief he saw only the darkness and shadows surrounding the mutilated trees. The wolf growled, and Magnus picked up his pace, aware that his companion still sensed great danger.

"What the hell were they, dog?" he said. The wolf merely continued to move onwards, as if like himself, desperate to be away from the trees, and the things they harboured.

They carried on, through yet more wooded areas, past huge expanses of obscene forest. Eventually they began to encounter occasional grasslands as the trees became less and less. Magnus looked at the sky, and was sure it was getting lighter by the minute, like a new dawn that washed the darkness away. They came to a stream; its clear gentle waters meandered along over a brilliant chalk bottom. They stopped briefly, the wolf greedily drinking the clear cool water. Magnus knelt down and scooped a handful of water into his mouth. Instantly he felt invigorated. The water tasted like nothing he had ever tasted before. He took another handful, devouring it with a furious appetite. When he had finished he noticed the wolf, already halfway across the stream. He got up and began to wade across the icy cool water that numbed his sodden feet. Once they had reached the other side, Magnus saw that it was now completely light, a brilliant sunrise now bursting over the horizon, bathing the land in a beautiful warmth. Stretching out all before him he saw fields of flowers, bright flowing colours of every spectrum.

"Whoa!" he shouted, surveying the scene with wondrous amazement. The wolf ignored his pleasure, and carried on, through the endless expanse of brilliant flowers towards a giant hill that rose from the ground like a colossal fortress. Magnus followed, surveying this new world as he went. Never had he seen such beauty. In fact he wondered just where on earth he actually was. The wolf seemed keenly oblivious to the wonderment of its surroundings, electing to amble on, as if guided by a sense no human could ever understand. Only as they reached the foot of the great hill did the wolf stop. It raised its mighty head, cautiously sniffing the air. Satisfied that they were now free from any danger, the wolf led Magnus to a rocky outcrop. Huge boulders, worn smooth by the weather of time concealed the entrance to a cave, still barely visible even as they approached.

"You live here, dog?" Magnus asked, ducking as he entered the cave. Inside only a small amount of light dared penetrate and Magnus had to squint his eyes as he made his way along a low passage. Suddenly from up ahead he heard a sound, like tiny feet scurrying along.

"I think you've got rats in the house, dog," he said. The wolf began to omit a high-pitched mewling sound, an almost tender, expectant call. Out of the darkness Magnus saw a small shape appear, scurrying madly as it approached. The wolf sprang on it, tail wagging wildly as it began to lick the small fury shape.

"Whoa, you've got a baby!" Magnus grinned broadly at the sight. The tiny package of fur barked furiously, obviously overwhelmed. The wolf suddenly gripped the tiny animal by the scruff of the neck, so tender with its massive lethal jaws. The pup swung comically as the massive beast began to carry it towards Magnus. He watched in amazement as the huge animal approached, stopping in front of him with the pup still hanging from its jaws. Carefully it lowered the tiny animal, placing it gently at his feet. Unsure of what to do, he stood awkwardly scratching his head. The wolf let out a heavy bark, a deep sound that echoed around the confines of the cave. Still unsure, Magnus looked at the tiny creature, sitting helplessly at his feet. Then, an overwhelming urge took over him. He reached down and picked the fury bundle up. A warmth began to spread through him, a magical feeling he couldn't explain. The pup stared at him, its tiny eyes melting him like a thaw after a long cold winter. Something was happening, an enlightenment that he could neither identify or understand. As he held the tiny pup in his hands, raw emotion began to pour from his heart. It was the most beautiful thing he had ever experienced. The pup looked at him, as if looking for reassurance, for safety. He didn't know why, and he realised he probably never would, but from nowhere tears of joy began to roll down his face, a stream of emotion that flowed endlessly, spilling a sense of love that Magnus Vandersar had never known before.

His breathing came slowly now, an even rhythmic beat that only comes with a deep peaceful sleep. In the early hours of morning, Magnus returned to the subconscious peacefulness that he had known before the storm of the nightmare. When he woke, he would know nothing of his restlessness, except for the spilled bedside table, and the discarded sheets. He would not know that omens come through dreams, and that danger lurked in the mutilated forests of civilisation. He would not know, nor would he remember. But the omen had been written, etched on the subconscious of his very mind, an inescapable and unavoidable passage in his life that he had yet to live, a battle in a war that he had yet to fight.

Chapter One

Confession

"I can't see a fucking thing!"

"Look harder then."

"It's the fog. I can't see three fucking feet in front of me."

"Keep looking, he'll be coming." Mags was getting pissed off. Two hours now, and they hadn't seen a thing. The fog had gotten thick, and now visibility was poor. The men kept their vigil, holed up in the unit they had broken into at seven that evening. Quite a surprise Mags had thought, wall-to-wall electrical good. Some enterprising bastards had been busy little boys. Mags made a note of the wide screen televisions in the corner. He'd be having a couple of those. It's hardly likely the owners would be too upset. Mags severely doubted they'd be calling the police.

"There!" Boris whispered.

"What?"

"Over there, it's him."

"Indeed it is. Lets go say hello." Mags felt the old ritual start; the left leg started shaking, his stomach turned to ice. He was ready. The two of them crept outside, out through the door they had carefully prised open earlier. Quietly, with the movement of nocturnal predators they made their way through the fog towards their prey. Mags paused behind a parked car, gave a hand signal to Boris, and then they moved. The prey, hands in pockets, head down, was oblivious to the menace behind. He'd had a good night, very good indeed. All the coke he'd collected the day before was gone. The mugs he sold it to didn't give a fuck what he'd cut it with; as long as the stuff was white they bought it. Business was good, very good. As he walked he began to smile. Things were beginning to go his way for a change. The tap on the back jolted him back to reality, the smile faded quickly. How had he not heard anyone behind him? He turned, and his bowels froze.

"Hello, John, how's things?"

"You. You're dead!"

"Not just yet, Johnny boy, not just yet." Mags stepped forward and grabbed his coat, then pulled him forward and head butted him in the face. As he sank into a deep sleep, John thought he saw another man appear, but then he reasoned he couldn't have, because the man he saw was Boris the Blade, and he was dead too. Mags and Boris dragged the limp body across the deserted street, through the thick fog towards the waiting car. The driver had seen them coming and was already opening the boot as his two friends arrived.

"In the fucking boot." Mags ordered.

The three of them manhandled the body into the boot, desperately forcing the body into the cramped space.

"He's too big; his legs won't go in," Boris complained.

"Break the fuckers then," Mags told him. Boris stepped back, and grabbing hold of the boot lid for balance he stamped on the legs hanging out of the back of the car. The right leg snapped just below the knee, the shin bone jutting at a horrific angle through the fabric of the well worn jeans. John woke with a scream, the intense pain bringing him back to life with a start.

"Shut him up!" Mags told the driver. The quiet thickset man leant over the screaming body and delivered a huge blow to John's head. All went silent again, but the quiet thickset man carried on punching. Mags watched as John's teeth started to break off, only stopping the brutality after several more heavy blows had landed.

"Mark, enough!"

"Let me kill the cunt."

"Later. Right now we need him alive," Mags told him.

Mark threw another punch, and Mags clearly heard a bone snap, probably a cheek or an eye socket.

"Enough!"

"Cunt, I want him dead." Mags lunged forward, grabbing Mark by the throat, pushing him into the side of another car, breaking the wing mirror off as the two of them wrestled.

"Listen to me. I feel your pain. I see it; I can taste it. Not yet, my friend; soon but not yet." Mags released his grip on Mark's throat, and he saw the tears welling up in his eyes. He leant into him, pulling him close.

"Soon, very soon. Hold it together for me" he whispered. He let Mark go, never breaking eye contact.

"Hold it," He whispered again. Mark nodded, then wiped the tears from his eyes.

"We've got to move; come on," Boris said. Mags grabbed Mark's arm, and they went back to the job at hand. Boris began stamping on the remaining leg, shattering it low, above the ankle. The three of them forced the broken legs into the cramped boot space. Mags slammed the boot shut.

"Let's go!"

Mark drove, through thick fog, through deserted back streets, across town towards their destination. Pulling up at a set of traffic lights Mark noticed a car approaching from behind. As it drew nearer he thought he could see luminescent writing on the cars bonnet.

"Shit. Mags, police," he shouted.

"Be normal," came the nonchalant reply.

"We don't need this," Mark added, panic audible in his voice.

Boris, apparently disinterested in the back, leant forward and brought his mouth level with Mark's ear.

"Calm down; be normal."

Mark thought he sensed a slight air of menace in that delivery. As the lights turned to green, he pulled away and quickly became normal. At the next intersection Mark turned off, taking the turning marked industrial area, whilst the following police car carried on by.

"You worry too much, boy," Boris commented. Mark threw him a look in the rear view mirror. Boris returned the stare. There was no joy behind those eyes. For a brief moment, Mark pitied the poor bastard in the boot, because there was no joy in any of their eyes tonight. Mags shifted forward from his position in the back. "How long?"

"Two minutes, boss," Mark told him. Mags pulled out his mobile, punched a key and spoke.

"On our way." He put the phone back into his jacket pocket, reached down to his belt and pulled out a pistol.

"What sort is it, boss?" Mark asked, craning his neck for a better look.

"It's a gun, Mark. It fires bullets and kills people. Now turn round and look at the fucking road." Mags looked at Boris, smiling. Boris shared the moment, then returned to inspecting his own weapon, checking the chamber, making sure it was ready for action. He flipped on the safety, tucked it back into his belt and decided it was. Mark pointed the car through streets lined with industrial units, turning into a side street, past an electrical wholesaler's, turning once again by a body paint shop, and finally pulling up outside a large drab looking building, the windows long boarded up. On the wall just above the single grey painted door was a sign. It read "Powerhouse Gym. Weightlifting, Powerlifting & Bodybuilding". The grey door, long in need of a paint job, swung open. A man appeared, nearly as wide as the door frame. In one hand he held a coffee cup, in the other he held a machete.

"Fucking hell. Where'd you get that motor?" he asked, walking towards the car. Climbing out, Mags threw him a frosty look.

"I bought it you thick fuck. Where do you think I got it?"

"Oh, I thought you nicked it."

"We did nick it, you fucking spanner." Mags shook his head and walked round to the boot. Boris was already dragging the broken body, still sound asleep, from the cramped compartment. The man with the machete sauntered over for a better look, swallowed the last dregs of his coffee and bent down over the broken victim.

"Hello, John, lad. It's me, the mad Scotsman. You tried to kill me remember?"

"Get him inside," Mags ordered.

"Mark, dump the motor round the corner," he added.

Boris and the Scotsman began dragging the body towards the open door of the powerhouse. Two more figures emerged to help, one bald headed and hugely built, the other slimmer, and very young looking. The bald headed man grabbed hold of John's hair, helping the others pull him through the door. This was Pat, and the younger looking man was Darryl. They had stayed behind along with the mad Scotsman to prepare the powerhouse, to set up the apparatus needed.

"Pat, everything set?" Mags asked.

"All ready." Pat heard footsteps. Looking round he saw Mark returning through the gloom.

"It's done. Parked it round the corner in front of the tyre depot," he said.

"Good. Right inside." Mags, the last one in, paused briefly to look up the deserted street, first left and then right. Satisfied, he shut the door and locked it.

Inside the gym, rows of training machines and weight benches lined the dusty floor. Here and there piles of weights had been absently left after use. On the wall, pictures of muscular men fought for space with naked women. In the middle of the floor, Boris and Mark had begun tying John to a chair.

"Wake him up," Mags told them.

Boris slapped him hard. It brought no response. He slapped him again, harder this time. Still no response. The Scotsman walked over, another cup of coffee in his hand, and kicked John hard in each leg. The pain from the shattered bones brought him screaming back to life.

"My legs!" he screamed.

"Shut the fuck up," the Scotsman shouted. Mags approached, drawing the pistol from his belt.

"Hello, Mr McGinn." He spoke quietly, bending to bring his face level with John's.

"We need to talk, John."

"My legs. My legs hurt bad," John whimpered.

"Forget about your legs, John. You won't be needing them anymore."

"Help me, please. The pain…" he pleaded.

"Rot, you cunt," Mark muttered, from his position perched on an old weight bench, its vinyl covering faded and tattered through years of use.

"Stop flapping, McGinn. Let's get down to business. Two weeks ago, two weeks and one day to be precise, you and a couple of other goons pulled up outside our nightclub and fucking shot us. Explain that."

"It wasn't me, I swear."

"Oh, but it was John. Cameras picked you up, clear as day. Now, I know in the past we've had our differences, but we don't like being shot. So why?"

"I swear…"

"Don't lie you fucking cunt! It was you," Mags screamed. He grabbed McGinn by the hair, pulling his head back.

"Why?" he demanded. He suddenly released his grip, and McGinns head dropped, his chin falling heavily onto his chest.

"Why?" Mags asked again, this time his voice hushed.

"They paid me." His reply came between sobs, his chest heaving.

One by one everybody came closer, forming a tight circle around McGinn.

"Who paid you?" Darryl asked. McGinns head fell back to his chest, the sobs became uncontrolled.

"Boris, get the saw," the Scotsman said, motioning to a chainsaw laying on a tattered bench. Boris walked over, picked up the saw, felt its weight, admiring its destructive potential. Once more Mags bent down to the sobbing McGinn.

"John. John, you fucking listening? Tell us who paid you, John, or Boris here is gonna cut your fucking arms off with that saw." The sobbing subsided momentarily, as real fear took hold.

"I don't know; I swear I don't know."

"You must at least know why, you scroungy fuck." The Scotsman viciously grabbed his throat, through gritted teeth he asked again.

"Why, what for?"

"I don't know why, I swear. I can't tell you who paid me; they'll kill me."

Mags nodded at Boris. The destructive sound of the chainsaw snapped McGinn into life, straining at the rope holding his wrists to the chair. Wide eyed with terror he stared as Boris approached with the saw. Mags merely nodded again. Boris brought the chainsaw down in a sweeping arc, severing tissue and flesh, pausing only briefly to cut through the bone of McGinn's upper arm. The men all stepped back as a spray of sinew and blood shot in all directions. McGinn tried desperately to scream, but only soundless pain escaped. His eyes bulged horrifically as the terror of the situation hit him. As he passed out once more, he saw his severed arm on the floor by his feet.

Dark blood was cascading in arcs across the floor, as Mark started tying a tourniquet, tightening the strap hard.

"Tighter, Mark. Don't let the fucking prick bleed to death," Mags told him.

Boris had begun kicking McGinn's left leg, driving his heal into the gaping wound where the bone sat protruding. Pat repeated the exercise on McGinn's right leg. It was enough to rouse McGinn once more.

"Please, please no more," he cried, his eyes bulging as terror enveloped him again.

"We wanna know why, John, and who?" Pat shouted, slapping him hard across the face.

"Johnny boy, we're gonna cut your other fucking arm off. You better start talking you miserable fucking prick," Boris added, almost casually.

"I don't, I can't." He stammered the words out.

"Cut it Boris," Mags said. The saw kicked into life again, the loud petrol engine drowning out McGinn's uncontrolled crying.

"Okay, I know who it was. I'll tell you," McGinn screamed.

Boris grudgingly lowered the saw, switching the setting to the idle position. For the moment the saw and Boris waited.

"I'm listening," Mags said. McGinn tried to control his sobs, breathing hard to regain control.

"The Russians paid me. A grand, they gave me the weapon."

"The Russians?" Mags looked around the room, puzzled expressions stood out on each face.

"Why the Russians? We've never had a beef with them."

"I don't know why. Ivanko set it up; he never said why. I had to get you all, especially you Mags. He made it clear I especially had to get you."

Mags walked away, deep in thought.

"What's it about, Mags?" Pat asked him.

"I don't know. I don't fucking understand it. Every other club around has had trouble with the pricks, but we've never had fuck all off 'em. Pat, how many clubs we got, twenty?"

"And at least forty pubs too."

"That's sixty places, and we've never had a murmur off the cunts. All of a sudden they want us dead. Why?"

"Fuck knows. You think he's lying?" Pat asked.

"Look at it this way, if you had your face smashed in, both legs shattered and an arm amputated, would you give them up?"

Pat thought for a moment.

"Yeah, reckon I might."

"So would I." Walking back to McGinn, he drew a hand across his throat, and Boris happily fired the saw into life.

"I believe you, John. You've been a good boy. I'll see you in fucking hell."

The saw came down onto the top of McGinn's head, tearing skin and scalp in an instant. The skull turned to pulp under the ferocious power of the searing blade. McGinn's eyes rolled back into their sockets. His mouth hung open in a vacant chasm as the blade ripped through brain matter, spraying the room, coating the walls in grey sticky lumps. McGinn began to convulse, his broken body jerking and heaving. The saw continued on its relentless passage, pulverising McGinn's brain. The muscles in Boris's forearms strained and stood out like steel cords as he ploughed the blade down with all his strength. His face a picture of maniacal frenzy, matched only by his hate of the man he was now killing.

"Enough, Boris, he's gone," Darryl said disgustedly. Boris lifted the saw, letting the blade spew its debris into the air. Finally he pressed the off switch, and the mechanical killer slowed, before dying completely.

Mags stood over McGinn's ruined body, the head blown apart, now unrecognisable as human. The sight of such carnage didn't worry him. The implications of McGinn's confession had. Deeply. The Scotsman and Mark had already begun untying McGinn from the chair. Darryl and Pat began laying sheets on the dusty gym floor. Boris cranked the saw into life again, before walking to the body now being laid on the sheets. Quickly and with dedicated skill he began dismembering McGinn's corpse, first cutting off the legs, then the remaining arm, and finally the shattered head. Pat began wrapping the remains, fighting hard to quell the nausea mounting inside his stomach. Mags sat alone on a bench, surveying the carnage, his mind numb. Mark walked over and sat down next to him. The bench creaked at the added strain.

"Guv, what now?" Mags looked up, but he didn't reply until he had the attention of everyone in the room.

"Well, I'd say we're at war. Wouldn't you?" Each man gave his answer via a simple nod, a small yet significant gesture. Mags stood up.

"Put the kettle on, Marky; we've got a lot to talk about."

Chapter Two

Two weeks and one day earlier

"You like that, you fucking bitch?"

"Keep going, baby, keep going."

Mags began pushing himself harder, driving his body into her, forcing her further across his desk. His rhythm increased. He gripped her harder, thrusting his entire body into her. Her breathing became laboured as she tightened her grip on the desk, her eyes half closed, her face a picture of ecstasy.

"Oh fuck, baby! Here I come, here it comes, baby," he screamed. Mags felt himself tighten. His body tensed as he released into her. Gripping her hair he slammed himself harder and harder until finally he collapsed onto her, exhausted. Breathing heavily, he pushed himself off her, wiping the beads of sweat that ran down his face. He stood over her for a moment, surveying the beauty stretched out across his desk.

"You're a dirty little slut," he told her, as a huge grin cracked his face.

"Only for you, lover; you know that," she replied, grinning as she reached for her bag.

"You better be, baby."

"Cigarette?" she offered.

"Nah, got work to do."

"Five minutes with me; come on," she pleaded.

"No. Get dressed and fuck off. I've got work to do."

"Well thanks for the shag, Penny; get dressed and fuck off why don't you!"

she said, reaching for her clothes. Mags sensed the resentment in her voice, dismissed it and carried on fastening his trousers.

"You know, you're such an arsehole sometimes, Mags."

"Put it in writing; I'll read it later," he offered, buttoning his shirt. Penny began fixing her dress, forcing her feet into her shoes at the same time. Mags eyed her up and down, agreeing with himself once again that indeed she was a gorgeous woman; just a pity she was married. He'd been banging her on and off for about four years, since before she married Ray, her policeman husband. Mags didn't blame her. Ray was the safe option. Mr reliable, he brought home a good pay cheque and provided for Penny and their kid, Jake. Straightening his jacket, he allowed himself another look at Penny, and just for a moment he felt a pang of jealousy. Maybe another time and place, he'd have kept Penny to himself. Still he reasoned, things had worked out alright,. Ray was in his pocket; he worked for Mags and the team. Ray was a boring fucker, but he'd done the lads some serious favours, and he'd lost some useful evidence along the way. The fact that Mags or any of his team had never done any time was Mags knew, down to Ray. He checked his hair in the mirror, and thought things weren't that bad at all. Ray kept the law sweet, Mags banged his wife. Everybody got a piece of the action. Mags took one last look in the mirror, decided he didn't look like he'd just pumped his bit on the side and headed for the door. Penny stepped between him and the door, squeezing her ample breast into his face.

"What, no goodbye even?" she demanded.

"Goodbye."

"Kiss me, Mags; don't be such a bastard." He grabbed her hair, pulled her mouth to his and probed her with his tongue. Her response once again drove a slight pang of jealousy through his heart. He pulled away, cupping her head in his hands. He took a second to bathe his eyes with her magical beauty.

"Tell Ray I need to speak. Organise a sit down," he told her.

"He'll know I've been here then."

"Tell him I rang. Sort it out for me." He pulled her forward again, tasting her lips.

"Right, now fuck off, you dirty little cow." Already he was pushing her out of the door, the music from the clubs gigantic speakers now making words meaningless. She touched his hand and started to leave, and he watched her as she descended the stairs, and chided himself for ogling her arse. Old habits died hard. At the bottom of the stairs she stopped and turned to give him a last lingering look, and then she was gone. Mags went back into his office, straight to the cabinet in the corner and opened it. The bottle of Jack Daniels, half empty, beckoned him for the umpteenth time that night. He necked another ample measure, savouring the warmth as it spread through him. He went to replace the bottle, but took another swig. Lately it had been his only solace. Sleep wouldn't come without it, and when it did, the dreams haunted him until the moment he woke. He looked up at a dusty picture on the wall, walked over and took it down. With his fingers he wiped the dust from the glass. The original team, Pat and Darryl, Boris, Mark, Mags, the Scotsman, and there in the middle Andy. Mags closed his eyes, remembering the good times they'd all enjoyed. There were too many to even begin to count. His eyes snapped open, the thought of that night stabbing his brain, like a knife. Reaching for the Jack again, he allowed himself to suffer the pain once more. Periodically he did this to himself, to sharpen his hatred, to heighten his contempt for those who'd helped in Andy's misery.

Andy had always been the life of the team, the natural leader. He fucked more women that was humanly possible. The man was a walking erection. Mags and Andy had started working the doors almost at the same time, a few days apart back in 1992. Straight away they'd clicked. Andy's laughter had been infectious, and it was the perfect anecdote for Mags, who had always been overly serious. Together they had set up the business, Guardian Leisure. At first there had been only the two of them, looking after one shitty pub in the less savoury area of Cambridge. Very quickly their reputation had grown. Within a year they employed thirty men, and ran fifteen pubs, and a nightclub. Mags slammed the Jack again, his mind running back to those early times. They had been good, the best of his life. Together they had recruited the best there was. At times they had gone out and poached doormen, selecting them from reputation and personal observation. Pat had been the first on their shopping list. A legend at twenty, with an awesome knockout punch. As the years had gone by, Mags had elevated him to his top man, his most loyal soldier. The selection had produced the best talent on offer, producing an awesome front line that had quickly established itself as the front runner for the best security company in the country. Admittedly the tactics used at times had been less than legal, the fact was the job had always been done. If a club had a problem, Guardian Leisure were brought in. The main team went in at first, then when the problems were dealt with a full time garrison of the company's' men were put in to run the place. It was this approach that earned the team its name, the Wolfpack. With the name came a reputation that few were willing to cross.

If they did, retribution was both swift, and brutal. The police had been all over them in the beginning, but soon even they'd realised that what the Wolfpack was doing might just save them a task, and even their lives. Mags pulled out a cigarette, lit it and took a long deep tug, reminding himself that he was meant to be quitting. He hung the picture back on the wall, allowing himself a smile as he thought about those early days. Raising the bottle he took another hard swig, and the warmth overtook him again. Those days would be hard to beat he thought, especially now Andy was gone. Gone. The word cut through him like an icy chill. Andy had been Mags' hero in so many ways, but the one vice they never shared had been Andy's fondness for drugs. Mags never questioned it. Andy was always his own man, and what he did was his choice. Besides, Andy never let it come in the way of business. If he had a problem he hid it well. Draining the remains of the bottle, Mags again relived the day that had haunted him ever since.

The police had woken him at two in the morning, banging on his door solidly for a good two minutes before finally Mags made his way drunkenly down the stairs. He'd opened the door, revolver hidden, to be greeted by two young officers. Mags knew them both well. By the time they had finished breaking the news Mags had been on his knees, revolver in hand, sobbing. When they had taken him to identify the body, he'd broken completely. It took five of them to hold him that night, before locking him in a cell where he'd spent the next five hours attacking the walls, driving himself relentlessly until his blood smeared every surface. Andy had been to a party, a regular occurrence for him. Someone had given him a hot dose. Mags knew Andy took a lot of coke, but he never had an idea he was into heroin. It had killed him. By the time anyone had realised Andy was in trouble, it was too late. He died in the back of an ambulance, an undignified death.

For a long time, Mags had been consumed with rage, hate and pain. He had pulled out all the stops to find the person who'd given Andy the dose. He'd paid Ray a fortune to find those responsible. When Ray delivered, Mags and the other members of the Wolfpack had mercilessly tortured them. The dealer, an eighteen-year-old girl called Sandy Martin, and her boyfriend, an addict himself had held out for twelve hours before finally confessing. Even after watching her boyfriend have his head smashed apart with hammers, Sandy Martin denied everything. Only when they'd taken out her right eye with a drill had she talked. Mags had almost admired her. Bravery and loyalty were the traits he so much loved in his own people. Before she'd blacked out and death had given her welcome relief, Sandy Martin had told him something that had eaten at him like a cancer ever since.

"Sandy, talk to me honey. Talk, or Mark is going to stick the drill in your other fucking eye. Come on, baby, tell me what I want to hear."

"Police," she had whispered.

"Police? What do you mean, Sandy?"

"Police…paid us." Then she'd started to drift away. Mags fought to keep her awake.

"Come on, Sandy, stay awake for me, honey," he had said, shaking her. She never regained her consciousness, and her confession went with her, to the grave.

Mags had tried to understand what Sandy Martin had meant. Police? They'd personally delivered both Sandy and her boyfriend to them, knowing full well what the outcome would be. Despite his love for Andy, Mags had always been very anti-drugs. Now he loathed both dealers and takers with a passion. Once he'd been tipped off that one of his men had been dealing in a club across town. He put Boris in there to keep an eye on things, and when Boris had witnessed several deals made, the man had sealed his own fate. The next morning, Alex Stanyard a thirty-five-year-old doorman was reported missing by his wife. The police, on investigation discovered Alex had been having affairs with a least four separate women, so therefore were not too concerned because an adulterous, suspected dealer hadn't come home to his wife. Alex Stanyard has never been seen again. Mags made it policy absolute; Guardian Leisure was the security company to rely on if an establishment had a drug situation. Some very big toes were stepped on by Mags' people. Most accepted the situation and moved on to a more permissible place of trade. One of two well-organised firms didn't take the hint so well.

The O'Donnell's had been a major player in organised crime in and around the Cambridge area for twenty years. A large Irish family whose roots lay in Dublin, Patrick O'Donnell had moved to England during the sixties to work in the booming construction industry. Patrick worked hard to bring up a young family, until his premature death aged fifty from a heart attack. Patrick O'Donnell was, and still is fondly remembered as a kind generous hard-working man who lived for his family. Despite such an early death, Patrick left a legacy, Seamus and Reardon. The two sons he'd adored and invested so much time in, had repaid their father by being expelled from every school they'd attended. By the time Seamus had reached seventeen, he had already earned a reputation as a reliable enforcer. Recruited by another local firm, the rising prospect moved up the underworld ladder at a swift pace. By age twenty Seamus had been implicated on at lease a dozen murders, including that of his cousin, Michael who had been impertinent enough to have crossed Seamus' employer, Leonard Grossman whose waste management consultancy company was a front for a whole list of illegal operations, ranging from prostitution to heroin distribution. Michael O'Donnell had decided to muscle in on the very lucrative and increasing heroin trade. His dismembered remains were found by a dog walker eight weeks after he was initially reported missing. His case remains open, although Seamus O'Donnell has always been the prime suspect. Lack of evidence meant he never stood trial, but the word was out on Seamus; he wasn't a man to fuck around with. Family ties meant nothing when it came down to business.

Reardon O'Donnell always lived in his brother's shadow. Two years younger, he lacked Seamus's penchant for violence. On his brothers recommendation, Leonard Grossman took Reardon on board, noticing his talent for management. Grossman methodically taught Reardon the tricks of the waste management business. Within two years Reardon knew it all, money laundering, tax evasion, and everything else needed to use a legitimate business as a front for several illegitimate businesses. Content that his brother had honed his skills to a satisfactory level, Seamus O'Donnell walked into his employer's office one evening to deliver some cash he had just picked up. While he was there Seamus stabbed Leonard Grossman twenty times. Leonard's whereabouts still remain unsolved.

Reardon and Seamus O'Donnell had arrived. The word was out. Cambridge had some real gangsters. The O'Donnell organisation grew like a momentous cancer, The heroin trade began to explode out of proportion. That's the way it remained, unchallenged and unchecked for nearly ten years. Nobody muscled in on O'Donnell territory and told the tale. That is, until a new firm had risen, seemingly from nothing to become very powerful. Seamus paid little, in fact no attention. This new firm he kept hearing about, they were a security company. They neither threatened his drug profits or his many other interests. Then in the summer of 1999, the two firms crossed paths. Under the new orders of their employer, the three doormen working the Red Lion in Cambridge city centre administered a severe kicking to a dealer they had caught, for the third time in as many weeks. The dealer was Alan Randal, an O'Donnell drug outlet.

"They kicked the fuck out of me, Seamus; look at me."

"Didn't you tell them who you were with?" Seamus demanded, pacing back and forth in his office.

"They said they didn't give a fuck," Randal whined.

"What!?" Seamus picked up the paperweight holding down a pile of invoices and threw it at Randal. The glass ball missed Randal's head by an inch, disintegrating against the wall behind him, showering his hair with glass.

"Cunts. Who the fuck do they think they are?"

"They seemed serious, Seamus," offered Randal, nervously awaiting the next flying object. Seamus moved across the room with venomous speed. Seizing Randal by the head, he forced his thumbs into Randal's eye sockets.

"What? You little fuck. Am I not serious enough for your liking?" Randal screamed, like a girl Seamus noted. Dropping the sobbing Randal, Seamus went to his desk. He picked up the telephone and after a brief moment barked his next move.

"Reardon. Get the fuck over here now. Bring some of the boys. And Reardon, come heavy." He hung up, and walked over to the now cowering Randal. Seamus began kicking the helpless Randal, and long after his doomed victim had lost consciousness Seamus began stamping on his head. Only when Randal's brain matter began spraying the walls of his office did Seamus stop. He surveyed his carnage, breathing heavily from the exertion. Seamus O'Donnell noticed how dirty the place was, making a note in his mind to sack the cleaner first thing tomorrow.

Reardon swung the Lexus into the car park, into a bay marked "Directors Parking". The idea pleased him. After all how many men his age could call themselves a company director? He got out, flanked by four men, all heavy set except for a small wiry individual who carried a large holdall. The men entered the foyer of O'Donnell Waste Management, along a narrow corridor to a door marked 'Private'. Reardon half opened the door, and stopped.

"What the fuck?" he muttered, quickly stepping back into the corridor. The sight of Alan Randal, or what he thought used to be Alan Randal greeted him.

"Seamus, Seamus," he called.

"What?" Seamus replied, pulling the door open.

"Everything alright?"

"Positively smashing, Reardon. There's a body on my office floor. What the fuck do you think?"

"Who did it; who done that to Alan?" Reardon asked the question while trying to determine whether in fact the remains at his feet were actually those of Alan Randal. Reardon had never seen a face kicked in so badly.

"I did, Reardon. I did," Seamus told him, regarding his brother with eyes as cold as steel.

An hour later the Lexus pulled to a halt at the rear of the Red Lion, a bustling pub situated in the Parkside area of the city. It was now eleven thirty, and the last stray drinkers were filing out into the cold night. Seamus waited ten more minutes, making sure the place was empty, save for the bar staff and the doormen. "Okay, let's go," he said opening the passenger side door. Reardon and the four men packed tightly into the back of the Lexus followed. The small wiry figure went to the cars boot. He retrieved a large holdall, a dusty worn green canvas bag. The holdall held an array of shotguns. One of the weapons, sawn off close to the butt, was handed to Seamus. He fingered the weapon almost lovingly, admiring the cold brutal contours. Seamus noticed with pleasure that he had the beginning of an erection. The five men entered the pubs rear door, quietly milling past the toilets until they came to the main lounge. Two men sat at the bar, both wearing black jackets with an embroidered logo across the back. Seamus mouthed the words 'Guardian Leisure', and quickened his pace. One of the doormen, Andrew Fennel noticed out of the corner of his eye a figure approaching.

"Sorry, lads, we're closed," he said swivelling in his seat. His eyes widened as he saw the sawn off barrels levelled at him. Seamus smiled.

"Goodnight, cunt!" he said, and squeezed the trigger. Andrew Fennel momentarily saw the flash, and then his world became dark forever. The blast removed his head completely from the bottom jaw upwards. The optics hanging from the wall behind him exploded under a hail of Fennels fragmented skull and brain. His partner that night, James Mailer dropped to the floor. He began to crawl along the bar towards the fire exit twenty feet away. Reardon O'Donnell blocked his path. James Mailer raised his head and looked up at the figure before him. It was the last image he would ever see. The force of the shotguns lethal power imploded Mailer's head like a ripe melon. To underline their message, and because Seamus O'Donnell now had a full aching erection, the O'Donnell crew shot and killed both the barmaids, and the publican.

The news reached Mags less than thirty minutes later. He had put the phone down, numb with disbelief. After downing a full quarter of a bottle of Napoleon brandy, Mags had summoned his most senior guard, the Wolfpack. The hastily arranged meeting at Mags' house had been a sombre affair. Each man lost for words, disbelieving. The arrival of Ray Callard, detective inspector, and an unofficial employee of Guardian Leisure confirmed what every man present had been unable, or unwilling to accept.

"Mags, I'm sorry, I really am."

"Fucking save it, Ray. I pay you to prevent this type of thing happening, unless you'd forgotten?"

"Mags, I had no idea those crazy fucking Irish bastards would go this far," Ray pleaded.

"Well, Ray, let me make this very fucking clear to you. I'm going to sort this little matter out and you Ray, are going to make sure our arses are covered. You clear on that Ray?" Mags put his face only inches from Ray's, noticing beads of perspiration beginning to form. "You understand what I'm saying, Ray?"

"It would make my job easy if there were no bodies, Mags, a lot easier." Mags pushed his face closer still.

"I'll see what I can do, Ray. Now leave us."

"Yeah, okay I understand.," he said nervously. He turned to leave, but Boris blocked his path.

"As long as you do, Ray," Boris warned. Ray saw the menacing intent in those eyes. He fully understood. Mags waited until Ray Callard had left before speaking. True, Ray had done them some real favours, unbelievable at times, but every man in the room shared Mags' deep loathing of the police, and besides Ray didn't need to know what was going to happen next.

"Lets bury the fuckers," Mags said, addressing his men, making eye contact with each man in turn. What he saw told him he didn't need to persuade them, not one bit.

Seamus sat on the toilet, stroking his erection, rhythmically pulling himself to the point of ecstasy. His breathing came harder; he fought to quieten himself knowing Reardon and his crew were sitting only yards away, drinking in his office. With eyes half closed, his intensity heightened as he drew to a shattering climax. Seamus gasped, his back arched as the excitement of the evening escaped him. Composing himself, Seamus washed his hands, wiped the sweat from his face before returning to the celebrations in his office. He should have noticed the silence as he walked down the corridor, but flushed from his own personal celebration only seconds before. Seamus entered his office, blissfully unaware that he was about to step straight into the gates of his own personal hell. Unable to digest exactly what he was seeing, Seamus stood, transfixed in the doorway. His brain numb with shock, incapable of taking in the scene. Reardon and his four associates, each man with his throat cut from ear to ear. Seamus looked at the floor, the blood ran in rivers at his feet. He made another mental note to do something about the cleaner; this wouldn't do. The ice pick hit him square in the back of his head, the force sending the pointed blade onwards exploding like a horn through his frontal lobe. Seamus O'Donnell died an instant later, standing in the doorway of his office, surveying the rivers of blood that snaked around his expensive Italian shoes. By dawn the next morning, O'Donnell Waste Management had burnt to the ground, the result of an electrical fire, according to the police reports. Just outside Cambridge, two lovers parked in a lay-by deep into some woods saw a group of men returning to their cars, carrying shovels and caked in mud. The two lovers paid little attention, preferring to continue their lovemaking undisturbed.

The knock woke him from his thoughts, the memory lost for the moment.

"Guv, you alright?" The door swung open. Darryl came in, displaying that huge smile he always seemed to wear. Still only twenty-three, Mags had recruited him when he was only seventeen. Darryl Hanlon had made an immediate impact on Mags. Driving home from work one night Mags saw a group of men surrounding a lone figure outside a takeaway. Mags had swung the car over to take a closer look. The odds had seemed way over the top to him, and bullies had always pissed him off. By the time Mags had got out of his car, four of the six attacking men were littered across the pavement. Two seconds later the fifth was freefalling through the kebab shop window. The sixth obviously an adept sprinter, ran for his life. Mags had seen, and worked with many martial arts experts in his time, but this kid standing before him would have beaten any one of them. And Mags had remembered, this good-looking kid before him was just that, a kid.

"Need a lift, mate?" Mags had asked.

Spinning round to face him, Darryl Hanlon met the gaze of this stranger who had seemingly come from nowhere.

"Who the fuck are you?"

"Me? I'm nobody. But you look to me like somebody who could do with a way out of here."

Darryl began to walk away, then stopped, hearing approaching sirens.

"Get in," Mags said. Darryl ran to the passenger side door, ripped it open and threw himself in as Mags started to accelerate away. Darryl snapped his seatbelt on, never taking his eyes off of the mysterious driver.

"Listen mate, you're not gay are you?" he'd asked. Mags had cracked up, almost losing control of the car.

"No, don't worry, kid," Mags replied between bouts of laughter. Still, the kid never took his eyes off of him.

"Guv, you alright?" Darryl asked again.

"Yeah, fine mate. What's up?"

"Dave Stevens just called in from Chicago's. Looks like they got some trouble brewing. He's asked for some back-up."

"What, again? Fucking place is more trouble than it's worth. Alright, run the van round. We'll shoot over there." Darryl was already on his way down the stairs, Mags a second behind him. The stairs led to the main foyer of the White Rooms, the club Mags and Andy had brought together. It was the headquarters of Guardian Leisure, and a place where the team generally hung out. In the event of any real trouble at any of the clubs and pubs they ran, Mags and the team could respond as back-up in minutes. Mags reached the foyer as Mark began handing out the vests. The Kevlar body armour had been an investment Mags had always believed in, and made it policy that every one of his employees wore one every time they went on duty. Pat was still fastening the straps on his vest as he went out the door. Mark and the Scotsman were already in the van. Mags, Boris and Darryl, along with Dave Foxton, a regular doorman at the White Room. He was also the van driver.

No one saw the white escort approaching slowly along Mill Road. Each man too preoccupied with the unfolding events at Chicago's. They had been there only a week earlier, and had ended up head to head with thirty squaddies from the nearby barracks. The outcome had been violent. Mags was the last to enter the van. He turned to close the sliding side door from the inside, and as he did he saw the escort slow across the street, the tinted windows hiding its occupants, and their intentions. Dave Foxton casually hit the ignition and threw the van into gear. Mags took another glance across the street, the concern registered in his eyes. Boris saw it and immediately turned to the source.

"Down!" Mags screamed, diving into the aisle, dragging Boris by the arm.

Across the road the gunman opened fire. From the passenger window the uzi jerked into life, spent casings falling to the ground like deadly rain. The first rounds slammed into the van, piercing the panelling like paper. Mark took three slugs in the chest. The impact took him through the passenger side window, leaving him sprawled across the pavement gasping for breath. Dave Foxton tried to pull the van away. He'd already made it twenty yards when the first of two rounds caught him in the right shoulder. The projectile cut upwards removing his collar bone, and blowing his throat apart. The second round impacted through his right temple, spreading the entire right side of his head across the vans interior.

Mags scrambled for the side door, opened it and began pulling Boris out with him. Darryl and Pat followed, and the four of them began a desperate dash for the safety of the White Rooms. The escort swung forward, mounting the pavement. The gunman opened fire once more. A wave of bullets cutting each man down at chest height. Mags was thrown through the foyer doors, landing unceremoniously at the feet of two young girls who were in the process of leaving the club. A hail of death cut them both nearly in half, painting the walls with blood and intestine. The uzi fell silent, its death dance still. On the pavement, unmoving lay the bodies of four senior ranking members of Guardian Leisure. In the blood-splattered van lay the fifth. Stretched out in the gore laden foyer of the White Rooms was its highest ranking member, Magnus Vandersar. The gunman allowed himself a smile, after all he'd just single-handedly killed the legendary Wolfpack.

Chapter Three

Aftermath

"Penny, it's me, Mags."

"Hi, you okay?"

"I'm fine. Is Ray there?"

"He's still at work. What happened? Why haven't you rung? I thought you were dead." Penny began to cry.

"Penny, I'm okay. Don't cry, please," Mags told her, trying to be sympathetic.

"You could have called, Mags," she scolded, the tears flowing.

"Look, we'll talk; I promise. I need to speak to Ray, and soon."

Penny wiped her eyes, trying to regain her composure. When she spoke the emotion returned.

"I love you, Mags," she blurted. The words cut into Mags' heart like a cold knife. He wasn't good at loving, and he wasn't good on being loved.

"I know, Pen, I know."

"What shall I tell Ray?" she asked, her voice still cracking with raw emotion.

"White Rooms, ten o'clock."

"Okay, Mags, I'll tell him." He went to hang up, stopped and spoke once more.

"Pen, I'm okay. Don't worry."

"But I do, Mags," she replied, but Mags had already hung up.

The Jaguar XK8 cruised to a halt outside the White Rooms. A queue at least two hundred strong stretched along Mill Road. Ray locked the car and hurried to the front of the queue, ignoring the complaints thrown his way.

"Hey, big shot, get in line." A blonde haired youth stepped in his way. Ray produced his warrant card and thrust it into his face.

"How about I turn your pockets out fuck features; see if I can't find anything interesting?" The youth took a step back, thought better of the offer and let Ray pass. The doorman at the front of the queue ushered Ray inside, and Ray entered the White Rooms to the chants of "pig". Mags stood at his office window, watching with interest Ray's defiant stand against the fearsome challenge of the blonde youth. Mags smiled. He knew Ray was a cowardly bastard who had always hidden behind his badge. Mags wondered how long Ray's new Jaguar would remain unscathed, and turning away from the window decided probably not very long. Ray entered the office, and Mags could see he wasn't in one of his better moods.

"Having trouble, Ray?"

"Wankers," Ray grumbled, plonking himself on the leather sofa. Mags stifled a grin. He wondered if Ray would be in a better mood if he knew how many times Penny had been naked on that very same sofa.

"So what's the news, Ray? What have you got for me?"

"Well, for all intents and purposes, Mags, nothing. I hear nothing. Nobody seems to know a thing," Ray answered, shifting uncomfortably.

"What am I paying you, Ray? Obviously too much looking at the car."

"Been promising myself that for a while." Ray shifted uncomfortably again.

"Why the fuck don't you just paint in foot high letters what a bent wank copper you are, Ray?" Mags went back to the office window.

"How many coppers of your rank can afford a motor like that?" Mags asked, staring out into the street below. When he turned, Ray was sitting looking at the floor.

"Don't fuck things up Ray; that's all I'm saying." Mags unscrewed a new bottle of Jack Daniels, and began to fill two glasses. He handed one to Ray, who greedily devoured the contents.

"Tell me Ray, why would the Russians want me dead?"

"What? They wouldn't." Ray looked up, bemused.

"That's what I thought. Apparently I was wrong." Mags poured them both another drink, and began to relay the details of McGinn's death to Ray. When he had finished, Mags waited for Ray's opinion.

"McGinn? Are you sure?" Ray asked, almost disbelieving. Mags produced a video tape; threw it onto the sofa beside Ray.

"Club camera's, clear as day."

"You never told me this, Mags. Why not?"

"We needed to fix this fucker ourselves, Ray. Trust me you couldn't pay him back like we did."

"And you believed him; I mean about the Russians?"

"Ray, he was telling the truth. We amputated the prick's arm. He couldn't have lied."

"But McGinn was a petty dealer. Hardly a top class hit man."

"Maybe. But McGinn did three years for possession, and it was my lads who caught him. That's a reason to hate us if nothing else. I just don't understand why the Russians would want us dead. I've known Sergatov for years. I can' say I like the man, but he's always stayed away from us Ray. I can't explain it." Ray got up from the sofa, went to the window. Satisfied that his car was still there, he sat down again.

"McGinn was a runner for Sergatov, but that's as far as it went," Ray said, pondering the situation.

"Fuck knows, but they've got to have it, Ray. That much I do know."

"Is that wise?" Ray asked.

"Don't take the piss, Ray. If they tried once and failed, they'll try again."

"This is mad, none of it adds up. McGinn, I mean he's hardly a reliable source, Mags. Anyway, Sergatov would never dare move against you. I don't believe it."

"Ray. We fucking dissected McGinn, bit by bit. He couldn't have lied."

"Look, Mags, hold fire for a bit. Let me take it up from here."

"No fucking way, Ray. That Russian motherfucker is going down. He wasted one of my men, a fucking good man, Ray, wife and three fucking kids."

Ray got to his feet, walked over to the half empty bottle of whisky. Pouring them a measure each, he returned to the sofa, mulling the options over in his mind.

"Mags, I've never let you down true?" he asked.

"I'll give you that much Ray. What's your fucking point?" Mags began refilling his glass.

"Give me forty eight hours. Hold firm on the Russians, and if I find out it was them, you do what you have to do."

"Why the fuck should I Ray?"

"I don't want to see you in a war for no reason, Mags. People are going to die," Ray pleaded. Mags took a sip from his glass.

"Count on it, Ray."

"Trust me, Mags. That's all I ask."

Mags drained the glass, got up and went to the window again.

"Okay, Ray, we'll do it your way. After that, people are going to die." Ray got up to leave, and Mags carried on looking down into the street.

"I'll be in touch, Mags."

"Close the door on the way out," Mags told him, never taking his eyes from the street below.

He watched Ray climb into his nice new car and sail away into the night. He knew Ray was right, but that didn't make Mags feel any better. He hated knowing Ray was right, almost as much as he hated Ray. The icy pain ran through his heart again. Penny. "I love you, Mags," she had told him. Secretly he knew he loved her, always had. He hated himself for allowing her to slip away, into a comfortable life with a devious little cunt like Ray. He pushed the thought from his mind. He simply could not allow it to cloud his vision right now. He was under attack. He'd lost a good man already, and almost lost his entire senior staff, his closest most trusted friends. Since the pain of Andy's death, he doubted whether he could take anymore. His drinking habits had gotten out of hand as it was. Mags knew he was always one step away from alcoholic oblivion; close to the edge. He went to the sofa, took off his shoes and lay down. He tried to put thoughts of revenge out of his mind for now. Ray was a prick, but he knew grudgingly, that he could be trusted. Ray would sort it out; he was sure of that. The icy pain struck his heart again as he thought of Penny, and when sleep finally came it brought darkness and relief.

The noise was shocking. Mags jolted from a deep peaceful sleep, rolled off the sofa banging his head hard on the floor.

"Bastard!" he shouted.

"Wake up, sleepy." Mags lifted his head, hung over and still groggy. Margaret the cleaning lady pushed the Hoover towards him, running over his hand. He felt like dogshit, and guessed he probably looked like it too. Margaret bent over to switch the Hoover off. The relief to Mags' head was enormous.

"Coffee?" she asked, already heading for the kitchen.

"And some aspirin," he called after her. Two minutes later Margaret returned, holding a steaming mug of black strong coffee, and a pack of aspirin. Mags devoured four tablets, before falling back onto the sofa.

At ten thirty Boris and Mark arrived. Boris took one short look at Mags, and shot him a wry grin.

"Fuck off!" Mags told him absently.

"You look like a bird I woke up with once. Only she had more of a beard," Boris quipped, heading for the kitchen.

"That don't all together surprise me, Boris," Mark cut in, slumping his huge frame down beside the still hung over Mags. Boris came in from the kitchen holding two fresh brews. Handing one to Mark he took a seat in Mags' office chair.

"Today, I am chairman of the board," he said, grinning like a child. Mags chuckled, feeling human for the first time that day.

"So what's on the agenda, Mags?" Mark asked in between slurping his coffee." Mags rose from his sofa, groaning at the pain throbbing in his temples. He walked to the window. Lifting the blind, he squinted out into the morning sunshine. The light felt like a thunderbolt in his head. He let the blind fall, relishing the relief it brought his eyes.

"I've got a job for you two. I want you both to keep an eye on the Russians. I want to know where they go, what they do & when they do it. Sergatov takes a shit. I want to know whether he enjoyed it. Understood?" Boris swivelled in Mags' chair, facing his boss.

"So we're going after them. About time."

"Not yet," Mags snapped.

"What? We know they did it, Mags. What the fuck are we waiting for?" Boris demanded. Mags turned on him, his eyes stoic.

"We'll hit them when I say. We need more proof."

"Proof! What the fuck?" Boris sat back in the chair, shaking his head in disbelief.

"Ray's checking it out. I gave him my word I'd give him forty eight hours," Mags offered, almost ashamed that Boris had questioned his commitment.

"Ray! That cheesy little cunt," Boris exploded from the chair, heading for the office door. Mags spun to stop him, anger now running through him like poison.

"Boris! Get the fuck back here."

"Sorry guv, I got a job to do, remember?" He pointed to the empty whiskey bottle Mags had discarded on the floor.

"If you want some advice, advice from a friend that is, you'll leave this shit alone, and concentrate on staying alive." With that he swung the door almost off its hinges, and stormed out. Mark got up to follow him, stopped and spoke softly.

"Don't worry, Mags, he doesn't mean anything by it."

"No, he does. And he's right."

Mark left him alone, but Mags never noticed him leaving. Magnus Vandersar was away somewhere else, battling the demons he'd been fighting for a long, long time.

Mark and Boris sat quietly in the front of the Cavalier. They'd been parked outside the Metropolis lounge for over an hour. They had followed Vasilly Sergatov, and two of his associates there. The Metropolis was one of Sergatov's strip clubs, and a major outlet for the Russian's primary business, heroin. Boris wanted to run in there and shoot everyone, from the Russian dog Sergatov, right down to the old men and fat city workers who came here every day to letch over the naked dancers. He knew he couldn't, and that made his blood boil even more. He consoled himself, knowing that when Mags snapped himself together and gave the order, he personally would blow the Russian prick's head off. He felt his blood boil again, the rage rising like a thermometer. Boris Hunter liked very few people. He hated many. Sergatov had tried to kill them all and had wasted Dave Foxton, one of the rare breed of person Boris actually liked. Fuck him, he thought. What goes around comes around. The thought soothed him slightly, and he felt his raging thermometer subsiding. For now anyway.

Boris let his mind wander off, to times long gone. He was already sorry for attacking Mags. The man was his friend. More than that, Mags was his brother. He remembered their first meeting. Boris had been twenty then, already a father. He'd left the army, his passion, because his young wife had fallen pregnant. He found himself burdened with responsibility, unemployed and barely still a kid himself. The only accommodation he and his wife Debbie could find was a tiny flat above a nightclub in the city centre. Weekends were a nightmare. Boris could do little but hang out of his bedroom window and watch the weekend circus perform. The drunks, the incessant pounding of the music, and the fights. Debbie would sit and watch the television, whilst Boris hung from his window and watched drunks punch the shit out of each other. He used to watch the doormen in battle; some impressed him, others he laughed at. It was while he was laughing at an inept performance from one of these doormen that the fighting broke off, and the embarrassed bouncer, in a vain attempt to save face issued a challenge to Boris. He ignored it. After all he had a young pregnant wife to think about. Then another challenge was thrown up at him. Standing in the shadows, Boris hadn't noticed him. The tall, well-built man stepped into the light cast by the neon sign of the club.

"Young man. Do you think you could do any better?" he asked.

"Fucking right I do," Boris had called back, defiantly.

"Well then, young man, come and show me," the tall stranger had challenged. Like most young men, Boris was ruled by testosterone, and a huge ego. He closed the window and headed for the stairs. Thirty seconds later he found himself outside the club, surrounded by six enormous doormen. The one who'd initially issued the challenge took his jacket off and prepared himself for battle.

"Come on then, you cunt!" he shouted, bearing down on Boris. The punch, a straight right hand, broke his jaw on impact. The now seriously embarrassed doorman fell like a stone. He hit the floor like a sack of shit, which is exactly what Boris thought he was. Boris tensed, the euphoria subsiding instantly. There was still five more to contend with, and he doubted his chances of making it back upstairs in one piece. He turned to face the inevitable, but all he saw was five doormen grinning. Confused, he began to relax, still wary but utterly confused. The tall stranger stepped forward, Boris noticed he was quite grey haired for a man probably only in his early thirties. He extended his hand to Boris, his face expressionless.

"My name is Magnus, and that was very impressive," he said. Warily Boris shook the hand.

"So, do you fancy the job then, or what?" Magnus asked, still expressionless. Boris thought for a second, and figured he might fancy the job. Yes he would indeed. An ambulance casually took the still comatose doorman away, like bin men tossing sacks of shit into a wagon. Boris started work that night, and within six months his reputation as a ruthless opponent and loyal brother in arms had elevated him from doorman to a fully-fledged member of Cambridgeshire's elite and mythical mercenaries, the Wolfpack.

Now sitting outside the Metropolis lounge, he regretted his outburst earlier. He knew Mags never really recovered from Andy's death. It had hit them all, but Mags never really got over it. Boris knew Mags loved his men like brothers, and hated himself for what he'd said. He owed Mags a lot; in fact he owed Mags everything. The rage thermometer began to rise again. This time however the only person he hated was himself.

Mark looked at his watch. Nearly four o'clock. The traffic increased as the evening rush hour began. Street lights began to flicker into life as the early evening gloom approached.

"Fuck me ragged. What are they up to in there?" Mark groaned, adjusting his bulk in the uncomfortable cramp of the cavaliers interior.

"God knows. Those fucking Russian heathens spend all day in this fucking place," Boris commented.

"Lucky cunts," Mark said, and the pair of them burst into a bout of hysterical laughter. Mark wiped tears from his face. His belly ached under the strain of the childish humour. Then something caught his eye through the stream of traffic. Walking through the endless procession of rush hour pedestrians, Mark caught a glimpse of a familiar figure.

"Fuck. Boris, ain't that Ray?" he said, pointing across the street to a figure hurrying along.

"Where?" Boris spun round, trying to make visual contact."

"There, black leather coat." Mark pointed. Boris fixed his gaze on the man Mark had pointed at. Indeed it was Ray Callard. The squat, balding figure was unmistakable to Boris, even in the early evening gloom.

"I fucking hate that short arsed little cocksucker; I really do," Boris said, following Ray with eyes of contempt.

"That's because he's old bill. You hate all coppers, Boris."

"True," Boris agreed. But he hated this one more than most. Boris didn't know why, nor did he care for a reason. From a young age he'd learnt to trust his instincts. There was something about Ray Callard that Boris found repulsive, and the thought made him uneasy.

"But copper or no copper, what the fuck is he doing in a strip club?" Boris asked, noting with interest Ray Callard looking both left, and then right as he entered the Metropolis lounge.

"Maybe he likes the décor," Mark said absently.

"Yeah, or maybe he likes Russian too," Boris added.

Mark turned the cars ignition, firing the cavalier into life. Boris flipped the heater to the fully 'on' position. The gloom had brought with it a biting chill. As the car headed out into the ever growing traffic, Boris looked back at the Metropolis lounge, and wondered what might be going on inside?

Mags was halfway through his fifth game of pool. Already he'd relieved Pat of thirty quid. At the pool table he took no prisoners, and friendship counted for little. The White Rooms was quiet tonight, as it normally was on a Wednesday. Mags and Pat usually played during the quieter evenings. Weekends barely afforded them a minute's peace. At the adjacent table, Darryl had just taken a crisp twenty from the Scotsman, who launched a tirade at him.

"You fucking lucky prick. Rack the fuckers up again." Darryl inserted two fifty pence pieces into the vending slot, pushed it forward and released the balls.

"You'll be living on handouts at this rate, you Scottish cunt," he taunted. The Scotsman slapped another twenty onto the table, ready for the challenge. The door to the poolroom swung open. Boris exploded through it, Mark a moment behind him.

"Guess who we've just seen visiting the Russians?" he shouted. All pool playing ceased, each man waiting for Boris to enlighten.

"Who?" Mags asked, taking a sip from his glass. Boris noticed it contained nothing more sinister than orange juice.

"Callard," he shouted.

"That slimy cunt copper," he added. In unison Pat, Darryl and the Scotsman gathered round him, eager for more details. Only Mags declined to hear more, content to take the two shots Pat had just gifted him.

"Let's waste the fucker," the Scotsman demanded.

"Yeah, fuck the bastard. Kill him," Darryl agreed.

Mags potted two reds, still paying no attention.

"I always knew that two-faced fuck couldn't be trusted. Mags how much do we pay that cunt?" Pat asked, watching as Mags sunk the black.

"Enough," Mags replied, picking up the three crisp ten pound notes Pat had wagered.

"Well what do you say, Mags, do we clip the cunt or what?" Pat demanded. Mags could see the anger on the faces now looking his way.

"We do nothing. I knew he'd be there," he told them.

"What?" Darryl asked, approaching.

"I left it to Ray to sort this out. I needed proof."

"Did we need anymore proof than we had boss?" Darryl asked him, perching himself on the pool table.

"You think McGinn was lying? After we fucking dismembered him, you honestly think he held the truth back. I don't wear it Mags, not for a second." Pat questioned. Mags picked up the cue ball, tossed it from one hand to the other, for the moment lost in thought. When the rhythmic tossing of the ball subsided, every man in the room held a fixed stare on Mags. He found it hard to look back at them. Instantly he wished he was in the confines of his office, alone with his whisky bottle. He dismissed the thought, knowing the growing dependence was a major factor as to why every man present was looking at him right now. The Wolfpack was a team built on mutual respect. Mags knew his was disappearing bit by bit in the eyes of his closest friends.

"Boss, we can't sit around forever on this one. We gotta act." Pat spoke, speaking unanimously for the entire gathering. Mags cupped his hands to his face, massaging the tense facial muscles. He took a deep breath and nodded.

"Get the weapons," he said, and like a well-oiled machine, the pack went into battle mode.

Four o'clock, that day

Ray Callard approached the doors of the Metropolis lounge. A tacky, heavily illuminated strip club surrounded by a vast assortment of sex shops and boarded-up premises. Ray knew Sergatov owned most of them. He reached for the handle, pulled the door open and paused to look left and then right. Satisfied he had not been followed, or recognised he went inside. He made his way to the dance floor, past two huge, very unfriendly looking bouncers. He stopped a few feet from the dance floor, watching as an obscenely large breasted redhead bent over and shook her assets in time to the rhythm of music blaring through huge speakers. Ray noticed a group of men seated at a table in the far corner by the bar. He made his way towards them, past men hunched over half empty glasses. Ray noticed another monstrous bouncer, a thick scar running from his right eye, down to his neck. The thick red tissue stood out like a pulsing vein, and Ray wondered briefly if the person who put it there was still alive? As he approached the group of men, one noticed him advancing, broke off from the conversation he had been holding and rose to meet him.

"Ray, long time since we saw you. How is it?" he asked.

"Vasilly, how are you; good I trust?"

"Me, good?" Vasilly Sergatov let out a roar of laughter. "Be seated, man, be seated," he said, pulling up a chair. He snapped his fingers and a young man who had been standing against the wall hurried over.

"Vitally, a drink for my friend."

"Of course, Vasilly," he answered, and hurried off to the bar.

Ray seated himself. Looking round the table he nodded his acknowledgements to those present. He noticed all of Sergatov's cronies were there, and for a moment he felt a wave of unease. At the end of the table, directly opposite him sat Andre Kansky, Sergatov's senior confidante. Ray knew that many of the bodies he personally had seen, often with only the dental records being the means of identification, could be attributed to this man's work. Ray felt an icy stabbing in his bowels.

"So my friend, how can I be of service to you?" Vasilly asked, snapping the spell the presence Kansky had cast over him. Ray lowered his voice, almost inaudible above the music.

"I mean you no disrespect, Vasilly, but I hear some rumours. Some friends of mine, someone tried to murder them. Those rumours tell me you had a hand in it." Sergatov's smile faded momentarily, then returned as bright as ever.

"Oh, you mean the doormen!" he laughed again. "The legendary wolf boys!" he bellowed. More laughter came from the end of the table, Kansky joined in his masters jovial chorus.

"You think I did it?" Vasilly asked, feigning mock amazement.

"No I don't, Vasilly. That's why I'm here." Kansky glared from his position at the far end of the table, no longer was there any humour on show.

"So why are you here then, policeman?" Kansky asked, coldly.

"I wanted to hear it from Vasilly himself. I trust his word," Ray replied. Kansky continued to glare. Ray felt the icy pain again. Sergatov grasped Ray's hands in his, squeezing them like a vice.

"Indeed, my friend, I have known you many years. Why would I possibly want to kill your friends?" he asked, loosening his embrace on Ray's hands.

"That's what I thought, Vasilly. Please don't take what I have said as an insult. I came here to reassure my friends and to avert any possible trouble."

"You think your little wolf boys could give us trouble?" Kansky asked. Ray wanted to tell him to go fuck his mother, but the idea of dying didn't appeal to him. Vitally arrived with a tray, unloading a bottle of vodka and several glasses. Ray was relieved at the respite, and he needed a drink. Vasilly poured the gin clear liquid into a glass, handed it to Ray and then poured himself one. The man on his left passed the bottle down the table, each man in turn pouring himself a shot. Ceremony over, a voice from his left started the proceedings again. It was Vanja Klitcho. Ray knew him quite well. In fact Vanja was a rather humble man who never seemed to raise his voice, unlike some of the other dubious characters seated at the table.

"Ray, we have no reason to attack your friends. I hope you realise our honesty in this matter."

"I do, Vanja. Its just I made a promise to a good friend, that I'd find out the truth."

"The truth is, Ray, it was not of our doing. I promise you that much my friend," Vanja assured him.

"Thank you, Vanja."

"Tell your friends they have nothing to fear from us, Ray. We are all brothers, yes?" Vasilly bellowed, raising his glass in a toast. Ray joined him, then emptied the contents in one large gulp. Turning to Sergatov, Ray felt embarrassment filling him.

"Vasilly, do you know who it could be then?" His face flushed, Sergatov regarded him with cold eyes, the smile now gone. Ray knew he was now outstaying his welcome.

"If I hear, Ray, you'll be the first to know. You have my word," he said, the smile still absent.

Ray got up to leave, extending his hand to Sergatov.

"Thank you, Vasilly." Sergatov rose, grasping Ray's hand, returning the gesture. The smile had returned to his face Ray noted, making the hard featured Russian seem approachable once more. Ray nodded to the men at the table, and turned to leave. He made his way through the growing evening crowd, who now sat viewing a pair of young girls, barely sixteen Ray guessed. Nearing the exit, he caught the glare of scar face, still standing fixed in the same position. Ray returned a fleeting stare, and then hurried his pace out to the familiarity of the bustling street. He was troubled, and his face wore the concern like a mask. Sergatov should have been incensed at such an insult. He hadn't been. Ray knew that normally such an accusation would have started a war. But Sergatov had no such ideas. "Disappointing," Ray muttered, as he walked. A war between the pack and the Russians was needed. He would have to start it.

Sergatov poured another vodka, savouring the rich flavour. Kansky rose from his chair and took up a position next to him.

"Well?" he asked, pouring himself a measure. Sergatov declined to reply, content to view the two young dancers, savouring every movement their lithe young full bodies made. Draining his glass, Vasilly turned to Kansky.

"Well what?" he demanded, irritated that this quiet moment alone with the two nimble forms had been interrupted.

"What about the Wolfboys?" Kansky impatiently questioned. Vasilly

42

reached for the vodka once more, then casually answered his subordinate.

"What about the Wolfboys, Andre? A misunderstanding, that's all," he said, before casting his gaze at the two young bodies once more.

Kansky left immediately, taking the back exit of the Metropolis. The waiting car swung forward to meet him, and Kansky took his position in the passenger seat, barely waiting for the car to stop.

"Go!" he commanded, and the car pulled out into the evening traffic. Within minutes the car's driver had negotiated the last of the evening congestion, and was heading to the exclusive rural properties situated on the outskirts of Cambridge itself. They turned into a maze of new houses, red brick and neatly kept lawns. The car pulled into the kerb, outside a new three-bedroom house, 141 London Crescent, Ray Callard's address.

Sergatov and Vanja received another vodka bottle from Vitally, greedily devouring the contents. Vasilly Sergatov noted with pleasure that business was good tonight. He raised his glass to Vanja.

"Prosperity, my friend, and good health."

"And to you, Vasilly." Vanja raised his glass, then swallowed the contents in a single gulp. Vasilly beckoned Vitally, who instantly appeared at the table.

"Vitally, have those two young creatures brought upstairs," he said, motioning to the naked girl gyrating around gleaming chrome poles.

"Of course," Vitally replied.

Vanja poured more vodka, handing a glass to Vasilly.

"Thank you, Vanja," Vasilly said, never taking his eyes from the young naked dancers.

Mags checked the weapon, adjusting the setting from auto to full auto. The gleaming Heckler Kosch felt satisfying in his hands. Seated behind him he heard the Scotsman loading cartridges into the pump action he held. Boris sat passively staring out the side window, lost somewhere with his own thoughts. Mark pushed the cavalier through Cambridge city centre, past the last remnants of workers returning home after a hard day. Mark checked his speed, mindful not to invite any police attention. The firepower on display in the car would raise more than an eyebrow should a curious traffic policeman decide to take a look. He kept the speed at an even thirty, and headed through the late evening towards a date with the Metropolis lounge.

Sergatov pushed his penis hard into the warmth of the young lady beneath him. He gazed at her with eyes of lust as he pumped his hips hard. Amanda Clayton received him with a mixture of warm pretence, and vile disgust. Barely past her fifteenth birthday, she was no stranger to such attentions. And now she hid her displeasure like the cool professional she had become. Sergatov, at fifty, cut a less than arousing figure to her. Fat and balding slightly, his feeble attempts to please her left her staring at the ceiling. In between bouts of boredom she dug her long nails into his fleshy buttocks, and called his name with well-rehearsed passion.

"Fuck me, Vasilly. Oh baby! Fuck me harder." He duly obliged, sweating heavily as he slammed into her, his flabby stomach slapping her like a wave. She kept her disgust well hidden.

"Oh baby, I'm gonna come!" she screamed, tearing his flesh with her nails. His breathing came in short gasping efforts as he let go inside her. She knew the screaming and nail digging always brought him to a premature climax. Tonight had been no different. He rolled off her, falling breathlessly onto the bed. Amanda pulled the sheets up to her chin, trying to cover herself from any further touch. She knew it was part of the game, and she played it well. Sergatov paid well, and kept her in a comfortable lifestyle. She had met him whilst still only fourteen, a runaway sleeping in doorways. He had offered her a room and a job. The price had been ending up as his personal whore, with a heroin habit she couldn't imagine living without. As she looked at him now, already asleep beside her, she wished she could break her habit, and her dependence on him. Making a fresh tourniquet for her arm, she reached into the bedside cabinet, producing a clean hypodermic. As she prepared her fix for the third time that day, thoughts of leaving this life were banished to the far reaches of her mind.

The huge doormen on duty at the Metropolis were not paying attention to the foyer doors. Both men were watching with delightful intent as a young dark-haired dancer ran her fingers over a neatly shaven pussy. Neither man noticed the three balaclava clad intruders enter. Both men died a second apart, a single silenced shot spreading each man's head across the walls. Seated inside the cloakroom, barely ten feet away, Pamela Mitchell looked up from her magazine. She had been reading the latest Hollywood gossip, noting with interest that Tom Cruise was heading towards divorce. She wondered if he'd give a second look to a forty-year-old divorced mother of two. She smiled, knowing that later, alone in bed Tom would visit her, as he did most nights. She put the magazine down. "Two quid for the coat please," she said. From where she sat the light was quite dim, and the punter looked odd to her. As he came into view, Pamela noticed he looked odd because he wore a balaclava. Oh well she thought, another night another sick pervert. The round entered her chest, pulverising her left breast and carving a path through her ribs, collapsing her lung before exiting her back. Pamela Mitchell tried to speak, but the only noise she heard was a wet sucking sound as the air escaped her torn chest. Before dying, Pamela wondered if she'd ever see Tom Cruise again.

Moving into the main bar, the three assassins began opening fire. The first, taller and much broader than the others, opened fire with a hand held uzi, spraying a hail of death indiscriminately. A buxom brunette, wrapped around a pole on the dance floor caught a barrage of the onslaught, the slugs entering her neck, spraying flesh and blood across the front row of customers. Before anyone registered anything, a savage volley cut through them, shattering glasses, cutting through tables, dismembering bodies.

Sultan Rachman, the forty three year old accountant who ran the financial side of Sergatov's empire, was in the process of returning from the toilets. Still zipping his trousers, his first sight as he re-entered the bar was the body of a man, his friend Vitally Krushtov, lying at his feet. Almost in disbelief, Sultan recoiled, falling back into the toilets. Vitally Krushtov reached out, a blood soaked hand desperate for help. Sultan nearly fainted. Vitally had a wound in his chest, the size of a man's fist. Under his jacket Sultan wore a leather holster. He reached inside and with trembling hands pulled out the Smith and Weston. As if waking from a dream, Sultan heard the murderous clatter of gunfire, still only just audible above the pounding music. He peered out from his position just inside the toilet, but he could see only panic and pandemonium.

Men were running frantically towards the fire exit. A girl, Sultan saw it was Katya, one of the barmaids, fell to the gunfire. Her head blown open like a ripe melon, the round shattering it and sending her fifteen feet, leaving the gruesome remains at his feet. Sultan froze. The shocking sights he was seeing was too much for his delicate mind. He noticed with further disgust that he had urinated. Amongst the carnage, he saw men firing seemingly at will. Three of them. Each man wore a hood, no a balaclava. A middle-aged man hidden under a table caught the attention of one of the gunmen, who kicked the table over, revealing the cowering victim. The gunman lowered a pistol, and a fraction of a second later, the man's head exploded in a cloud of fine spray. Sultan felt his bowels loosening, and as fear gripped him with its all-powering hand, Sultan lost the battle with his bowels. Alone inside the toilets, Sultan cowered in fear, anguished by shame, as a foul wetness spread down his legs.

In the luxurious apartment above, Natalie Cox woke with a start, loud popping noises interrupting her dreams.

"Vanja, Vanja!" She shook him.

"What, what is it, dear child?" He woke from his deep vodka induced sleep, startled yet still in the embrace of a deep warm dream.

"Listen, Vanja!" she screamed.

He lifted his head, propping himself grudgingly onto his elbow. Instantly his senses snapped into life. Screams and gunfire, he flew from the comfort of the bed, instinctively reaching for his jacket. Fumbling in the dark he found his weapon. With trembling hands he flipped off the safety catch, before heading for the next room where Sergatov lay, seemingly unaware.

The door swung open, Sergatov had time to notice a dark figure filling its frame. He too had heard the gunfire, and now he realised he might have woken too late. On the bedside table lay his only salvation, a nine millimetre Beretta. His hand reached it just as a massive force hit him in the back, lifting him upwards and throwing him off the bed to end up crashing into the wall. He tried to fumble in the darkness for his weapon, but found he couldn't move. He felt no pain but knew instinctively he was badly hurt. He looked on helplessly as the figure approached, unable to utter even a protest. He watched paralysed as his attacker paused by the bed. Three flashes and a deafening noise sent Amanda into a permanent state of sleep. Sergatov hoped she had not woken at all, and that she had felt no pain. Turning his attention once more to Sergatov, the gunman raised his weapon, levelling it only inches from his face.

"Goodbye, Vasilly," the gunman uttered. Despite the impossibility of his situation, Sergatov cocked his head. He knew that voice, recognised its distinct accent. In his mind he put a face to this unseen killer, and then he began to cry, tears rolling down his face as the muzzle flash ended his torment forever.

Vanja heard the first shot, pausing at the door linking Sergatov's room to his. He heard three more, and he knew he was too late to save his great friend. The anger began to swell inside of him. Vasilly had saved his life, many years before in the harsh mountains of Afghanistan. Vasilly, Vanja and Andre Kansky had served there for three long bastard years. They had forged a strong friendship, born out of adversity on the barren killing fields of that godforsaken land. Vasilly had taken a rebel's bullet intended for Vanja, a favour he would not, and had not forgotten.

They had returned to Russia and been greeted no better than dogs. Forgotten was their debt to the Motherland. They were like many thousands of other conscripts, useable and expendable. Sergatov had changed that. Fuelled by a divine hatred for the communist regime, he had quickly begun to establish himself as a player in Russia's largest growth area, the black market. Initially food and clothing, then pharmaceuticals, and eventually drugs. Sergatov recruited only his close friends, all former conscripts. They had quickly made a huge fortune smuggling much needed stolen medicines into the country, where they were sold at large profits. When Vasilly saw the opening for a more demandable substance, heroin, he exploited it fully. Rival operations were swept aside with consummate and ruthless ease. Nobody stood in his way, and lived. Vanja greatly admired this iron resolve in his comrade, and had subsequently been at his side throughout. With the fall of communism, the possibilities for business had become limitless. Soon Vasilly had established links with organised crime in England, overseeing heroin smuggled out of Afghanistan and into Europe. With profits soaring, Sergatov saw a possibility to increase his wealth further. With the elimination of his paymasters in England, he would no longer be merely a middleman. In the summer of ninety six, Vasilly Sergatov, Vanja and Andre Kansky visited the city of Cambridge on a business trip. By the time they left three days later, the police had fifteen unsolved murders on their hands, and Vasilly Sergatov had established a new base of operations.

Now as Vanja leant against the door, his ear pressed hard to detect any further sound, he prayed his friend was still alive. He fought hard to suppress his breathing, taking short low breaths. He prepared himself to make an assault into the next room, wishing Andre was there. He knew Andre would have cut through the door; he would have dealt with the situation. Vanja cursed himself silently, his lack of nerve at this moment costing valuable time, but then he realised never before had he been in a position such as this without Vasilly or Andre by his side. He drew a short steadying breath and prepared to go in. Another shot rang out. Vanja recoiled as if he himself had been hit. He raised the weapon, felt for the door handle.

"Be careful, Vanja," Natalie called. Vanja turned, finger to his lips.

The killer pushed his boot into the lifeless corpse. Satisfied there was no more life left in Sergatov, he wiped his bloodstained boot on the expensive silk sheet, now crimson red with the girl's blood. Suddenly a voice broke the silence.

"Be careful, Vanja." He spun towards the sound. Raising his gun, instantly emptying the magazine through the door separating the two rooms. Vanja turned to Natalie, finger held to his lips, a gesture of silence. The wooden door exploded in a shower of splinters. Vanja was hurled backwards onto the bed. Natalie let out a long hysterical scream, as Vanja was flung onto her by the force of the impacting rounds. Quickly she clambered from the bed, running to the bathroom. Inside she locked the door, pushing herself into the furthest corner. She looked down at her naked body, and then broke into hysterics again at the sight of Vanja's blood which had covered her. Natalie continued to scream, even as the bathroom door was kicked from its hinges. The man standing in front of her lifted his balaclava, and Natalie Cox froze in disbelief. Then she pleaded for her life, for the man standing before her she knew well and she begged for his leniency. None came. She called out his name and begged for her life, and she died that way, a single bullet that penetrated her sternum, sending her lung tissue cascading across the clean white tiles behind her.

Chapter Four

Second-hand motors

"Fuck me senseless!" Mark shouted, smashing his huge fist into the steering wheel.

"Mark, tell me this is a fucking wind up. Tell me we haven't just broken down in the middle of the busiest road in fucking Cambridge." Mags was leaning over, shouting in his ear.

"Sort it out, mate," Boris moaned.

"I'm not a mechanic," Mark replied, winding the key again. "Nothing. Fucking thing's dead," he added.

"Well this looks fucking suspicious. Six armed men pushing a fucking Vauxhall Cavalier up the road." Mags slammed his hand on the dashboard.

"Hang on. Darryl, you know about cars," Mark suggested.

"You fucking muppet. I read the exchange and mart. That doesn't mean I'm a mechanic, Mark."

"Right, stow the fucking guns away, and Mark, pop the fucking bonnet," Mags ordered, already halfway out of the car. Together they pushed the lifeless vehicle over to the hard shoulder, as passing cars sounding their horns with impatience.

"Fuck off, you cunts!" Boris screamed at a passing Mercedes, its driver flooring the accelerator at the sight of six huge men, all brandishing a middle finger. Mags looked down into the engine compartment, not understanding what the fuck he was looking at.

"Where the fuck did you get this piece of fucking shit, Mark?"

"The auction, what's wrong with it?"

"It's a piece of fucking shit Mark, that's what's wrong with it."

"Mags, I paid two grand for this," he whined.

"You were ripped off, you mug," Mags replied, shaking a bunch of wires in the vain hope it might actually do some good.

"Careful, Mags, careful."

"Mark, fucking go over there; stop fucking moaning."

"Yeah but…," he began, but Mags cut him off in mid-sentence.

"Over there. You're giving me the fucking hump. Some getaway car this is. We may as well have brought a fucking bike."

Mark stomped off, taking a seat on a nearby rubbish bin.

"You've upset him now." Pat laughed.

"Fucking divvy cunt," the Scotsman chipped in. Meanwhile Mags tugged at some more wires, beginning to lose his temper.

Mark sat on his bin, shaking his head as Mags got medieval with his wiring. They always blamed him he mused; always had and probably always would. He didn't complain. He knew they embraced him as a brother. Markus North was different, that much he knew. He was a member of the pack, an honour he wore like a medal. But he didn't have the killer instinct the others possessed. He just didn't have it. There had been times when he'd been called upon to inflict pain, and he'd carried it out to the letter. Inside though he didn't relish the idea, not in the same way that Boris or even the Scotsman did. He knew they didn't judge him because of it He had a sensitive side and they accepted it, and he was grateful for that. He had been with Mags virtually from the beginning, because Mags used to go out with his sister. Because of his natural size Mags had offered him a job on one of his doors. From there he had become the company driver, ferrying the main team around trouble spots, backing up the front line doormen. When Andy had died, Mags had hit the bottle hard, and Mark had become his personal chauffer and general dogsbody. Everyday he had to drive to Mags' house, let himself in, wake up the severely hung over Mags, then basically bring him back to life. During those dark times Mags had treated everybody like shit, especially Mark. Even now he was prone to bingeing on whisky, which left him in a foul mood for days. Markus North had never answered Mags back, never complained, and he realised that Mags had repaid him by moving him up to the pack. Mags lived by the idea of loyalty, and Mark understood that it was his way of saying thank you for sticking around, and putting up with the shit.

"Try it now, Mark," Mags said, wiping grease off of his hands onto an old shirt.

"Mags, that's my shirt you've got there," Mark pointed out, a look of disgust across his face. Mags rolled his eyes.

"Try the fucking motor."

Mark squeezed his bulk behind the wheel. Turning the ignition, he got the same response; nothing.

"Still dead," he said. Mags kicked the passenger side wheel arch, denting it and hurting his foot.

"Bastard!"

"Careful," Mark shouted at him. The Scotsman leant under the bonnet, rubbing his chin thoughtfully.

"Let's get a taxi," he said after a moment.

"What? Hang on a minute. Does anyone know the number of terrorist taxis?" Darryl answered.

"Well it was a thought," the Scotsman said, going back to looking at the engine. Mags, who had been massaging his swelling foot, stopped and pondered the idea.

"Actually, that's not such a stupid idea. Who do we know who's got a taxi?" he asked. In unison, Darryl and Pat answered the question.

"Mohamed!"

"Fuck me, yes," Boris agreed.

"Get on the phone, Mark. Get that big nosed cunt out here sharpish," Mags snapped.

Thirty minutes later a gleaming yellow and black cab pulled to a halt behind the cavalier.

"Hey boys, how you doing?" The driver stuck his head out of the cabs window. A broad grin covered his face.

"'Bout fucking time, just as well we ain't paying," Boris told him, opening the passenger side door.

"You ain't paying?" The grin disappeared from his face. Mohamed watched as the six men crammed themselves into his cab, then started to shake at the sight of the weaponry.

"Oh dear God, what is this in my taxi? A bloody revolution."

Mags poked the barrel of his Heckler Kosch into the back of Mohamed's head.

"Drive on. Metropolis lounge. Make it quick." Mohamed eased the overweight vehicle into the now dwindling traffic, constantly eyeing his passenger warily. He knew them well, too well for his wife's liking. Aisha was a devout Muslim. She frowned at his association with these men, the all night card schools, and drinking marathons that lasted for days. For his part, Mohamed enjoyed their company immensely, free of his strict family ties. Indeed, it had been these very passengers who had financed his taxi company. He also knew that the closure of many rival firms was their work too. He owed them. Still, he'd never been in their company before in such bizarre circumstances. He wanted to ask, but after studying each man he thought better of it. He scratched his large nose, then checked to see if anyone was looking. His rear view mirror told him they weren't. He fingered his nostril, emptying a large finger full of snot. He wiped it discretely on his trouser leg.

"So, how's it all going, boys?"

"Just wonderful, Mo, absolutely fucking tip top," Pat replied sarcastically. Mohamed gave up on the conversation, and concentrated on his driving instead.

Mohamed approached the Metropolis, through dimly lit back streets, where retail outlets gave way to sex shops. Boris saw the flashing lights first. Blue light bathing the night sky in waves. A speeding police car overtook them, sirens wailing.

"Drive by, keep going," Mags whispered. Mohamed kept a constant speed, slowly negotiating the fleet of emergency vehicles littered in front of the Metropolis lounge.

"Holy fucking shit. What the fuck has been happening here?" Mohamed asked, his thick Pakistani accent rising to a screech.

"Keep going, straight on," Boris reminded him.

"Will there be something you boys would like to be sharing with me?" Mohamed asked. Boris threw him a withering look, and Mohamed figured there wasn't.

"Back to the White Rooms, Mo," Mags said from his cramped position in the back.

"Okay dokey, Magnus. Anything you say." Mohamed threw the car into a left turn and headed for the White Rooms, just relieved that he hadn't been asked to stop at the Metropolis lounge. Relieved to be free of the confines of Mohamed's cramped taxi, Mags paused to breathe some life into his numb legs. He waited until the car was empty before poking his head through the open driver's side window.

"Thanks, Mo."

"No problem, my friend."

"Forget what you've seen or heard tonight Mo, understand?"

Mohamed nodded. He'd already forgotten.

Boris came in from the kitchen, entering Mags' office with a tray of drinks. He handed them out, before taking a seat. A silent calm filled the room as they watched the late evening news.

"And now to local news. Police have released a statement regarding a shooting at a city nightspot. It is believed as many as twelve people have been killed, in what police say could be a drug related incident. Live at the scene is our city correspondent Jane Yakamato…"

Mags leant forward and switched the television off. He sat back into the sofa, taking a sip from his coffee cup. He wished he had a whisky.

"Well lads, it looks as though someone beat us to it," he said rubbing his throbbing temple.

"Yeah, indeed it does. But who?" Pat asked. Mags felt his headache intensifying, and could not offer an answer.

Hell's Gate

"Sweet mother of God." Detective Inspector Bradley Killian knelt down, taking a closer look at the grisly remains of the body, headless and with most of its upper torso shredded. Killian had been a copper for twenty-eight years, fifteen as a murder squad detective. During those years, Killian had seen some disturbing sights, scenes of heart wrenching and insane violence. He stood up, his arthritic joints groaning. Surveying the remains of the Metropolis lounge, he believed this scene topped them all. The remains of at least eight bodies lay littered around. He knew four more were to be found upstairs. Photographers busily documented the gruesome scene, whilst his fellow officers like himself tried to begin piecing together the events that had gone on.

"Guv, it's twelve. That's official." His colleague, Andy Slater handed him a slip of paper. Killian read it, a frown creasing his face.

"Seventeen wounded. Five critical," he said absently, folding the slip and handing it back to Slater.

"Some fucking night out," Slater remarked, stepping over a bloody mess. He looked and noticed it was a piece of skull, the owner's ear still attached. Slater deposited his last meal noisily across the dance floor. Killian looked away, fighting an overwhelming urge to do the same.

"Let's go get some air, Andy." Slater wiped his mouth on his sleeve, before following Killian outside.

The cool evening air washed over them, and thankfully Killian felt the urge to vomit begin to pass.

"Inspector, can you tell us what happened?" Killian instantly regretted his need for air. Jane Yakamato, the evening news on-the-spot presenter rushed him, her crew in tow.

"What happened Inspector? Was this a drug-related attack?" she asked, thrusting a microphone inches from his face.

"At this stage of the investigation we have no comments to make," he answered, walking away.

"Is it true Vasilly Sergatov was among those killed?" she asked, following him.

"No comment." Killian began to feel the irritation rising within himself. He had no time, or patience for reporters. He saw them as vultures. He'd lost count of the times that they had arrived at a murder scene before he even knew about it. Jane Yakamato hurried behind him, cameraman and sound engineer a step behind. Killian knew her well. They had clashed before.

"Inspector, can you…" He cut her off, spinning with an agility that belonged to a man much younger than his fifty-two years. Jane Yakamato stopped dead in her tracks. Her cameraman less observant ran into her, the camera lens slamming her in the head. She reeled away massaging her scalp. Killian smiled, finding some light relief at her discomfort. He fixed her with his deadpan expression.

"Miss Yakamato. Do I have your unbridled attention?" he asked.

"Yes, what can you tell us?" she replied, rubbing the bump on her head.

"Right, I'm going to release a statement, just for you, young lady."

"Start rolling," she shouted to her cameraman.

"Ready?" Killian asked. The cameraman gave him a thumbs up signal. Jane thrust an expectant microphone into his face.

"Okay. At ten twenty three this evening, we received a call regarding an incident at a city centre strip club. There had been a series of shootings, resulting in the deaths of at least twelve people. Seventeen others received injuries and were admitted to hospital. We cannot for obvious reasons release names of the victims." Killian began to walk away.

"Inspector, that's it?" Jane stood with the microphone still in her outstretched hand.

"That's it," he answered heading for his car. Slater followed, fumbling in his trouser pocket for the keys.

"I'm beginning to think you don't like her, Guv," Slater said, threading the key into the lock. Killian gave him a cheeky smile, before examining Jane Yakamato once more. She still held out her hand. This time only the middle finger extended.

Slater pulled the car into the parking bay at the rear of Parkside police station. Killian was already halfway out of the door as Slater killed the ignition. He hurried after Killian, through the custody area towards the stairwell leading to their office. Slater found himself breathing heavily at the exertion of the stairs, silently reminding himself to quit smoking, as he did every time he became aware of his poor conditioning. As always, Killian bounded them two at a time. When Slater caught up, Killian was already at his desk. A mountain of paperwork littered its surface.

"So what have we got, Andy?"

"God knows, Guv. Sergatov made a lot of enemies in his worthless life," Andy answered, fighting to maintain his breathing. He reached into his pocket and took out a fresh packet of cigarettes.

"True, but I'll bet my life it had something to do with heroin," Killian mused. Slater lit a cigarette, nodding his agreement.

"So what are we looking at here? New firm looking to take over?" Slater offered. Killian leant back in his chair, rubbing his tired eyes.

"We'd have known about them, Andy. Besides, Sergatov would have crushed any rivals long before it came to this." Killian reached for a large folder in amongst the clutter on his desk. The dog-eared cover bulging at the seams. Bradley Killian opened it, the first page devoid of anything but the name of his long-term nemesis, Vasilly Ivanovich Sergatov.

Killian had first encountered Sergatov back in the summer of ninety six. Then the biggest heroin dealers in the city had all been murdered, within days of each other. Each murder had been brutal, and professional. The point blank head shot executions had been the first Killian had seen. In the five years since, he had seen at least twenty more. Russian mafia trademark executions stood out in a city like Cambridge. Linking Sergatov and his vile henchmen to the crimes had been easy. Taking the cases any further had been difficult, and a conviction had proved an impossibility. Only once had Sergatov actually stood facing a charge in court, and then Bradley Killian and his team had been forced to watch helplessly as a string of technicalities brought the trial to a halt. Long ago Killian recognised the ruthlessness of his adversary, and for all his loathing of the man and his methods, Killian admired the brain that kept Sergatov a mile in front of the law. He was a cold-hearted killer, but Bradley Killian understood that Sergatov outmatched him in every way. The bottom line was clear to Killian, Sergatov made him feel inadequate. It was a shame he carried around everyday of his life, further fuelling his quest to put the man behind bars. Now as he reflected on the evening's events, he felt a mixture of jubilation, and resentment. He was unashamedly happy that Vasilly Sergatov now lay in a cold mortuary, a hole in his back the size of a mans hand, his head blown into a fragmented mess. The jubilation was tainted by the realisation that someone had robbed him of his very reason for getting out of bed each day.

At fifty-two Bradley Killian lived a regimented, yet lonely existence. His wife had left him ten years before, unable to cope with his selfishness. Rarely had he spent a day away from his office, and even then he usually brought a mountain of paperwork home with him, working late into the night. Even with her departure, Bradley had barely altered his pace. The only inconvenience being the bind of performing his own household chores. In the rare periods he did reflect on his marriage, he realised with a sense of shame that he had probably never loved his wife, not in the true sense anyway. He held her no malice after returning from work late one night to find an empty house and a letter informing him of her departure. In truth he was secretly happy for her; it was no less that she deserved. He knew he would always be married to the force, and to do that required a single-minded approach to life, and marriage would never allow that. Bradley was and always would be a loner, and he was more than happy with that.

Slater looked at his watch, now past two in the morning. Angie would be pissed off, again. She tolerated the hours; she knew how much the job meant to him. He looked at the framed picture of them both. He kept it on his desk, amongst the growing mountains of paperwork. It was taken in Paris, during their honeymoon. It had been an idyllic two weeks, he thought affectionately. Since being transferred to work with Bradley Killian such periods of relaxation spent with Angie had been scarce. Killian was a fully-fledged workaholic, and expected the same from his staff. Slater lit another Marlboro, wincing at the sight of the overflowing ashtray. He figured now was the wrong time to quit smoking.

"Brad, this is just a hunch, but do you remember that shooting incident a couple of weeks ago, you know those bouncers?" he said.

"What about it?" Killian replied from behind his own paperwork mountain.

"Never came to anything did it? I mean, one of them pegged it, but we had no leads. Reckon these two incidents might tie in?"

Killian rubbed his chin, feeling the rough stubble, reminding himself to get a much-needed shave.

"Who's dealing with that,? Callard, isn't it?" he asked.

"Yeah, Ray knows the owner of the company. What's it called, Guardian Security?"

"Guardian Leisure I think," Killian responded, absently rubbing his chin again, lost in thought.

"But what could tie them together? Sergatov dealt in heroin, we know that much. These guys at whotsit, Guardian Leisure, from what I know of them, they do a good job of keeping the dealers out of the clubs," Killian added, trying to make something of Slater's idea.

"Ray reckons they don't fuck about either."

"Yeah, I've read some of the complaint forms." Killian thought hard, but still found no link. Slater reached for another Marlboro, shaking his head at the sight of the near empty packet.

"Anyway, let's call it a day. I'm fucked." Killian rose from his chair, his creaking back protesting.

"I'm all for that," Slater agreed, reaching for his jacket.

"I'll speak to Ray in the morning. See what he's got on his mates at Guardian Leisure," Killian said to Slater. But Andy Slater was already heading for the stairs, with the thoughts of his bed and Angie filling his tired mind.

Killian drove through the deserted city centre. He opened his window, allowing the chilly air to overwhelm him. Something nagged at the back of his mind and it bothered him as he drove out towards Histon. Was it the death of Sergatov, his great enemy? He didn't know. Maybe, he thought, but there still remained a great relief knowing his hometown would be a safer place to live. He switched on his car stereo, breaking the early morning silence with the stirring sounds of Rachmananov. The classics were one of his only true passions. Killian often drove endlessly at night, absorbed in their peaceful moods. Tonight he needed to drive and be absorbed. He thought of what he'd seen earlier that evening, the mutilated bodies blown apart, beyond recognition. A wave of nausea crept upon him, and fighting an urge to lose his stomach, he took a deep breath of the cold morning air. He headed through the quiet streets of Histon, deserted save for a stray mongrel feasting on a discarded take away. Again the nagging crept into the recess of his mind. Had it been what Slater had said? Was there a connection somewhere. He tried to dismiss the thought as he left the quiet streets and headed out into the still countryside. He turned the volume up to full and wound up his window. He drove on absorbed, trying hard to forget the events of the last few hours, convinced that if hell existed, he indeed had been through the gates tonight.

Chapter Five

Killers come with smiles

Mags looked at the alarm clock sitting on his bedside table. Nine fifteen. He wondered if he was still asleep. After all he hadn't been awake this early in years. For a moment he thought it might be nine fifteen at night. He got up and went to the window. Pulling the curtains back a wash of bright sunlight bathed the room. His amazement complete, it was indeed morning. He wandered into the bathroom, relishing the relief as he sent a long steady stream of urine down the toilet. Something was different. He wasn't quite sure what. Even as he entered the warm water of the shower he didn't know what it was, but all the same something had changed. Mags let the warm jets soothe his body, rousing him from a still sleepy daze, enjoying the water's warmth. Reaching for a towel, Mags stopped in mid-motion, his hand inches away from the towel rail. It hit him like a bolt of lightning, and he realised what had changed. For the first time in probably three years Magnus had woken up without a hangover.

The Jaguars throaty roar pierced the quiet morning air. Ray Callard eased the powerful machine to a halt outside Mags' house. Mags peered through the kitchen window, watching as Ray leant into the cars vast boot. He watched with interest as Ray made his way towards the house carrying a large cardboard box. Ray didn't pause to knock, opting to ease the door handle open with his knee, pushing himself cardboard box first into the kitchen.

"How the fuck did you know I was up?" Mags asked, reaching for the

---

kettle.

"Saw you nosing out the window," Ray replied, dumping the box onto the kitchen table.

"Fuck me. No wonder you're a fucking copper." Mags laughed. Grinning, Ray began opening the box.

"Got you some new toys," he said.

"Fuck me, Ray, how much is this going to set me back?" Mags asked him, eyeing the weapons Ray was now unpacking.

"Consider it a gift my old mate. Besides, you might be needing them soon," he said, holding an uzi in his right hand.

"Why?" Mags asked, spooning coffee into two mugs.

"Unless you've been on Mars for the last twenty-four hours, I'm sure you've heard what happened last night."

"I heard. What the fuck did happen, anyway?" Mags poured the boiling water into the mugs, before hunting for some milk.

"We don't know yet, but it's looking like a new firm made a play for the cup."

"You think we might be next?" Mags asked, handing Ray his coffee.

"Someone out there had the bollocks to step up and take Sergatov out. No disrespect Mags, but if that's the case no firm in the city can afford to sit back." Mags sipped the hot coffee, mulling Ray's words over.

"But who, Ray? Where the fuck did they come from?"

"No idea. But whoever it is meant business; that's for sure."

"That bad?"

"Mags, that's why I got you these fuckers," he said passing Mags an uzi.

"Where the fuck did you get these; lost property?" Mags asked, feeling the weapons' weight in his hand.

"I confiscated them off of some rogue Jehovah's witnesses," Ray told him, breaking into a chuckle.

"Cheers. They'll come in handy no doubt." Mags held the uzi up to the kitchen window, pretending to fire out into the street. Ray finished unloading the box, another uzi, followed by three handguns, each fitted with a silencer.

"What is it, fucking Christmas?" Mags asked, lowering his uzi and looking at the impressive arms cache laid out on his kitchen table.

"Do I look like Santa?"

"No, Santa ain't as fat as you." Mags laughed, reaching for the kettle again.

They sat at the table, the refilled cups steaming in their hands.

"We went to whack them last night, Ray, just to put the record straight," Mags told him. Ray stopped the cup short of his lips.

"What? You fucking told me you'd wait, Mags," Ray shouted, slamming the cup down, spilling its contents.

"I know. Don't fucking panic; we didn't do it. It was all over before we got there. Marks fucking motor broke down on the way. Useless cunt."

"You should've waited. I went there yesterday evening you impatient bastard. Sergatov denied everything, and I believed him too," Ray snapped. Mags declined to mention the fact that he knew Ray had been seen at the Metropolis.

"Really, Ray. Fuck, I'm sorry."

"It wasn't him, and I never thought it was anyway." Ray spoke in between sips of his coffee. He took a tissue from his pocket, wiping the spilt liquid now running across the table.

"We've got to consider that whoever clipped the Russians, tried to clip you guys," he added.

"Yeah, but McGinn worked for Sergatov. Explain that fucker, Ray?"

"McGinn was a dirty cunt who'd have sold his mother for a fix. He'd have worked for anyone who paid him a dime. You knew the bloke, Mags. He was no more loyal to Sergatov then he was to anyone else. He was a fucking degenerate."

"True, but he told us it was the Russians, Ray. We were cutting him into sections at the time, so don't bother telling me he was lying."

"Maybe we've got another Russian firm moving in. Let's fucking face facts, Mags. Sergatov came out of nowhere, killed every cunt and took over. History repeating maybe?"

"Perhaps, Ray, perhaps. I'm still inclined to believe McGinn. You should've seen what we did to him, Ray. That cocksucker Sergatov had us clipped, no doubt about it. Last night somebody caught up with him, and be honest, those fucking Russian pricks have pissed one or two people off down the years. I'm only fucked off because they beat us to it that's all." Mags lifted his cup, draining its contents.

"I hadn't looked at it that way. You've got a point though," Ray agreed.

"Cunts, I wanted to kill that prick myself. He cost me a good man, Ray, I wanted him personally."

"Well he's gone now. We'll have to keep our ears to the ground; see who's doing what," Ray said, helping himself to a piece of half eaten toast Mags had left over from breakfast.

"Let me tell you this much. I don't want another firm like that in my manor. I can't have a repeat of all this. If another firm pops up, Ray, you'd better take them down. If you don't, bet your life we fucking will."

Killian had slept less than four hours, yet he still looked remarkably fresh. Slater looked and felt like shit. He wondered how Killian did it? Slater handed his boss a coffee.

"Thanks Andy, I need it." Slater knew he didn't. He'd been with Killian for nearly two years and knew the man could exist on little, or no sleep at all. He envied him for his stamina. Slater was twenty years his junior, yet often felt ready for retirement.

"Andy, I've been thinking about what you said, about the Russians connection with Guardian Leisure."

"How's that then guv?" Slater felt pleased. It wasn't often Killian considered any ideas but his own.

"I don't know, but there's something. Call it a hunch, but there's a connection in there. What was it, two weeks apart, the shootings?"

"Something like that. You think last night was a revenge hit by the bouncers?" Slater asked.

"Could be. They've used force in the past. We can link them to one or two violent crimes if we look, I'm sure."

"Ray should be in soon. He's got a file of them as thick as the Bible guv. Want me to send him in when he gets here?"

"Straight away," Killian told him, before turning his attention to the morning newspaper.

Ray arrived in his office shortly after eleven. He barely had time to take off his jacket before Slater knocked and came in.

"Morning, Ray," he said closing the door behind him.

"Hello mate, how's Angie?"

"Oh, you know, alright I guess."

"Good. You'll have to come over soon. Penny always asks how you both are."

"Love to, mate. Be nice if I had the time."

"Oh yeah! I forgot about Killian. How many hours you working these days?" Ray asked, genuine concern etched across his face.

"Fuck knows. Sixty maybe seventy hours a week. Now we've got this murder case to sort out, I'll be ready for the fucking nut house at this rate, Ray."

Ray shook his head. He knew Killian well, a brilliant detective, but not particularly popular. He had a reputation for burning out colleagues at an alarming pace. Ray worked mainly in drug enforcement, and had turned down promotion, and a healthy salary rise because it meant joining Killian.

"Anyway, Ray, can Brad have a word?"

"Yeah, no problem. He's not going to offer me a job is he?" Ray asked, grinning. Andy went to leave, pausing at the door.

"I fucking hope so, Ray. Then I can get a real job."

Ray made his way through the myriad of corridors that made up the upper floors of Parkside station. A huge square building, lined with smoke glass windows, it stood casting an intimidating shadow across the lush green common that sprawled across the road. Ray came to a row of faded wooden doors, each fitted with a simple nameplate. He stopped outside the end door, looking briefly at the blue plastic plate. 'Detective Inspector B. Killian', he read before entering.

"Raymond! Is that you?" Killian sprung from his seat, ignoring the stiffness in his back.

"Bradley, long time no see." Ray extended his hand, and Killian grasped it firmly in exchange.

"Bloody hell, Ray,; I thought you'd defected." Killian told him, taking his seat once more. Ray found himself one and dropped himself into it.

"No, I'm still here, Brad. Fully paid up member of her majesty's finest," Ray cackled. Killian shot him a grin, before reaching into his desk. He pulled out a small metal flask.

"Brandy? Its not too early is it?" he said, offering the flask to Ray.

"Why not." Ray took the flask, unscrewed the cap and took a deep swig. Instantly the muscles in his neck tensed as the fiery liquid cut its path through him.

"Shit, that's some strong stuff," he said, handing Killian the flask. Ray watched with disguised interest as Killian took a hefty mouthful, noticing almost admirably how the brandy had no effect.

"That it is, my son," Killian said, screwing the top back on.

"So, Brad, what can I do for you?" Ray asked.

"Guardian Leisure, your department isn't it Ray?" Killian watched as Ray loosened his tie.

"Yeah, I know them well. What's up?"

"Probably nothing, mate. We, well Andy, actually wondered if there was a connection between the attempt on their lives the other week, and last night's shootings?

"I heard. Russians got it eh?"

"Just slightly, Ray. Fucking bloodbath." Killian briefly felt the wave of nausea rise in his throat, remembering last night's carnage.

"Fuck, I don't pity you have to sort this lot out." Ray pointed at the mountain of paperwork.

"Shit, this is existing cases, Ray. I haven't even started on last night's yet," Killian pointed out. Ray frowned, glad once more he wasn't on Killian's team.

"So what have you got on these bouncers, Ray? That's what they are I take it?"

"Thugs. I've been inside them for years. Clever fuckers though, Brad; can't pin anything big on them."

"I know that feeling, Ray, believe me." Killian thought briefly of Sergatov, still annoyed he hadn't brought him down himself.

"It's mostly violence, but it's the heroin we want, Brad. I'll take them down soon; matter of time," Ray added. Killian's ears pricked at Ray's last statement.

"Heroin?"

"That's what they're shifting."

"No shit, Ray. Well that's an interesting little snippet." Killian reached for the phone, clearing several pieces of paperwork to find it. Ray wondered how he knew what was important and what wasn't. He realised Killian probably didn't know either.

"Andy, get up here now," he ordered, slamming the phone down.

"Ray, I need everything you've got on these boys, post haste."

"No problem, I'll have it sent down." Ray got up to leave, pausing to straighten his tie. Killian stopped him at the door.

"One more thing, Ray. Are these clowns likely to have access to automatic weapons?"

"Oh yes, they don't fuck about, Brad. Serious fucking people. We've linked at least ten incidents to them in the last five years. All shootings," Ray told him before leaving.

"Well there's a thing," Killian muttered to himself as Ray closed his office door.

Slater found Killian at his desk. The paperwork mountain had grown, verging on the ridiculous.

"Fucking hell, Brad, that stuff's breeding." Killian looked up, shaking his head.

"I think we've got some real candidates here, Andy."

"The Guardian boys?" Slater asked.

The very ones," Killian replied.

Slater quietly congratulated himself. His idea might just turn out to be a case solver. And this case probably meant promotion to Slater. Angie would be pleased.

"Andy, I need a ballistics report on every weapon used. I want to know makes and models by dinner time." Slater looked at his watch, eleven fifty three. A second later he was heading for the door.

Ray pulled the Jaguar out of the car park, heading away from the station and into the city centre. The pre-lunch time traffic had already begun to clog the narrow roads. Ray found himself grid locked, not two hundred metres from the station. He reached into his jacket pocket, produced his mobile and began punching the keys. He raised the phone to his ear, idly watching two blondes leaving a clothing boutique. He marvelled at the huge breasts sported by the taller of the two.

"Ray?"

"It's done, the wheels are in motion," Ray answered, before switching the phone off and replacing it back into his pocket. The traffic began to move, and Ray crawled along, keeping pace with the two blondes. The bigger breasted of the two noticed the Jaguar crawling beside them, saw the driver staring at her. Uncomfortable with the attention she hurried her pace, her friend turning to see the source of her concern. Ray kept pace, causing a slight tailback behind him. The taller of the two blondes stopped, turned to the occupant of the gleaming blue Jaguar and extended her middle finger before heading into a chemists. Ray stepped the pace of his Jaguar, rejoining the lunch time traffic, a broad grin plastered across his face.

Mags arrived at the White Rooms at eleven. He kicked open his office door and made his way to his desk. Pat sat taking a call. He moved the phone as Mags relieved himself of the large cardboard box he was carrying.

"No problems, Bill; I'll make sure they're there. Yeah, I'll stick it on your monthly account statement." Pat began scribbling on a pad as he spoke.

"Okay then, Bill, consider it done. See you later mate, goodbye."

Pat replaced the receiver, continuing to scribble.

"Who was that?" Mags asked, delving into the box.

"Bill Hancock at the city arms. There's a home game tomorrow; he's expecting five hundred Peterborough fans to tear his pub apart. He wants extra men on."

"Is it sorted?" Mags unpacked an Uzi, handing it to Pat.

"Yeah, I've got Fred and his lads covering," he said, examining the weapon.

"Good idea. Fred's a tasty little bastard," Mags agreed.

"Where the fuck did you get these from?" Pat enquired.

"Ray." Mags produced another Uzi.

"Where the fuck did Ray Callard get these?"

"Jehovah witnesses apparently." Mags laughed.

Pat didn't share the joke, and went back to scribbling on the pad.

"This is some interesting reading, Andy."

"Isn't it just." Slater nodded his agreement, flicking through the pages of the file he now held. Killian also had a file, which he now sat intently reading. He found it absorbing, and at the same time wondered how he'd never crossed their paths. He stopped at a section devoted to one man, Magnus Vandersar. A founding member of Guardian Leisure, Killian read his background with interest. The only son of Icelandic parents, they had divorced when he was eleven. His mother had taken him to England, where she had relatives. They had initially settled in Bristol, but Magnus' mother Anka, had met Harry Caddick, a travelling salesman. After a brief courtship Anka had moved to Cambridge with Harry. Magnus had grudgingly left the warmth of his new home in Bristol to live in Cambridge with his mother.

At first life had been bearable for the young Magnus, almost enjoyable. He still greatly missed his father Magnus senior, who he had been extremely close to. Harry Caddick had little time for the boy, resenting his mother's doting. Harry initially tried his best to tolerate the boy's presence. But then, as Magnus reached his teenage years, Harry found his presence too much of an intrusion into his relationship with Anka. Harry had never known his parents. His father, an armed robber had been killed by police when he was less than a year old. His mother had put him up for adoption shortly afterwards, finding herself a widowed single parent at the age of only seventeen. Harry had spent his entire life being pushed from foster homes to social services shelters. He had grown up hating his parents even though he had never really known them. Now as he watched Anka doting over her beloved child, he found years of suppressed hatred boiling within himself.

"You're a fucking mummy's boy, you know that, you little cunt?" Harry had taunted him whenever they were alone. By his fourteenth birthday, Magnus no longer had to endure taunts. Harry switched to beating him instead.

"Does that hurt you, huh?" Harry would shout in-between blows with a heavy leather strap. Anka never knew of her son's torment. Magnus rarely spoke and he always managed to explain away the bruises he regularly sported.

"Rugby's a rough sport mum.," he would tell her if she looked concerned at the appearance of a fresh wound. By his sixteenth year, Magnus already stood six feet tall, and tipped the scales at a little over fifteen stone. He outweighed Harry Caddick by over fifty pounds, and towered over him by a good three inches. In the spring of his seventeenth year, Magnus decided he didn't want to put up with Harry's brutality anymore. He had arrived home late from taking his girlfriend to see a movie. Harry was waiting for him as he walked into the house.

"Let me guess, you fucking mistook my house for a fucking four star hotel?" Harry had asked him, the familiar leather strap hanging from his left hand.

"Leave it, Harry, I want to go to bed," Magnus had told him, heading for the stairs. The strap had caught him full in the face. Magnus dropped to his knees clutching his mouth that now poured blood profusely.

"Don't take the fucking piss kid. This is my fucking house. I call the fucking shots. I'm the fucking weight in this building you cunt." Harry brought the strap down again. It struck with a sickening crack across Magnus' back. Despite the pain, Magnus clambered to his feet.

"What, you want some you cheeky little fuck?" Harry closed in on him, the strap drawn back ready for another assault. Magnus fixed Harry with cold steel blue eyes, an intensity burning inside that Harry Caddick could not hope to match. Magnus approached him, the hatred intensifying with each purposeful step. Harry inexplicably noticed that his bowels had failed him. He had just enough time to register the warm feeling running down the back of his legs before Magnus changed the balance of power within the Caddick household. Magnus had woken his mother, telling her to come quickly as Harry had fallen down the stairs. Anka had ridden in the ambulance with Harry, and sat patiently through the night as surgeons rebuilt his shattered face. Harry Caddick never lifted another hand to Magnus again.

Slater handed Killian another cup of coffee. He'd lost count of how much caffeine they'd consumed already. Slater doubted he would sleep because of it, then reminded himself that he wasn't getting much sleep anyway.

"Look at this, Andy. It's like a fucking Mafia structure. Vandersar is obviously the boss, but then you've got this character, Patrick Glover who's his top captain. This guy runs the whole operation; he's like the under boss. Then we have Boris Hunter, Vandersar's muscle, aka 'Boris the Blade'. Got a real talent for inflicting pain this fella.

"He sounds a right mad cunt guv," Slater agreed, reading his own copy.

"What have we here? McRae Miller, otherwise known as the mad Scotsman. Another mad fucker, he's got a record stretching back right into the dark ages."

"All for violence?" Slater asked.

"Each and every one of them. Then we have Darryl Hanlon, and Markus North. They make up the rest of the team, although I think these two are the least violent of the bunch. Neither of them got much previous."

"Markus North, done for car theft in ninety-four, that's it though. This kid Hanlon though, prime suspect in a killing outside a kebab shop some years back, killed a bloke with a single kick, seriously injured a few others too." Slater read from his file, studying the black and white picture of Darryl Hanlon.

"And these bastards control a whole army of bouncers?" Killian wondered.

"Who in turn control a major slice of Cambridge's pub and club trade," Slater added.

"So if they wanted to distribute large quantities of heroin?"

"Well then they've got only a small hurdle to get over haven't they? And let's face it guv, it looks like they've already crossed it." Slater spelt it out to Killian.

"So if we were betting men, Andy, we'd stake a whole bunch of money of these pricks taking the Russians out to corner the heroin market, wouldn't you agree?" Andy Slater looked across the crowded desk at Killian, and both men knew who they'd be going after next.

The Takedown

Killian looked at his watch, six forty. He sat in the unmarked van, Slater beside him. Behind him in the back sat Detective Sergeant Vinny Hills, and two regular beat coppers. In front of their van, another was parked, unmarked and loaded with eight more coppers, all armed with Heckler Kosch sub machine guns. Parked unseen a hundred metres from the White Rooms, they sat in silence and waited. Killian watched as the tail end of the rush hour traffic crept by, people busily making towards home after a hard day's work. Slater nudged him, then pointed towards a Vauxhall cavalier now pulling to a halt outside the White Rooms. Markus North and Darryl Hanlon got out and went inside.

"That's it, guv, they're all here." Slater noted.

"Okay, lads, standby for my signal," Killian whispered into his radio.

Mark and Darryl walked into the pool room, the familiar midweek sight greeted them. Pat was on the wrong end of another beating at the hands of Mags.

"Fuck me, you're a fucking degenerate pool player, Patrick," Mags gloated.

"You're a cheating cunt," Pat replied, handing over another twenty pound note.

"Now now, children," the Scotsman called from the next table, where he was in the process of emptying Boris' wallet. Darryl went to the bar, poured himself a measure of Southern Comfort.

"Anyone else?" he asked, dropping ice into his glass.

"I'll have a bud," Boris told him, raising an empty bottle.

"Fuck!" Pat slammed his cue into the floor, cursing at potting the black.

"Another twenty I believe?" Mags laughed, holding his hand out.

"That's it. I've had enough of this. Mark, give the bastard a beating." Pat threw his cue to Mark, who produced two ten pound notes from his pocket.

"Get ready to be poor, Mags," he said, slamming the money down.

"In your fucking dreams, in your fucking dreams," Mags challenged. Mark began racking the balls, whilst Mags chalked his cue. It was turning out to be a typical midweek night at the White Rooms. Mags was glad. He needed some normality back in his life. The last few weeks had drained him both physically and emotionally. He replaced the chalk and found his mind drifting to thoughts of Penny. His heart missed a beat as he realised he wished he was with her, and suddenly felt for a moment, an overwhelming urge to go to her house and see her. Ray or no Ray.

Killian lifted the radio to his mouth, pressed the squelch button and spoke.

"Okay let's go," he said, and simultaneously the two vans emptied. Killian held back as the armed officers made their way towards the White Rooms. An old man walking his dog stopped and looked on in amazement as the armed police ran down the pavement. Killian and Slater followed, along with Vinny

Hills and the two uniformed coppers. Silently the armed policemen entered the White Rooms, catching the two doormen totally unaware. The lead officer raised his weapon, and the two doormen backed off, arms outstretched in a gesture of surrender.

"Where are they?" the officer asked.

Henry Gillian, who often covered the door at the White Rooms, pointed at a door marked 'pool room'.

"Right, now fuck off," another armed officer told them, motioning at the door. Henry and his colleague Mark Vallard needed no further invitation. They fell out of the White Rooms, almost knocking Killian over in their haste. The eight armed policemen took up a defensive position outside the pool room. As if an unspoken signal had been given, one of them launched himself at the door.

Mags folded the two ten pound notes, placing them in his pocket.

"You know what, I don't know why I bother paying you pricks. You give it all back to me anyway," Mags told the whole room.

"Piss taking cunt," Mark muttered heading for the bar. The door exploded under the weight of the lead policeman. Instantly more spilled into the room.

"Armed police, hands in the air now!" one of them shouted. Boris swung his cue, breaking it across the policeman's face, shattering his jaw and removing all of the teeth on his left side, some breaking off at the jaw line and spinning across the room. Another policeman next to him levelled his weapon at Boris.

"Down, down, get the fuck down now!" Boris dropped the remains of the shattered cue, before slowly and defiantly falling to his knees, his hands clamped behind his head.

"Cuff that cunt," the officer ordered, and another ran over brandishing a set of handcuffs. He snapped them on Boris' left wrist before pulling it down behind his back where he then cuffed the right wrist too. Satisfied Boris was no longer a danger, he raised his weapon before smashing the butt down into his helpless victims face. Mags was forced over the pool table, both hands locked in position behind his back. He felt an incredible pain in his shoulders, but fought any urges to show the pain. From his position on the table, Mags watched as each of his men were cuffed and taken outside to the waiting vans. He was kept there, a gun held to his temple. Two men entered the room. Both wore suits Mags noticed, and he knew instantly that these were the real coppers. The older of the two spoke, leaning over so that he fixed Mags' eyes with his own.

"Mr Vandersar, I presume? I've heard all about you, and now you're in some deep shit sunshine."

"Suck my fucking cock," Mags told him. The butt smashed into his head just at the base of his skull. For a fraction of a second a splitting pain splintered through his brain, and then all he knew was darkness.

Killian sat in the interview room, one of three situated along a corridor from the stations detention area. Slater entered the room, grinning broadly.

"Things are looking up, Brad. Those weapons we found in their office match the ballistics description of the weapons used. We should know within the hour if they were the ones. I'm trying to get a positive match right now."

"Good work, Andy. Have them bring Vandersar in. See what he's got to tell us." Killian sat back in his chair, rocking back and forth thoughtfully. Slater headed down the corridor, stopping at the custody area to recruit four uniformed officers. Slater had been shocked at his first meeting with Magnus Vandersar. He hadn't expected a man of such size. He guessed Vandersar's weight at around two hundred and eighty pounds, and if he carried any fat Slater hadn't seen it. Andy Slater was not a big man, and didn't rate his chances of bringing Vandersar out of his cell in one piece. He stopped at a row of dull grey doors, heavy metal with small hatches at eye level. Slater went to the third door along, lifted the hatch and peered inside. There sat Magnus Vandersar, his huge frame dwarfing the tiny wooden bed he was using as a makeshift chair. At the sound of the hatch being lifted, he looked up, cold blue eyes locking Slater's momentarily. Slater pulled away, letting the hatch fall shut. He looked at the four officers now standing behind him, and they looked as nervous as he did. Taking a deep breath he fumbled with a large bunch of keys, finally selecting one and inserting it into the lock. He pushed the door open with his shoulder, the cold metal grudgingly giving to his demand. The four officers filed inside, forming a semicircle around the wooded bed that Magnus occupied.

"Vandersar, we're taking you to be interviewed. Are you going to behave?" Slater asked from the relative safety of the doorway.

"I always behave," Magnus replied, standing up. Slater backed out of the cell into the corridor.

"Okay then, let's go." One of the officers began handcuffing Magnus's wrist behind his back. Satisfied he was behaving, they led him out of the cell.

Killian sat rocking in his chair as the door opened. Slater led Magnus into the interview room, accompanied by one of the officers. The other three stood guard outside.

"Ah, Mr Vandersar, we meet again. How's the head?" Killian asked.

"The name is Mags," he replied, looking around the room.

"So, Mags, how is the head?" Killian asked again.

"What do you want fuck features?" Mags replied, still looking round the room.

"You. I want you, Mags. You see, it turns out you and I have something in common."

"I fucking doubt that. Unless of course you mean we've both fucked your mother." Mags ceased gazing round the interview room, instead focusing his attention on Killian. Mags noticed his sarcasm had disappeared. A scowl now sat on his face. Pretending to be unperturbed, Killian carried on.

"It would appear, Mags, that you and I have, no let me correct that, *had* a common enemy."

"I have many enemies," Mags told him.

"Vasilly Sergatov. He was your enemy, and mine I should add. But you blew his brains out, whereas I didn't." Killian leant forward over the veneer covered table, waiting for Mags' response. Mags began to laugh, a low chuckle developing into a booming roar. Killian watched as Mags doubled over, tears beginning to fall down his face.

"You think this is fucking funny you sick fuck?" Killian slammed his fist into the table. Slater looked at his boss. Rarely had he seen him lose his calm laid-back approach.

"You're a sick fucking inividual, Vandersar, you know that?" He slammed his fist into the table again, harder this time. Mags continued to laugh, taking great satisfaction from Killian's irritation. Finally Mags began to compose himself. Smiling broadly he locked eyes with Killian.

"You stupid fuck. Is that the best you can come up with?" Mags shouted. Killian felt his irritation mount again.

"I know it was you, Mags, so why don't we make this easy?" Killian snapped. Mags fought the laughter welling within him. Instead he began to shake his head.

"Have no doubts about it, you prick. I was going to do the Russian, but believe it or not, our car broke down on the way." Mags began to laugh again, the image of six heavily armed hit men clambering into the back of Mohamed's taxi he found particularly amusing.

"That's some alibi," Killian observed.

"It's the truth. That's how funny it is. We must be the worst fucking hit men in the world." Mags again began to roar with laughter. A knock on the door brought a distraction to Killian's frustration. Slater got up and left the room, glad to be out of the feud now brewing between Killian and Mags. A tall grey haired officer – Slater saw he was the duty sergeant – handed him a slip of paper.

"Ballistics sent it down; said it was urgent," he said.

"Thanks." Slater unfolded the slip, and looked at it before hurrying back into the interview room. He was relieved to see that Mags had stopped laughing, and had now gone back to absently looking at the floor. Slater handed the slip to Killian, noticing he still looked irritated. Slater knew that was about to change. Killian looked at the slip of paper, a broad smile spreading across his hard face.

"Well, Mags. You did say I could call you Mags didn't you? Well anyway, according to this piece of paper I'm holding, you and your cronies are all well and truly fucked. Killian waved the piece of paper at him. Mags sat impassively, wishing he wasn't bound by the handcuffs that now held him. Killian continued to smile, a look of pleasure etched across his features.

"Not laughing now, are you?" he said, before reaching across the table and smashing his fist into Mags' face.

Slater sipped his coffee, the bland liquid leaving a stale taste in his throat. He reached into his pocket for his cigarettes, produced an empty packet and cursed loudly. He needed one right now, more than he normally craved, and Slater knew that must be bad. As he stood in his office, looking out of the window into the dark street below, he knew something was wrong with what he had just witnessed. He'd seen Killian get rough before. He put it down to his single-minded pursuit of getting a conviction. Andy Slater didn't like it, but he knew he lacked the courage to challenge Killian. Neither did he agree with Killian denying Mags and the other five suspects the right to a solicitor. He sipped his coffee, silently ashamed with himself. There was something else that bothered him, yet he could not identify it. He told himself he was tired, which he was. He finished his coffee – the dour liquid making him cringe – and carried on looking down into the dark street below.

James Reagan had only been in the job for three months, and he hated it. Being a policeman hadn't turned out to be what he expected. Secretly he had dreamt of chasing bad guys through crowded streets, sirens wailing. In reality he found himself chained to a desk, endlessly filling out paperwork. Save for chasing a bag snatcher through Woolworth's, the level of excitement he had experienced so far had been disappointing. Now here he was, releasing Magnus Vandersar from his handcuffs, wishing he was anywhere but here. James knew all about Magnus. He understood that if he decided to misbehave now, all the restraining moves he had been taught at training school would count for nothing. He released the cuffs, instantly stepping away. His three companions backed away warily towards the cell door. James hurried to join them.

"Hey kid," Mags called after him. James reached the door before turning to face Mags.

"Yes?" he asked nervously. Mags wiped fresh blood from his nose, bloodied by Killian's fist.

"See this, kid?" he held up two blood stained fingers. "You tell your boss I'm going to kill him for this," he said.

James nodded nervously, before closing the cell door. He turned the key, relieved as the lock clicked into place. Secretly he was glad he wasn't Killian. He didn't doubt what Magnus Vandersar had just told him had been the truth.

Slater tore at the clear packaging, fighting his way into the cigarette packet with the skilful hands of a professional smoker. He nimbly removed one, flipped it with precision into the corner of his mouth and lit it. Inhaling deeply, the smoke cut a warm trail into his chest. He examined his watch, nearly midnight. He hadn't had a cigarette for nearly two hours, and Slater proudly considered that as some achievement. He was on his way home, taking a long detour to find a late night shop that was still open. Now standing in the cold gloom outside an off license situated along a dirty back street, one of many Slater had trawled looking for cigarettes, he wondered if Angie was asleep? He hoped she wasn't. He had barely spoken to her in the last three days; he'd barely seen her in fact. Getting in his car, he wondered where he was. In fact Slater didn't really know whether to go left or right, or turn back the way he had come. Gunning the engine into life, he switched on the headlights, put on his seatbelt and reached for another cigarette. He knew tonight was going to be another late one.

Killian stopped outside the cell door. He felt his pulse quicken, the blood pumping through his temples creating an echo that ran through his head. Behind the cell door he knew Magnus Vandersar waited. Killian hated him. He knew Sergatov had mocked him time and time again, but Killian was a patient man. He reasoned that sooner or later the Russian would have made a mistake, and

Bradley Killian would have been waiting. It was that thought that had occupied his mind for a long time. Too long. He had worked hard, sacrificed too much in his pursuit of Sergatov to be denied of the final prize, his conviction and subsequent long prison sentence. But it had all been in vain, years of work and sacrifice for nothing. The reason for that lay behind this cell door, Vandersar. Killian lifted the hatch. A potent odour of stale urine and disinfectant instantly assaulted his nostrils. Magnus lay on the hard wooden bench, seemingly asleep.

"Get used to the inside of one of these," Killian shouted, hoping to rouse Mags. He got no response. Footsteps in the corridor made him look to the source of the sound. A young policewoman carried two plastic cups of tea towards the operations room deep inside the station. When he turned his attention back to Magnus, he noticed with surprise and alarm that the bench was empty. Killian recoiled as Mags appeared, his face inches from his.

"What do you want with me, policeman?" Killian felt those cold blue eyes boring into his, and felt uneasy. They were separated by the heavy steel door, so Killian kept his hard exterior, not allowing Mags to see his unease.

"You're a murderer, and I'm going to take you down. People like you disgust me," Killian spat through the hatch, the wet spittle coating Mags' face. Killian began to laugh. Mags stepped back, wiping the drool from his face, hatred running through his veins like a fire out of control.

"Not so fucking big now are you, Mags? In prison you'll be nobody. In fact you'll probably end up as someone's bitch." Killian laughed again, a loud mocking cackle. The fire in Mags' veins now burnt out of control like a raging inferno. He went back to the bench, away from his tormentor at the door. The mocking laughter continued, and Mags felt like a caged animal, a tiger. He lay down, trying to ignore Killian. The torment continued.

"You'll have an arsehole the size of a dustbin lid by the time you get out tough guy."

The raging inferno threatened to explode, but Mags fought to control his anger, knowing it would get him nowhere in the confines of his cell.

"Pretty fucking blonde boy like you. Yeah I bet shower time will be a real giggle."

Mags exploded, the fire swept through him, out of control. He leapt from the bench, reaching the door in an instant.

"You're a dead man, do you understand? I am going to prison for murder, but I promise you it's going to be yours." Mags sneered through the hatch, teeth gritted, his top lip pulled back. Killian didn't move, the steel door impenetrable even to a man such as Mags, Killian reassured himself.

"I wouldn't bet on that," he mocked, a thin smile creased his face.

"Oh I'm not a betting man!" Mags told him, before returning to the comfort of the hard wooden bench.

Slater found a familiar landmark, the shop and save on the corner of Brooks Road. He stopped there regularly to buy cigarettes, and now wondered how the hell he had gotten so far off the beaten track? He gauged his position before throwing a left and finally heading for home. He glanced at the digital clock display on the dashboard; twelve twenty. He cursed, then reached for the nearly half empty packet of Marlboro's. He cursed again before lighting one. Reaching the familiarity of the city once more, he passed darkened shop fronts and pubs long closed. He noticed three figures leaving the heavily illuminated Illusion nightclub. Slater smiled. The last time he had been to a club they had been called discos. He absently glanced at the figures now getting into a white Mercedes, three men, all over the limit Slater betted. Suddenly a familiar face caught his attention. He nearly lost control of the car such was his surprise.

"Ray Callard," he muttered. He craned his neck for another view of the Mercedes, now twenty metres behind him. It was Ray Callard, getting into the passenger side of the car. Slater drove on, an uneasy feeling chilling him as he looked again at the now distant Mercedes in his rear view mirror. The fact that Ray Callard had been leaving a nightclub at such a late hour neither bothered or surprised him one bit. The man getting into the driver's side of the Mercedes had been Andre Kansky, and that bothered Andy quite a bit indeed.

"He's fucked; they all are." Ray took a mouthful of champagne, savouring the expensive liquid. From now on he intended to be drinking plenty of it.

"Good work, my friend. Now perhaps we can get on with business." Andre Kansky lifted his glass before swallowing its contents. Kansky reached for the half empty bottle in the middle of the table, filled his glass and then topped up Ray's. Seated in the quiet corner of Illusion nightclub's private lounge, only the muffled sound of music intruded on their privacy. Kansky raised his hand, and motioned to a lone figure standing at the bar. Ray watched as the figure approached, feeling a sense of unease at the presence of the man now standing at the table.

"What is it, Andre?"

"Marco, more champagne."

"Of course." The man headed back towards the bar, and Ray felt an order of calm return. He had known Marco Karpov for some time. Yet without fail whenever in his company Ray felt decidedly uneasy. Karpov was Kansky's personal bodyguard, a man of considerable size who oozed menace. The huge thick scar that ran the length of his face completed the vision of menace. Karpov was a natural killer, Ray knew that much. He was also a man of few words, and Ray found it very hard to make conversation with him. Kansky went everywhere with Karpov never far behind. Ray watched Karpov return. The champagne bottle looked like a miniature version in his huge hands.

"Thank you, Marco." Kansky took the bottle, already opened. Ray marvelled again at the size of Karpov, at least six feet ten, probably a good three hundred pounds Ray guessed. In truth Karpov not only made him uneasy, he scared Ray too. He had a friend who worked for the foreign office check Karpov's background, and when Ray had read the discreetly delivered printout, his blood had run cold. Marco Karpov, forty-two years of age, a former Russian special forces commando who had been linked to atrocities against civilians during his tours of Chechnya. The crimes included the massacre of women and children.

He was recruited by Sergatov and Kansky, and swiftly established himself as a brutal servant. He had originally stayed behind in Russia to look after Sergatov's business links there while he and Kansky had moved to England. Three months later he had murdered two Moscow traffic policemen who had been impertinent enough to search his car during a routine stop and search. In the rear of Karpov's Mercedes had been seven assault rifles and three kilograms of pure heroin. Sergatov had understood that Karpov had been left with no other option. Karpov had slipped across the border into the Ukraine where he had been kept in a safe house owned by one of Kansky's associates. Karpov repaid the favour of the associate, Vladimir Klevar, by raping his wife Mira, then killing Klevar himself. Sergatov then brought him to England where he could at least keep an eye on him. Sergatov for his many sins, and they were indeed many, found Karpov little more than an embarrassment. In July nineteen ninety-nine, he finally lost patience with him, ordering his execution.

Andre Kansky, knowing the value of a good killer, and secretly admiring Karpov's talent, pleaded with Sergatov to spare his life. Sergatov grudgingly agreed through persistent persuasion. Kansky understood how easily Karpov could be moulded; after all he lacked any real intellect. So was born a sinister alliance; one that Sergatov chose to ignore, one that ultimately led to his brutal death. Ray felt a cold shiver run through him. He poured himself another glass of champagne in the vain hope that the succulent liquid may take the unease from him. He glanced at Karpov, leaning at the bar, and doubted any amount of alcohol could shake the feeling the Marco Karpov always instilled within him.

Slater finally arrived home, the darkened windows of his three bedroomed terrace a depressing home coming. Tired fingers inserted a key into the front door lock. Quietly he pushed the door open, entering a dark hallway. Slater crept upstairs, avoiding the third step, always creaky, but deafeningly loud in the quiet of night. Angie lay peacefully asleep, her gentle breathing the only real sign of life. Slater quickly undressed, throwing his crumpled suit over the end of the bed. For a long while he simply stood and looked down at her, admiring her beauty. Even after twelve years together he still found her stunning, the blonde hair always beautifully kept, those slim long legs, and the breasts. Andy doubted he would ever see any better. When Slater finally climbed in beside her, exhaustion fought to claim him, but sleep would not come. Even in the embrace of deathly fatigue, he found himself conspiring to put Ray Callard and Andre Kansky into perspective. Something was sorely wrong Andy reasoned, and for some unknown reason he felt consumed by finding the answer. As the dark fingers of sleep pulled him under, Andy Slater began to wonder if Ray Callard might be the answer.

"The pack is now out of business. Sergatov is gone. Now is out time." Kansky stroked the thigh of a young blonde girl, now seated on his lap.

"So, what now?" Ray Callard asked, absently staring at the girl's ample breasts. She smiled, as if to acknowledge his attention.

"Now we move our product, my friend. Every fucking club in this great city is ours. My people are in place. Soon we will both be very rich men." Kansky slid his hand inside the girl's skirt, his fingers probing the warm soft flesh.

"I'll drink to that." Ray lifted his glass, toasting the idea.

"And now, Ray, you will have to excuse me, I have other matters to attend to." Kansky rose from his chair, leading the girl by the hand. Ray watched them leave, heading upstairs for the privacy of Kansky's own personal flat. Ray couldn't wait to be rich. He envied Kansky, and more to the point his lifestyle. Now as he sat alone at the table, he reflected on the recent events that had led to his new partnership with Kansky.

In a way he felt almost sorry for framing Mags. He detested the rest of them, but Mags had earned a degree of respect, he had always paid him, and

Ray thought that deep down Mags actually liked him. But Kansky had come up with a far more attractive offer, and Ray decided that being rich far outweighed being popular. When he Kansky and Karpov had entered the Metropolis lounge, Ray doubted that he could actually pull a trigger, let alone murder people. Kansky and Karpov had set about the task with real zest, and Ray strangely found the act of killing reasonably easy, and somewhat alluring. He felt no remorse, and now he understood why killers killed. But then Ray knew he would never stand trial, or indeed go to prison. Mags and the Wolfpack would shoulder that burden for him. Business after all, was business. Mags would never make him rich, and Sergatov would never have made Kansky rich. Out with the old, Ray thought as he refilled his glass; in with the new.

Mags paced the confines of the cold cell, counting twelve steps from wall to wall, then repeating the process over and over again, an endlessly frustrating game. He had found himself performing the same task on his first night of incarceration behind the walls of Parkhurst. He had repeated the ritual every night for two years until his release. Whenever he found himself confined in a small room Mags forced himself to pace its length, counting each step in a macabre religious ceremony. It was his way of dealing with confinement. Those lonely nights at Parkhurst, the screams of inmates sending him to a point he could only describe as the abyss of insanity.

Two years of his life wasted, for a crime he shouldn't have even been convicted for. He was a rookie doorman then, on his way home from another Thursday night shift at the shitty little club he covered. He had just reached his car, situated behind the nearby police station off all places. A loud desperate scream had washed the tiredness from him, and he homed in quickly on its source. Mags located the now hysterical woman, a bingo caller also on her way home from a late shift. A young heavily built man, his hands round her throat, was in the process of raping her. He sat alone in the coldness, deep in the bowels of Parkside police station and remembered those events. He had reacted swiftly pulling the attacker away with venomous force. His concern, sixty-year-old widower Deirdre Hammet had been his main priority.

Mags shook his head as he recalled the look of sheer terror on her face, the disgust, bewilderment. The blade had struck hard, embedding deep into Mags' left shoulder, the force of impact so strong the blade had snapped, leaving four inches of cold death inside of him. Spinning instinctively Mags had broken Mark Allit's jaw with a reaction left hook. Allit had been asleep long before Mags kicked his ribs through, puncturing both lungs, and rupturing his spleen.

He gave a small cynical laugh, his mind still not able to work out how Allit only served a twelve-month prison sentence, whereas he, Deirdre Hammets saviour that night, had served exactly double the time. British justice had always pissed him off, that's why he made sure the issue was settled out of court. Mark Allit was found, decomposing. His remains a hive of maggots, two months after his release. Someone had taken the liberty of dismembering him with a meat cleaver before dumping his remains in a disused quarry ten miles from Cambridge. The police never did find his killer, and unofficially they never really looked too hard either. Cambridge would always be a safer place without Mark Allit anyway. That was in ninety-three, and Magnus Vandersar had received a card every Christmas since from Deirdre Hammet, without fail. He counted carefully each step, to the wall and back again, one foot at a time, laborious, yet clinically thorough. He looked around the depression that now housed him, remembered Parkhurst and its life-sapping monotony, and knew he could never go back to prison.

The heavy lock clanked as the key stubbornly made it yield. James Reagan entered the cell, the tray held in front of him. Ten minutes to two, handing out luke warm tea would be the last job of his shift.

"Brought you some tea, Vandersar," he said, alarm crossing his face at the sight of the empty bench. Mags, hidden behind the door, moved in with lethal speed. The heavy door swung, lifting Reagan off his feet, hurling his ten stone frame, now drenched in tea, across the corridor, dumping him violently against the far wall.

"You can call me Mags." The boot landed square on Reagan's head, his nose imploding into his face, the sound of bone snapping loudly. James Reagan felt his bowels let go as the intense pain shocked his system. The last thing he saw before his fragile mind shut down was Magnus Vandersar heading along the corridor towards the custody area.

Derek Softly felt his erection stir beneath his trousers. He flipped another page, the sight of a young man, maybe eighteen at best, Derek imagined him to be younger, brought on a full state of arousal. He hurriedly flipped the tattered pages, greedily searching for more images. The next picture showed the young man naked, on his knees with a huge penis filling his mouth. Derek Softly decided he needed the toilet urgently. He would wait until the boy returned from playing tea lady, then he could do something about the matter stirring in his trousers. He heard footsteps approaching. Hurriedly he slid the tatty magazine inside his photographers' weekly.

"Hurry up James lad, I need a shit mate…" Softly lost any capacity for speech. Now bearing down on him was Magnus Vandersar. He felt his erection subside, and now he urgently needed to urinate.

"Keys!" Mags ordered, quickly closing the distance between himself and the fat ruddy-faced sergeant seated at the desk in the custody area. Softly fumbled for the large collection of keys clipped to his belt. He handed them to Mags, his chubby hand trembling.

"Right, open the fucking cells fatso!"

"But, I can't," Softly protested, a thin sliver of spittle escaping from his heavy mouth.

"Open the fucking doors now you fat fuck. Two fucking seconds, that's how long you've got fat boy." Softly moved with the grace of a gymnast, almost leaping from his chair. A magazine was knocked from the desk. It spilled its contents onto the tiled floor. Mags noticed with a measure of amusement and disgust that the photography magazine had spewed out a gay porn brochure.

"You fucking sick fat cunt. Move!" Mags shouted, driving a heavy foot into his ample buttocks. Softly began opening the cell doors at speed, each one revealing one of his own men. Boris was the first one to emerge. Mags noticed he looked meaner than normal.

"Boris, this fat cunt likes young boys, don't you lard arse?" he said, pointing at Softly. Sweating profusely, the overweight sergeant backed his considerable girth into a now open cell. Boris followed him in, his face pure menace.

"Please, please don't hurt me," Softly begged, the sweat running down his flabby jowls in rivers. Boris brought his knee up to Softly's groin, his left testicle exploded on impact. Softly tried to scream, the intensity of the pain like nothing he had ever experienced before. He dropped to his knees, mouth open in a silent scream. Boris delivered a thudding kick. The force snapped Softly's jaw in five places, spraying droplets of sweat and dark blood across the cell walls. Darkness took him, and Derek Softly was able to dream peacefully about the young man in his magazine.

Killian woke with a start, his senses scrambling back into the conscious world. The phone, it was the phone he realised reaching across to his bedside cabinet.

"Hello?" He fumbled the receiver to his ear.

"Bradley, sorry to wake you mate, but we've got a problem." It was Gordon

Randall, a beat copper Killian had worked with for years. Instantly Killian was wide awake. Gordon Randall didn't make a habit of ringing at – Killian reached for his watch – two twenty in the morning.

"What is it, Gordon?"

"Those blokes you had in for the Russian murders, well they seem to of escaped."

"What!" Killian was already well on his way to getting dressed as Gordon Randall replaced the receiver.

Mags waited impatiently, the phone receiver pressed hard to his ear. "Answer!" he shouted. Still no reply. He waited impatiently anyway, willing someone to answer.

"Yeah what?" Ray Callard finally woke from a drunken stupor, the incessant ringing finally reaching him.

"Ray, its me Mags."

"Mags?"

"Listen, Ray, we're in some deep fucking shit here. Get us some fucking help."

"Whoa, slow down, Mags, slow down. Where the fuck are you mate?" Callard reached into his jacket pocket casually discarded on the bedroom floor. He pulled out a scrap of paper, fumbled some more and produced a well-chewed biro.

"Ray, we had to do a runner. We're sitting behind a fucking bush in a field down Coldhams Lane, by the bridge." Mags pulled his shirt collar up as a car passed, desperately trying to remain hidden. Mags realised he almost filled the phone box he presently occupied, and felt slightly embarrassed with himself

"I take it you're in the phone box by the bridge then?" Ray asked. Mags pulled the receiver away from his face, held it up and looked at it.

"No, Ray. Presently I'm ringing from the house across the road; number twenty-two. Wake up, Ray. Of course I'm in the fucking phone box you dumb fucking shit. Get the fuck down here and get us the hell out." Mags slammed the receiver down, and not for the first time in their relationship Mags questioned Ray's common sense levels. He pushed the door open, and sprinted across the road towards the field. He caught his shirt on the rusty barbed wire fence as he tried to duck under it. "Fuck!" he shouted, feeling a warm stream of blood snake its way down his back.

"Over here, Mags."

"Where?" Mags answered, trying to locate the sound in the dark field.

"Here, you blind bastard." Pat walked towards him, coming out of the gloom like a huge menacing spectre.

"I'm not a fucking bat you know. I don't see so fucking good when it's pitch black," Mags responded, skidding on a thick pile of wet cow shit.

"Fucking hell," he moaned.

"Careful," Pat said grinning.

"Fuck off, cunt," he said, before skidding over again on another pile.

Killian stormed into the custody area. Gordon Randall was waiting to meet him.

"What happened, Gordon?"

"Poor kid, James Reagan. Vandersar jumped him. Broken nose by all accounts. I was out on patrol Brad. I heard the call go out over the radio and figured you'd want to know. Killian stared at the open cell doors almost in disbelief. In all his years on the force, no one had ever broken out of the custody cells, and then sprung five others too. It just didn't happen. He shook his head, anger rippled through his body. Perhaps he had underestimated this man as he had Sergatov. Killian didn't like the thought, not one little bit.

"I want this fucker and his mates found, Gordon. You do understand me don't you?"

Randall sensed the serious tone in Killian's voice, and he knew all too well that he wouldn't be going home when his shift ended at six o'clock.

"Everybody we've got is out there now Brad. We're doing all we can," Randall replied. Killian looked at the still fresh pool of blood against the wall outside of Vandersar's cell. He knew James Reagan quite well, nice kid. But he also understood that he was no match for a person of Magnus Vandersar's stature.

"How's the kid, Gordon?"

"Shook up pretty badly. I just rang the hospital. They reckon he'll need surgery on the nose."

"What the fuck happened in there?" Killian pointed inside the cell adjacent to him, blood splattered across the walls.

"Derek Softly, fractured skull by the look of it."

"Fucking hells bells. Derek wouldn't hurt a fly." Killian pictured Softly, seriously overweight granted, but a gentle man all the same. Softly even turned out most weeks to coach his local under elevens football team. Randall scratched his head, a furrow of concern ploughed across his forehead.

"Well the thing is, Brad, we've got another little problem, concerning

Derek." Randall went to the custody desk, producing a magazine that he handed to Killian.

"Sweet fucking Jesus." Killian spoke to no one in particular as he flicked through the pages, many sealed together with what Killian guessed was dried sperm.

"Well I think we can safely say that Derek won't be coaching the under elevens anymore, Gordon." Killian muttered as he flicked through the magazine.

"I hope not, Brad, I really do." Randall looked away as Killian stopped at a page showing a young boy, probably no more than ten or eleven being buggered by a much older male.

"The filthy bastard," Killian uttered, and for the first time is his entire career Bradley Killian wished he had not come in to work.

Slater thought for a brief moment he was in the middle of a nasty dream. Angie was shaking him, bringing his protesting body back to the waking world.

"Andy, wake up darling."

"What? What's the matter, have I overslept?" he asked, already falling out of bed.

"It's Bradley on the phone." Angie passed him the receiver. Andy glanced at the luminous dial on his bedside clock, wondering once more if this was all a surreal nightmare. He took the receiver, hoping it was indeed a dream, and Killian was about to order him to take a month's paid leave.

"Andy, its me, Brad."

"What's up? It's the middle of the night," Slater protested.

"I know that,. I need you here now. We've got big trouble."

"Oh, for fuck's sake, Brad...!" Slater heard Killian hang up, now only a monotonous tone coming from the phone. Slater slumped back onto the warm bed, dropping the receiver on the floor.

"What's up, baby?" Angie asked, switching on the bedside lamp.

"Bradley Killian, that's what's up honey."

"Oh no! You haven't got to go back to work now have you?" she asked, laying her head on his chest. He relished her contact, realising again just how much he missed her lately. She began to rub her hand across his stomach, small rhythmic circles working their way down towards his groin. Slater began to feel his penis twitch, hardening as his wife's hand brushed against it. She reached up and kissed him gently, her hand taking his fully hard member in its warm embrace. Slater responded, his hands greedily devouring her firm warm body.

As Slater entered his wife, Bradley Killian was but a distant memory. For now at least he would have to wait.

Shivering in the darkness, six cold men waited, hidden behind a row of bushes deep inside a wet muddy cow field.

"Where the fuck is that prick?" Mark asked, hopping from foot to foot in a vain attempt to get warm.

"Mark, stop jumping about, you fat cunt, you're splashing shit up my legs," Boris growled.

"I'm cold," Mark protested.

"You're a fucking degenerate, that's what you are," Boris told him, kicking a pile of cow shit up Mark's back.

"Bastard!" Mark walked away, seeking the protection of Mags.

"Behave, you fucking children. This isn't the school sandpit for fuck's sake," Mags chided.

"What the fuck is Ray driving, a fucking pushbike? He should've been here by now, the Scotsman wondered, trying to catch a clear glimpse of his watch in the moonlight.

"Probably got lost, the dumb fuck," Mags offered. He did wonder though, after all Ray Callard was driving around in a brand new Jaguar, probably fifty grand's worth Mags figured. Somewhere in the back of his mind a nagging thought battled to be heard. Mags tried to calculate Ray's earnings. He reasoned a copper of his rank would probably be earning around thirty grand a year. He also lived in one of the most sought after areas in the whole county, and that didn't come cheap. The nagging thought troubled him greatly. Magnus Vandersar had never been a mathematician, but from where he was standing, ankle deep in cow shit, the maths surrounding Ray Callard just didn't add up, not even close.

The white Mercedes cruised slowly along Coldhams Lane, past houses cloaked in darkness. The driver spotted a phone box, its dim illumination a beacon in the dark gloomy shadow of a huge road bridge.

"There's the phone box, by the bridge," Karpov noted, turning to his passenger, Andre Kansky.

"Turn down there," Kansky ordered, pointing to a side road twenty metres past the phone box. Karpov spun the steering wheel. The Mercedes responded with screeching tyres, before coming to a halt. Karpov got out of the car, pulling a revolver from his waistband. Kansky remained seated in the passenger side of the Mercedes, screwing a silencer to the barrel of his weapon. He wanted the job carried out properly this time, with no fuck ups, and no noise. Satisfied the silencer was fitted correctly, he stepped out of the car into the coldness of the night. Suddenly the sound of an approaching car broke the serene quietness. Kansky instantly tucked the weapon into his waistband, covering it with his jacket. Karpov, less concerned simply stood and waited for the approaching vehicle. Headlights cut through the gloom, illuminating the Mercedes. Kansky watched the gleaming new Jaguar approach, relaxing slightly as Ray Callard stopped inches behind his own car.

"Sorry I'm late," Ray offered, stepping from the Jaguar.

"You'll be late for your own fucking funeral policeman," Karpov commented. Ray felt his blood chill at Karpov's statement. He wondered if it had been wishful thinking.

Mags raised his hand, bringing a halt to the bickering still going on between Boris and Mark.

"Ssh, shut the fuck up!" he told them. He craned his neck, hoping to locate the sound.

"Mags? Mags, where are you?" The voice was unmistakable. Mags left the sanctuary of the bushes. Squelching through the wet ground he headed for Ray Callard who he could now see standing by the phone box.

"Ray?" he called.

"Over here, mate." Mags could see Ray waving.

"Let's go, lads," he shouted at the five shivering figures behind him.

"About fucking time," one of them shouted back. He was beginning to agree. The cold had begun to penetrate his bones. Ray watched as the six figures emerged from the darkness, like a ghostly spectacle. He smiled, content in the knowledge that very soon they would all be indeed just that, ghosts.

Slater knew from the second he entered the rear door of Parkside station that something big and probably bad had happened. Chief Inspector John O'Neil was the first person he saw. Chief Inspectors were rarely to be found on duty at this time of night. O'Neil was busily barking orders to anybody in his vicinity. Slater noticed with amusement that Killian was one of them. Killian saw Slater approaching, and immediately waved him over.

"Hello, sir," Slater said, shaking hands with O'Neil.

"How are you, Andy? Well, I hope.

"Fine, sir. What on earth is going on?" Slater asked. O'Neil shook his head, his sharp angular features cutting the air like a knife. Always a very serious man, Slater saw that now he looked positively suicidal.

"We've got some serious problems Andy. Bradley will give you the details. Let's just say you are all in for some heavy overtime." Slater felt his shoulders drop, almost crying at the news he had been dreading. Randal walked over and handed O'Neil a piece of paper. He read it and immediately headed for the nearest telephone. Killian took the opportunity to slip away. Slater followed with the look of a condemned man.

"So?" Slater asked as they headed for Killian's office.

"Vandersar and his mates escaped, Andy. They fucking jumped the duty copper."

"What? You're kidding, aren't you?"

"Do I look like I'm joking about, Andy?" Killian pointed out, his face almost as miserable looking as O'Neil's Slater noticed. They entered the office, and Killian slumped behind his desk and began rummaging through his top drawer. He produced his metal flask and set about half filling two dirty coffee mugs.

"Understandably O'Neil's not a happy bunny," he said passing a stained mug to Slater.

"Press will have a fucking field day with this, Brad."

"Don't I know it," Killian agreed, remembering his special relationship with journalists, and especially news reporters. Slater downed the contents of his mug in one giant gulp, ignoring the heat generated in his throat. He needed the courage, because something weighed heavily on his thoughts, and he decided Killian needed to share that weight.

"Brad, there's something I've got to tell you." Slater watched Killian, waiting until he had his full attention.

"What's up, not pregnant are you?" Killian answered, cackling like an old woman, much to Slater's annoyance.

"No, Brad, I'm not pregnant. But I'll tell you this much, I don't think Vandersar and his crew killed Sergatov. I think you've overlooked the obvious." Slater studied Killian's face, a wave of amazement washed over it. He also noticed Killian wasn't laughing anymore either.

Ray watched the bedraggled shivering assortment of bodies approach, Mags leading the way, his huge feet squelching through the wet mud.

"You look like you could use a drink, mate," Ray commented as Mags ducked under the barbed wire fence. He made it through without tearing any more holes in his shirt, and began lifting the top strand so Boris could squeeze his large frame through.

"I've quit drinking, Ray, in case you haven't heard," Mags replied, helping Boris untangle his trousers from a stray barb.

"Fuck the chitchat, Ray. Where's the fucking wheels?" Darryl asked, purposely kicking wet cow shit across Callard's shoes. Ray looked down at his brand new loafers. He had bought them only a week before. Now the suede glistened with foul wet cow shit in the bright yellow streetlight.

"Thanks, Darryl mate." Ray tried to shake the bigger lumps off, hoping they might stick to Darryl's already filthy trousers.

"Don't mention it, Ray," Darryl told him, slapping him hard on the back with a snigger. Ray couldn't see the wet black muddy handprint neatly plastered on the back of his beige jacket.

"Cut it out, you two," Mags snapped, releasing the barbed wire as Mark finally eased his considerable bulk through the gap.

"I'm parked up the road, Mags," Ray said, pointing towards a side street situated in the shadow of Coldhams Lane's hugely forbidding road bridge.

"Funnily enough, Ray, I'm not in the mood for a long distance walk. Couldn't you have parked a bit fucking closer?" Mags grumbled, looking over towards where Ray had pointed. He reasoned it must be two hundred metres away at least. Ray set off, leading the pack hurriedly across the deserted road. Mags stamped his feet loudly as he crossed, shaking large lumps of mud and cow shit across the tarmac. Instantly five other sets of feet began the same noisy routine. Ray stopped, turned and watched with a sense of bewilderment as the six of them, all highly sought after fugitives, stood in the middle of a deserted road kicking and stamping mud off of their caked shoes.

"Why don't you lot make a bit more fucking noise?" he asked sarcastically.

"You want this fucking mess in your nice new motor, Ray?" Pat asked him, swinging his left foot and launching a clump of mud over Ray's shoulder.

"I've borrowed a van. How could I get you lot in my motor?"

"Good point, Ray," Pat noted.

"It hasn't got police written on it has it, Ray?" the Scotsman asked, and simultaneously every one except Ray burst into laughter.

In the darkness of the bridge, hidden by impenetrable blackness, Kansky and Karpov waited silently. They could hear laughter breaking the silence, and loud foot stamping. Kansky wondered what the hell they were up to? He gripped the weapon hanging by his side, longing to silence the laughter piercing the quiet night stillness.

"Get ready, Marco," he whispered. Karpov flipped the safety catch off of his silenced revolver with his thumb.

"What are they doing, Andre?" he asked, his booming voice echoing loudly under the bridge.

"Ssh! Quiet, Marco." Kansky nudged him in the ribs, doubting whether his huge companion actually registered it, and went back to waiting silently.

As they approached the bridge, Mags thought he heard a voice, the dull echo carrying through the night. He was shoulder to shoulder with Ray when he heard it, and stopped instantly. Ray carried on unaware.

"Ray, hold up," Mags whispered. Ray kept on walking, pretending not to hear.

"Ray!" This time Mags shouted, and Ray turned to see Mags and the others backing into the gardens of a row of council houses.

"What's up with you lot?" Ray asked, holding his arms out in mock amazement.

"Get over here, dickhead. There's someone under that bridge," Mags told him, waving him over furiously.

"It's probably a tramp, Mags. Come on, lets fucking get out of here."

"I don't like it, guv," Pat whispered from behind a privet hedge.

"No, I don't either," Darryl added.

"Ray, get the van and we'll wait here," Pat shouted through the bush.

"Suit yourselves," Ray muttered walking away. As he neared the opening to the side street, he saw movement in amongst the gloomy shadows of the bridge. He broke into a run, eager to get out of the impending line of fire. Mags saw the flash, a yellow plume of fire leaping out from beneath the bridge. A fraction of a second later he heard a dull thud as the Scotsman was literally lifted from his feet. Initially Mags couldn't make his brain understand why the Scotsman was flying backwards through a privet hedge. The screaming then began, and Mags made the connection.

"Everybody down!" he bellowed, dropping flat on his stomach.

"Fuck, I'm hit!" the Scotsman screamed, clutching his right shoulder. Pat left his position from behind a low garden wall and ran to the Scotsman's aide. Mags scanned the bridge, ignoring the screaming. He saw first one, then two figures emerging from the shadows. Another flash, then another. Mags buried his face into the cold earth of a flowerbed. He actually heard a loud whizzing as the rounds sped only inches over his head. Another sickening thud followed by a grisly scream told him another of his men had been hit. He lifted his head and saw Pat stretched out on the pavement, his left leg twitching as a rapidly expanding pool of blood spread from his side, an open gaping hole that spewed intestines. Mags didn't know who the two approaching figures were, but he knew they were all dead within the next thirty seconds if they didn't act. He jumped to his feet, felt the air part as another shot came perilously close to his face, and ran full on at the front door of the house whose garden they were now being slaughtered in. The wooden frame exploded as two hundred and sixty five pounds of Icelandic muscle hit the door at speed. Splinters of wood peppered his face as he landed with a sickening thump at the foot of a set of stairs.

"Come on!" he screamed. Darryl burst in a moment later, with Boris right behind him. Mark struggled to drag the Scotsman along the garden path to the sanctuary of the house. Another round slammed into the Scotsman, the force ripping him from his arms. Mark watched in disbelief as a chunk of flesh the size of a fist exploded out the back of the Scotsman's head. Suddenly he was being dragged along, his shirt almost ripping as a strong hand tugged frantically.

"Leave him, he's gone. He's gone!" Darryl shouted pulling him into the broken doorway.

"We've gotta move, lads; come on," Mags screamed. Heading along the hallway, he kicked open a shabby door that led to a grimy kitchen. Mags could clearly smell the odour of a recently cooked curry. He hated curry, and thought the place stank. He started ripping open drawers, throwing the contents onto the kitchen floor. Boris kicked the contents about, bending over and picking up a huge steak knife, its ten-inch blade glimmered in the moonlight that penetrated through the window.

"You two, get going." Mags pointed at Mark and Darryl.

"What about you and Boris?" Mark asked, tears beginning to well in his eyes.

"Go!" Mags ordered. Darryl unlatched the kitchen door, revealing a patio that led to a long expanse of lawn.

"What about Pat?" Mark snapped, tears streaming down his cheeks.

"He's gone, Mark. Now save yourself. Go!" Boris told him, picking up another smaller blade that Mags had just deposited from a drawer. Darryl grabbed Mark by the arm, leading him out onto the patio. Mark took one last look back at Mags and Boris, and wondered if he would ever see them again?

Kansky stood over the twitching body, watching with grim fascination as

Pat fought vainly to cling to life. He knelt down, and poked the silencer of his weapon into the mass of protruding intestines. In the cold air Kansky noticed with childlike wonder that the steaming organs looked like the sausages he bought from his favourite delicatessen. Pat's breathing came in short desperate gasps, his face contorted with pain. Kansky stood up, lowered his pistol and shot Pat in the face twice from near point blank range. The first shell impacted on the left side of his face, removing most of his jaw in an explosion of bone, flesh and teeth. The second round entered through Pat's right eye, obliterating the soft organ before spinning through his brain. The pack of Patrick Glover's head came apart, spraying grey chunks of brain matter across the bloody pavement. Karpov was already peering through the shattered doorway, into the darkness of the hallway.

"Careful, Marco," Kansky warned, approaching with his weapon held outstretched in front of him. Karpov entered the darkness, almost tripping on a large chunk of broken doorframe. All was quiet as he approached the kitchen door. He tentatively pushed it open with his foot. In the darkness he could see the open door leading to the garden. Karpov lowered his gun, realising that the open door meant they had already escaped. He cursed silently to himself.

"Andre, they have gone," he called. Then Karpov felt an immense pain pierce his chest, the shocking intensity forcing him backwards into the hallway. Boris followed, rage consuming him as he plunged the lethal ten-inch blade once more into Karpov. The force of the ferocious assault nearly severed his head. Boris pulled the knife out of Karpov's throat and plunged it again and again into his chest. Karpov collapsed, his hands clutching his severed throat, fountains of warm blood spewing through his fingers. He fought for breath as his lungs began to fill with blood, his life ebbing away as Boris rained more savage blows into him. Karpov could vaguely make out a dark figure standing over him, a glimmering object moving back and forth in time with fresh bolts of pain. Boris wildly delivered another violent blow, the full length of the steel blade penetrating Karpov's left eye, severing his brain in one swift fatal movement. Boris continued pushing the blade into Karpov's lifeless body, only stopping as a large chunk of wall exploded inches from his face. Kansky unleashed another round. It exploded less than an inch from Boris's head, showering him with masonry.

Mags grabbed him by the arm, hauling him into the kitchen. Another round exploded, shattering a pile of dishes left drying by the sink. Mags dragged Boris out through the open door onto the patio as another pile of dishes disintegrated behind them. Kansky made his was along the darkened hallway, pausing briefly at the body of Karpov. He saw with grisly wonder, that his loyal friend was no longer recognisable, his face little more than a butchered husk of raw meat. He let off two more shots as he entered the kitchen, firing into the dark corners where an ambush might be lurking. He glanced back quickly at Karpov, realising his friend had been too hasty, and had paid dearly. From the distant corners of the night Kansky heard sirens. He cocked his head to intercept the sound more clearly. There it was, definitely sirens, and growing closer. He backed up, emptied the remainder of his magazine into the dark kitchen before hurrying back through the ruined doorway and into the night.

George Ridley had snored every night of his life since he was eighteen years old. He married Maylene when he was twenty, and she hadn't slept a full night since, forty years almost to the day. Maylene looked up from her word search book, trying to think. Her husband's booming snoring had made her lose her concentration in the middle of a line of celebrity names. She looked at him lying beside her, on his back with his mouth hung open. Same pose for forty years she told herself. He was a good man; she had always loved him dearly, but as she looked at him now, his chest falling and rising in perfect rhythm with the baritone noise, she wondered how on earth she had put up with him. Shaking her head in dismay, Maylene went back to her puzzle. Finding a familiar name, she circled Elton John and quietly congratulated herself. Suddenly a huge explosion shook the house. Maylene was in the process of circling Terry Wogan's name. The shock caused the pen to deviate across the page, snaking indiscriminately.

"George, George wake up." She shook him as hard as she could.

"Uh, wha…" George woke with a start. A stream of saliva fell from his mouth and hung off his chin.

"There's somebody downstairs, George. I think there's been an explosion." She clung to him, her word search strewn across the bed.

"Get off, woman." He struggled to free himself from her limpet embrace. George had stopped enjoying Maylene's physical attentions long ago.

"It's burglars, George, downstairs."

"Get off me, you bloody old fool," he said, prising himself away from her, and almost falling out of bed. A muffled thudding came from downstairs, another followed and George decided burglar or no burglar, he wasn't happy about having his sleep interrupted. Heaving his pyjama bottoms up over his massive belly, he headed for the bedroom door.

"Be careful, love," Maylene called, now almost hidden under a pile of bed linen. As George opened the door, a bright flash of light lit up the darkened hallway, a fraction of a second later a muffled thud followed. George could clearly see a figure standing in the open doorway at the bottom of the stairs. The figure held something in his outstretched hand. George couldn't figure out what it was, until a stream of fire escaped followed by another dull thud. George Ridley had lived a quiet reasonably unexciting life, just how he liked it, but he had watched plenty of good gangster movies, and he knew from James Cagney flicks that the figure standing in his hallway was firing a gun.

George closed the bedroom door, hurriedly wedging Maylene's dressing table chair up against it, knowing how futile a gesture it was, because when James Cagney let loose, a flimsy chair never got in his way. He peered through a slight crack in the curtains, out onto the darkened road. In the dim streetlight he made out something lying on the pavement. He strained his eyes, unable to believe that what he was seeing really was a body. He felt his blood running cold, ice water through his veins. George thought he had seen just about every good gangster movie ever made, except in the films the bodies didn't look like the one lying outside his house. The body George was now looking at didn't have a head. As he staggered over to his bedside table, fumbling for the telephone his stomach gave in, and an eruption of warm bile showered the bed, and Maylene.

Killian looked up sharply as Slater burst into his office, the door nearly leaving its hinges.

"Guv, call just came in. Old fella in Coldhams Lane reckons there's a man shooting his house up."

"Oh yeah, and there's a body outside in his front garden," Slater added. Killian reached for his jacket, the puzzled look still etched in his features as he left the office. Once again he wondered if getting out of bed this morning had been a big mistake.

Killian sat patiently with Slater. In the growing dawn light they watched as a number of armed police officers entered the house with military precision. Torches taped to the barrels of Heckler Kosch sub machine guns cut a path into the gloomy hallway like neon lasers. Slater watched intently, but also glad he wasn't a firearms officer. He wound down the passenger side window, reached into his trouser pocket and produced a crumpled packet of cigarettes.

"I'd rather you didn't, Andy," Killian said, never taking his eyes from the unfolding scene. Slater threw the packet onto the dashboard, and wound his window back up.

"About what you said earlier, Andy, do you really believe that?" Killian asked, referring to the conversation they had both shared.

"What, do you mean the bit about Callard?"

"Yeah, about Ray." Killian nodded.

"It stinks, Brad; something's not right. Sergatov and most of his top men get themselves murdered, and then low and behold Callard's out on the piss with Karpov and Kansky."

"What's he up to then? What's you gut feeling?" Killian asked, and Slater thought that just for a moment his all-knowing boss might have been yielding to his theory.

"I've already told you," Slater answered, ready to watch Killian crawl, beg if need be.

"Tell me again. Please." There it was Slater noted. 'Please'. Killian never ever said please. He realised that in Bradley Killian's self-righteous mind, 'please' was a degrading word.

"Well look, why the fuck would Vandersar and his crew walk into Sergatov's own club and shoot everyone in sight? There's no motive is there? I mean, from what we know they never even knew each other."

"Heroin?" Killian suggested.

"Look, Ray handed us a big pile of shit on Vandersar. Admittedly he's a violent bastard, but if he was into heroin trafficking how come we never heard about it? In fact nobody in the whole station knew that Vandersar was moving heroin. That's because he's not."

"That's a good point, I'll admit that." Killian told him.

"Damn right it is, Brad. There's no motive there at all, and tell me the truth, does Vandersar come across as a stupid man to you?" Killian shook his head. True, he didn't particularly like the man, but then when he thought about it, he didn't really like anyone at all that much.

"But the weapons, Andy, they matched?" He quipped, looking to gain some respect and tear Slater's theory down.

"I can't answer that just yet," Slater admitted.

"Looking at it from your point of view Andy, I'll admit I might have been a bit hasty. But if it wasn't him and his buddies, we've got a multiple killer, or killers on the loose still."

"Yeah, and I'm still willing to bet that body over there is the latest victim," Slater added, nodding at the corpse lying fifty yards away.

"Well I think we need to sort this mess out Andy, and then go and pay Ray an early morning call."

"I'm up for that, guv," Slater agreed, reaching for his cigarettes.

The first officer entered the dark hallway, instantly swinging his sub machine-gun from side to side in a sweeping motion. The beam of his mounted torch picked up pools of liquid, reflecting light back in hazy patterns. A second officer flanked him as he stepped closer to investigate. He stepped over the wreckage of Marco Karpov's body, slipping slightly in a puddle of rapidly spreading blood. He entered the kitchen, sweeping left to right, arching rapidly for a target. Nothing hid in the darkened corners; only a cold morning breeze rippled through the room.

"Clear," he said, lowering his weapon. He heard his fellow officers running up the stairs as he stood over the body of Marco Karpov. He shone his torch slowly and carefully over the butchered remains, and was left in no doubt that there was little point in calling for an ambulance.

"Armed police." The chair flew across the bedroom as the door was kicked open with almighty force. The first officer through the door clicked his safety catch, realising the old couple lying huddled on the bed were no threat. He almost burst out laughing at the sight of the old woman, her face was covered in cream. She looked downright comical he thought. Then he noticed what looked like bits of carrot stuck to her hair, and the smell hit his nostrils. He had to fight hard to stop his own stomach from rebelling.

Slater sat in a crouched position, examining the corpse lying half in the hallway, and half in kitchen. The wounds he had witnessed at the carnage of the Metropolis lounge had been shocking, almost too much to take in. But looking now at the butchered remains of Marco Karpov, Slater knew he would suffer nightmares for the rest of his life.

"Jesus fucking wept," he uttered, at the sight of Karpov's head, almost split in two. Killian walked over, being careful not to step in the congealing pools of thick dark blood.

"Fitting end to a bastard like him," he said. He had known and stalked Karpov from the moment he first stepped into the country. He knew all too well what a psychotic monster Karpov was, and that his life would end this way.

"Live by the sword, die by the sword," Slater added.

"It looks that way Andy."

"This is some weird shit guv. What the hell on earth is a Russian mafia hit

95

man doing lying stabbed to death in the hallway of a council house?" Slater asked, puzzled at such a bizarre set of circumstances.

"My sentiments exactly." Killian wondered much as Slater did, and knew the two shared the honour of being totally lost in a plot that was seemingly motiveless. Killian left Slater, glued with a grisly fascination to Karpov's remains, while he made his way through the growing number of forensic technicians and uniformed officers.

"Where's the old couple?" Killian asked Gordon Ridley, who was in the process of wiping blood from the soles of his boots on the wet grassy lawn.

"Fucking stuff," he moaned.

"Gordon, the old couple?" Killian snapped impatiently.

"Oh yeah, in the van," he replied pointing to a police van parked twenty metres away in amongst a veritable convoy of police and forensic vehicles. Killian left Gordon to clean his boots, noting with a sense of disgust red patches staining the green turf.

Ritchie Lang hated his job, he hated his workmates, and he hated having to start work at seven in the morning. He glanced at his watch, and knew instantly he was never going to make it on time. He swore at himself for not leaving the pub until nearly midnight, he always overslept after a skin full, and that he knew was almost every night. Since his wife had left him nearly two years ago, taking their three children with her, Ritchie had progressed from a regular drinker who came home drunk and beat his wife and children, to a fully-fledged drinker who simply beat up anyone who even mildly irritated him. At thirty-four Ritchie had a string of convictions stretching back to his early teens, all of them for violent offences. Now, almost relieved not to be burdened by a young family, his life was dedicated to drinking and supporting the real love of his life, Cambridge United. As a token of his love, he'd had 'love' and 'hate' tattooed across his knuckles. He proudly took the status of the headman at the Abbey Stadium, seriously indeed. Ritchie and his mates, all dedicated thugs themselves, lived for the violence they inflicted. He overtook a milk float on a blind bend, almost forcing it into a kerb. Ritchie glanced once more at his watch, three minutes past seven. "Cunt!" he shouted. Never mind, he reassured himself. If that prick of a foreman starts today, Ritchie planned on breaking the fuckers jaw. Long overdue he concluded, long overdue. Besides, he was Ritchie Lang; everybody knew that. Nobody fucked with Ritchie. Nobody.

Killian peered into the back of the police van, a young copper sat holding the old girl's hand. She looked in shock. The old fella with her, Killian presumed it was her husband. He sat shivering under a blanket, his huge swollen gut protruding like an obscene pregnancy. Killian decided now wasn't the time for a question and answer session and left them alone.

"Any joy?" Killian found Slater standing behind him, peering over his shoulder into the van.

"No, leave them," Killian told him. Walking back towards the house, he wanted to check out the other body lying on the pavement. A tarpaulin had been hastily erected to cover the body, and when Killian and Slater entered the makeshift covering, they could immediately see just why.

"Bloody hell." Killian felt his stomach tighten and convulse. Slater took one short look at the corpse and then made his way out into the cold fresh air. Enough was enough he told himself, lighting a cigarette. Killian joined him a second later, and looking at Slater he wondered why on earth he himself didn't smoke.

Ritchie stood on the brake. The metro's rear end rebelled, sliding at a crazy angle as its tyres fought and lost their battle with the wet tarmac. With a dull thud the Metro came to a halt, sideways on against a stationary transit van. Ritchie looked on in utter disbelief. Two men had just jumped out in front of his car. It was a miracle he hadn't run straight over them. Rage consumed him like a dark veil. What the hell were they thinking of? Well he was Ritchie Lang, and these two clowns were about to pay for any damage, with interest. He kicked his door open, falling from the cramped confines of the Metro.

"You stupid fucking cunts!" he bellowed, bearing down on the two men, now standing innocently by the wreckage. Ritchie readied his meaty fists, love and hate about to administer their own brand of retribution. The two men held their ground as Ritchie pulled back his right arm. The taller of the two swiftly and with sublime precision launched a hefty foot straight between Ritchie's legs. All thoughts of violence left his mind as he dropped to his knees. The pain throbbed through his testicles like a hot fire. Fear and disbelief merged as Ritchie could do nothing more than spectate as the two men jumped into his car and wheel spinned away. Vainly he tried to get to his feet, but couldn't and fell over face first, his head landing in a pile of fresh dogshit. If this got out he reasoned, he was finished at the Abbey Stadium. The indignity of it all.

O'Neil looked at the screen. The computer enhanced the fingerprint until it was almost filling the screen.

"Definitely the one; it's a match," he said.

"Patrick Glover, twenty-eight, five ten. He's our man," Jenny McAllister added. The young policewoman punched up Patrick Glover's details confirming his personal statistics.

"Wolfpack," O'Neil spoke quietly.

"What was that sir?" McAllister asked.

"What's his form, Jenny?" he said urgently. She tapped the computer consul with consummate ease, her fingers moving with rapid speed and dexterity. The screen came to life with a whole list of dates and convictions. Patrick Glover had been a busy boy O'Neil noticed.

"Theft, ninety-two. Actual bodily harm, ninety-four and ninety-five. Lots of assaults, petty stuff really sir."

"What about drugs, Jenny, anything?"

"No, nothing," she said, guiding the mouse to reveal all of Patrick Glover's previous form.

"That's interesting. Jenny, be a love and get me Brad Killian on the phone. He'll want to know all this."

"Yes, sir." She began dialling Killian's number.

"Hang on. Is he still in Coldhams Lane?" O'Neil asked.

"I think he is, with Andy Slater."

"Don't worry, I'll shoot down there myself."

"Okay, sir," she said, but O'Neil was already on his way out of the incident room.

Boris and Mags filled the entire front of the Metro. It looked like a toy car. Boris drove, and the two of them headed through the growing traffic in silence, both still stunned by the events of the last few hours. Mags recalled the madness of the last couple of weeks: two attempts on their lives, the death of his men, arrested for murder. He hoped he was still drunk and the whole thing was nothing more than a bad nightmare. He glanced at Boris, his normally fierce exterior now crushed into a state of dazed shock and confusion, and he knew it was no dream. Pat and the Scotsman gone, dead. Mags fought an overwhelming urge to break down and cry, to simply give in to the emotion spinning through his battered mind. Pat, his most senior man. He'd loved the guy like a brother. Pat had been with him from the very beginning. He was one of the toughest men Mags had ever known, with a never say die attitude. Early in his career as a doorman Mags had fallen foul of a local gang, thugs who sold shit to kids. Pat had been their muscle, and he had been sent to sort the new

98

doorman out. They had both gone round to the back of the club Mags worked at and gone head to head. Forty minutes later they were still at it, both bloody and bruised but neither willing to lose. Mags remembered how a large crowd had gathered, people were actually sitting around drinking beers and eating bags of chips, just like being at the fights. After nearly three quarters of an hour of brutal action, the exhausted pair had finally ended up in a heap, lying in a puddle totally spent. They agreed to call it a draw. The crowd, so impressed gave the two a standing ovation, much to the dismay of Pat and Mags. There had been very few people in Mags' life who could take what he had to offer and still stand up, but Pat had done just that, and nearly beaten him in the process. As a gesture of respect he jokingly offered Pat a job, and when he accepted Mags knew he had found the right hand man he needed. The memories flooded through him as they drove quietly towards the outskirts of the city. Mags knew he couldn't grieve just yet, because before this bad dream was over, he knew there would be more deaths to mourn.

O'Neil pulled the squad car to a halt behind the convoy of vehicles. He couldn't remember seeing so many of his men at the scene of crime before. The night shift had stayed on, merging with the morning shift who had arrived at six o'clock. Slater and Killian were milling about amongst the throng. Both looked tired O'Neil noticed.

"Brad," O'Neil called, dodging an officer decked out in a white one piece overall.

"Sir, over here." Killian waved him over.

"I've got you an identification on one of these bodies. Patrick Glover, aka fully paid up member of the Wolfpack." O'Neil handed Killian a computer print out. A photo fit of Patrick Glover stared up from the sheet, Killian saw with a sense of relief that the photo was an old picture, Patrick Glover with his head still intact.

"We think the other body belongs to McRae Miller, formerly known as the Scotsman," O'Neil added, surveying the scene.

"Holy shit, what the hell is this all about?" Killian read through the printout, shaking his head.

"One other thing, Brad. This guy Glover has nothing against him that would mark him down as an associate, or an enemy of Sergatov. Everything but drug offences in fact."

"Yeah, isn't that strange," Slater cut in.

"Sir, we need a bit of time on this one. We've got something we want to follow up. Probably nothing but we'll need to check it out," Killian told him, folding the print out and handing it back to O'Neil.

"Do whatever you have to do, Brad, just put an end to this." O'Neil's tone changed as he punctuated the last point, leaving Killian and Slater with no delusions that their boss was being very clear about his orders. Killian watched O'Neil leave, the tall serious looking man casting his gaze across the scene of carnage. He knew failure or success in this case would determine whether he rose or fell through the ranks. O'Neil was a decent bloke he concluded, but results mattered, and O'Neil was a man who liked results. Cambridge had enjoyed more murders in two weeks than it had in years, and Killian knew O'Neil definitely didn't view that as a result; not at all.

The blue Metro cruised to a halt outside Ray Callard's home. Its leaking loud exhaust signalling its arrival. Mags looked around, the new houses of London Crescent looking oddly out of place against the leafy backdrop of the surrounding farmland. Mags wondered what a house like this must have cost, and once again decided Callard's personal income figures didn't match up. Boris stepped out of the car, admiring the dents running all the way down its length. White paint from the transit scored the blue paintwork. Boris thought it looked quite good. Mags ran his hands through his hair, looked at his reflection in the Metro's side door mirror, decided he looked like a sack of shit, and headed up the path towards Ray's house. Boris pressed the doorbell as Mags tried to straighten his torn shirt. The solid wooden door opened, rich dark oak adorned with polished brass fittings. Mags felt his heart leap as the door revealed Penny, her blonde hair hanging loosely. If ever he needed a pick-me-up, now was it, and Penny was better than any drink he'd ever had.

"Hi, Pen," Mags stuttered.

"Mags, what the hell happened to you? I've been worried sick," she pleaded, already starting to cry.

"Don't get upset, Pen. I'm okay. Where's Ray?" he asked, as he and Boris entered the house, stale clumps of mud and cow shit littering the white deep hallway carpet.

"I heard you were dead." She threw her arms round him. Mags winced as she hugged him, the deep slash from the barbed wire fence flaring up signals of fresh pain.

"You heard wrong, baby. Pat and the Scotsman didn't make it." She squeezed him tighter still, more spasms of pain jolted through him. Suddenly he pushed her away. She stood looking at him, shaken like a scolded child.

"What? What's wrong?" she asked, tears flowing freely down her flushed cheeks.

"Who told you I was dead?" he demanded. She looked at him with confusion, his sudden outburst catching her totally unaware.

"Ray did. He phoned about an hour or so after you called him."

"Where is he now?"

"He said he had to go straight into work, sort out what had happened."

"Penny, go and make us some coffee, love," he told her, almost lost within himself. She hurried into the kitchen. Mags waited until she was out of earshot before speaking.

"Boris?"

"Yeah, I'm with you. How the fuck did Ray know we were dead if he'd already legged it?" Boris nodded, his mind already working at overtime speed. He pieced together the last moments before the shooting, remembering how Ray had left them to get the van.

"Why didn't he come back for us, Mags?" Boris asked.

"Because he's a gutless cunt." Mags fired back. The two stood in Ray Callard's hallway, eye to eye trying hard not to find Ray guilty for selling them out.

"Tell you what I think, Boris. I think the man earns at best thirty grand a year. He drives a sixty grand motor. This house must be worth what, quarter of a million?"

"Easy," Boris agreed.

"So, it would seem to me that our friend Ray must be earning a bit extra on the side, and I don't pay him that much, Boris; about four hundred a month to look out for us, that's all."

"Kansky?" Boris already knew the answer.

"Looks that way, mate, doesn't it?" Mags replied, a fire of hatred now simmering behind those cold blue eyes.

"Promise me one thing, Boris." Mags hushed his voice to a whisper.

"What's that?" Boris came closer still to hear.

"When we kill him, we do it slow, really slow." Mags raised his left arm, gripping Boris' shoulder in a gesture of strength. He wanted now more than ever the loyalty of his men.

"Fucking right, Mags, fucking right." Boris gripped his hand, and from that moment on Ray Callard's life was on borrowed time.

Chapter Six

"Andre, what happened?" Ray Callard sat parked behind the Red Lion Pub, on Hills Road, the place long empty and now the windows revealing only darkness.

"Marco, they got Marco the motherless fucking bastards," Kansky shouted, and Ray had to pull his mobile away from his ear.

"Shit, what happened?" Ray feigned mock concern. Secretly he was jubilant.

"They were waiting inside that house. They kicked the door down and hid like the rat fucks they are. Marco, they killed him." Ray could hear the emotion in Kansky's voice, trembling with each word he spat out.

"Did you get them?"

"I think so. Two for sure, the rest I think I got." Kansky replied, his voice regaining some poise.

"You think so? You either did or you fucking didn't, Andre. This is quite a serious fucking matter here, in case you've forgotten?" Ray found himself shouting down his mobile, his own emotions rising.

"Hey, fuck head, I just lost a great friend. Maybe you should fucking shoot them?" Kansky ranted.

"Okay, I'm sorry, Andre It's just these guys are not people to fuck around with." Ray rubbed his temple, the frustration now beginning to make his head pound.

"Neither am I, Ray. Look, I got two definitely. I'm sure I hit the others too." Kansky was now raging, Ray could clearly hear every word with his phone held a foot away from his ear.

"Okay, Andre, calm down. I'll get to the station and find out what's happening. You lay low for a while."

"Keep me informed, Ray. I'll be at home for a while." Kansky had returned to a calmer state, much to Ray's relief.

"Will do, Andre; speak to you later," Ray told him, before snapping his phone shut. He hoped for their sake Magnus Vandersar had been one of those killed. Ray knew he would soon start putting two and two together, and that meant his death. He was certain of that. He rubbed his temples again, desperate to stave off the now throbbing pain in his head. Flipping his mobile open again he pushed in his home number and waited for Penny to answer.

"Hello, Ray?"

"Yeah, it's me, honey."

"What's happening?" she asked, rubbing the effects of deep sleep from her eyes.

"There's been a shooting. Mags is dead I think."

"What?" Penny felt her blood run cold, an icy ball welled up in her stomach.

"Yeah, I always told you he'd end up dead didn't I?" Ray asked smugly. Penny tried to remain calm. Despite the tears falling freely she kept up the pretence of disinterest.

"You did, Ray," she told him, hating him for his smugness.

"Anyway, I won't be home. I'm going straight into work to sort this out. I'll see you later, honey."

"See you later." Penny hung up, and instantly her pain erupted. She began sobbing almost hysterically, rocking back and forth. The only man she had ever loved, and he was gone. Why hadn't she gone to him when she had the chance? He had told her he could never offer her security, so she had found it with Ray. But she had never loved him, not even remotely. His touch she found unbearable, almost disgusting. When they did make love, which was very rare, she switched herself off and acted like an adoring wife, which is exactly what Ray wanted. When Mags had made her pregnant she had simply lied to Ray and told him her pill had failed. The fact that they hadn't had sex in months hadn't alerted Ray to anything, so she let him believe he was the father.

When Jake was born she knew straight away there could be no doubt who the real father was, his blue eyes and fair hair almost a carbon copy of Mags. Ray suspected nothing, and that added to her pain. She inwardly hoped that he would question her, knowing that she would probably cave in and tell him the truth. Then at least she wouldn't have to live everyday of her life as a lie. Jake brought her nothing but love and affection, but with each passing day he reminded her more and more of the man she truly loved. It was an unbearable pain she fought to live with, her only hope that someday they might actually be together. Now that hope was gone forever, her husband bringing the news with his usual sense of uncaring detachment. Penny sobbed hysterically, curled up in a tight ball on the bed. Only when the dawn began to break did she finally fall into a deep traumatised sleep.

Slater pointed to a signpost up ahead, Weldon Homes new estates.

"Down there?" Killian asked, guiding the Mondeo into the turning.

"London Crescent, guv, I think that's the place anyway," Slater told him, looking at the rows of new red-bricked houses, white picket fences bordering each house from the next.

"Bit posh, guv," Slater noted, wondering how Callard could afford to live in such an exclusive area.

"Not bad for a copper," Killian added, his voice heavy with sarcasm. They crawled past finely built houses, drives filled with expensive cars. Slater could see an elderly man peering through the bay window of a large house as they rounded a bend. His wrinkled face following their car as it drove by. Neighbourhood watch Slater thought, bet on it. He returned the stare, and the face withdrew to the sanctuary of expensive handmade curtains.

"Fucking nosey old cunt." Slater gave him a middle finger salute for good measure. Killian glanced at the source of Slater's annoyance, saw only an empty house, and wondered for a second if his partner had actually been talking to him. He thought better of asking, and carried on trying to negotiate the warren that passed for London Crescent.

"I'll know the fucking place when I see it, guv." Slater began examining each house in turn for a glimmer of recognition.

"They're all the same; it's a bloody maze," he added. The bleeping of Killian's mobile interrupted the hunt for Ray Callard's elusive residence. Slowing almost to a crawl, Killian fumbled inside his jacket until he could find the phone, now busily playing a rendition of the Mission Impossible theme tune. Slater glanced across and smiled. That tune always cracked him up. He'd always had Killian down as a bit of a Mozart man.

"Hello?" Killian slowed the car to a halt, noticing at least two sets of curtains twitch in a house opposite.

"Brad, its O'Neil."

"Hello, sir, what's up?"

"Just to put you onto the latest Brad. The second body was McRae Miller.

Massive internal injuries. Died instantly so the chaps at the morgue tell us."

"He didn't look too well, sir." Killian winced at his reply, remembering too late that O'Neil didn't appreciate his humour the way Slater did.

"Very good, Brad. Anyway, two characters fitting the descriptions of Vandersar and Hunter stole a car early this morning, left the driver needing surgery on his testicles.

"Bloody hell!" Killian winced.

"Exactly my thoughts. Just keep your eyes open for a blue Metro, licence plate unknown. Apparently the driver was too drunk, and in too much pain to be very helpful. Mind you it had just crashed into a stationary transit van, so it's probably a bit banged up."

"Will do, sir; we'll keep our eyes open."

"Okay, keep me informed, Brad. I want these idiots found."

"No problem, bye, sir." Killian lowered the phone, eyes wide open, almost transfixed. Slater followed his gaze, his own eyes coming to rest on a battered blue Metro parked not fifty feet away. Suddenly recognition snapped him back to life.

"That's it, that's the house there. Where that blue Metro is." Slater looked back at Killian, who still sat transfixed on the blue car ahead.

"What's up, guv?" he asked, wondering if Killian had perhaps seen a ghost.

"Do you believe in coincidence, Andy?" Killian broke his gaze from the battered Metro.

"I suppose, why?" Slater was looking at Killian now like he had grown an extra head.

"O'Neil just told me two things, Andy. One, the second body was McRae Miller. Two, Vandersar and Hunter hijacked a blue Metro early this morning."

Now as Killian looked over at Slater, he saw his partner's eyes locked on the battered car.

"Fuck!" Slater reached for his own mobile, intent on calling for backup. Killian put his hand on Slater's arm, stopping him in mid-motion.

"No, Andy."

"What?" Slater looked on in amazement.

"Do you believe in this theory of yours?" Killian asked, withdrawing his hand.

"Yeah, I do as it goes."

"Well then let's think about this, shall we?"

"Yeah, but O'Neil…"

"Fuck him, big nosed cunt," Killian snapped. Andy Slater sat dumbstruck.

He'd never seen his boss like this.

"But, I mean…" he protested.

"What? What, Andy? Look, whoever's behind all this obviously wants Vandersar dead, correct?"

"Correct." Slater nodded.

"Then let's get to him before he dies Andy. We don't know who's behind this yet, but I'll bet my life he does," Killian told him, turning to make sure the Metro was still there. It was, with flecks of white paint decorating the dented panels.

"What do you want us to do, go over there and knock on the fucking door?" Slater asked almost incredulously.

"Yep."

"You must be fucking nuts. The fuckers are probably armed guv."

"If they were armed, Andy, why did they stab the Russian to death with an old kitchen knife?" Slater's eyes narrowed at the question. It was a point he hadn't considered.

"True, very true," he had to admit.

"I think you're right, Andy. Ray's in on this, and I don't think Vandersar is here for a social visit."

"You think he's here to kill him?" Slater's eyes widened at the thought.

"Something along those lines anyway," Killian offered, already reaching for the door handle.

Mags needed the coffee. In fact his thoughts turned to the idea of something stronger, but he quickly dismissed them. Penny refilled his cup, watching as he greedily began to devour the contents.

"Rough night?" She leant over and kissed his cheek.

"We lost Pat and the Scotsman Pen." He could barely disguise the emotion in his voice. He looked across the kitchen table at Boris, who sat staring into his coffee mug.

"Oh God!" She hugged him. The tenderness of her embrace almost tipped his fragile emotions, and he fought the urge to cry. Mags looked at Boris who lifted his head to meet his friend's tear-filled eyes. He felt the tears welling in his own, and returned to staring into his cup.

"Who, why?" Penny asked.

"Doesn't matter, Pen, but there's one thing I need to know."

"What? Anything, Mags, what is it?" He noticed the concern creeping into her voice, and knew he would have to be careful about how he broached the next question.

"Sit down," he said, gesturing at the vacant chair between himself and Boris. She sat down, facing him innocently and momentarily he lost his composure.

"Penny, has Ray had any calls lately, from a Russian bloke?"

"Yes, he has. What was his name?" She pinched her mouth, trying hard to remember the name.

"They came round the other night," she added, still trying to put names to faces. Something she remembered with a sense of embarrassment that she had never been good at.

"They?" Boris asked, pushing the empty cup away.

"Two of them; one was huge with a massive scar running down his face."

"Karpov, he's the cunt who we nailed," Boris told her.

"What about the other guy, Pen?" Mags asked, gently squeezing her hand.

"Much smaller. To be honest he was a bit scary looking, shifty."

"Andre Kansky, Russian mafia hit man, all round bastard." Boris remarked.

"Sounds like it, mate." Mags sat nodding.

"What have they got to do with Ray?" Penny asked. Mags loosened his hold on her hand. She watched as his eyes narrowed, cruel furrows creasing his tired brow.

"Ray's gone over the hill on us, Pen. He set us up to be clipped." Mags watched as she physically caved in right in front of him. Her shoulders dropped as if she'd been punched hard in the chest.

"No!" she cried.

"Yes." Boris slammed a huge fist into the pine table.

"Easy mate." Mags winked at Boris, who looked ready to vent his fury. Boris relaxed slightly, leaning back in his chair.

"It can't be. Ray would never betray you, Mags," Penny whimpered.

"Honey, look around. You know how much I pay Ray to keep an eye on our business?" She shook her head, spilling tears onto the polished table surface.

"Four hundred a month. That doesn't finance all this, Pen, neither does a copper's fucking salary."

"He fucked us, and you know what that means?" Boris chipped in.

"But he wouldn't, would he?" She looked pleading, first at Boris and then at Mags. The two stoic faces told her the answer. She broke down and began to sob.

Slater thought he was going to have a coronary,. His breathing became even more laboured as he tried to keep pace with Killian.

"Guv, hold up."

"What's up?" Killian stopped to let Slater catch up. "You okay, Andy?" he asked.

"Nothing, guv. Well, tell a lie, I'm a bit, you know?"

"What, scared?"

"Sort of. Well yeah, I'm scared," he admitted. Killian turned away, picking up his pace again.

"So am I, son, so am I," he called back. Slater wiped the sweat from his forehead, praying he wasn't actually in the process of a heart attack, and began to follow his fitter, and much calmer boss. He finally caught up with him at the end of Ray Callard's garden. Killian had stopped and was now looking over the battered Metro.

"You ready to put your theory to the test, Andy?" he asked, still peering into the Metro's scruffy interior.

"I think so," he replied.

"Yes or no, yea or nay, in or out?" Killian snapped, the old venom returning to his voice. Slater knew he had to make his mind up, or Killian would make one quick call and an army of armed police would swoop down and finish the situation.

"I'm with you, Brad, I'm in."

"Good," Killian told him.

"Let's fucking do it then," he added, before striding up the block-paved drive towards Ray Callard's house.

Mags stroked her hair. With each tender caress her sobs grew weaker, until finally dying.

"Come on, baby, don't cry," he whispered. A knock at the front door threw the serenity into a state of alert. Mags jumped to his feet, Boris already reaching for a steak knife neatly holstered in a cutlery rack.

"Stay hidden, Boris. Penny, get the door. Fuck them off quick, whoever it is." Penny hurriedly began wiping her face, before heading down the hallway towards the front door. She paused for a second, using her sleeve to dab at her puffy eyes. She opened the door, and a face she hadn't seen for a long time greeted her.

"Brad, Bradley Killian?"

"In the flesh. How are you Penny?" He wanted to tell her she looked well, but the swelling around her eyes deterred the idea.

"I'm fine, Brad." She looked over his shoulder, where Andy Slater stood behind him.

"Andy, how are you? How's Angie?"

"We're both fine, Pen. Never see each other, but apart from that," he said, grinning.

"Look, Ray's not in and I'm kind of busy at the moment, I'm…"

"Vandersar." Killian cut her off in mid-sentence, all of the humour and pleasantness now gone from his voice.

"But, I…" she stuttered to get her words out.

"Penny, go back indoors and tell Magnus we believe him. If he tries to run we'll hunt him down. If he talks to us, well I think you get the picture," he said calmly. Penny nodded, tears once again running down her face.

"Come in," she told them, opening the door. Killian stepped through. Slater paused warily, a wave of panic causing him to breath rapidly again.

"Stay here," Penny told them, leaving them both at the end of the hallway, within the relative safety of the front door. She made her way into the kitchen. Boris was pressed flat against the wall next to the kitchen door, the huge steak knife held tightly in his left hand. Mags sat calmly on the kitchen worktop, kicking his feet back and forth.

"There's someone…" she began.

"I heard. Send them in," Mags cut in. Penny turned and waved Killian and Slater in, nervously eyeing Boris. Killian purposely strode into the kitchen, his eyes switching from left to right. He caught sight of Boris at the last moment, lurching away as the big man lunged for him. Boris missed, but a second later caught sight of another target. Andy Slater, panting with the stress of the fraught situation, froze. Boris wrapped his near twenty-inch bicep around Slater's throat, almost crushing his windpipe. The knife stopped its murderous journey a fraction away from Slater's left eye.

"No!" Killian shouted.

"Boris, easy," Mags snapped. Boris held firm, but the knife dropped to a safe distance, coming to a rest at Slater's throat.

"Put the knife away," Killian barked. Boris paid no attention. He intensified his grip on Slater's windpipe, watching intently as his victim began to turn blue.

"I give the fucking orders," Mags said, jumping down from his position on the worktop. He nodded at Boris, and Killian watched with relief as the big man loosened his grip and let Slater slip semi-conscious to the shiny tiled kitchen floor. Mags looked on as Killian rushed to Slater's aid.

"Andy, you okay, mate?" he asked, cradling Slater's head.

"I'm alright, honest, guv," Slater told him between huge gasps of air. Penny handed Killian a glass of water. He knelt down and helped Slater as he tried to take a mouthful.

"Sit him in the chair," Mags ordered. He watched as Killian manhandled him into position at the kitchen table. Slater devoured the glass of water, wiping the drips from his chin.

"You alone?" Boris asked. Slater nodded, still unable to speak.

"We weren't followed. We came alone," Killian confirmed, eyeing the knife Boris still held.

"What the fuck do you want?" Mags asked.

"We – he I should say – doesn't believe you topped the Russians," Killian replied.

"Oh no?"

"No."

"Tell me, Mr Killian, what does he think?" Mags said patting Slater on the back.

"Well, Mr Vandersar, he's stupid enough to think you're all innocent. For my sins, so do I."

"What is this, a wind up?" Mags asked, not sure what to make of Killian.

"I think we have a mutual friend, Magnus, and I think he's balls deep in all this."

"Raymond Callard I presume?" Mags offered.

"The very one."

"Sit down, Mr Killian." Mags pulled him up a chair. Killian took the seat, watching Boris cautiously as he seated himself. Mags noted his nervousness.

"Lose the knife, Boris. It's okay," he said, watching as he handed the knife to Penny. She racked it in its rightful place alongside several others.

"Put the kettle on, Pen," he told her, cursing himself for his insensitiveness. After all the coming conversation would be all about her husband's final days, one way or the other.

The water looked almost pleasant in the early morning sunshine Kansky thought. He watched a group of ducks making their way downstream, the quivering tails creating bow waves that befitted a much larger creature. Kansky watched in amusement, and wondered if life might be easier being a duck? God knows it had to be.

"Andre?"

"What?" He looked towards his bedroom. Katylana his latest sex toy lay waiting for him.

"Andre, come back to bed," she called. He poured himself a shot of vodka, then made his way to the bedroom. He stood in the doorway, mulling the warm clear liquid. Katylana was tempting, no doubt about that he thought. Stretched out across the sumptuous bed, her long finely kept blonde hair covering her young firm breasts. Her shaven vagina looked ripe, like a flowering rose. From beneath his dressing gown he felt his penis beginning to grow. Katylana watched with interest, parting her long legs to reveal the soft pink lips of her plump labia. Andre now had a full erection, his considerable penis jutting up at an angle through his gown.

"Come to bed, baby," she said, stroking herself with a perfectly manicured finger. The red nail parting her lips to reveal a swollen shiny wet opening. Andre swallowed the remainder of his vodka, before slipping from his gown. Katylana shifted her position, bringing her knees high to receive him. Anticipation coursed through her veins like a drug as he climbed between her legs, his hardness lightly brushing her swollen flower. Gently he pushed his hips forward, her lips parting easily as he entered her for the second time that morning. She let out a deep sigh, her back arching as the full length of his penis filled her. Her excitement pleased him, and he began driving in and out of her in deep rhythmic strokes, watching as her magnificent breasts shook with each thrust. She pulled him to her and began to probe his mouth with her hungry tongue. As he pounded her with deep orgasmic strokes, Andre Kansky began to forget about the worries in his life, and just for a while he was as free as a bird, gently coursing along the river on a bright winter's morning.

Ray Callard sat in a coffee shop, drinking his third cup in the last ten minutes. The waitress had looked at him strangely when he had ordered his last refill. Ray looked at the pricelist in front of him. Two twenty for a cup of coffee? Fucking liberty. The fat cunt waitress could look all she wanted. At these prices she could suck his cock. He sat close to the glass-fronted entrance, watching the human traffic coursing through the typically busy Grafton Centre. He followed a young mother, struggling with an irate and obnoxious young boy, probably no more than three years old. She fought to control the child who was intent on entering a toy shop situated across the precinct from where Ray now sat. The young mother lost her grip on the child, and ran after him as he bolted clumsily for an action man display. Her huge breasts heaved back and forth beneath her heavy black sweater. Ray pictured her naked, those massive bosoms swinging like swollen udders.

"Matthew, come here you little sod," she shouted, catching the child by the arm. Fucking kids he thought. He had one. He didn't really want it though. It kept Penny happy, but Ray figured kids should be seen and not heard. His own father had taught him that, and whereas Ray had enjoyed a loveless childhood, he reasoned his father had known best. After all, Ray had made a success of his life. His own son Jake was a quiet boy, and Ray paid little attention to him. He didn't like the way he clung to Penny though; he found it all a little disturbing. He wouldn't have minded too much if she showed him the same level of affection, but contact between him and his wife had ground almost to a halt.

He sipped his coffee, lost in thought. Ray tried to remember the last time he and Penny had sex. He drained his cup, counting back the months, finally coming to the conclusion that he couldn't actually remember when. Some fucking life he thought, once again eyeing the young mother, now bent over trying to strap the child back into his pushchair. He imagined her naked again, her large rounded backside waiting invitingly for him. Visions of ramming his hard cock up her arse filled his head. He wondered if she took it up the arse? Women today liked that sort of thing, didn't they? He had tried it once with Penny, forcibly entering her while she slept. He remembered with a smile how she had struggled, forcing him to get a little heavy with her. When he'd ejaculated in her, it had felt like fucking a virgin. He had left her crying on the bed as he went to the bathroom to clean himself up. Finding his penis coated in fresh blood had excited him more than the act itself. He masturbated there and then in front of the bathroom mirror. Penny had never really been very responsive to him before that, and she had been a cold whore bitch ever since. Never mind he thought. Kansky had fed him a continual supply of top-drawer whores, far more adventurous than Penny could ever be. He didn't need a wife; he could make it without her. He raised his hand, catching the attention of the waitress. She made her way over with a fresh pot.

"Thirsty today?" she asked, filling his cup once more.

"Just do your fucking job, woman," he snapped.

"I beg your pardon?"

"What, are you deaf as well as fucking ugly?" A thin smile crept across his lips. She finished pouring and hurried away, tears visibly welling behind her large brown eyes. Good, he thought to himself. Nosey fat cunt, fuck off.

"If I wanted to talk I'd phone the fucking Samaritans," he shouted after her. He looked into his cup, the black liquid throwing hot steam up that assaulted his eyes. He began to drift back to the events of the night before, wondering how Kansky and that dumb fuck Karpov had managed to fuck things up. He just hoped Mags had got it. Without him the pack was leaderless, an army without a general. If he had survived, he would be just slightly pissed off. Ray also understood that Mags would be out there now hunting down those responsible. He wouldn't kill Kansky until he'd tortured every possible connection out of him. He shivered at the thought. Rumours had circulated on how that drug-dealing piece of shit McGinn had met his end. Ray was under no illusions that those rumours had been true. If he had survived, Kansky was soon to be one dead Russian, that was for sure. That didn't worry Ray too much. Kansky was merely a business partner, in a business that had failed to get off the ground. True, with Sergatov and the Wolfpack out of the way, Ray and Kansky would have been free to run heroin wherever they wanted, and become extremely rich in the process. But now he knew all bets were off. Back to being a copper, two weeks in Spain with a wife and kid who couldn't stand him. Fuck it, those were the breaks. Ray knew he could live with that, for now anyway.

The trouble was he knew Mags too well, and if he was still alive, Kansky would end up telling him all he needed to know, before ending up being butchered to death. Ray knew that if that happened, he too would end up being carved like a Sunday roast, and he didn't like the idea one little bit. He hated his boring life quite intently, but he wasn't ready to be dismembered. No, he had to put himself as far away from all of this as possible. He took a mouthful of hot coffee, the bland liquid making him wince. Ray Callard weighed up his options. Kansky as a business partner was now an unattractive marriage, whores and three grand a month in his back pocket included. Mags paid peanuts, but if he was still walking around, that was the team Ray needed to be playing for. The only problem standing in his way seemed to be Andre Kansky, and his soon-to-be tortured confession. Ray emptied his cup, left a handful of coins on the table, and made his way out into the bustle of the Grafton Centre. In the multi-storey car park above, his car lay waiting. He made his way through crowds of shoppers towards the car park exit, planning his next move as he went.

Boris shook his head in disgust, the murderous rage inside of him threatening to escape.

"The cunt!" he screamed, rising from his chair.

"Calm down, Boris. Sit back down," Mags told him.

"The fucking bastard, he's fucked!" Boris exclaimed, straightening his chair before sitting down again.

"You sure about this, Slater?" Mags asked, his cool eyes piercing Slater's.

"I saw him, with the two Russian goons, leaving their club," Slater replied.

"Jesus fucking Christ." Mags sighed, leaning back in his chair.

"Bit of a coincidence don't you think?" Killian cut in.

"Slightly," Boris snapped.

"Look, we're still not sure. I mean we don't have total proof do we?" Mags offered, trying to lessen the impact of the conversation on Penny, who stood leaning against the kitchen doorway, her face swollen from crying.

"What about this?" Killian pulled a piece of paper from his jacket pocket, and handed it to Mags.

"What's this?" Mags asked, unfolding it.

"Read it," Killian told him. Mags studied the paper intently, reading a list of offences ranging from violent assault to drug dealing and trafficking allegations. As the top of the page he saw his own name printed.

"What the fuck!?" he stammered.

"Ray gave us this. That's the intelligence he has on you," Killian said.

"This is shit. I've done some things, but drugs, no fucking way." Mags snapped.

"Ray handed that to us, Magnus, when it looked like you guys were in the frame for Sergatov's murder," Slater told him.

"I don't fucking believe it. The cunt." Boris slammed his fist into the table again. Penny began to sob once more. Mags rose from the table and went over to her, taking her in his arms.

"Then the motherfucker has to die," Mags told them all, pulling Penny closer to him.

"You know I can't let you do that, Magnus. He's got to stand trial," Killian said, a serious edge entering his voice.

"Well then, Mr policeman, you'd better find him before we do," Mags replied, and the edge in his own voice left Killian in no doubt what that might mean.

Katylana stirred beside him, as Kansky lay wide awake staring at the ceiling. Sleep would not come, despite the overwhelming fatigue that tried to envelop him. He reached to his cigarettes, thrown earlier onto the floor beside his bed. As he reached over his left leg kicked Katylana, causing her to moan lightly. Fumbling amongst his discarded clothes Kansky found with a sense of relief that his cigarettes were still there. He repositioned himself back in bed before lighting a Marlboro. Kansky blew a lazy ring of blue smoke towards the ceiling, watching with fascination as it exploded like a wave as it hit. "Boom," he whispered as the smoke rippled away in ever increasing circles. Kansky half closed his eyes, his mind wandering. What would his next move be? Karpov's loss was a body blow to his future aspirations, but certainly not the killer punch. Marco had been loyal, a great friend and servant, but Kansky now controlled the entire heroin trade of a whole city, and he still had plenty more loyal subjects under his command. Now Sergatov was gone, every member of the organisation would answer to him.

He blew another curling billow of smoke. It drifted lazily upwards before impacting across the ceiling. *Sergatov, my dear friend* he thought, a thin smile creasing his mouth. "No more fucking errands," he uttered. The thought pleased him, very much indeed. True enough, he and Sergatov had a long history together, right back from when as conscripts they had shared the bloody kills in the wastelands of Afghanistan. Together they had fought the odds to survive, only the dreams of one day having their own personal empire keeping them going through three years of horror. Somehow the dreams had given birth to everything they'd ever wanted; all except one small detail. Sergatov was the boss, and Kansky had always remained little more than a hired killer, never really rising to the rank Sergatov had always promised. Andre was by his own admission more of a killer than a business executive, so he had patiently waited until Sergatov had woven his magic and established a very, no Kansky corrected, an extremely profitable business. When everything was in place he had struck with venom. Any loyalty he might have had thrown aside in the pursuit of wealth. Greed was a great motivator he thought, flicking ash onto the floor beside the bed. It had all been so easy. The old fucks had been so busy counting their fucking money they hadn't seen anything coming. Complacency was a far greater sin than greed, that much he understood. All he had needed was a fall guy, someone to take the rap. Cambridge had been notoriously easy to flood with heroin, easier that any of them had anticipated in fact. Yet there existed a large number of outlets, pubs and nightclubs that could have provided them with even further wealth, yet for a band of bouncer who gave no quarter to the drug trade. They ran their business with military precision, and a ruthlessness that Kansky almost admired.

Shit, if he hadn't needed to destroy them he would have tried to recruit them instead. But they had to go. More and more of Sergatov's business was being interrupted by them. Not that the stupid fuck had noticed. Kansky saw a chance to kill two birds with one stone, and eliminate the bouncers and Sergatov and his old fucking allies in one go. He had paid one of his top dealers, McGinn to kill the bouncers while they were totally unaware. The dumb fuck had managed to screw it up. But then things had actually turned out alright, because indeed the rumours surrounding the legendary Wolfpack had turned out to be pleasantly true. They had found McGinn and cut him into pieces. Kansky didn't blame McGinn for giving up his employers. In fact it had worked out just fine. When the Metropolis had been hit, the police had assumed that the bouncers had paid Sergatov back in kind, even though in reality the old fuck had known nothing. Perfect, he thought stubbing his cigarette out into a nearly full ashtray.

Katylana turned over and snuggled up to him, her warm body so inviting. And that had been his bait to catch the dipshit policeman Callard. He had regularly been visiting the Metropolis, like many other lonely sex-starved husbands. When Marco had tipped him off that the short balding man who regularly spent his evenings tucked away in a dark side booth had been a member of Cambridge police, notably the serious crime department, Kansky had made it his personal policy to entertain him. When, after countless evenings entertaining him with pretty whores and fine vodka the prick had let it slip that he personally managed the legal services of Guardian Leisure, Kansky's ears had turned like a radar.

"Me and Vandersar are like brothers," he had boasted.

"Really?" Kansky had replied, showing how impressed he was by a man with such connections. From then on the whores had been dirtier, giving in to every whim Callard demanded. Apparently he had a serious fascination with punishing the girls anally, much to their disgust. In time Kansky asked for small favours, lose a parking ticket, check out a name, stuff any policeman working for Sergatov would have done for free. Instead Kansky paid him well, so well that when he finally asked him to become his new business partner, Ray Callard couldn't possibly say no. The whores, and nearly forty grand in kickbacks in the first year alone had been sufficient to convince Callard that running huge errands for Magnus Vandesar and his friends for pocket money wasn't all it was made out to be. When he had left his house one morning to find a gleaming brand new Jaguar, his dream car, parked on his drive with the keys in it, Callard decided being connected meant getting into bed with Kansky. Andre lit another cigarette, deeply inhaling the warm smoke. Now wide awake, he again watched the blue smoke curling upwards, and realised he could lie here all day, and maybe he would, why not? After all he was the boss.

He flicked ash onto the floor, thinking about Vandersar. The stupid fucking police had picked them up, and then what had happened? The pricks had staged a jailbreak! Kansky shook his head, annoyed. Such things only happened in Westerns surely? Still, they trusted Callard, and they had turned to him for help. *Big mistake,* he thought taking a deep pull on his Marlboro. "Dumb shits!" He laughed. The laughter faded as he remembered how things had gone wrong, Marco was dead, and some of them had escaped. Fine, a setback maybe, but Kansky mulled the facts over in his mind. They were still out there, some of them anyway. But the truth was they were wanted for multiple murder, breaking out of jail, and a whole host of other offences. They wouldn't last long, and he smiled at the thought, because then nothing and no one would be left to stand in his way. He dumped the cigarette, looked down at Katylana and decided she should benefit from his steadily rising penis.

Ray searched for his mobile, keeping his eyes on the road as he located it under the clutter of discarded paperwork littering his passenger seat. He clumsily thumbed the digits, almost running into a bus pulling over in front of him.

"Fuck!" He stood on the brake, almost skidding into a row of parked cars.

"Hey, fuck face, look where you're fucking going!" A man about to cross between the cars and the bus shouted, jumping back sharply as the nose of the Jaguar nearly clipped him. Ray gave him a smile and showed him his middle finger before powering back into the mounting midmorning traffic. He fiddled with his phone again, this time successfully negotiating the keypad without any near misses. He sat impatiently in the grid locked city centre, waiting for Penny to answer.

"Hello?"

"Penny, its me. Have you heard anything?" he asked, almost casually. Penny's failure to answer alerted his mind. Had something happened?

"Pen?"

"What, Ray?"

"What's the matter?" he demanded, growing impatient.

"I know, Ray, I know what you did," she hissed.

"What the fuck are you on about, woman?" Ray searched his memory. When was the last time he banged a whore?. How could she have known?

"If you put out a bit more I wouldn't need to, would I?" he added, his temper flaring.

"What? Stop babbling, Ray. I know, Mags knows. You fucking bastard,

117

how could you?" she screamed, flecks of saliva spraying the telephone. Ray froze. The traffic in front of him moved on but the Jaguar remained still. The driver of a black cab behind tooted his horn impatiently. Ray never heard it. The blood rushed through his veins, pounding through his temples like a raging flood out of control.

"What? What are you on about, Pen?" he whispered, afraid somebody might be listening in. Paranoia gripped him like a vice, its icy hands crushing him.

"You bastard! You tried to kill him. Pat is dead, Ray, and so is McRae. They were your friends for Christ sake.

"I didn't, I mean…" he began to stutter wildly.

"Fuck you, Ray," she wailed.

"Who else knows?" he asked, trying to regain some composure.

"Andy Slater and Brad Killian are looking for you. Oh and so is Mags, funnily enough!"

"Killian? Fuck!" He felt the sweat breaking out on his forehead. Absently he wiped it away with his sleeve.

"Has he told anyone? Had Brad told anyone?" he pleaded.

"Not yet, Ray. He's more concerned with saving your worthless life," she told him, a bitter sarcasm etched into her voice.

"What the fuck does that mean?"

"Think about it you spineless twat. Mags is coming for you." Ray thumped the steering wheel of the Jaguar, venting his anger, wishing his bitch of a wife were here beside him. He knew she wouldn't be so fucking lippy then.

"Mags? Fuck him," he snapped. There was a lengthy pause before Penny came back with an answer.

"I already have, dear husband. Where do you think your son came from?" she told him, a deep satisfaction built on years of frustration finally breaking free. She put the phone down and for the first time in her married life, Penny Callard actually felt happy.

Tap, tap tap. Ray spun to look out of his car window. Tap tap tap, a huge fist, knuckles decorated with gaudy tattoos shook the toughened glass. Ray pressed the automatic window release. As it slid smoothly down a face appeared, a man probably in his early thirties, a face heavily adorned with scar tissue.

"Oi, have you broken down or what?" he asked. Ray could clearly see the man had two broken front teeth, both jutting jaggedly from his jaw.

"What?" Ray replied, still holding the mobile uselessly in his hand.

"You fucking deaf, you cunt? Move your fucking motor!"

"Piss off, you prick," Ray snapped.

"What? You want me to knock you the fuck out?" Ray ignored the question. Instead he reached into his pocket, producing his wallet. He opened it and took out his warrant card.

"See this, you mug? Police." He thrust the card into the face now halfway through his car window.

"I might have known. Fucking old Bill."

"Yeah, now fuck off, you ugly cunt," Ray told him, pressing the automatic window rewind. He threw the Jaguar into drive, pulling off into the traffic and narrowly missing an old lady awkwardly making her way across the busy road. Ray swerved at the last moment, missing her by an inch. She carried on oblivious, shuffling with two heavy bags of shopping. Ray glanced in his rear view mirror, wishing he had run the old bitch over. It might have cheered him up a bit. God knows he needed it.

"Fuck, fuck!" he shouted, slamming his fist into the wheel again. What now? He tried to rationalise his options, thinking at light speed he knew instantly he had to act fast. Penny had just told him that Killian and Slater knew, but no one else. Fuck it he thought. There's only one option. Killian and Slater couldn't live to tell, simple as that. If no one knew, then he was out of the woods. Kansky was his only living link, but Ray was on his way to rectify that little problem right now. The meddling cunts from the nick, Killian and Andy Slater would be next on his busy schedule. He neared the exclusive apartments of Jesus Green, luxury flats overlooking the river Cam. He would be seeing Andre Kansky any minute now. He could pick up all the weapons he needed. As he pulled into the car park beneath the Jesus Green apartments, his mind selected the last words she had spoken to him, the last words he intended her to ever speak. So Mags and the slut he married had been taking the piss behind his back? When he'd taken care of the others, he'd be sorting Mags out, once and for all. After all he reasoned, friends just don't do that to each other.

Penny walked into the kitchen, her face puffy from crying, but Mags noticed instantly the anguish had disappeared.

"That was him," she said.

"Ray?" Killian asked.

"Yes."

"What did he say?" Slater probed, rubbing his bruised throat.

"I told him, I told him everything," she said, a serene smile lighting up her face.

"What did he say to that?" Mags wondered, eyeing Penny curiously.

"He said for you to go fuck yourself."

"Did he now?"

"I told him I'd take care of that." She smiled, a knowing look sending shivers of emotion down his spine.

"You told him? He knows?" Mags asked. She sat on his lap, slipped her hands round his neck and kissed him gently on the lips.

"I told him," she whispered, before kissing him again.

"So what now?" he asked, breaking away from her tender lips. She kissed him again, with even more emotion, daring not to answer. For now she just wanted to hold the moment, unsure of what the future held.

Ray jogged the two flights of stairs, taking three steps at a time. Breathlessly he paused at the landing of level two, anxiously facing the door of Andre Kansky's apartment. Collecting himself, he pressed the doorbell of apartment eleven, and waited.

"Fuck," Kansky moaned, looking at his watch. Finally he'd managed an hour's sleep, and now the piercing tone of the doorbell had interrupted it. He hated the sound it made anyway, a high-pitched wail that always made him jump. As he searched for his robe he decided he would disconnect the wires. In future people who came to his house would simply have to knock. The bell rang again, slightly longer this time, an impatient annoying din.

"I'm coming, you motherless whore!" he shouted in annoyance. Andre decided he really wasn't in the mood for visitors, and elected to turn whoever it was away. He made his way through the spacious lounge, tripping on Katylana's discarded underwear.

"Cunt," he muttered, before kicking the offending item away, watching satisfied as the red lace panties came to rest on top of his huge wide screen television. The doorbell pierced into life again, just as he reached the door.

"Who the fuck is it?" he snapped, cautiously waiting for a reply.

"It's me, Ray." Andre recognised the voice, and groaned tiredly as he slipped the lock off before letting Ray through.

"Don't you ever sleep?" he asked, leaving Ray to shut the door behind himself.

"We've got a problem," Ray told him, quietly closing the door.

"Problems, problems, problems!" Kansky replied, falling lazily onto the green leather upholstered sofa that took centre stage of the lounge.

"It's no joke, Andre. You missed Vandersar. He's alive."

"Fuck him. The police will get to him soon. Relax, Ray."

"How the fuck can I relax? He's looking for me, and you." Ray took a seat on the sofa; the deep luxurious upholstery swallowed him.

"Stay low for a day or two, Ray. He won't last that long," Kansky reassured, yawning heavily.

"I've got a better idea, but I need a weapon." Ray spoke quietly, as if the room was crowded and ears might be listening.

"You? Kill him?" Kansky sat himself up, suddenly alert.

"Yeah me." There was an assertiveness to Ray Callard that Kansky had never seen, and had doubted ever existed.

"Way to go, Ray." He mockingly punched him in the arm, suddenly finding that he might have been wrong about his business partner. Without a word, Kansky leapt from the sofa and headed towards the huge kitchen the apartment boasted. Expensive Italian marble worktops blended into fine oak cabinets. Kansky pulled a chair from beneath the kitchen table, before positioning it at the foot of a huge handmade oak dresser. He climbed onto the chair and reaching up, his hand barely made it to the top of the dresser. His fingers strained along the top, finally finding something solid. He stood on tiptoes to get a hold of the object, reached it and brought it down. In his hands he held a towel, carefully wrapped around a long awkwardly shaped package. Unwrapping the towel he exposed the dark sinister form of a Kalashnikov assault rifle. He stepped down off of the chair, admiring the deadly beauty of the weapon, finding a familiar satisfaction from holding it in his hands. He walked back to the lounge. A broad smile adorned his face.

"Will this do?" he asked, offering the weapon to Ray.

"Bloody hell!" he said. Ray held the Kalashnikov, marvelling at its destruction capabilities.

"Good, yes?"

"Fucking lovely," Ray replied, and Kansky could see by the childlike wonderment in his eyes that Ray no longer seemed to be worried about Vandersar.

"Is it loaded?" Ray asked.

"Ready to go, my friend," Kansky told him, slumping back down into the sofa. He watched amused as Ray pretended to take aim at objects around the room, wondering if perhaps he should have given him something else instead, like an air pistol perhaps? He laughed as Ray levelled the barrel only inches from his face.

"Goodbye," Ray told him, before squeezing the trigger. Kansky was still smiling broadly as a 7.62mm round entered his forehead. The round spun a deadly path through his frontal lobe, before exiting the top of his head, sending huge chunks of grey brain tissue spinning through the air. In an instant the wall behind him was plastered with blood and brain matter. The force of the impact threw Kansky backwards off the end of the sofa. Ray watched as he spun like a rag doll before landing in a heap on the expensive carpet. He saw that Kansky no longer had much of a head left. Nothing remained except jagged reaches of skull that jutted out awkwardly. The sight reminded him of a broken egg, the yolk now splattered across satin finished walls.

"Andre? What was that, Andre?" Katylana had been robbed of her deep sleep by a concussive bang. Now as she sat up in bed startled, she found her lover gone.

"Andre?" she called again. She heard movement coming from the lounge, and wondered what the hell Andre was up to? When Ray Callard appeared through the bedroom doorway, immediately she knew something was wrong. The assault rifle he held in his hands confirmed the idea.

"Ray? What are you doing here? Where is Andre?" she asked, nervously pulling the bedcovers closer to herself. Ray lay the weapon on a bedside table, and wordlessly approached.

"Andre, Andre?" she called, glancing over Ray's shoulder willing her lover to appear.

"Shut the fuck up, whore!" he snapped, grabbing a handful of her blonde hair. She grabbed his arm, desperately trying to free herself. Ray swung his right fist directly into her face, the force breaking her nose and sending the bone awkwardly up towards her right eye. The skin parted, revealing a jagged shard of pure white bone, and a fine fountain of blood erupted from the wound. Katylana tried to scream, but the second punch landed with such power that it snapped her lower jaw in three places, removing seven of her teeth. Ray tightened his grip on her hair, pulling her head back at an alarming angle. He punched her hard again, and heard a loud crack as her left cheekbone collapsed. In desperation she tried to pull her head from his grip. A handful of hair gave way but he pulled even harder dragging her down flat onto the bed.

"Please!" she begged, through mouthfuls of blood that threatened to choke her.

"Fucking slag whore!" he shouted, punching her again and again. He let her hair go, noticing with great delight that a huge handful had become entwined around his fingers. Ray rolled on top of her barely conscious body, delighting at her firm breasts. He lowered his head into her chest and cupped her right breast in his hands. He began to suck her nipple excitedly, coating her with thick saliva. She began to stir, her consciousness returning. Ray took her breast in his mouth and bit down as hard as he could. As her body began to spasm with intense pain he bit down harder still, the warmth of fresh blood flooded his mouth. He pulled away to survey the sight, delighting at the scene that he saw. Her mutilated breast pumped rich dark blood across her chest, where it ran down her body in rivers.

"Cunty whore!" he shouted, driving his hand between her legs.

"You fucking Russian slut," he said, forcing his fingers into her vagina. Kansky's recently deposited sperm lubricated her as he drove his entire hand into her. She began to jerk and spasm frantically, her eyes open wildly in a mask of terror.

"Like that, cunt?" he asked, as his fist disappeared inside her. As he began to fist her back and forth Katylana began to moan loudly, her broken jaw slightly open to reveal dark froth.

"Whores, all women are fucking whores!" he screamed, pumping his arm further inside of her. Katylana's body jerked violently, her head began to shake from side to side. Then as her fragile mind could no longer deal with the horror, mercifully she slipped into a deep dark passageway.

"Wake up, you cunt," he said, annoyed at her lack of tolerance. He pushed his arm up into her womb, feeling the warm fleshy texture of her insides. Her vagina began to tear, small droplets of blood ran a path down her buttocks before staining the sheets crimson. He pulled his arm out of her. A loud wet sloppy noise followed as her vagina fought to return to its normal size.

"Wake up, you whore." He slapped her hard, slashing blood across the silk pillows. Her unresponsive body angered him greatly. He got off the bed and removed his trousers, hurriedly stepping out of them. His erection jutted out awkwardly from his body as he rolled her over onto her front, blood staining the pillows further as it seeped from her battered face. Ray climbed onto her and angrily pushed his penis against the opening of her anus. The tight flesh refused to yield to him so he pushed his full weight into her. Suddenly her opening parted, the flesh splitting as he pushed the heavy girth of his erection deep into her bowels.

"Oh, baby," he murmured, his eyes half closed. Frantically he began to pump her, slapping his belly into her buttocks as he quickly neared his orgasm. His pace altered, short fast strokes as his testicles tightened in anticipation.

"Oh you bitch, you fucking bitch!" he cried, as his penis spurted hot semen deep inside her. He fell onto her body, still pumping madly as he reached for her throat with his hands. As the last spurts of semen left his penis, Ray tightened his grip on her throat, his strong hands pressing hard on her windpipe. Katylana never woke. The last ounce of life left her body as Ray Callard pushed his now dying erection in and out of her torn back passage. Sperm and blood mixed together and ran down her vagina, forming a glue-like patch on the sheets beneath her. He tenderly kissed her back as he released his grip on her throat, lightly caressing her soft skin with his lips. He felt good again, better than he had done in weeks he realized. He kissed the back of Katylana's neck, taking in the musky scent of her young body, and decided he needed to meet women like Katylana more often.

Chapter Seven

Peering tentatively through the blinds, Mark kept his body as far back from the window as he could, trying not to create a silhouette with his prestigious size.

"Nothing?" Darryl asked from his comfortable position on the sofa.

"Nah, fuck all. Anyway, why don't you have a go at being look out?"

"Stop whingeing, Mark. You're doing a great job," Darryl told him, adjusting his position. They had made their way back to the White Rooms as soon as Mags had told them to go early that morning. They had climbed over garden fences and trampled blindly through neatly kept gardens trying to make their way to the nearest road. There they had dodged any cars, hiding behind bushes, ducking out of sight in case any approaching vehicle had been a police car. As they had hurried away from the scene of the shootings they had heard more gunshots, and had no way of knowing if Mags and Boris were dead or alive. Now Mark kept his vigil, peering out into the busy traffic, expecting hordes of armed police to appear at any moment. He hoped Mags and Boris would come strolling casually down the street, and every time he spied two men approaching his heart leapt, only to fall again when he saw that they were merely a couple of shoppers.

"What do you reckon?" Mark asked, straining to look across the busy street at two men getting out of a black cab.

"About what exactly?" Darryl snapped, annoyed with Mark's chitchat.

"Mags and Boris, did they make it?"

"Fuck knows," Darryl told him tiredly.

"Surely we would have heard, I mean someone…" Mark began.

"Look, just fucking shut up about it will you, you're giving me the fucking hump," Darryl shouted, throwing a pillow at him.

"Fucking hell, Darryl, I'm worried that's all." Darryl noticed a slight quiver in his voice, and decided to back off a little. He pushed himself up, his tired body protesting.

"Mark, it'll be okay. Just don't worry, mate, alright?" he said, patting Mark gently across the back. Suddenly Mark's face began to quiver, his mouth creased awkwardly as he began to sob.

"Easy, big fella, easy." Darryl put his arm round him, offering some comfort. He mentally slapped himself for being so hard with him. He knew how emotional the lad could be.

"Come on, mate, we'll be alright," he added, rubbing his hand over Mark's huge shoulders.

"I'm sorry, Darryl, it's just…"

"Yeah I know, mate, I know," Darryl replied, and found himself fighting his own battle with emotion. Both men suddenly jumped as the phone began to ring. Darryl reached for it, but paused wondering if it was such a good idea. It could be the police.

"Get it!" Mark snapped.

"It might be old Bill," Darryl offered.

"Nah, they'd have stormed the place if they thought we were here."

"True," Darryl agreed, snatching the receiver.

"Hello?"

"Darryl, its me." Mark watched as Darryl broke into a broad grin.

"Mags, you're alive!" he exclaimed, smiling madly at Mark.

"Definitely. Look, mate, stay put; we're going to meet you there soon. Don't answer the door or the phone to anyone from now on, okay?"

"Right, we'll see you soon. Mags, one thing before you go." Darryl felt a sense of dread creeping over him as he thought about his next question.

"What?"

"Pat? The Scotsman?" he asked, hoping.

"Gone." He could feel the emotion in Mags' voice as he spoke that single word, 'gone'. Darryl replaced the receiver, vaguely aware that Mark was talking to him, but the numbness running through him like a cold river had drowned his senses.

"Darryl, Darryl. What happened?" Mark asked, impatiently from the window. Darryl put his head in his hand, and his own tears cascaded down his cheeks like waves of sadness.

"Darryl?" Mark left his vigil at the window, already knowing the cause of his friend's distress.

"They're gone." Darryl sobbed. Mark reached over and pulled Darryl into an almighty hug, and this time the two of them wept together.

Killian drained the lukewarm dregs of his coffee, his stomach protesting noisily as it always did after too much caffeine.

"So you'll make your way back to your club, and stay put?" Slater asked Mags.

"Scouts honour," he replied.

"Make sure you do, Mags. Until we can pin something concrete on Ray, our boys will be looking everywhere for you," Killian cut in.

"Alright, alright, I promise." Mags threw his hands up in the air in mock surrender.

"And just remember, it's our balls on the block here lads. If our guvnor finds out we've even seen you, we'll be signing on by tomorrow morning," Killian added, genuine concern now entering his voice. Mags took the hint, realising that for whatever reason the two policemen sat at the table had staked a lot on a hunch. Mags traditionally hated police, and everything they stood for. Only hours previously he had been willing to murder Killian with his bare hands. Now he grudgingly accepted that perhaps he had been wrong, and not all coppers were that bad. He toyed with the idea, throwing it around in his brain. He hated being wrong, hated it.

"Look, I understand. I appreciate what you're doing." Mags looked first at Slater, then at Killian before reinforcing his acknowledgement.

"You have my word."

"Thanks," Killian said, rising from his chair. Slater followed suite, rubbing his bruised throat gingerly. Mags followed the two men down the hallway towards the front door.

"Lose that motor, Magnus, every squad car in Cambridge is looking for it," Slater told him, pausing as he reached for the door latch.

"Sorted, don't worry," Mags replied. Slater opened the door. Bright cold sunlight bathed the hallway. Mags gently grabbed Killian by the arm, pulling him back into the hall.

"Find him," he whispered, leaning down until he was only inches from Killian's face. Bradley Killian fixed Mags with a serious glare, his face a mixture of determination and unease at being alone with Mags, who towered over him, and outweighed him by probably one hundred and fifty pounds.

"We'll find him, don't worry about that," he replied, pulling his arm from Mags' grasp and heading out into the bright sunlight.

Ray Callard entered the rear of Parkside police station, nodding as he held the door open for two young beat officers.

"Morning, sir," one of them said, before slipping through the door. Ray watched them go, wincing at the acne both sported in abundance. Had he gotten old, or were the recruits getting younger? He figured it was probably a bit of both.

"Ray, how are you?" He turned to see O'Neil bounding along the corridor towards him.

"Morning, sir," he acknowledged. Suddenly he felt totally at ease. Penny hadn't lied. Those cunts Killian and Slater hadn't told anybody yet. If they had, the big nosed prick wouldn't be heading towards him with a hard on.

"Sir, have you seen Brad Killian?" he asked pleasantly.

"Ah, Brad. He's a bit busy at the moment. I take it you've heard there was more shootings last night?"

"Yeah, I heard. Shocking. Glad I'm not on murder. I'll stick to drugs any day."

"Yes I see your point, Ray. Brad and Andy have got their work cut out at the moment," O'Neil said, shaking his head. Ray watched as his beaked nose cut through the air like a sharpened blade.

"Vandersar broke out I hear?" Ray enquired.

"Bastards!" O'Neil snapped, the embarrassment returning, like it had never left.

"He won't get far, sir," Ray added, trying to inject some support.

"Bastards!" O'Neil repeated.

"Look, I must be off, Ray. Things are a bit…well you know," he added.

"Yeah, sure. Nice to see you, sir."

"Likewise, Ray," O'Neil replied, before making his way towards his office. Ray smirked, watching the stuffy jumped up senior officer as he strutted down the corridor.

"Twat" he muttered to himself. He secretly wished he could run up behind O'Neil and punch him in the back of the head. He smirked again, finding the idea very pleasing indeed. *Maybe another time,* he told himself. Shaking the idea away, Ray headed down the long corridor towards the control room. The room consisted of rows of tables, each adorned with computers and telephones.

At one such table, situated at the far end of the room, Ray saw Hillary Birch. The fifty-three year old civilian administrator had been at Parkside longer than Ray had. She was a widow. Her husband Jim had been a highly respected beat copper who was stabbed to death by a drunk outside a nightclub five years earlier. Ray remembered it well. Jim only had eighteen months left until he retired. Any policeman whose life was lost in the line of duty was always a sad time, but Jim Birch had been a great man, a copper of the old school who had rebuffed promotion on numerous occasions because he loved being a policeman. He had lived to tutor the new recruits who learned everything they would ever need to know from him. He had been a street bobby, and proud at that. His death had shattered everybody who had ever come to know him.

Hillary had taken his death as she took everything else that happened in her life, with no fuss. Still, Ray had been damn close to Jim, and he had gone out of his way to keep an eye out for Hillary. Rarely a week passed without him visiting her. Right now he knew she would be the person to see if he needed to know the whereabouts of anybody who worked at Parkside. Hillary ran the control room, both civilian and police personnel alike. She was due to retire at fifty-five, and Ray, like everyone else knew that replacing her would be almost impossible.

"Hello, young lady," he said as he crept up behind her, grabbing her round the waist.

"Less of the young," she responded, turning to kiss his cheek.

"How are you, sweetheart?" she asked.

"Fine, Hillary."

"And Penny and Jake?"

"Just fine, I took them to the cinema last night. Saw that new Disney picture."

"Oh lovely, Ray!" The thought delighted her.

"I just wish I could spend more time with Jake, but work." He rolled his eyes.

"I know, you should go home at five, Ray. Forget the overtime," she scolded.

"Gotta pay the bills," he said, shrugging his shoulders. She looked at him disapprovingly, narrowing her eyes.

"Anyway, sweetheart, I need a favour," he asked, putting an arm round her.

"Well there's a surprise, and there was me thinking you were chatting me up," she teased.

"Oh, but I am." He winked, squeezing her tightly.

"So what do you need?"

"I've got some information for Brad, pretty urgent. Couldn't find him for me, could you?"

"I'll see what I can do," she said, tapping expertly into the computer keyboard.

"I've got his mobile number here, Ray. Do you want that instead?"

"Yeah, that's fine. I can speak to him myself," he replied. Hillary jotted the number down onto a slip of paper, before handing it to Ray.

"Thanks," he said, leaning to kiss her cheek.

"Stop it. People will talk," she mocked.

"Let 'em talk!" he shouted, kissing her again. She wriggled free, smiling broadly.

"Be gone, young man," she told him.

"Okay, but don't say I didn't try." He stepped back, arms outstretched in mock surrender.

"I know when I'm beat," he said, backing towards the door. Hillary laughed and waved him away, glad that Ray had popped in and made her day, as he always did. She watched as he left, wishing she was twenty years younger, knowing that Penny wouldn't stand a chance.

Killian cursed, the traffic got worse. Five minutes now and they hadn't moved an inch.

"What the fuck is going on up there?" he demanded, craning his neck to see past the procession of cars.

"Bloody roadworks I should think," Slater said, drumming his fingers impatiently on the dashboard.

"Pisses me the fuck off," Killian moaned. His frustration was forgotten momentarily as his mobile began to ring. Absently he took it out of his jacket pocket, still searching ahead for the source of the hold up.

"Killian, who's that?" he snapped impatiently.

"This is Ray. How are you, you fucking Judas?"

"Ray!" Killian jolted stiffly in his seat. He noticed Slater watching him intently.

"Yeah, it's me alright."

"Where the fuck are you?"

"What, like I'm going to tell you?" Ray taunted.

"Ray, I suggest you hand yourself in, before things get worse," Killian growled.

"Do you now?"

"Ray, stop fucking about and meet me at the station. See if we can sort this out."

"You think I'm fucking stupid, Brad, is that it?" Ray laughed.

"No I don't, but Ray we've got a situation here," Killian said, trying to keep the situation rational.

"I'll tell you what, Brad,; I'll meet you, but not at the station." Ray laughed again, much to Killian's annoyance.

"Then where, name a place?" Killian asked.

"There's a place in Cherry Hinton, Lime Kilne Hill, you know it?"

"Yeah, I know the place."

"Halfway up on the left there's a caravan park. It's deserted at this time of year. I'll be there at six."

"I'll be there, six o'clock," Killian agreed.

"And Brad, don't come with your fucking mates hiding in the bushes. If you do, me and you are gonna fall out badly, understand?" Ray let a sinister edge fall into his words, leaving Killian in no doubt about his intentions.

"How the fuck do I know you won't shoot me anyway?" Killian asked, a tinge of anguish rippling through him.

"You don't. Listen, don't fucking worry, Brad. I won't kill you, but there's more to this story than you understand."

"I'm sure there is. Look, Ray, we go back a long way. If I can help you I will," Killian reassured.

"Good. Be there at six."

"I will, but…" Killian began, but Ray Callard had hung up already.

"What did he say? Where is he?" Slater asked expectantly. Killian ran a hand through his hair, sighed heavily and turned to Slater.

"Andy, I think he's fucking lost the plot."

"Why, what did he say?"

"I've got to meet him at six, Cherry Hinton," Killian told him.

"Have we?" Slater asked.

"No, Andy, just me."

"What? Brad don't you think that's a little dangerous?"

"Of course, but Andy, if I don't meet him, we'll never get to the bottom of this. We haven't got enough to go to O'Neil with. The word of Vandersar just ain't enough, is it? Besides, O'Neil thinks the sun shines out of Ray's arsehole anyway."

"Yeah, that's true I suppose. But we can link him to the Russians," Slater said, annoyed that Killian was prepared to put himself at such a risk.

"How can we?" You saw them together. That's not a crime now is it? And think about it, Andy, only one of the Russians is still alive, and Kansky's not going to be easy to find, and he won't give us fuck all even if we did find him. No, I think Ray wants to tell me. He'll give everyone else up if it means he doesn't have to take the fall.

"And he knows Vandersar's going to come looking for him," Slater added.

"Exactly. He's looking for a way out, Andy, and he trusts me to help him find it."

"And?"

"And I'll watch the fucking prick swing when the time comes," Killian replied, anger crossing his face like a dark shadow.

"He's a copper, Andy, a bent copper," he added for effect.

"Yeah I know, I know," Slater replied sombrely, remembering how Ray had been a good friend.

"Look, Andy, I know you and Ray were mates, but believe me this bloke ain't the nice man you used to have dinner parties with," Killian told him, almost reading his thoughts.

"Yeah, you're right." Slater sighed. Killian jabbed him in the arm playfully, smiling. Slater returned the punch, a little harder Killian thought, but declined to take the point up. He noticed with relief that finally the grid locked traffic had begun to move at a crawl.

"Thank fuck!" he murmured, and began to prepare his thoughts for the coming evening.

The explosion shook the foundations of the house. Ornaments neatly placed over the marble fireplace wobbled, teetered briefly before crashing noisily onto a beautifully tiled hearth. Bertram Fulton always took a nap around midday, and now like always he sat snoozing in his leather recliner, mouth ajar with a thin sliver of saliva running down his chin.

"What, what was that?" He jolted upright, saliva spraying onto his worn cardigan. With an agility that belied his seventy years, Bertram sprang from the comfort of his chair. Initially he thought there had been a plane crash, but thought better of it when he looked out of his front room window. There, on the magnificently tailored lawn stretching from his house to the quiet road ahead, sat the mangled burning remains of a car. Bertram thought it looked like a Metro. Quickly he pushed the insignificance of such trivia out of his head, and started to try and get his head round the idea of why, and what? Suddenly from behind the burning carnage Bertram saw a figure, hugely built with a near shaven head. The figure calmly, almost casually gave him a cheerful wave, before walking off down the road, as if out for a gentle stroll on a bright, but cold winter's morning. Bertram stood, oddly transfixed by the whole bizarre episode. He was the chairman of the local neighbourhood watch association, but somehow the police hadn't been able to prepare him, or his fellow members for such an incident. As the car burnt fiercely on his neatly kept lawn, Bertram Fulton stood numbly watching, his mouth ajar, a fine stream of drool snaking down his chin.

Mags heard the door open. He peered tentatively round the kitchen doorway to make sure it was Boris, and not a surprise visitor.

"All sorted?" he asked, as Boris trudged into the kitchen, his usual brooding scowl visible.

"Done," he replied, falling heavily into a chair, the pine legs creaking in protest under his weight.

"Right. That silly fucker Mohamed will be here any minute," Mags told him, glancing at a clock hanging neatly from the kitchen wall.

"When will I see you?" Penny asked, concern crossing her face.

"Come with us," he replied, gently squeezing her hand. She returned the gesture, a little harder.

"I can't. I've got to collect Jake from playschool this afternoon." He could see the sadness in her eyes, but he understood and didn't push her any further. Boris went into the lounge, leaving them alone.

"I love you," he whispered, pulling her close. Her eyes lit up, an animated glow behind them that reached out and touched him.

"I love you too, Magnus," she replied, pulling his head down to hers. He could smell her scent, the warm musky odour that made his senses dance.

"I'll come back for you, when this is done," he told her, before kissing her gently.

"Promise?"

"I promise, baby, I won't ever leave you again." Despite his life being a war zone, he felt like a spotty teenager in love for the first time. It was then that it actually hit him, the damning fact that perhaps for the first time in his crazy, and somewhat turbulent life, he was in love for the first time.

"Mags, the mad cabby's here." Boris came storming into the kitchen, somewhat embarrassed at catching the two of them in an embrace.

"Gotta go Pen," Mags said, kissing her forehead gently. He released her from his embrace, and followed Boris down the hallway. Pausing at the door, he turned for a last lingering look at Penny, before heading out into the winter sun. Mohamed greeted them in his usual manner, a huge toothy grin that radiated.

"Hello my favourite gangster friends," he quipped as Boris and Mags filed into the back seats.

"How's it hanging Mo?" Mags asked.

"Oh you know, ten inches long and thick as a white boy's leg." He cackled, rows of pure white teeth gleaming.

"Drive!" Boris snapped impatiently.

"Okey dokey, guv!" Mohamed chuckled, pulling the cab noisily out into the deserted street. Mags watched intrigued as they passed rows of identical houses, each manicured so neatly. He wondered if this was what Penny wanted, and if so could he give it to her? He certainly had the money, but was this really him? He decided not to dwell on the idea. After all there were much more pressing matters to deal with, and deal with them he would.

"Holy mother of…" Mohamed slowed briefly as they rounded a bend. He stared amazed at what looked like the remains of a Metro smouldering on some old duffers lawn. Several fire fighters were still dousing the blaze, while an old man stood looking on helplessly. Mags shot Boris a quick steely glare, then burst into laughter, his huge chest heaving with amusement.

"Silly old cunt," Boris snapped.

"Why there?" Mags managed in-between bouts of hoarse coughing.

"The old fucking was nosing out of the window as we went by earlier. Nosy old cunt!" he moaned, seemingly unable to appreciate the humour of the situation.

"Man, that's fucking weak," Mohamed cut in, guiding the cab gently round two fire-fighters who were in the process of rolling a thick hose into a tidy ball.

"Fuck off, Mo," Boris told him, and then Mags cracked up completely, roaring heartily. Mohamed flashed his toothy white grin, shaking his head in amusement.

"Fucking weak man, fucking weak," he quipped, before pulling out of London Crescent, and into the busy traffic heading into Cambridge.

Mags thought his spine might be broken, and wasn't so sure about the ribs on his left side either.

"Fuck, Mark put me down you big cunt," he begged, breathing with relief as Mark released him. Still, he was happy to see Mark and Darryl again.

134

"How's it going, lads?" he asked, pulling Darryl into a hug.

"All the better now you two are back," Mark replied, his big round face visibly beaming. Mags playfully put a fist to Mark's chin, giving him an encouraging wink.

"So what now?" Boris asked, his intense expression giving no clues to the happiness he felt at seeing his friends.

"I reckon you read my mind, Boris," Mags said, slapping him on the back.

"First of all, I promised Killian we'd leave Ray to them. My word is final; I made a promise," he added.

"So we waste Kansky?" Boris asked expectantly.

"Fucking right we do. Let's go," Mags replied, already heading for the steps that led to the foyer of the White Rooms. He took the steps two at a time, bounding urgently. He quickly headed into the foyer's cloakroom, a large dull room lined with rails that sported rows and rows of coat hangers. Hanging on the sparse walls, pictures of movie stars hung smartly in gold trimmed frames. Mags slid the signed portrait of Robert DeNiro aside, pausing for a moment to admire his hero. The frame had been hiding a small wall safe, discreetly kept from view by DeNiro in a pose from Mags' favourite film, Raging Bull. Deftly he pressed in a four-digit number, and the door sprung open. Inside lay his hidden weapon, kept for special occasions where the police would be very unlikely to look. He took out the heavy Desert Eagle special, admiring the weight in his hand. Satisfied that now was a special occasion, he slid the weapon into the waistband of his trousers, took an old leather coat long left behind by a punter, and headed out into the busy street. He kept the coat pressed against himself, careful to keep the desert eagle hidden. Boris held the door of Mohamed's cab open before climbing in behind him.

"Where to, guv?" Mohamed asked, eyeing the coat suspiciously.

"Jesus Green, Mo," he replied.

"That's a fair run, Mags," Mohamed said, looking ruefully at the cabs metre.

"Don't worry, Mo; you'll get your money," Boris growled. The cab pushed into the afternoon traffic. The driver of a rival cab firm gave Mohamed the finger for cutting in. He flashed a broad grin before returning the compliment. Mohamed looked at the metre again, the smile gone from his face. He knew he wouldn't get his money. Like always he'd be working for the love of it.

Penny moved swiftly, selecting only bare essentials, underwear and toiletries hurriedly thrown into a suitcase. She opened the double-doored wardrobe that kept her finest clothes, quickly snatching two pairs of faded blue jeans and a worn sweatshirt. She took one last look at her enviable collection of dresses: Gucci, Prada, and even a little black number by Chanel, the favourite item of clothing in her collection; the one she usually wore when she could get away to meet Mags. Her cheeks flushed at the though, but at the same time a warm feeling spread its way from her stomach down towards her genitals. She found herself stroking the black Chanel dress. The memories it held made her smile. She had done things whilst wearing it that she never thought she could do. But that was the attraction of Mags, the animalistic instincts he brought out in her. Ray had never made her come, let alone excited her she mused. Magnus Vandersar made her come with his eyes. He merely had to look at her and she felt a fire running through her body.

She closed the wardrobe doors, and let the memories go with her designer clothes. She knew she was about to start a new life, the life she had always wanted, her with Mags and their son Jake. Jake, the child she had always wanted, the love that had made her life bearable. She sat down on the edge of the handmade pine bed Ray had bought when they had married. A dark cloud crossed her mind, and now she knew it was nearly time to step out into the rain that would surely come. Penny had told Mags that she had revealed the truth about their relationship. He had been shocked, but there was a ray of happiness omitting from him that she couldn't fail to notice. But there was one thing that Mags didn't know, and she hated herself for keeping it from him. Jake was his son, and soon she would have to tell him the truth. She had known Mags a long time. She understood his moods and his ways, but he had never expressed any interest in fatherhood. The thought worried her. It probed deep into her subconscious mind, leaving doubts that she couldn't shake. Penny sighed deeply, a heavy burdened breath that emptied her lungs. She tried to concentrate on the good side to the whole affair. At least she wouldn't have to contend with Ray and his sexual demands anymore. She picked herself up, and made her way towards Jake's bedroom. She could easily fit plenty of his clothes into the case. Penny was about to open the door to Jake's room when a shocking, blackening pain exploded through her head. She tried to cry out, but her voice deserted her. Instead her knees buckled and she fell in a heap. A second explosion crashed through her brain, sending dizzying light shooting past her eyes. She desperately tried to find the source of the pain, pawing frantically at her head. Rivers of warmth ran between her fingers, before pulsing down her hands. Instinctively she knew it was blood, and a terror ran through her heart, even though she didn't know why or what had happened.

She fought to stay conscious, blinking madly to clear her eyes. She looked up and saw a figure looming over her in the dim light of the fading afternoon.

"Hello, cunt!" the figure shouted, grabbing her by the hair and forcibly lifting her to her feet. Her legs wouldn't support her weight, but the force dragging her by the hair was too strong and she found herself stumbling blindly trying to keep pace.

"Now then whore, what am I going to do with you?" Penny knew the voice, and her bowels turned to ice as she heard the words echoing through her shattered mind. Numbly she tried to speak, but only a weak crackling noise escaped her. Ray kicked the bathroom door open, dragging Penny in by her blood-soaked hair. He threw her headlong into the spacious walk in shower room, her blood splattering the peach coloured tiles.

"You fucking whore bitch. I'm going to make you fucking pay, you slut," he shouted, kicking her hard in the ribs. She curled up in agony, her eyes wide in terror.

"See this, see this, you cunt?" he snarled, holding up a bloodstained claw hammer.

"This is going to fuck you better than the big blonde prick ever could," he added, through gritted teeth. She tried again to speak, but only a low guttural whimper escaped.

"Say your prayers whore, I'll see you in hell." He came at her in slow motion. She watched helplessly as he raised the hammer, her own fresh dark blood dripping for the vicious claw.

"Please..." she croaked.

"Save it, baby," he said, bringing the hammer down with brutal force. The blow landed high on her skull, cutting an easy and unchallenged path through her outstretched hands.

"Fucking whore!" he screamed, clubbing her time and time again. Blood cascaded with force into the clean tiles, rivulets running awkwardly to form macabre murals. Ray kept swinging the hammer, even when Penny's brain exploded in small grey fragments that stuck to his hammer, and clogged the lethal claw. Penny Callard had been dead for at least three minutes before her husband finally ran out of breath. Ray was actually quite impressed with his fitness levels, and even more so when he noticed the throbbing bulge protruding from his trousers. Breathlessly he released his hard penis and began to masturbate furiously over Penny's butchered remains. As he ejaculated over her bloody smashed face, Ray decided things were going to be alright after all.

Angie Slater opened the front door, worry etched across her plainly attractive face.

"Andy, what are you doing home?" she asked, her concern intensified when she saw Bradley Killian standing beside him.

"Nothing, babe, we just need to hole up here for a while," he said kissing her cheek before sliding past her into the house.

"What's happened honey?" she asked, knowing he would never be home this early. Killian eased past her, nodding politely. She slammed the door shut and followed them into their cramped kitchen. Andy Slater was in the process of filling two brandy glasses when she confronted him again.

"Darling, what's happened?" she asked, glaring at Killian as she spoke.

"Ray Callard, that's what's happened, babe," he replied, handing Killian a half filled glass.

"Ray? Is he okay?" Her concern now visible.

"Well, we think he's behind at least a dozen murders, maybe more. Oh yeah, and it seems the nice bloke we have round here for dinner parties is a bent copper working for the Russian mafia, who incidentally are a bunch of fucking murdering drug peddling psychopaths. Other than that Angie, he's just fine," he said, emptying his glass in one hit. The fire water burnt his throat and he winced heavily.

"Ray?" She looked staggered.

"That's the way it's looking, honey. I'd like to think its all a big misunderstanding, but I think that's pretty fucking unlikely," he added, pouring himself another shot. He raised the bottle to Killian, but noticed his boss had a vacant look and seemed lost with his own thoughts.

"What are you going to do?" she asked, producing a cigarette.

"Nail the fucker. But, and here's the problem, we haven't got enough on him yet. At the minute this whole mess is hanging over the heads of six blokes who I'm sad to say are innocent," he said, rubbing his bruised throat.

"Four," Killian cut in.

"Pardon?"

"It's four, Andy, remember?"

"Oh yeah, four innocent blokes. Ray had the other two horribly murdered," he corrected.

"Dear God," Angie whispered, drawing nervously on her cigarette.

"Brad here is meeting Ray in an hour or so. Maybe then we might get the truth out of him."

"Is that wise, Brad?" Angie asked, putting her dislike for the man aside.

"It's all we've got. Right now me and Andy are guilty of helping suspected murderers, who this morning broke out of Parkside station, hospitalising two coppers I might add. Without Ray's confession we've got very little, in fact nothing much at all. To be honest Angie, this is all your husbands fault. This is his hunch. No one else twigged it, except him." Killian raised his glass, for once needing no prompting to acknowledge Slater's excellent perceptiveness.

"Thanks, Brad, thanks," Slater said, feeling almost proud that Killian had complimented him in front of his wife. He looked into Killian's eyes, and saw the hard edge the old bastard normally displayed had disappeared.

"One for the road?" Slater asked, raising the bottle.

"Yeah, why not." Killian smiled, accepting the offer. He needed something to calm the nervousness that now gripped him, and being picked up for drink driving was about the least of his worries right now.

Lime Kilne hill sat impressively towering over the border between Cambridge city and the sprawling agricultural heartlands that surrounded it. A dark lonely road traversed it, snaking endlessly like a slow winding river. At its origin, which began on the outskirts of Cherry Hinton village, a dark wooded lay-by offered refuge for lovers, unseen from the road but in turn leaving them the opportunity to view any approaching vehicles. Constable Nigel Coston now sat parked in the lay-by, his trousers hanging idly at his ankles. Leaning over him, with his penis fully erect in her mouth, was constable Claire Coxton. She was his newest probationary, only six weeks into her initial ten week assessment. For the last five years his job had been to assess new recruits, grading their performance which in turn weighed heavily on their future in the police force. Not many male recruits received good marks from Nigel Coston, and the few women that did, always went that extra mile in pleasing their tutor. He grinned with satisfaction. Claire Coxton obviously liked to please.

"That's good baby, take the whole length," he encouraged, pushing her head down forcibly. No two ways about it he thought. This little blonde bitch was going to end up as chief commissioner.

"Suck it, baby, oh yeah wrap your fucking tongue round my helmet," he begged, gripping her hair. A set of headlights illuminated the road in front of the lay-by. Nigel Coston tensed, ready to push Claire's head away. He watched the lights approach, growing stronger as they came. He stayed taught as the road became fully awash with light. He hoped the sight of a parked squad car might deter anybody from pulling in. To his relief, a blue car slowly drove by, heading steadily up the hill until it disappeared into the black night. Wasn't that the new Jag? That prick Callard had got one he remembered, flash fucker. He couldn't stand the smug twat. Like most people in the station he saw Callard as a slimy arse licker who lived up that stuffy prick O'Neil's arse. There was something strange about Callard too, Coston thought. Never mind. He relaxed and concentrated on the lovely thing now sucking his cock.

"Get your tits out, baby. Wrap them round my hard prick," he said tugging at her shirt. Oh! yes indeed, he mused, this girl was going to make a great copper.

Killian stopped as the lights hit red, skidding slightly on the already freezing road surface. He revved the Mondeo's engine hard, nerves and impatience mixing.

"Come on, come on," he snapped, willing the lights to hurry up. As they flashed to amber he was already crossing the junction, turning right into the dark forebode of Lime Kilne Hill. He flicked the lights onto full beam, his eyes strained hard to see the entrance of the caravan park. He passed a lay-by on his left, heavily wooded.

Just for a fraction of a second, he thought he saw the familiar luminescence of a squad car. He carried on, dismissing the idea. After all only Slater knew he was here, and why would a squad car be parked in a wooded lay-by out here anyway? He saw a sign illuminated up ahead on the right. Slowing carefully he squinted his eyes trying to read the working. 'Caravan Club of Great Britain', he read before slowing almost to a halt. He took a deep breath, trying hard to expel any nerves. Failing miserably he pushed the Mondeo into the entrance of the caravan park.

All he could see was darkness, black and unsettling. He followed a narrow dirt track through tall intimidating trees, until eventually arriving at a sprawling expanse of grassland. Fifty metres in front of him sat a wooden lodge, almost colonial in its design. Parked beside it sat the gleaming blue Jaguar XK8 that he knew belonged to Ray Callard. Slowly he cruised over to the lodge, apprehension turning his blood to ice. He pulled the Mondeo alongside the bigger Jaguar, clearly making out the silhouette of a figure seated behind the wheel. As the Mondeo pulled to a stop, Killian once more fought to control his overactive nervous system. His blood vessels now swelled madly as the huge adrenaline dump crashed into his bloodstream. He closed his eyes briefly, took a long deep heavy breath, before opening the car door and stepping out into the freezing night.

He heard another car door slam, and the adrenaline rush increased, heightening his senses, bringing on a state of alertness that he'd never known before.

"Brad, how you been?" Ray Callard asked, barely visible to Killian in the darkness.

"Oh, not bad, Ray! Can't complain," he replied nervously.

"Good, then lets cut the shit shall we?" Killian began to tense further at the menace in Ray Callard's voice.

"Sure. What do you want to talk about, Ray?"

"I want to know, Brad, why the fuck you have to stick your fucking nose into my fucking business?" he growled. Killian flinched as he saw the weapon being raised. It looked like an extension of his arms in the darkness.

"Steady, Ray, steady mate!" he begged, backing up to the lodge. He felt trapped as the balcony rails pressed hard against him.

"Easy Ray, come on mate," he said, trying hard to keep his voice low.

"Why the fuck should I, Brad? I mean, after all only a week ago I was well on my way to becoming a very rich man. Now, well let's just say my predicament is a bit piss poor."

"We can sort it out, mate. Just put the gun down," Killian pleaded.

"And I'll tell you something else Brad. I could live with being poor, at least for the moment anyway. But then today I find out my wife's been fucking Vandersar. Oh, and he's the father of my son. Well fuck me, Brad, I don't think I will put the gun down."

"Ray, they'll find you, mate. You'll spend the rest of your life behind bars. Think about it," Killian said, keeping the calmness to his voice. Over the years he had faced some very nasty and highly dangerous individuals. His rule had always been to keep a calm voice, no matter what. Now, he figured wasn't a good time to change his tactics. Still, he had never seen Ray Callard behave anything remotely like this, and the thought seriously disturbed him.

"Prison? I don't fucking think so, Brad. I mean, the way I see it, only you and that panty-wetting partner of yours know the score. Correct?" he asked, still chuckling lightly.

"Penny, Penny knows, Ray," Killian replied, vainly hoping the mention of Penny might alter his thoughts.

"That fucking whore? I shouldn't worry too much about her, Brad."

Why, what have you done, Ray?" Killian snapped, his calm giving way to an angry rage.

"Well, I fucking killed her as it happens." He chuckled heavily, a long throaty laugh that chilled Killian to the bone.

"That's your wife for God's sake, man," Killian bellowed, the anger welling inside of him.

"She was a cunt, a no good two bit whore."

"Dear God!" Killian raged, carefully measuring the distance between himself and Ray. Maybe he could make it if he was quick, snatch the gun and…

"So that leaves you and the prick Slater. Oh, not forgetting Vandersar and his buddies of course. But I don't suppose anyone is really going to believe a word they say, do you, Brad?" Killian readied himself, the adrenaline sharpening him like a steel blade.

"Now then, I believe I've got two little problems left. You and Slater. So, goodbye, Bradley." Ray raised the Kalishnakov. As Killian started his run, he pulled the trigger, releasing a burst of 7.62 millimetre rounds. The projectiles cut through the night air at six hundred miles per hour, reaching Killian in an instant. The four and a half kilogram weapon kicked heavily in Ray's hands, knocking him backwards slightly as he fought to control his pattern of fire. The first dozen rounds hit Killian square in the chest, obliterating his rib cage and shredding his lungs in an awesome burst of power. Killian was thrown back violently, slamming hard into the wooden railings of the lodge's balcony. The second volley of rounds caught him full in the head, exploding it like a ripe succulent melon. Spinning fragments of skull and mucous plastered the external walls of the lodge, a huge fist size lump of Killian's skull blew off and blasted a whole through the glass fronted lodge door. Ray lowered the smoking Kalishnakov, walking calmly to the fragmented remains of his former colleague. He studied the unrecognisable remains of Killian's head, marvelling at the complexity of the human brain. The silence of the cold night once again engulfed the deserted caravan park. Ray Callard delighted at the peace.

"Only one more left," he uttered, in reference to Andy Slater, before loading the Kalishnakov into the boot of his Jaguar. He was about to head off in pursuit of Slater and lose the last little problem still alive in his life when he paused. Fumbling between his legs he noticed that his raging erection had returned. Unzipping his trousers, Ray released his swollen penis, and once again practiced his celebration ritual, as only he knew how.

Nigel Coston strained hard, gripping the door handle of his squad car with some force.

"Oh fuck! Oh baby, here it comes!" he whimpered, as he ejaculated into Claire Coxton's warm inviting mouth.

"Oh sweet fucking Jesus!" he added, gently stroking her fine blonde hair.

"Good?" she asked, grinning as she wiped a stray stream of sperm from her chin with her hand.

"Oh yes! I'm gonna promote you right now," he quipped.

"Is that a promise?" she said, laughing as she slipped her bra back over her pert breasts. A volley of rapid explosions cracked through the still night air, jolting them both.

"What was that?" she asked, scanning the woods around them.

"That sounded like fucking gunfire," he replied, rapidly pulling his trousers up.

"Better call this in," he added, zipping his fly.

"Was that really gunfire, Nige?" Claire asked, suddenly quite shaken.

"I think so. I spent eight years in the infantry before the police. You don't forget the sound of automatic gunfire," he said, reaching for the car's radio.

"Seven five nine to control, do you read me, over?"

"Roger seven five nine, go ahead." The controller's voice crackled into life, Nigel recognised the voice as belonging to Martha Finley, another former probationary he had passed with flying colours.

"Martha, I'm out at Cherry Hinton, around the Lime Kilne hill area. I think I've just heard gunfire."

"Roger seven five nine, stay put and I'll despatch backup. Be advised armed response will attend, over."

"Thanks Martha, over." He replaced the mike, pondering his actions. What if it had been nothing? Kids letting off fireworks perhaps? No way, he reasoned, after all he'd seen combat action in the Falklands, and he knew automatic gunfire when he heard it.

The door wasn't even locked. Boris couldn't believe his luck. Gently he eased it open, only a gentle click betrayed him as the latch gave way.

"We're in," he whispered to Mags.

"Okay, on three. One, two, three." Boris hit the door with his huge shoulder, exploding it against the wall in the hallway. Mags sprinted in first, the desert eagle held out at arms length, moving from left to right searching for a target. Nothing entered his sights as he moved into Kansky's lounge.

"Boris, get the fuck in here!" he shouted.

"I'm here. Fuck me ragged." Boris stepped by Mags, cautiously approaching the bloody remains sprawled awkwardly against the lounge wall.

"Somebody beat us to it, Mags. I don't fucking believe it," he said, kicking the remnants of Andre Kansky's head. "Done a grand job too. I like it," he added, wiping a lump of clotting brain tissue off of his shoe.

"What the fuck is going on, Boris?" Mags wondered, kneeling down beside the body.

"Don't know, but there's some strange shit happening," he replied.

"Pass me that pillow," Mags said, pointing to the sofa. Boris reached over, gingerly snatching the expensive green leather cushion, ornately decorated with gold stitching.

"What do you want that for?" Boris asked, handing over the cushion.

"I owe this fucker, dead or alive," Mags growled, placing the cushion over the remains of Kansky's shattered head. He took the desert eagle out of his waistband, using his thumb to release the slide safety catch.

"Mags?" Boris gave him a quizzical look.

"Die again you cunt!" he roared, pushing the guns ten-inch barrel into the cushion, before squeezing the trigger. An awesome explosion shook the room, a deafening roar that shook the apartment's window frames. A dazzling dance of fire ripped the cushion to shreds as the bullet, driven by over a thousand pounds of energy cut a path, spreading the remnants of Kansky's skull across the expensively carpeted floor. The gas operated pistol recoiling in his hand, juddering his entire body with its awesome firepower.

"Fucking hell," Boris said, staggering backwards at the deafening explosion. He nearly fell over the edge of the sofa, but caught his balance at the last moment, steadying himself.

"That was for Pat and the Scotsman, you Russian wanker," Mags whispered, thumbing the safety catch and rising to his feet.

"Fuck! I can't believe you just did that, Mags. I'm fucking impressed." Boris told him, his eyes alight with respectful wonderment.

"I feel a bit better now," Mags replied, before kicking Kansky's corpse hard between the legs. Boris watched with a horrified respect, wondering why he hadn't thought of the idea?

"Let's check the other rooms, see if there's anymore little surprises laying about?"

"Good idea, Mags. Nothing much would surprise me anymore," Boris said, already heading for an open door that led to Kansky's bedroom. The curtains were still drawn, and only the light from the lounge gave any illumination to the darkened room. Boris ran his hand along the wall, searching carefully for the light switch. His palm caught on something sharp. Quickly he fingered the object, and the room became bathed with light. The bright ceiling lights forced Boris to squint, his pupils shrivelling with the sudden intensity. Carefully he scanned the room, forcing his eyes to adapt to the contrast. His eyes stopped at the bed, the huge sprawling bed that now held the lifeless body of a young woman, her flesh now blue and bruised as blood began to clot and solidify in her veins. Masses of dried blood clung like rust to her backside, her genitals caked.

"Shit me, Mags, in here!" he called, unable to avert his eyes. The desert eagle entered the room, Mags a fraction of a second later. He froze momentarily as he surveyed the scene.

"Christ almighty," he said, lowering the gun as he approached the body.

"This is some bizarre fucking shit."

"Tell me," Boris said, the disgust clear in his voice.

"Who the fuck could do this?" Mags asked, closely examining the girls torn genitals.

"Somebody fucking sick by the looks of it." Boris shifted his gaze, unable to deal with the concept. He knew he had seen worse, had done some terrible things himself, but this was the body of a woman.

"Boris, let's get the fuck out of Dodge city," Mags said, already backing out of the bedroom, an unsettled look crossing his face.

"I heard that," Boris replied, already wiping his fingerprints off of the light switch with his shirt sleeve. He spared the body one last pitying look, before leaving the room, glad to be away from the poor girls undignified resting place. A shiver ran down his spine. Debbie, his wife, was barely older than the girl in that room. He hoped he got to meet the person responsible for the outrage he had just seen. He would avenge the poor child's death as if she had been family.

The playground was deserted. Only leaves driven idly by the cold winter wind stirred. The deafening rush of children had passed an hour earlier. Morley Memorial primary school now stood cloaked in early evening gloom, deserted save for overworked teachers and the school caretaker. Deputy head Margaret Lishner impatiently replaced the receiver, annoyed. For a full twenty minutes now she had tried to reach Penny Callard, with little success. Her son Jake now sat in the staff room, amongst teachers marking papers, and tired gossip shared over coffee. Margaret was surprised, and slightly annoyed. Penny Callard always collected her son on time. She looked at her watch. She was an hour late. What had got into the woman? There would be words exchanged when she finally arrived, Margaret was sure about that.

Huffing with irritation, she left her office and crossed the long winding corridor and entered the staff room. Sally Barrington, her English teacher sat busily studying form books. An overflowing ashtray littered the table beside her. Gordon Ritchie, the fat balding maths tutor sat angrily as always, taking up an entire sofa. She threw him a withering glance, wondering how on earth he had managed to become a teacher. He hated kids and made no secret of it. Jake Callard sat in a beaten leather chair, innocently watching the old black and white television that always played from its position in the corner of the room. What a beautiful child she thought. His deep steely blue eyes transfixed, as he gazed at the antique television. Margaret studied the boy, his blonde curly hair adding to his beauty. She smiled. In a few years he would be a real heartbreaker.

"Sally, can I have a word?" she called.

"Sorry, Margaret, I didn't see you there," she apologised, wearily rising from her comfortable chair.

"I can't get hold of his mother; I've been trying for ages," Margaret said, nodding discretely at Jake. Sally looked at the clock on the wall, stained yellow with nicotine and coated with a heavy layer of dust.

"Do you think something's happened?" she asked, noting the time.

"I don't know."

"Perhaps, well maybe you ought to think about calling the police," Sally said tentatively, gazing at Jake.

"The police?" Margaret asked, a little shocked.

"Well, it is getting late," Sally reminded. Margaret looked at the clock; nearly five o'clock.

"Oh well, I suppose better safe than sorry!" She sighed, wishing she had gone home early like she had intended.

"Thanks, Sally," she added, before leaving the smoke-filled confines of the staff room. As she entered her office, Margaret thought she could feel the beginning of a headache making its way across her temple. She closed the door wearily, and settled in for a long tired evening.

Slater sat at the kitchen table, drumming his fingers heavily against the badly scratched pine surface. He drew deeply on a Marlboro, noticing with disgust that the ashtray now spilled its contents. He blew a cloud of smoke towards the kitchen ceiling, catching a glimpse of the clock hanging crookedly on the wall in front of him. Seven o'clock.

"Fuck it," he murmured, stubbing the cigarette out into the overflowing ashtray. "Angie, I'm going out," he called.

"Where?" she shouted from her position on the worn sofa in their living room.

"To find Brad. He ought to have phoned by now Angie. She left the comfort of the sofa, drew her dressing gown together and hurried into the kitchen.

"But what if it's dangerous, Andy?" she pleaded, hugging him lightly.

"Angie, Brad might be in trouble, I've got to check it out," he told her, kissing her forehead.

"Please, Andy," she begged, pulling him close.

"I've got to, honey, I've got to," he replied, pulling away. He could see the tears in her eyes, and pain and love washed through him like a wave.

"Sorry, Angie," he said, gently pushing her away. He tried not to look at her. The tears that would surely come bound to change his mind. Closing the door on his wife, his life and everything that went with it was the hardest thing he had ever had to do. As he headed off into the cold dark night, his car headlights cutting a path through the gloom, Slater doubted whether he would ever see his wife again. He hoped it was just a bad feeling, something that would pass like a dark rain cloud as soon as this whole affair was over.

Anyway, knowing Killian the old fart probably had Callard in custody, and was busily milking the honours all for himself. Slater laughed. It was probably true he told himself. His mood lifted slightly as he negotiated the late evening traffic. He had never really taken to Killian, probably because the old bugger wouldn't let anyone take to him. However, for the first time in their working relationship he found himself wondering what he would do if perhaps anything did happen to the old sod? He dismissed the idea. Killian would live to be ninety, and would still be fitter than he was.

Slater lit another cigarette, grudgingly accepting that he actually quite liked his boss, even if it was only slightly. An approaching road sign told him Cherry Hinton was only a mile away. He drew deeply on his cigarette, the bitter smoke cutting a path down his throat that made him cough heavily. Time to quit Andy, he told himself, taking another heavy drag. Blue lights broke the darkness up ahead. Slater began to slow as he approached, noting with concern that the road was littered with police vehicles. A uniformed officer waved him over, his bright yellow jacket glowing in his headlights. Slater pulled over, winding his window down.

"Sorry sir, this road is closed I'm afraid. There's a diversion…." Slater produced his warrant card, cutting the officer off in mid-sentence.

"Oh, go on through detective," he said, stepping aside. Slater felt his heart begin to race, the blood crashed through his chest like a tidal wave. Nervously he lit yet another Marlboro, steering the car through the mass of vehicles with one hand while he did so. He followed the blue lights. They stretched endlessly, as he made his way up Lime Kilne hill. What had happened here? He wondered. Killian must have started a war by the looks of it. He smiled at the idea. He saw a turning on his right. An armed policeman stood in the gateway, his Heckler Kosch fully automatic assault rifle crossing his chest. The German made weapon gleamed as Slater's headlights bathed the gateway.

He produced his warrant card, and threw it on the seat beside him as the armed policeman waved him through. He expected to find Killian holding court, explaining how he single-handily brought down the most corrupt copper in British history. He swung lazily round a narrow dirt track, emerging into an expanse of grass, sprawling out in front of a large building, which Slater thought looked very much like an old wooden cabin. An ambulance was now parked in front of it, next to several other vehicles. Killian's Mondeo was there. Slater saw men in white overalls pawing over it. As he pulled to a halt behind the ambulance, Slater saw O'Neil bounding towards him. "Shit," he moaned. If O'Neil knew, they were both fucked. Where the hell was Killian? O'Neil opened his driver side door. Slater waited in preparation of the severe arse kicking that was about to be delivered.

"Andy, stay there," O'Neil said, gently putting his hand on Slater's arm.

"What's up, sir?" he asked, surprised at O'Neil's calm manner. Perhaps it was a ploy, he thought.

"It's Brad. There's been a shooting," O'Neil explained, his eyes creased. Slater felt his bowels loosen, ice water stirred in the pit of his stomach.

"He's dead, Andy, Bradley's dead." O'Neil moved his hand, gently laying it on Slater's. "I'm sorry, I'm really sorry," he added, bowing his head. A wave of nausea washed through Slater. He felt the urge to be sick, but fought it.

"No," he whispered, tears rolling silently down his cheeks. O'Neil watched helplessly as Slater began to sob, his body racked with heavy spasms as his emotions folded.

"I know you were close, Andy," O'Neil whispered quietly. Slater nodded, tears spilling onto his trousers. O'Neil released Slater's hand, electing to leave him alone with his grief. The sight of Bradley Killian's body, blown apart horrifically would stay with him forever. The sound of Andy Slater's sobbing would haunt his dreams for a long time to come.

"So, where to now, guv?"

"Mo, just fucking drive. Get us the fuck out of here," Mags snapped, slamming the cab door as he and Boris hurriedly leapt in.

"Back to the club?" Mohamed asked, grinning at the comical entry Mags and Boris had just made. The hard pressure of the desert eagle's barrel cut into the soft flesh of Mohamed's neck, the audible click as Mags thumbed the slide safety ran his blood cold. The toothy white grin evaporated, a concerned grimace replaced his usual quirky smile.

"Mo, if this fucking cab ain't rolling in three seconds flat, you'll be taking a shit out of the back of your fucking head," Boris said, leaning into the front, making sure Mohamed understood clearly. The cab swung briskly out of the Jesus Green apartment car park, clipping the brick flowerbed that bordered its perimeter. Boris settled back into his seat, a wry smile pressed across his lips.

"So how did it go?" Darryl asked, wincing as Mohamed narrowly missed an old man wobbling along the verge, his antique cycle long past its road safety capabilities.

"Somebody beat us to it. The cocksucker was already dead. Messy too," Mags replied, noticing the old man waving his fist as they swerved by.

"Fucking hell. You sure?"

"No, Darryl, I'm not sure. The fact that the prick didn't have a fucking head didn't convince me. What the fuck?" Mags threw him a withering look.

"Sorry, guv, I didn't..." Darryl began, but Mags cut in.

"Anyway, he was already dead. His girlfriend too. It wasn't pretty."

"Damn, this is all fucking strange man," Mohamed quipped.

"Shut up, Mo," Boris said, reaching over to flick his ear.

"Anyway, there's someone else out there with the same intention as us. But who?" Mags asked, pondering the situation.

"The Albanians maybe?" Mark offered. Mags shook his head gently, unconvinced.

"Nah, bunch of fucking thieves, but this is grown up stuff. I don't see it Mark. Heroin ain't their game."

"Maybe they're branching out," Mark said, searching the cab for an alliance.

"No way. Gutless fuckers. They wouldn't dare step up and take on the Russians," Boris cut in.

"Listen guys, its none of my business but..." Mohamed started.

"Shut up, Mo," Boris snapped, attempting to flick Mohamed's ear again, but missing when Mohamed leaned forward, almost ramming the windscreen with his face.

"Hah, missed," he said gleefully.

"No I don't wear that either. This is the work of someone in the know. Kansky wouldn't fall for a stranger turning up to clip him. The man was a cunt, but he was a professional cunt," Mags decided.

"How about…"

"Shut up, Mo. Drive, you twat." Mark flicked his other ear, catching Mohamed unaware.

"Bollocks!" he whined.

"Well I'm lost, I know that much," Mags said, scratching his head absently.

"Can I just say, that if…" Mohamed tried again.

"Mo, will-you-shut-the-fuck-up." Mark deliberated each word carefully. Mags smiled, he always got a kick out of the piss take they had with Mo.

"Let him speak," he said, chuckling. Mohamed checked his rear view mirror, making sure a stray hand wasn't looming, ready to flick his ears.

"All I was going to say is, from the bits I've overheard, you know the stuff about Ray? Well if I was him I'd be taking care of any loose ends, no witnesses, no evidence, if you know what I mean?"

"Carry on, Mo," Mags told him, listening intently.

"Well look, boys, if there are no loose ends, it'll all come down to Ray's word against you lot. He's a copper boys, whereas you lot, well let's be honest here; you lot are a bunch of degenerate fuckers," he said, his massive teeth gleaming as a broad smile stretched across his round face. The four men crammed into the back of his cab sat impatiently, the only sound audible came from the heavy traffic clogging the road.

"Don't get me wrong, boys, I don't think you guys are a bunch of degenerates. Well Boris is, but who are the police going to believe, you lot or one of their own? Right now you dipshits are wanted for fuck knows how many murders, amongst other things. How the hell are you going to convince the old bill that one of their best detectives is behind it all? Face it you fucking losers; it's not happening now is it?" He grinned heavily again, satisfied that for once he had shut the piss-taking liberty takers up.

"Well, thank you for that, Mohamed. I'm touched. We all are aren't we lads?" Mags replied, looking at his companions, but all he saw was three open-mouthed individuals, each man lost in silence.

"That's okay, guv. What are friends for after all?" The grin stretched obscenely, almost reaching his stinging ears. They rode on in silence, Mags like the others lost in deep thought. How had they overlooked the obvious? But surely Ray Callard wasn't capable of such things, surely not? A thought stabbed his mind like a hot knife, and he remembered that only a day before he wouldn't have believed Ray Callard capable of betrayal, let alone murder. He had been wrong about that too, and it had cost him dearly. As Mohamed swerved unsteadily through bustling traffic, Mags realised that he couldn't afford to underestimate Ray again. The sooner Killian and Slater nailed the fucker, the better. Otherwise Mags knew he couldn't wait for the legal system to work, and he and his men would have to settle out of court.

"Fucking hell on a moped!"

"What, what's the matter?"

"In here, oh fucking hell!" Frank Killray, twenty-seven years on the force, sank to his knees. Vomit began its upward escape from the pit of his stomach, before bursting through his gritted teeth.

"Frank, what the hell's the matter?" James Reagan burst through the half open bathroom door, skidded on a fresh stream of Frank Killray's vomit, and landed awkwardly in a heap beside the toilet. A loud cracking sound echoed through the tiled room, audible even above Frank Killray's heaving nausea. In the brightly illuminated room, James Reagan could clearly make out the gleaming whiteness of his shattered femur, sticking proudly through the torn material of his trousers. A weak stream of pulsing dark blood pumped from the wound like a fountain, as James watched fascinated, the pain for the moment numbed by the massive adrenaline dump that had just been released into his bloodstream.

"Fuck!" he said weakly, running his hand over his swollen nose, wincing slightly as he caught the bruised puffy flesh. The doctors had told him to stay off work for at least two weeks, but he had returned as soon as he had been discharged. He looked at the bone protruding like an alien from his leg, and wished that just for once in his life he had done as he had been told.

"Uurgh!" He turned his attention to Frank, his tutor. Frank had just deposited another stream of vomit, some of it splashing over his wound. A stinging sensation began to spread as Frank's stomach acids mixed with half digested food began to eat at the fresh injury like battery acid.

"Frank, why did you just do that?" he asked, confusion and shock spreading through him like a sedative. Frank wiped a thin stream of mucous from his chin, watching disgustedly as it smeared an ugly stain along his jacket sleeve.

"There. In there," he said weakly, pointing at the shower. James shook the mist of darkness off that was threatening to cloak him. He strained his eyes against the bulb that so brightly illuminated the room. He could see a body curled awkwardly into a ball. Blood clung to the tiled shower walls like a crimson glue. It was everywhere, and James had never seen so much of it. He thought the body belonged to a woman, but he couldn't really be sure. The head wasn't all there. It had been smashed in, and now much of it hung lazily on strands of clotted blood, smeared across the interior of the shower room. James wished he had done what the doctor ordered. He could have been sitting at home, feet up watching sky sports. He closed his eyes, mentally reminding himself what a prick he could be at times. His mother had always said his stubbornness would get him into trouble. By God the moaning bitch had been right, he thought grudgingly. Suddenly the pain in his leg began to pulse like it had its own life force, the initial adrenaline dump now subsiding.

"Frank, call an ambulance," he said, gritting his teeth as a fresh wave of agony rippled through his shattered leg.

"She'd dead, James. It's too late for an ambulance son," he replied, taking short hard breaths, vainly trying to control his rebellious stomach.

"Frank, I need the ambulance," James told him incredulously.

"What?"

"My leg, Frank, look at my leg." Frank Killray shifted his glazed eyes to James' leg. The bone stood proudly, splintered like a piece of broken timber.

"Oh fucking shit," he whimpered, before his stomach erupted again, spraying chunks of unrecognisable food, bound together with milky white digestive juices all over James Reagan's leg. The acidic liquid burnt into the wound, burning into James like a white hot knife. Bravely he fought the pain with a conviction that belied his youthful status, but the switch that kept his conscious mind alive through times of extreme stress could take no more, and it tripped sending him into a peaceful dark world, where pain no longer tormented him, and where his mother's words could no longer taunt him.

O'Neil knew that his career wasn't going to go any further, not after this. He'd be a laughing stock, especially at the rotary club. Now as the latest report rang though his head like a bell, he wondered what the hell had happened? Penny Callard, horribly murdered, he just couldn't take it in. So far nobody could locate Ray, poor bastard. How the hell would he tell him? And O'Neil knew it would have to be he who broke the news. He sat at his desk, used coffee cups crowded it along with countless reports of murders, violent assaults, and many other offences he couldn't even be bothered to look at. He did know however, that he could clear the whole thing up in one go, if only he could find Vandersar. He'd rot in prison for this; O'Neil would see to it personally. He began to drift lightly into a semi-conscious daze, his tired body rebelling against the sleep depravation he had been forced to endure. The gentle knock at his office door snapped him awake. He bolted upright, alertness returning.

"Sir?" Andy Slater entered the office, his eyes ringed with heavy dark circles.

"Andy, come in, mate." O'Neil began to rise from his seat, but gave up and motioned Slater to sit down in the leather sofa that stretched along the far wall of his spacious office.

"Sir, I need to talk to you," Slater said, slumping tiredly into the sumptuous leather.

"Andy, why don't you go home mate; get some rest."

"Look, sir this is important."

"It can wait, Andy. You've been through a lot. Go home, we'll talk tomorrow," O'Neil insisted, his voice tired.

"No. We need to talk now," Slater replied, an edge entering his tone. O'Neil shot him a glare, but under the circumstances he was prepared to understand that Andy was in a highly emotional state.

"Tomorrow mate, tomorrow," O'Neil repeated. Slater took a deep breath; his shoulders rose with the effort. He steadied himself, took another heavy breath before addressing O'Neil once more.

"It was Ray," he said, feeling the blood rushing powerfully through his temples. O'Neil stared at him absently, seemingly unaware of what Slater had just said.

"Ray did it. He Killed Brad, and he was in on the Sergatov murders too," Slater added.

"What?" O'Neil looked at him, a barely disguised veil of anger cloaked his face.

"You heard me. He had Vandersar's men killed too. Oh, and I've just heard about Penny. Bet your life he did that."

"Andy, are you bloody insane? Do you understand what you're saying?" Now O'Neil couldn't hide his anger. All traces of tiredness disappeared as he listened to Slater's disgusting outbursts.

"Andy, I'll forget you've just said any of that. Now I suggest you go home, get some sleep and we'll review this in the morning," he snapped, urging Slater to drop the subject.

"Have I touched a nerve, sir?" Slater repeated. O'Neil's face reddened, the inner rage he had been trying to suppress suddenly found an escape route.

"What? Andy, I'm not asking you to go home, I'm ordering."

"Have I touched a nerve, sir? Is the idea that Ray might be a sadistic murdering bastard too much to take?" Slater asked, now fixing O'Neil with an icy glare.

"Get out, Slater. Fuck off home," O'Neil demanded, slamming his bony fist into his desktop. Several coffee cups shook before spilling cold liquid across the scattering of paperwork.

"He's been on the take for years, first for Vandersar, then for Kansky. But Kansky made him a better offer obviously, and Vandersar became, well, surplus to requirements." Slater spat the words out, emphasising his disgust.

"You expect me to believe that?" O'Neil asked, shaking his head with disbelief.

"No, sir, I don't. But when this is all over, don't say you didn't know," Slater replied, pushing himself up from the sofa. "And when you're checking parking metres in the city centre, don't say I didn't warn you," he added. O'Neil stared at Slater intently, looking for something, anything that might betray what his real motives were. He had known Slater for a long time, and he knew his record was impeccable. In fact O'Neil thought he was an outstanding copper. He searched Slater's eyes, probing his deepest thoughts for an ulterior motive, but he found nothing behind those sad bloodshot eyes but honesty and integrity. He let Slater reach the office door before giving in to his inner belief.

"Andy, don't go," he said softly.

"Why, so you can tell me what a great bloke Ray is?" he replied sarcastically.

"No, I'll listen," O'Neil told him, an image of himself handing out parking tickets flashed through his mind as he spoke.

"Killian knew; he knew everything, and it cost him his life," Slater said, leaning heavily against the door. O'Neil sighed, a tired heavy movement that left him deflated.

"He was a grumpy old cunt you know? But I'll tell you sir, Brad was the best copper I've ever known," Slater added, his eyes welling heavily.

"I know, Andy. He was a good man," O'Neil replied, running a hand across his stubbled chin. "Sit down then; tell me what you know."

"You'll listen?" Slater asked, a thin smile pressing his lips.

"I promise, I give you my word," O'Neil said, extending his hand. Slater looked at the outstretched hand, regarding it suspiciously. Finally he reached out with his right hand and the pair shook.

"Where do you want to start?" Slater asked.

"From the beginning," O'Neil told him. Slater released O'Neil's hand, before dropping heavily into the deep leather sofa.

"First of all, sir, I want your word on something."

"Of course, Andy, what is it?"

"Vandersar. Call everyone off. He's innocent," Slater said, reaching for his cigarettes.

"You are joking, Andy?" O'Neil asked incredulously.

"No I'm not. This was all a set up. He was nothing to do with it."

"He assaulted two police officers, Andy, before breaking out of the cells. On top of that he hijacked a car, and he put the driver in hospital."

"Let it go, sir."

"Why?"

"If you had been framed for all those murders, and you knew you were looking at life in prison, wouldn't you act a little irrationally?" Slater asked, blowing a cloud of blue smoke up into the air.

"Maybe I would, Andy, but…"

"He was desperate, sir! Think about it," Slater shouted, cutting O'Neil off in mid-sentence. "What was he supposed to do; trust in the legal system?" Slater asked angrily.

"Why are you so intent on protecting him, Andy?" O'Neil demanded. The question forced a heavy laugh from Slater.

"Why? Because I believe in wrong and right, sir. Remember that? It's what we joined the police for isn't it?"

"Yes, it is, Andy," O'Neil agreed, playing the question over in his mind.

"Okay, Andy, I'll do it," he said, instantly reaching for the phone sitting on his desk hidden beneath pages of paperwork.

"I'd hurry up and find Callard too, sir, before Vandersar does."

O'Neil hesitated with the received held in his hand.

"You think Vandersar will kill him?" he asked, a look of shock spreading across his tired face.

"Slowly, very slowly," Slater told him, reaching for another cigarette. He lit it as he watched O'Neil frantically giving orders to the control room. He winced as he bellowed into the receiver.

"Yes! Ray Callard, you heard me right. I want every officer we've got looking for him," he shouted angrily. Slater drew heavily on his Marlboro, glad that he wasn't the poor girl on the other end of O'Neil's tongue-lashing.

"Just do it!" O'Neil snapped, before slamming the receiver down.

"I hope you're right about this, Andy," he said, massaging his throbbing temple.

"So do I sir, so do I," Slater replied, blowing a heavy cloud of smoke towards the ceiling. He stubbed the cigarette out in a glass ashtray balanced beside him on the leather sofa.

"Right, tell me what you know," O'Neil said, leaning back in his chair. Slater regarded him, wondering how O'Neil was going to react to what he was about to hear? He studied the tired face, lined with stress and lack of sleep. Not very well Slater decided, but he was going to tell him anyway. He owed Killian that much.

The city centre was alive. Pubs spilled revellers out into the cold late evening, whilst nearby takeaways filled the chilly air with the aroma of fast food. Ray drove through the busy streets, the brightly illuminated shop fronts lighting the dark sky. He edged through a crowd of drunken women, crossing the road unsteadily, teetering drunkenly on stilettoed heels. The Jaguar's huge engine roared as it swung into Catherine Street, narrowly missing a black taxi parked in the middle of the road, discharging two drunk middle-aged men. Further along the street, standing under the glare of a heavily illuminated shop front, Ray saw what he had been searching for. Deftly he swung the Jaguar into the curb, bringing it to a smooth halt outside the Gold Rush, a glass-fronted pawn shop. A metal security shutter hid the interior from unwanted scrutiny during the times the shop was closed. Now the only item on view stood under the bright neon sign.

Beverly Jenson had been working Catherine Street for nearly two years. At only twenty-one, her lithe subtle body meant she found no shortage of work. The extra income had already put her through college, and was about to put her on a plane for a two-week holiday in Jamaica. Two more days, and she'd be lying on a beach, just what she needed after the long English winter nights, standing out wearing no more than the barest amount of clothes. Beverly was about to go home. Business had been very slow on this particular evening, and the biting cold had begun to eat into her bones like a freezing disease. Suddenly a large gleaming Jaguar cruised to a halt in front of her. She welcomed the attention and walked over as the passenger side door was opened for her.

"You working, love?" Ray Callard asked, peering through the open door.

"Yes, darling," she replied, sliding her slim bottom into the passenger seat.

"How much?" he asked, admiring her long stockinged legs.

"Ten for a hand job, oral is twenty five. If you want the lot, it's forty quid."

"It's a deal," he said, pulling out into the quiet road. Catherine Street gave way to the busier fringe streets of the city centre. Like any multicultural city,

Cambridge truly came to life after darkness. Students wobbled merrily from one pub to another, while the homeless took up residence in shop doorways. Ray saw a young girl, probably no more than twenty, huddled in the draughty doorway of a department store. A filthy blanket pulled up to her chin, the only defence she had from the biting cold. A mange-riddled mongrel sat huddled beside her, tied to the doors by a withered piece of rope. Momentarily he was swept with pity, but the though passed quickly when his passenger interrupted.

"Nice car. What do you do then?" she asked, gently running a long red fingernail along his leg.

"I'm a copper," he said absently.

"You're joking," she stuttered, concern cutting into her voice. He laughed at her response, amused as her hand jumped away from his leg.

"Don't worry, sweetheart; I'm off duty. Anyway, I have my needs." He grinned as he spoke, pleased with her nervousness. She seemed to relax at his humour, and her slender fingers again began snaking along his leg, tracing an enticing path towards his stiffening penis.

"Married?" she asked, finding his erection.

"No, not anymore," he replied.

"Divorced?"

"Widowed; she died recently."

"Oh, I'm sorry," she said, genuine sorrow creeping into her words. Ray left the conversation there, content to drive onwards through the rural outskirts of the city.

"Where are we going?" she asked, massaging his penis.

"Somewhere quiet," he replied, glancing over at her pert breasts. Passing the industrial areas, he stared impressively at the huge glassed expanse of the city's science park. Ahead lay the main A10 road, linking Cambridge to the overflows of rural villages. He gunned the Jaguar, hitting nearly ninety with ease as he made the most of the deserted highway.

"Hurry up, honey," she said, gently unzipping his trousers.

"Nearly there," he replied, slowing to take a side exit on the left hand side of the road. Slowly the huge car snaked through a tree-lined valley, the only illumination coming from the headlights and the dull moon breaking periodically through darkened clouds. The road suddenly came to a final halt, a large lay-by used as an illegal dumpsite. Ray saw the remains of an old sofa, tattered and torn, now coated with a fine layer of damp moss. He swung the Jaguar into a gap between piles of brick rubble, narrowly avoiding scratching the cars sleek angled wing. Satisfied with his position, Ray killed the engine, returning the lay-by into darkness.

Beverly wasted no time, releasing his erect penis. She leant over, engulfing his stiffened member with her painted lips. Ray let out a low groan, marveling as her tongue toyed with his swollen gland. He moved his left hand down to her flowing blonde hair. The silky texture felt good to his touch. Greedily he took a handful and pushed her head down, choking her as his penis forced its way into her throat. She tried to push her head upwards, unable to breathe as his penis choked her, cutting off her air supply. Her struggle excited him greatly, and he felt his orgasm nearing. Ray grabbed her hair violently, ripping her head from his penis. Gasping, she began to cough heavily, taking in air in huge gulps. Her eyes widened in horror as he punched her hard in the face. She was dimly aware of the cracking noise as her nose shattered, the bone bursting awkwardly through her pale skin.

"Bitch!" he screamed, punching her again. Beverly Jenson reeled as the blow broke her jaw in five places, forcing her head into the passenger side window with such force, the safety glass shattered into a million star shaped fragments. Suddenly he released his grip on her hair, before jumping briskly out of the car. He stumbled across broken bricks, hurriedly making his way round to the passenger side. Beverly lay slumped against the passenger door, and when he opened it she fell helplessly out onto the muddied rubble strewn ground.

"Come here, you fucking whore cunt," he said, dragging her by the hair. With terrific violence Ray lifted her clean off the ground by her long blonde hair, now matted with dark blood. He threw her head first onto the Jaguar's bonnet, her face denting it as her mangled features bounced heavily against the warm metal.

"You're gonna give me what I want now, ain't you bitch?" he said, tearing her skimpy black knickers off. The thin material cut into her legs as Ray pulled, forcing the lace to snap.

"Oh yeah, you're gonna take it, you fucking whore," he shouted, pushing his erection hard against the opening of her anus. In her semiconscious state, Beverly became aware of the painful sensation now spreading through her back passage. She tried to scream, but her broken jaw, now swelling to three times its normal size, refused to open. Only a muffled groan escaped as blood bubbled through her gaping nose. Her obvious pain pleased him enormously, and shifting his bodyweight forward Ray pushed his penis hard into her anus, the delicate skin surrounding it gave way, and a mist of fine blood began spraying across his groin as he excitedly pumped into her. Again she tried to protest as the mind-blowing pain spread through her. Only an empty scream escaped her as her jaw swelled further, locking her face into a fixed grimace. Ray heightened his pace, hurriedly and wantonly he pushed faster and faster. His breathing became heavy, his chest rising and falling as he neared ejaculation. Gripping her by the back of the neck, he stiffened as his penis began its familiar pumping, spurting streams of hot sperm deep into her torn bowel.

"Oh, you fucking slag," he muttered, falling heavily onto her. He lay there, panting for a minute or more as he tried to compose himself. Once his breathing had returned to normal, Ray pushed himself up, returning his now flaccid penis to his underpants. He smiled gleefully as he noticed the blood path around his groin. Beverly lay across the bonnet, motionless except for sporadic twitches as her body reacted to the intense pain that ran out of control through her ruptured bowel. Ray eyed her casually, like a predator surveying its prey. He grabbed her by the arm, pulling her like a limp rag doll until she flopped awkwardly to the ground. She lay helplessly at his feet. Her eyes pleaded with him, begging for clemency. Ray spat at her, a large glob of spittle landed across her chest. Beverly knew her life was running out, the force leaving her by the second as her eyes fixed intently on the figure now towering over her.

"Ple-ase," she begged, the pain excruciated her as she managed to force the broken word through her shattered face. Ray lifted his right foot, forced his body forward and stamped on her head. The blow caved in her left eye socket, the bones giving in under the intense pressure. Her eye exploded, an oozing running liquid cascaded down her cheek. Again he stamped, this time on her chest, his bodyweight followed the blow, shattering the ribs on her right side like twigs. Her lung collapsed and an audible rush of air escaped as the organ punctured. Excited now, Ray again felt the stirring of an erection as he jumped up and down on her lifeless body. Her spleen exploded as his body landed squarely on her midsection, rupturing her liver in the process. Ray carried on with his frenzy, kicking her now dead body into an unrecognisable mess. Even as he took his fully aroused penis out through his bloodied trousers and began to masturbate, Ray kept on kicking and stamping on Beverly Jenson's limp body.

Chapter Eight

The rest was a welcome release, all problems forgotten, if only temporarily. Mags sat in his reclining office chair, feet perched lazily on the mahogany desk now lifeless and redundant. Being a gang of fugitives had put paid to any new business. Now the office phone sat quietly on the desk, along with piles of invoices and enquiries. He glanced at Boris, now heavily asleep on the sofa. Mark and Darryl wedged either side of him, both lost in their own dreams. He watched as Boris snored heavily, his huge muscular chest rising with each massive intake of air. *Sleep well, my friend,* he thought. There would be many more battles to fight yet, that much Mags was sure of. His men needed the rest. They hadn't had much of late.

Boris whimpered lightly, a small cry of anguish that interrupted his bellowed snores. Mags smiled lightly. The big man looked so peaceful for a change. He thought about the battles they had fought together; so many wars. Boris had been an unstoppable force through those encounters, an unyielding entity who never took a backward step. Mags had learnt from a very early age the power of loyalty, the unity it gave, the strength it brought. Boris personified loyalty. Outwardly he was the most unhappy person Mags had ever met, but inside somebody else existed altogether. His love for the team knew no bounds. It was a genuine unconditional love that few men would ever be lucky enough to experience. The deaths of Pat and the Scotsman had devastated them all, but Boris had hardly acknowledged the incident. Like a warrior he had battled on, business as usual. Somewhere in the future, when this war was over, Boris would go away and grieve alone. He would say his farewells in his own place, in his own time. Another loud snore broke the quietness. Boris spluttered and stirred briefly before once again settling back into a deep sleep.

"I can't afford to lose you guys," Mags whispered, gazing at the three sleeping giants. Now more than ever he was aware of their vulnerability, their nakedness. Mags didn't want to lose another of his men, and knew he couldn't afford to either. Mags closed his tired eyes, leant back in the heavily padded recliner and tried to lose himself in sleep. The dark fingers of tiredness probed at his mind eagerly and he welcomed them gladly. In seconds he was deep in dreams, lost to the conscious world where brutality and misery plagued his every waking moment. In his dream the world was peaceful, he stood in a flowing field of flowers, red and yellow roses flooded his senses, swallowing his view in every direction. He glanced to movement far away in the distance, a figure waving. He squinted his eyes against the bright warm sun, making out faintly the figure of a woman, running towards him. It was Penny, her golden hair flowing as she made her way through fields of colourful roses.

"Mags, Mags I love you," she called as she drew closer.

"Penny, I love you too," he replied, heading towards her. The emotion swept over him, flooding his senses with warmth. How much he wanted to hold her, to touch her. Suddenly the sun began to dim, dark clouds gathered, sending the beautiful landscape into perpetual gloom. Mags stopped in his tracks, the air had become cold, almost freezing. He watched in horror as the roses began to whither and die. The brightly tinted petals turning black before falling lifelessly to the ground. An overwhelming sense of panic spread through him, goose bumps pimpled his skin and his hair stiffened on the back of his neck. He scanned the horizon. Where was the sense of fear coming from? Penny was near now, her smiling face so reassuring.

"Hurry, Pen," he called, looking around at the dead flowers. He wanted to be away from this place. "Run Penny!" he shouted, but when he turned to her she was gone. "Pen?" he called, scanning the fields. "Penny, where are you?" Only the harsh coldness replied. The wind had begun to pick up, echoing darkly around the expanse of emptiness.

"Mags, here they come."

"What?" He turned to the voice now addressing him. Boris stood behind him, but this wasn't the Boris he knew. The person standing here now was decked in armour, heavily plated with a huge breastplate adorned with symbols Mags had never seen before, almost hieroglyphic. His head was encased in a gleaming helmet, the face tapering away to revel Boris' features. In his hand he held a huge lethal looking sword.

"Boris, what the fuck?"

"Mags, wake up, they're here," Boris replied coldly. "They're here," he repeated, nodding to the horizon. Mags slowly turned to where Boris had nodded. The darkening skies had given the landscape a forbidding look, almost evil. There, not fifty metres away, lined up as far as the eye could see, stood thousands and thousands of cloaked figures. Each figure held a lethal looking sword, and Mags could clearly see some of those swords dripped blood.

"Who the hell are they, Boris?" he asked.

"It's time, General, it's time," Boris told him, raising his sword.

"General? Boris what the…" Mags lost his words as he looked behind Boris. The fields were black with men, more people than he had ever seen in his life before. Their shining armour glinting in the dim half light, each man held his sword to the ready.

"Who the fuck are they?" Mags wondered aloud.

"They are your men, General, the army of good," a voice replied. Mags searched for the person who had spoken. His eyes stopped when they fell on familiarity.

"Pat, is that you?" he asked incredulously.

"Yes, sir, I'm here." Mags ran over and embraced him, tears flowing down his face as he did so.

"Not now, sir, we've got to finish this," Pat said, pulling away.

"But Pat, I…"

"Sir, they're coming," Boris shouted. Mags looked and saw the army of hooded figures moving forward like a filthy black tide, slowing surging onwards. Fear began to creep into his stomach, his bowels lurched wildly.

"Sir, give the order," Pat said, raising his sword. Mags looked around, unable to take the situation in. His eyes fell on Mark, a stoic look pressed across his face. Next to him Darryl looked towards the approaching army with a hated determination. The Scotsman stood behind them, a banner held in his hands. Mags saw the red flag waving wildly in the cold wind, a black wolf's head emblazoned across the red material.

"He's yours, you cunt!" Mags spun sharply, the croaking voice snapping him into life.

"Judas! He's yours," the voice shouted. Mags saw the army of cloaked figures getting nearer, a lone figure at the front, his face hidden by a dark hood.

"The bitch betrayed me. He's yours, Judas."

"Who are you?" Mags shouted.

"I was your friend, Judas," the figure replied. Mags watched in shock as gnarled hands slipped the hood back, revealing a dark evil face, wrinkled by age. Red eyes stared out from beneath hollow sockets as they bored into Mags. A flicker of recognition swept through his mind. He knew who that was, didn't he?

"Ray, is that you?"

"Judas, you betrayed me."

"Ray, you set us up. Why?" Mags pleaded.

"He's yours, you cunt," the dark crackling voice replied.

"Who?"

"The boy, he's yours." The thing that was Ray Callard was now only a few metres away,. Mags saw oozing puss running out of blistering sores that covered his face.

"Sir, we've got to fight now," Boris said.

"Now I'm going to kill you, Judas," Ray snapped, holding out clawed hands. Mags saw with disgust that they looked like the talons of a bird.

"Sir!" Boris shouted.

"I don't understand, Ray?" Mags said, confusion running madly out of control in his mind.

"He's yours, the bastard cunt is yours," Ray bellowed, his lips pulling back to reveal a mouth full of jagged lethal looking white fangs.

"Ray, what do you mean, I don't..." Mags began, but the thing now only two paces away from him reached into its dark cloak and produced a curved deadly looking dagger.

"He's yours, the cunt boy is your Judas, and now I'm going to eat your heart," the Ray thing wailed.

"Sir!" Boris screamed. Suddenly a bright white pain shot through Mags' brain, a blinding jolt that stiffened his entire body. From instinct Mags knew he was moments from death, and he swung his right arm forward with great power. His amazement was complete when he saw a huge broad-edged sword fixed in his hand. The blade sliced through the Ray thing's neck with absolute ease, severing his head in one swift powerful move. The Ray thing's head spun through the air, rolling like a ball, evil red eyes still burning their bright hatred. The cloaked army stopped its approach, their leader now slain.

"*Vae victis!* Woe to the vanquished!" Boris bellowed, his sword held defiantly in the air. Mags heard the deafening rumble as his army moved as one, armour clanking as many thousands of metal clad bodies advanced ready for battle. The red banner, its wolf's head insignia passed him waving madly in the icy wind. The cloaked army now composed began its dark advance once more. Mags could clearly see an infinite number of bright red eyes burning from under those hooded cloaks. An icy hand reached into his stomach as one by one each cloaked figure raised a curved, murderous-looking sabre. Boris and the lead element had already reached them. Mags saw a dozen figures fall, limbs severed, a foul green blue liquid spraying from the hideous wounds. Men poured past him, crying battle shrills as their armour clanked heavily. Suddenly a hand gripped Mags' leg. He instantly jerked away, but the force held its grip causing him to stumble over, landing heavily. He looked down to his leg. A scaly clawed talon held him, the filthy yellow nails biting into his flesh. The headless body began pulling him forward. Frantically Mags fumbled for his sword, lost behind him as he fell.

"Judas, cunty fucking whore Judas!" Mags heard the vile words even over the deafening noise of battle. The horror froze him as he saw the Ray thing's severed head, now smiling at him.

"He's yours, the cunt is yours," it spoke, spitting globs of green blue liquid across Mags' feet. The spell broke. Mags threw his weight backwards and reached out for his sword. The heavy cold steel reassuring to his touch. His fingers wrapped round the handle, and with a swift arching movement he swung his body upright, slamming the blade downwards with venomous power. The scaly talon bit deeper into his flesh as the blade severed it from its disgusting body. A foul stench hit Mags' nostrils as the noxious liquid pumped from the wound.

"She's a slut, a cunt, a whore!" the head shouted, its scabbed lips stretching to reveal those razor sharp teeth.

"Fuck her, fuck the bitch in the arse," it cackled. Mags rolled away from the headless corpse before pushing himself up off the cold muddy ground.

"Whore! Whore! Whore!" Cackling laughter pierced his brain, a painful feeling spreading through his head. Mags bent down and ripped the talon from his leg, the razor sharp nails tearing his skin. Disgust rippled through him as blood began to trickle from the wounds. He threw the talon to the ground before stamping on it. An audible series of snaps greeted his ears as the bones shattered.

"Whore! She's a cunt."

"Shut the fuck up!" Mags snapped.

"Judas, you're a fucking Judas." The Ray thing began to cackle again, but Mags had already begun to raise his sword. The cackling mouth froze to a grimace as the cold steel began its final descent. A heavy sickening thud rang out as the blade severed the head in two, carrying onwards before embedding in the muddy field.

"Die, you fucker," Mags whispered, pulling the blade out of the blue-green mess. His disgust became nausea as swarms of maggots crept and wriggled out of the mangled brain. He backed away from the mess as the maggots began to wriggle towards him, forcing a path through his feet. He carried on backing away, and the sounds of battle once more caught his attention. He saw his men slicing hooded figures to pieces. In amongst the chaos he saw Boris smashing a cloaked head repeatedly with his sword. Boris' armour became painted with the vile blood as he cut the brains to a pulp. Everywhere he looked he saw pain and misery. To his left one of his men fell to his knees, a curved sabre jutting out of his back. The hooded figure that stood over him yanked the blade out and then severed the man's head in one final movement. Mags could clearly see the battle was far from one sided. He counted dozens of armoured bodies littering the battlefield.

"Mags, wake up!" Heavy hands shook him, bringing him back to the conscious world. His eyes snapped open. Boris was there looming over him.

"What?" he asked, still groggy.

"There's someone at the door. Listen," Boris said. Mags could hear the heavy thuds of a fist banging into the front doors of the White Rooms.

"Police?" Mags asked, jumping from the comfort of his chair.

"Don't know," Boris replied, already at the top of the stairs. Mags pulled the desert eagle from his waistband, thumbed the safety and followed Boris.

"It's that fucking copper!" Mark called from his position by the front window. "Slater," he added.

"Is he alone?" Darryl asked, peering over Marks huge shoulder. "Yeah, on his own," Darryl said, scanning the street in each direction. Only the late night traffic, now very thin shared the road below. Mags descended the stairs, Boris a step behind. The foyer now stood unusually silent, shrouded in darkness. The White Rooms had never been shut before Mags mused as he slipped the deadlocks from the main door, not even Christmas day. The stiff heavy door opened grudgingly, letting in a blast of freezing air. Andy Slater stood outside on the concrete step, his thin raincoat pulled up tightly to his chin, a vain gesture against the cold night.

"Slater, what you doing here?" Mags asked, ushering him in quickly.

"We need to talk," he replied. Even in the poor light of the foyer, Mags could see Andy Slater looked a mess.

"You look like shit, Slater. Boris, get him a stiff drink."

"A double," Slater added, before following Mags back up the stairs towards the office. Mark still stood by the window, making sure Slater hadn't been followed. Slater nodded at Darryl, then Mark.

"I'm alone. Don't worry, son," he said, watching as Mark kept his vigil at the window.

"So you say. And I'm not your fucking son either," Mark cut back before peering through the blinds again.

"Cool it, Mark," Mags said, grateful that Boris had returned, a hefty measure of brandy held in his hand. Slater took the glass greedily.

"Thanks then," Boris said sarcastically.

"Thank you," Slater quipped, before downing the brandy in one hungry gulp.

"Fucking hell, are things that bad?" Darryl asked, staring in amazement as Slater sank the fiery liquid.

"Worse than bad," Slater replied taking a seat on the sofa. Mags sat back in his recliner, slightly intrigued at Slater's dishevelled appearance.

"I've got some bad new," Slater told them, fighting the urge to cry. Concerned, Mags leant forward, almost upset at Slater's state.

"What's up, mate?" he asked.

"Killian's dead, so is Penny Callard."

"What?" Mags thought he had misheard Slater. "What did you say?" he repeated.

"I'm sorry, Mags, she's gone. Ray killed Killian; I think you can put money on him being Penny's killer too." Slater spluttered the words out, embarrassed that a tear had begun to snake its way down his cheek.

"Oh shit," Boris said, making his way to Mags, who now sat in stunned silence.

"I'm sorry, Mags, so sorry," he said, putting his hand on his shoulder.

"You must have it wrong. She can't be dead Slater; I fucking love the woman!" Mags screamed, jumping out of his chair. Instantly Boris wrapped his arms round Mags' chest, and heavily the two wrestled to the floor, knocking the office table aside. Mark ran over from his position by the window, lending his considerable weight to help restrain Mags. From his position on the sofa, Andy Slater began to weep. Tears rolled freely down his face. His body shook under the weight of saddened emotion.

"NO!" Mags' agonising scream rocked the room as Boris and Mark fought to hold him down.

"Easy mate, easy," Boris said gently.

"No, please, not Penny," Mags wailed. Under the weight of his friends, Mags fought desperately to escape and confront Slater. Knowing his efforts were useless, Magnus Vandersar slackened, his body lifelessly slack on the floor of his office. For the first time in his violent and turbulent life, he began to sob, every ounce of emotion released, as the reality of Penny's death swept over him like a blackness that offered no glimmer of light.

George Atkins fiddled with the tiny buttons of his mobile phone. Now fifty-four, the telecommunications revolution had come late in life for him. He pressed the 'send' button, and smiled like a naughty boy as the message was sent. Marion, his long suffering wife of thirty years had bought him the phone for his birthday, and despite his initial distrust of modern gadgets, he now never left home without it. He laughed loudly. Marion would blush when she received the message. It was the fifth one he had sent her this evening as he sat parked in a lay-by just outside Cambridge science park. He glanced at his watch; nearly midnight. He groaned, knowing he still had over two hours to go until his shift ended. George took a small measure of comfort from the knowledge that he only had three more months left to complete in the force, and then he could retire. He had been a copper for twenty-six years, the last fifteen as a traffic policeman. Handing out speeding fines was about all he wanted to do nowadays anyway. The job suited him just fine. He sat back comfortably in the drivers seat of his police Volvo, watching idly as the odd car sped by. He closed his eyes and dreamt of retirement, long lazy days tending his prized allotment, a cold beer and his old transistor radio to listen to cricket. George figured he could put up with three more months of checking dodgy tyres and giving the odd breath test. Easy as pie.

His comfort suddenly blurred as the high-powered whine of a massive engine roared past at speed. George just made out the make of the car as it sped past. The gleaming Jaguar touched something in his mind, but what was it? He tapped his fingers on the steering wheel, trying to remember what it was about that model of car. "Shit!" he said, suddenly realising that he had been briefed earlier in the evening to be on the look out for Ray Callard, and he drove a Jaguar XK8. The Volvo roared into life, the powerful engines kicking the car out into the quiet road. George flicked a switch on the dash, and instantly the darkened sky became awash with the deafening blue of the Volvo's roof mounted lights. He floored the accelerator, reeling back in his seat as the car climbed rapidly to eighty miles an hour. Up ahead he could see the Jaguar's tail lights, burning bright luminous red as the car entered the outskirts of the city.

To George Atkins surprise, and slight disappointment, the Jaguar began to slow, carefully pulling over into the nearside kerb outside a row of neat terraced houses. George sighed with displeasure. He was hoping for a bit of a chase. He loved the fast pursuits. He pulled the Volvo into the kerb, twenty feet behind the now dormant Jaguar. He watched hesitantly as the driver's door opened, already reaching for his radio handset to call in for the Jaguar's registration details. When he saw that the figure now walking to the rear of the Jaguar was in fact Ray Callard, George momentarily wondered what to do. Besides, what was Ray doing? George decided to radio in. After all he had little time for Ray Callard. Nobody he knew did, except for the old girl in the control room, and George thought she was going senile anyway.

"Sierra Oscar, this is five three six over," he said, thumbing the talk button on the radio mike. A burst of static crackled back, before any reply came.

"Go ahead five three six, this is control, over," a petite voice spoke. George tried to put a face to the voice, figuring that it was probably that little blonde thing everyone kept trying to pull.

"Control, I've got…" George stopped in mid-sentence, his jaw ajar as he watched Ray Callard approaching his driver's side window. With a sense of fascinated fear, George realised Ray was holding a gun in his hands, a big gun like he'd seen in action movies. The mike slipped from his hand as he watched Ray Callard level the weapon up to his head, only dimly aware that the pretty blonde thing at control was trying to reach him.

"Go ahead five three six, over," she said urgently. George felt his bowels loosening as he realised the enormity of the situation. This couldn't be happening. After all he only had three months left to do. Easy as pie. The last thing he saw in his life was a bright flash. He never knew that the single round hit him above the right eye, obliterating his brain in a split second. The interior of the Volvo suffered an explosion of bloodied tissue as fragmented grey gelatine globs of brain exited George Atkins' head through a wound carved viciously by the 7.62 millimetre round. As George died slumped into the passenger seat of his police Volvo, at home Marion his long suffering wife read a saucy text message, the fifth one that evening. She glanced at the clock hanging above the open fireplace, and decided she might give the silly old bugger an early retirement present when he got home.

"Find him, punish him and then gut the cunt like a fish," Boris said, taking Darryl out into the hallway. Behind them they could still hear sporadic sobs.

"He's in a bad fucking way," Boris added.

"Yeah, no sweat. We'll find the fucker alright." Darryl could feel the hatred welling within himself as he spoke. He had always hated Ray Callard and could never quite understand why Mags had kept him around.

"Kill him, Darryl, and when he's dead kill him again."

"Don't worry, I'll drip dry him."

"Good, man. Take Mark along for the ride. I'll stay with Mags." Boris patted Darryl on the arm, giving him a knowing look, leaving no doubt as to what he wanted done to Ray Callard. Darryl pushed the office door open and motioned Mark to join him. Mags sat at his desk, his head buried in his hands with despair. Andy Slater still sat on the sofa, another brandy wedged firmly in his hand. Mark closed the door behind himself as he joined Boris and Darryl in the hallway.

"We can't leave him like that," he said.

"Don't worry, Mark, I'm staying with him," Boris said. Mark gave him a bemused look, huge frown lines spreading across his round face.

"Where are we going then?"

"Mark, we're going to clip Callard," Darryl informed him.

"Fuck! Who gave the order?" Mark asked.

"I did," Boris snapped.

"Yeah but Mags wants him," Mark whined. Boris grabbed him by the scruff of the neck, pulling him roughly down the hallway.

"Listen to me, you fat cunt. I'm next in charge, understand?"

"Yeah okay, steady, Boris," Mark stuttered.

"That fucking man in there is my friend. I love that fucking guy. Now listen to him in there sobbing, you hear it?"

"I hear it, Boris. I didn't mean anything, honest."

"Then show some fucking respect, burger boy!" Boris dug his hands into Mark's flesh. Red welts began forming on his throat.

"Easy, blade, easy." Darryl gently rubbed Boris' huge shoulders trying to calm him down. Slowly he began to release his grip, but still the fire of menace stayed in his eyes. Mark fell back into the wall, his large cheeks reddening as tears began welling.

"I'm sorry, mate," he said, rubbing a huge hand to his watery eyes.

"Right then, get the fuck out there and do some killing. Butcher the cunt. Do it for him in there!" Boris shouted, pointing at the office door. Darryl grabbed Mark by the arm, leading him briskly down the dark stairs towards the foyer of the White Rooms. In the gloom of the dimly lit reception area, Mark paused briefly to wipe a stream of tears from his red face. Darryl held the door open for him, choosing to stare out into the night rather than add to his friend's misery.

Chapter Nine

Another table of glasses crashed noisily to the floor. Splinters of jagged daggers littered the carpet. Howls of laughter greeted the ears of the two doormen as they entered the bar.

"Oops," someone called from a crowd at the far end of the oak-panelled bar. Winston Morgan glanced over, feeling decidedly uneasy.

"Not good," he said to his partner, Andy Kellar.

"I count eight of them, Win," Kellar noted uneasily. Eight skinheaded men stared back. Winston could clearly make out Nazi tattoos. Swastikas and black eagles adorned arms hanging under Fred Perry shirts.

"Whatcha looking at, nigger?" From the crowd stepped a squat heavily muscled individual. A thick black swastika decorated his left forearm. Winston felt his blood running cold. He had heard about the minority of skinhead thugs that littered the city, but until now he had been fortunate enough never to have met any of them.

"Nigger, what you looking at then?"

"Ignore them, Win. I'll call for some help," Andy Kellar said, producing a mobile from his bomber jacket pocket.

"Who the fuck are you going to call, Andy? Mags and the boys are on the run remember?" Winston replied, nervously watching as the squat muscular skinhead rolled a bottle around in his hand.

"I've got to try, Win. We'll never get this lot out on our own," Kellar said, tapping the phones keypad. He held it to his ear, willing for an answer, all the while aware that the crowd at the end of the bar were watching intently.

"What are you doing, calling your fucking girlfriend?" a voice called out.

Kellar noticed it came from a tall lanky individual. He sported a black eagle on the left side of his shaken head. A round of laughter greeted the comment and Kellar silently willed someone to answer the phone. In his office above the White Rooms, Magnus Vandersar sat silently and stared at the telephone as it rang. The pulsating tone hypnotized him, pushing his mind further away from reality.

"I'll get it," Boris said, entering the office with another glass of brandy for Andy Slater. He thrust the glass into Slater's eager hand before snatching the receiver.

"What?" he snapped impatiently, remembering why Mags rarely let him deal with customers. Fuck them, he mused. Right now he was the only secretary they or anyone was going to speak to.

"Boris, is that you?"

"No, its Clint fucking Eastwood. Who the fuck is this?"

"Boris, its Andy Kellar. I'm at the Railway Tavern and it's about to go tits up."

"Deal with it then," Boris replied impatiently.

"There's only me and Winston here, and we're up against a fucking gang of skinheads," Kellar pleaded.

"Skinheads?"

"Yeah, Nazi's by the looks." Boris could hear Andy becoming decidedly panicked. He knew why.

"Andy, has one of them got a swastika on the side of his head, real lanky cunt?"

"Yeah, that's right. Why?" Now Kellar panicked. He had heard the urgency in Boris' voice and knew that very little bothered him.

"Right, Andy, get the fuck out of there now."

"What?"

"What you've got there is Jake the biscuit, small time H dealer, and a right nasty cunt. And by the way, Andy, that lot hate blacks. Get out. I'll be there in ten minutes."

"Boris, what about…" Kellar stopped in mid-sentence. Boris had already hung up. A cold panic began clawing into his stomach. He looked at his watch. Ten minutes was a long time to be sinking in a world of shit. Besides he only had half an hour left on his shift. He shook his head in annoyance. This just about summed his luck up.

"What did they say?" Winston probed.

"It was Boris. He said we're fucked," Kellar replied, slipping the phone back into his pocket.

"Do what?" Winston had now taken his eyes off of the skinheads and was busy studying his partner.

"You heard me right, Win. That's Jake the biscuit over there, and his equally sick fuck mates."

"Oh shit!" Winston groaned. His whole body sank at the thought of being face to face with such a notoriously famous thug.

"Hang on, Andy, I thought he was inside?"

"Obviously he's not, Win, is he now?"

"What we gonna do then?" Winston asked, fighting to control his shaking legs.

"Well, Winston, I'm going to calmly walk to the door, then on the pretence of going to the toilet, I'm going to run like fuck. Now then, if you want to race me, you're more than fucking welcome."

"I can outrun you any day, you fat cunt."

"Let's go then," Kellar challenged.

"Fucking right," Winston agreed, already making tracks.

Boris took the brandy glass out of Slater's hand, before throwing it absently onto the floor.

"Stand up," he barked.

"What for?" Slater protested, but Boris already had him by the coat and was lifting him out of the comfort of the sofa.

"Stand up, you mug," he said again. Satisfied that Slater was suitably erect, Boris smacked him hard across the face with his open hand. Slater left his feet and tumbled backwards over the sofa before landing unceremoniously in a heap.

"What the fuck was that for?" he wailed. He looked up and saw Boris looming over him menacingly.

"Are you sober now?" he asked, punting Slater between the legs.

"Fuck!" Slater curled into a ball, his hands clamped over his swollen testicles.

"Are you sober?"

"Yeah, I'm sober," Slater pleaded, desperately trying to shield against another attack.

"Right then, get up you silly cunt. I need you to help me."

"What for?" Slater asked.

"We're going hunting. Ever been hunting, Andy?"

"What? You mean like shooting deer and stuff?"

"Yeah, something like that. Now get the fuck up. We've got to go." Boris gently prodded Slater again with his boot, watching with a sense of amusement as Slater recoiled into a ball.

"Get up, you muppet," he added, before walking over to Mags.

"Mags, can you hear me, buddy?" Boris saw with pity that Mags remained motionless, staring blankly at the telephone.

"I've got to go, boss. Andy Kellar and Winston have stepped into the shit. They need help."

"He's in shock," Slater said, climbing up from his foetal position. Boris gave him a baleful glare.

"I can see that, fuck nuts. What am I, fucking stupid?" Slater carried on rubbing his testicles, mindful that Boris was quite capable of much worse.

"Sorry, I just thought…"

"You shouldn't think too much, Slater. It gets you a big kick in the bollocks."

"Sorry, Boris."

"Get your motor by the front doors, Slater, I'll meet you there in a minute." He watched as Slater hurried down the stairs, grinning as he heard him stumble in the darkness and tumble.

"Mags, I'm off. Get yourself sorted, mate," Boris whispered into his ear. Gently he lifted the desert eagle from Mags' waistband, aware that Mags still sat hypnotised. He made his way to the door, pausing to look back at his great friend. Normally he found it very hard to feel pity for anyone, but then the stark thought hit him. How would he feel if somebody murdered his beloved Debbie? Closing the door as he left, Boris gripped the coldness of the desert eagle, knowing the answer to that little question lay in his hands right now.

Kellar never saw the punch coming. His front teeth sheered off at the jaw line and tumbled into the back of his throat. Blackness tried to engulf him as he stumbled wildly before collapsing in a tangled mess. The huge fat skinhead had been waiting at the door for them, just in case he and Winston had tried to leave. Desperately he fought to stay awake, but a huge fat leg swung into his view before connecting with his head. The shocking impact shattered his nose wildly, sending white lights shooting through his eyes. The last thing Andy Kellar saw before blackness mercifully took him was a huge fat fist bearing down towards his shattered face.

"Seth, enough."

"Let me take the cunt, Jake."

"Enough. We want them alive." Jake the biscuit stepped over the unconscious body of Andy Kellar, absently treading in blood as he did so. The near thirty stones of his henchman, Seth Arnold heaved as he gave the prostate body another kick for good measure.

"Listen, lads, leave him; he's had enough," Winston pleaded. Four skinheads held him roughly, and were now in the process of dragging him back into the bar.

"I don't believe anyone asked for your opinion, nigger," one of them said, punching Winston hard in the back of the head.

"What's this all about?" Winston pleaded.

"You'll find out, coon. Now shut up." Winston was thrown savagely onto the floor, smashing a bar stool as he fell.

"Ah, what have we here then?" Winston looked up and saw Jake the biscuit looming over him. His six feet seven frame cutting an imposing figure.

"What do you want?" Winston asked. A huge fat-gutted man came into the bar. Winston almost laughed at the near comical sight as the man's gut quivered as he walked.

"What I want is to give you and all your mates a fucking message," Jake the biscuit said, kneeling down beside Winston. He picked up a piece of splintered bar stool, admiring the jagged weapon.

"I hear that your guvnors are out of business," he said tossing the splintered wood from hand to hand.

"So, the way I see it, you and your mates are unemployed. Now, that puts me in a position where I can do whatever the fuck I please."

"What are you getting at?" Winston asked, nervously watching as Jake tossed it to and fro.

"What I'm getting at, you fucking black cunt, is that from now on this pub is mine. My boys are running it now, understand?"

"Whatever you say, mate."

"Don't call me your fucking mate. I don't have fucking niggers as my mates, you disgusting black bastard."

"Okay, easy. I don't want no trouble, alright?" Winston tried to push himself hard against the bar, desperate to put as much distance between himself and the decidedly evil nutter now kneeling over him. Jake laughed wildly, his lips exposing rows of yellowed rotting teeth. Winston could smell his breath and nearly brought up his last meal.

"You hear that, Seth? He reckons he don't want any trouble. What a nice man. What shall we do with him?"

"I reckon we should cut his black balls off, Jake," Seth heaved as a heavy chuckle escaped. Winston watched with a mixture of disgust and comic amusement as his massive belly jiggled under his white shirt.

"Cut his balls off? I don't know,, Seth. I mean he is a nice man after all."

"Please lads, don't hurt me." Winston looked pleadingly at both men.

"Oh dear, don't hurt him, Jake," Seth chuckled.

"Fuck the black bastard," Jake cackled, before plunging the jagged splinter into Winston's right eye. A jet of clear liquid squirted out, splashing his hand. Jake twisted the wood, feeling the soft flesh squelching. Winston let out a loud frozen scream, but the throng of skinheads only began to laugh wildly. Jake pulled the splinter out of the shattered eye, watching like a fascinated child as the crumpled organ came out with the jagged wood.

"Fuck, Seth, look at that," he beamed, holding the stick up for inspection.

"Whoa!" Seth exclaimed, laughing wildly.

"A one-eyed nigger!" he added, his gut jiggling. As Winston screamed a long guttural howl, Jake passed the shattered eye around for inspection while the skinheaded throng applauded.

Slater looked nervously at the gun Boris now toyed with in his hands. A series of conflicts began battle in his mind. After all, here he was a serving policeman riding along just as casually as could be, while his passenger fiddled with a huge gun, an illegal gun at that.

"I ought to arrest you right now," he said.

"You could try, but then I don't think you will," Boris replied, never taking his eyes from the weapon. Carefully he checked each moving part. Slater juggled his vision between driving and watching his passenger, noting that Boris possessed a deft working knowledge of the firearm.

"Listen, Boris, where are we going exactly?"

"Railway Tavern. You know it?"

"Yeah, I know it. I used to drink in there when I was younger."

"Good, then step on the fucking pedal."

"Just promise me you're not going to use that bloody gun," Slater said nervously.

Boris threw him a black look, his eyes creased under his heavy brow.

"Yeah, I promise," he said, before returning his attention to the weapon.

"It's just that, well, I'm a copper and it won't look too good if you start waving that fucking thing about will it?"

"Don't worry, Slater, I promised you, didn't I?" An uncomfortable silence followed as they sped through the quiet streets, now almost devoid of any real traffic. Slater saw groups of people hurrying home, wrapped against the coldness of the night.

"What do you know about Jake the biscuit?" Boris asked, breaking the silence. Slater glanced at him, surprise written all over his face.

"Fuck me, there's a name from the past."

"So?" Boris said impatiently.

"What do you want to know?"

"Look, do you know the fucking prick or not?" The agitation in his voice growing as Boris spoke. Slater laughed before speaking.

"Jake the biscuit, aka Jake Robinson. Heroin dealer, nasty cunt, and self-proclaimed leader of the black eagles." Slater reeled the list off with sublime ease, leaving Boris in no doubt that Slater knew the man very well.

"Black eagles?" he asked quizzically.

"Yeah, the black eagles. During the eighties these fucking idiots were quite a force; a Nazi outfit who ran all the city drug trade. They ran the lot: drugs, protection, extortion – need I go on?"

"And?" Boris barked. Slater jumped at the order, mindful that Boris was still holding a gun, loaded at that.

"One of my first collars. Nicked him for supplying. Eighty-nine I think it was. Anyway, he got four years. That wasn't his speciality though, oh no. Jake liked selling drugs, taking them too, but what he really liked to do was hurt anyone who wasn't white. He really believes in all that white supremist shit, and he had quite a following too."

"And?" Boris snapped again.

"Fucking hell, Boris, it's been a while. Anyway he's still in prison. What's the problem?"

"The problem, Slater, is that Jake the Nazi is right now stood in the Railway Tavern with his storm troopers."

"What?" Slater said, almost losing control of the steering wheel.

"You heard me right."

"But he cut up an Asian girl. I mean he got ten years for it," Slater pleaded, feeling very disturbed at what Boris had just said.

"Yeah well he's probably been a well-behaved Nazi, because he's waiting for us right now."

"But…" Slater stopped his words at the thought. Waiting for us. "I can't do this Boris, no way."

"You don't have to. I'll sort it," Boris reassured, but Slater couldn't shake the feeling of fear that now gripped his insides like a vice.

"Let's call for back up, get some more police down here," Slater whined.

"Shut up, Slater. Just drive for fuck's sake."

"But, let's be reasonable about this, Boris."

"This is just a hunch, Slater, but bravery isn't a requirement of joining the old bill is it?" Boris looked at Slater, his dark eyes boring into his head, daring, challenging for an answer. Slater fixed his attention on the road ahead, his face burning brightly with a mixture of shame and embarrassment. He so wanted to shut Boris up, but knew he didn't have the courage or the honesty to form a truthful reply. They drove on in silence, speeding through the cold night towards a destiny Slater dared not dwell on. As they turned into Trumpington Road, the brightly lit sign of the Railway Tavern stood out like a neon torch in amongst rows of darkened shop fronts. Boris unclipped his seatbelt, already reaching for the door handle long before Slater slowed the car.

"Right, wait here, Slater. If you fucking drive off, I'll hunt you down and fucking murder you, do you understand?"

"I'll be here. Remember your promise," Slater replied hopefully. Boris jumped out, slamming the Mondeo's passenger door hard. Slater watched him casually disappear through the front door of the Railway Tavern. He looked no different to Mr Average popping in for a late drink after a hard day's work. Somehow Slater knew that very shortly, Jake the biscuit was about to have a bad night.

Laughter echoed around the room, loud howls merging with high-pitched cackles.

"What's up, black boy, you got a sore eye?" Seth bellowed, his huge gut wobbling madly as he heaved under the laughter. Winston moaned softly, consciousness coming back to him.

"He's coming round, Jake. What shall we do with him?" Seth asked.

"Put him back to sleep, Seth," Jake said coldly reaching into his jacket pocket. He produced a gleaming silver switchblade, and handed it to Seth.

"Put him out of his misery," he added. Seth dropped heavily to his knees, his mountainous bulk quivering endlessly as the shock rippled through rivers of fat. His huge bloated hand grabbed Winston's hair, roughly lifting his head off the floor. Seth admired the lethal double-edged blade, finding a soothing beauty in its destructive power.

"Night then, nigger," he said, before plunging the five-inch blade into the side of Winston's neck. With one powerful cut the blade opened his throat, almost severing his head. Seth recoiled as a gush of hot blood spurted across his fat hands, watching with fascination as the life ebbed from his victim.

"You fucking see that, Jake?" he yelled excitedly. Annoyed that no one else had acknowledged his delight, Seth turned to his friends. What the hell was up with them?

"What's up with you…" Fear gripped his bowels like an icy tentacle. Only inches away from his fat jowls, the barrel of a gun held him in a hypnotic trance. Jake and the rest of the gang now stood against the bar, fear frozen across their faces.

"Goodnight, burger boy." Boris squeezed the trigger, and felt the power of the desert eagle as it recoiled in his hand. The round struck Seth in the left temple, disintegrating his brain cavity in a microsecond. Blood mixed with the solids of Seth's brain plastered the mirrored wall behind the bar, coating the optics with fragmented skull and tissue. Boris stepped back as the huge body teetered and fell heavily. Disgust hit his stomach as he watched the rolls of fat rippling as the body landed.

"What a fat fuck," he murmured before turning his attention to the other skinheads now cowering at the bar.

"Jake, long time no see," he said.

"Boris, look mate, I didn't know you looked after this place, honest."

"Yes you did, Jake. But never mind, that's not important now. What is important though, is the fact that you've just killed one of my best men. Now that's a fucking liberty." Boris levelled the weapon at Jake's chest, before squeezing off another round. The back of Jake's white shirt exploded as his left lung disintegrated through an exit hole eight inches across. The impact threw his willowy body hard into the worn wooden bar top, severing his spine at waist height. Boris looked on with great pleasure as Jake fell, almost in slow motion before landing awkwardly like a rag doll. Only the fresh bitter smell of spent gunpowder filled the air,. Silence now cloaked the bar like a heavy veil.

"Right then, which one of you fucking degenerates is next in charge?" Boris asked calmly. Trembling under shaking legs, the squat muscular skinhead who only moments earlier had been so vocal, raised his right hand.

"And you are?" Boris asked, eyeing the shaken figure with contempt.

"Carl, my name's Carl Housden," he spluttered. Boris tilted his head as if measuring his quarry.

"Bye then, Carl." Boris squeezed the trigger once more, visibly jolting as the weapon discharged its deadly cargo. Carl Housden spun backwards wildly as his head shattered. His fellow skinheads, as if one being, ducked as a fine spray of sickly matter splashed across them.

"Okay then, so who's next in charge?" Boris asked, grinning broadly. Nobody raised a hand. Instead the cowering skinheads remained where they were, huddled together with terror.

"Now then, you fucking dickheads are out of business. If I see any one of you dildos again, I'll fucking kill each and every one of you. Now get the fuck out of here." Boris barked his order, and he saw them visibly shake at his tone. The five skinheads began rushing for the doors, stumbling over each other as they fought for the sanctuary of the night. A tall gangly individual fell as he caught the leg of a heavier skinhead, landing unceremoniously in the doorway. Boris wandered over, annoyed at the lack of speed the man had shown in vacating the premises.

"Hey, baldy," he said, bending down to make sure he had the full attention of his stricken foe. "So you're a Nazi then?" he asked curiously. The gangly skinhead stopped rubbing his twisted ankle, now frozen with fear.

"Yeah, I'm a Nazi, so what?" he asked, defiantly.

"No reason. I'm just curious. Does that ankle hurt?"

"A bit."

"Oh dear," Boris said, pushing the barrel of the desert eagle into the swollen ankle. He grinned warmly as he pulled the trigger, and cackled happily as the gangly skinhead's foot blew away from his leg. Boris was already heading out of the Railway Tavern as the gangly skinhead stared in disbelief as a fountain of dark blood shot from his shattered limb.

Slater jumped in his seat, visibly shaken at the crashing sound coming from within the Railway Tavern.

"Fuck!" he shouted, knowing he had just heard gunfire. "Stupid lying cunt!" When the second bang rang out, Slater instinctively began to start the Mondeo. He paused with the key in his hand, very mindful that to leave Boris now might mean his own death. Seconds later he heard another shot ring out, and he had to physically fight the urge to start the engine and speed off into the night. The sight of four very terrified skinheads barging through the Railway Tavern's doors broke the urge.

"What the fuck?" he whispered to himself. Another blast rocked the night, and seconds later Boris, cool as the night air strolled out towards the waiting Mondeo.

"What the fuck have you done?" Slater shouted as Boris climbed into the car.

"Drive," he snapped, ignoring Slater's question.

"What have you done?"

"I told you to drive." Boris threw him a steely glare, and Slater grudgingly kicked the Mondeo into life. They had travelled only fifty metres before Slater summoned the courage to challenge Boris again.

"What went on in there?"

"Stop fucking whining, Slater. I had to sort a problem out."

"You used that gun, you promised you wouldn't," Slater snapped angrily. Boris ignored him, electing to peer out of his side window.

"You promised me, Boris."

"I lied."

"Well thanks, mate, you've just implicated me in what you've just done. Thanks a fucking lot, you cunt." Slater felt the rage boiling over within himself, as he pulled the Mondeo over into the kerb, finally stopping outside a bus shelter.

"I ought to fucking arrest you now!" he shouted.

"Fuck off, Slater, you're starting to fucking annoy me."

"Annoy you? Well I'm fucking sorry, pal," Slater quipped sarcastically. Boris spun in his seat, whipping a heavy left cross into Slater's face. The blow drove his head back into the door, cracking the driver's side window. Instinct took Slater by the scruff of the neck. Never a violent man even he was surprised beyond belief as his reflexes drove his right arm forward, catching Boris square in the face. As the massive rush of adrenaline left him, Slater knew he was in big trouble. Boris gently wiped a trickle of blood from his nose, holding his hand up to inspect the blood. Casually he raised the desert eagle, levelling the weapon only inches from Slater's chest. Fear never gripped him, only a heavy sadness that he would never see his wife again. Slater chided himself for not getting out of the job when he first started losing faith in what he was doing. Even under the present circumstances, he tried to remember exactly when that had started to happen.

"Holy fucking dogshit!" Boris shouted. Slater's spell broke. Instinctively he flinched expecting to feel indescribable pain. Boris pointed at a car heading at speed along the now deserted road.

"That's Callard. Drive, Slater, get going," he demanded.

Slater followed the cars tail lights as they disappeared over the brow of a bridge.

"Go, Slater, get going. Wake up, you muppet!" Boris screamed. Frenziedly Slater pulled the Mondeo out from the kerb, wheel spinning the car on the near freezing road surface.

"I don't fucking believe it," Boris said, shaking his head. Slater floored the accelerator, quickly gaining speed. He shot Boris a sly glance, careful not to distract him from his new source of interest.

"Listen, I'm sorry about that back there," he said meekly.

"Forget it. It was a good punch; you ought to be proud," Boris replied, smiling. Slater saw his humour, and breathed a quiet sigh of relief.

"Would you really have shot me back there?" he asked, jokingly. Boris kept his vigil, straining his eyes to make out the tail lights far up ahead.

"Of course," he replied. Slater felt a chill run down his spine, and silently thanked Ray Callard for his perfect timing.

Mark eased the last mouthful of burger down his throat, barely tasting a thing as he devoured it greedily. Satisfied, he let out a long deep fart, lifting his buttocks and wincing to dramatise the effect.

"Okay, Brown, you're through," he said laughing wildly. Darryl grinned, a little ashamed that he shared Mark's juvenile humour. He watched in fascination, and honest admiration as Mark unwrapped another quarter pounder.

"Fucking hell, Mark, that's the fifth one you've had in the last ten minutes. That's one every two fucking minutes. How do you manage to eat that much?"

"Easy, practise makes perfect." Another loud fart coincided with hefty bites of greedy burger. Darryl shook his head in disgust, then opened his driver's side window, hopeful to escape the dismal smell seeping from his passenger's backside.

"You're a dirty fucking bastard, Mark, do you know that?" he said, welcoming the rush of cold air.

"Yep."

"Stop farting will you, for Christ's sake," Darryl complained.

"Can't help it." Mark finished the burger, before rubbing his swollen stomach with pride.

"Right, can we be off now then. I mean unless you want to nip back in there and buy another whole cow?" Darryl nodded at the brightly lit Burger King they now sat parked in front of.

"Nah, I'm full for now," Mark told him, letting out a long rancid smelling fart. Darryl eased his Calibra out into the quiet night, welcoming the sudden blast of freezing air that cleared the noxious foul smell from the cars interior.

"Where to now?" Mark asked, wiping his greasy hands on his black trousers.

"Back to base I suppose. I don't reckon we'll find Callard tonight."

"No, I don't either. Fuck it then. Back to base. See how Mags is holding up." Mark knew it would be a while before Mags bounced back from this little setback. It was bad enough losing Pat and the Scotsman, but everyone knew how he felt about Penny. Both Mark and Darryl knew very well that Ray Callard's time on this earth was at best, limited. His death when it came, as it surely would, was going to be painful and drawn out. The idea quite appealed to him. He hated Callard, always had. Mags wouldn't tolerate a bad word about him, but Mark knew he was a bag of shit. The two of them had been riding around vainly looking for Callard's flash Jaguar. They would have killed him on the spot if they had found him. But they had been unlucky. Two fruitless hours had produced nothing. Mark wasn't too bothered. They could afford to be patient after all. If Ray Callard was still alive one week from now, Mark would be very impressed.

"I knew he was a cunt," he said absently.

"Who?" Darryl asked, looking puzzled.

"Callard."

"Definitely. I hate the fucker, always have," Darryl agreed.

"I hope I get the chance to do him."

"Why?" Darryl asked, amused.

"Cos he always took the fucking piss out of me."

"Everyone takes the piss out of you."

"Fuck off," Mark snapped.

"I know what you mean, Mark, don't worry. Look, if we get him first, you can have him."

"Cheers. I fucking hate the prick," Mark said, before expelling another burst of foul air.

He had fought too many battles, been in so many wars that he couldn't even begin to remember what most of them were even over. Magnus Vandersar had always been victorious. Not in his life had he taken a backward step. Now the possibility of defeat loomed over him like a dark foreboding cloud, a black cancer that ate into his mind like a ferocious predatory beast. He had no answer to the pain; he couldn't fight it, couldn't kill it. It was a true warrior, a formidable opponent that knew no pain, that couldn't be beaten. Mags leant back in his chair, aware now for the first time that he was alone. He looked slowly around his office. Where had they all gone? He hadn't noticed them leave, and he wasn't bothered by the solitude either. Penny entered his thoughts again, a white light shining through the turmoil of blackness. What if?

"Fuck!" he screamed, slamming his fists into the office desk. The force reverberated along the wooden surface, shaking the telephone, until it teetered precariously on the edge, ready to crash heavily to the floor. Through gritted teeth, he called her name. Why had he let Ray marry her? Why had he been such an arsehole, so afraid of commitment? He had known many women, too many over the years. But Penny, she had been different, and how he had loved her. The thought stirred raw emotion in his heart. The tears began again, falling heavily down his sad face before pooling on the desktop. Mags exploded from his chair, hurling the desk over angrily. The telephone flew through the air like a missile before smashing against the door.

"Motherfucker!" he bellowed, picking his chair up and throwing it against the wall. He stood, heaving under the weight of anger and hatred. He turned and tore the blinds away from the window with one savage swipe. Eyes forged in hell burned out into the dark winter's night. He scanned the city, as far as he could see. Out there somewhere, Ray Callard preyed under the cover of darkness. Mags could sense him, he could taste him with every breath he took. He had taken the thing he lived for, and now he had to pay.

"My name is vengeance. I have many faces, I take many forms, I move in many ways. I will find you Ray, somewhere, somehow. When I kill you, as I surely will, I'm taking your soul with me straight through the gates of hell."

His eyes glowed with pure fire as he spoke, the eyes of a rogue wolf, delivered by Satan to put hell on earth. Mags knew he couldn't win this war. The loss of his men and then Penny had made a victory meaningless. But he could at least even the score, and Ray Callard would soon find out that the wolf from hell could deliver vengeance better than anyone else. He was the master.

"Only one life left to take, and the score is even," he whispered, scanning the darkness with those fired eyes.

The rear of the White Rooms lay in total blackness, surrounded by taller buildings, not even the stray light cast from street lamps penetrated. The sleek Jaguar cruised into the small parking area, its light switched off. Ray peered through the gloom, unable to see anything other than shadows and darkened walls. Perfect cover he deduced. Switching the engine off, he quickly made his way to the Jaguar's boot. He fumbled with the catch, finally releasing it after several attempts. Fishing around inside, he caught hold of the Kalashnikov, before taking it out and quickly closing the boot.

"The place to catch a wolf, is asleep in its lair," he said quietly, scanning through the gloom for the rear doors. He spotted them through the darkness, two blue wooden fire doors, with 'Keep Clear' painted on them in large white letters. Slowly and quietly he made his way across the car park, the Kalashnikov held ready in his hands. He felt up and down the doors, searching for a handle or a lock. Unable to find any, he stepped back and levelled the rifle at waist height. He would shoot the internal locking system away. His finger squeezed gently on the trigger, but suddenly a battle of bright light began to illuminate the darkness. Turning suddenly, he saw the headlights as they began to enter the parking area.

"Shit," Ray muttered angrily, before scrambling for cover behind the refuge of a huge industrial bottle bin. He made it just as the car park became fully illuminated. Ray peered out from his hiding place, and saw the familiar green Calibra of Darryl Hanlon. He cursed the inconvenience, but decided a moment later that perhaps this might be a dual opportunity.

"Two birds with one stone," he whispered. Through the gloom he made out a passenger inside the Calibra. It was Mark, the butt of much of Ray's humour.

"Three birds then," he added, the darkness concealing his delight. Behind the cover of the bottle bank, Ray Callard hid under the gloom, an automatic weapon held in his hands, and the early stirring of an erection beginning to raise itself in anticipation of the kill.

"You're a dirty fat cunt," Darryl said, gagging.

"I can't help it," Mark moaned, also disgusted by the foul smell his bowels kept emitting.

"You can, that's just it. Stop fucking eating so much junk, you greedy great cunt."

"I don't eat a lot, not really."

"What! How the fuck can you say that without laughing?"

"Well I don't."

"Fuck me, Mark, you've eaten more tonight than I'll eat in a week."

"I was hungry."

"Hungry? Fucking hell, you could feed a family of five on what you've just eaten."

"I was starving."

"No you weren't. You're just a greedy fucking bastard farting machine."

"Everyone farts," Mark protested.

"Not every ten seconds, Mark. You're an animal," Darryl said, wincing as a ripping sound escaped from between Mark's legs.

"Oh my God! You are a fifthly fucking degenerate.

"Sorry."

"Don't say sorry, you dirty fucker. Just stop your arse from spewing out that foul fucking smell."

"Sorry," Mark repeated, looking sheepish. Darryl threw him a withered look, almost colliding with the high wall that bordered the rear car park of the White Rooms.

"Shit, that's Ray's motor," Mark shouted, as the Calibra swung into a parking bay.

"Fucking hell, so it is," Darryl acknowledged, feeling the hair raise on the back of his neck. For a moment the two men sat in stunned silence, unable to decide their next move. Suddenly Darryl saw a movement out of the corner of his eye, a dark blur moving rapidly from behind the bottle bank. By the time his brain engaged to danger mode, Ray Callard had closed the distance between them.

"Get down!" he shouted, grabbing Mark by the arm and pulling him forward. The burst of gunfire echoed loudly in the confines of the car park. A rain of glass fell onto Darryl, showering him with tiny icicles of razor sharp fragments. Frantically he scrambled to start the Calibra, fumbling madly with the key.

"Go Darryl, fucking drive!" Mark began screaming. The Calibra's engine roared into life. Instantly Darryl slammed it into reverse, crunching the gearbox noisily. Darryl expertly swung the car backwards in a sweeping arc, instantly finding first gear before the car had even stopped its backward descent. He began to breath a sigh of relief as they screamed out of the darkened car park. Just as the car began its turn into the main road, another burst of gunfire shattered the rear window, showering glass everywhere.

"Hold on," Darryl said, accelerating heavily. The car's back wheel slid across the freezing road. Darryl had to fight hard with the steering wheel to avoid losing control. He dared to glance into his rear view mirror, praying a gunman wasn't lining them up for another shot. His nerves relaxed slightly when he saw nothing behind but empty road.

"We're clear," he said, but kept the car's speed at a constant seventy as a precaution.

"Callard, the cunt was waiting for us. Had to have been him, the little rat fuck bastard." Darryl glanced over at Mark, half expecting him to be wiping away a flood of tears. Mark sat motionless, his huge hands clutched tightly to his chest. A dark shiny liquid seeped through his clasped hands. A look of shock settled across his face like a sombre mask.

"Shit," Darryl muttered, slowing the Calibra, and bringing it to a halt in the middle of the road.

"I'm hit, Darryl. I'm fucking shot, mate."

"Don't worry, hang on," Darryl said, barely concealing his own panic. "Let me see. Move your hands," he shouted leaning over to inspect the wound. Grudgingly Mark slowly withdrew his hands, and instantly blood began to flow freely. Even in the darkened car, Darryl could clearly see the glistening white of shattered ribs poking viciously through Mark's skin.

"Oh fuck, put your hands back," he said, slamming first gear into place.

"Is it bad?" Mark asked weakly.

"I wouldn't want it."

"Oh fuck, I'm gonna die."

"No you're not, Mark. Don't worry I'll have you at the hospital in five minutes."

"Have I got five minutes?" Mark asked grimly. Darryl declined to answer. Instead he floored the Calibra, wheel spinning madly as the car fought for traction on the slippery road surface.

Mags jumped visibly at the sound. Gunfire, and close. He ran to his office door. Carefully opening it, he peered down the stairs and into the White Rooms' foyer. Nothing stirred but shadows and cold silence. Suddenly another burst. Mags dropped instinctively to a crouch, expecting to see an armed figure burst from the shadows at any moment. His brain switched to alert mode; instantly his senses heightened. Never moving a muscle, Mags sat silently watching the darkness.

After a minute or more had passed, he was satisfied that no one had penetrated the White Rooms, and began to make his way stealthily down the dark stairs to the foyer. Like a shadow he moved quickly and unseen across the black empty foyer. He checked the main front doors, found they were secure and began carefully exploring the rest of the building. He entered the main bar lounge, now strangely silent. Across the dance floor he could see the imposing outline of the car park exit doors, and quietly he made his was towards them. He stopped ten feet away, alert and straining as he thought he heard muffled footsteps. Automatically he reached into the rear of his waistband, seeking the familiar comfort of the desert eagle. Panic began to sweep through him as his hand found only his untucked shirt.

"Fuck!" he whispered angrily. Then the darkness disappeared as a burst of white light flooded his vision. The wooden fire doors exploded and splintered as the Kalashnikov cut through the flimsy doors with contemptuous ease. Mags dived to the floor, landing heavily as lethal wooden splinters showered all around him. When the firing had stopped, he gently lifted his head, straining his eyes through the darkness to see. A figure emerged through the shattered doorway, stepping over the remains of the safety rails that had locked the doors. Mags could see the figure holding something in his hands, long, sleek and lethal. He had no doubts as to what it could be. The figure walked along the nearest wall, and began running his hand along the surface, almost as if looking for a light switch Mags thought. In an instant the world illuminated, bathed in brightness as the overhead lights came to life. A sickening thought ran over Mags' mind. Whoever the figure was, knew exactly where the light switches were, which meant they knew the layout of the building. As his eyes adjusted to the brightness, Mags squinted from his position spread eagled across the dance floor.

When he saw Ray Callard approaching with a Kalashnikov held in his hands, fear should have gripped him in its icy vice. Instead Magnus Vandersar scrambled madly to his feet, fuelled by anger, feeding off hate.

"Well, what a result this is. Mags my old mate, how the devil are you?" Ray cackled.

"You fucking Judas. I'm going to kill you, Ray, slowly," Mags ranted.

"No I don't think you are, Mags. In fact it's me who's going to kill you."

"Really, Ray? I thought you could only handle women. Why don't you fucking put the gun down and fight me?"

"That's not nice, Mags, is it now?" Ray said, raising the Kalashnikov. He squeezed the trigger, letting of a single round. The bullet hit Mags in the left shoulder, shattering his collarbone and spraying blood across the dance floor behind him. The impact lifted Mags visibly two feet off the ground, dumping him like a rag doll in a broken heap. He winced as the pain ran through the wound like a mad demon.

"So, Mags, how's it been?" Ray asked, laughing as he walked over carrying a wooden chair.

"Suck my cock, Judas," Mags snapped through gritted teeth.

"Like my wife did you mean?" Ray quipped, taking a seat ten feet away.

"Now then Magnus, there are a few things I want you to hear before I let you die."

"Save it," Mags told him.

"No, God forbid Magnus, I think you should hear what I have to say."

"Fucking kill me you cunt, then fuck off."

"Oh, I intend to, Mags, don't worry about that. She died in pain, real pain did you know that Mags? The slut deserved it, and to tell you the truth I enjoyed wasting the whore."

"Fuck you!" Mags desperately tried to get to his feet, but Ray already had the Kalashnikov ready. A single round entered Mags' midsection, cutting through his abdominal wall, before slicing through his colon. Mags tumbled back wildly, clutching desperately at the horrific wound. He looked on helplessly as blood poured through his fingers, pooling into a vast puddle beside him.

"As I was saying before you interrupted me, Mags, she died like a two-bit whore. Then I wanked over her. How does that sound, Mags?"

"I'll see you in hell," Mags managed through the pain.

"And you will, Magnus, no doubt. By the way, I expect you'll be seeing your old mates there too; Pat and what's his name, the Scotsman? Mind you, I think I've just got the fat boy too. Fucking hell, Mags, you won't be lonely down there." Ray let out a long bellowing laugh, his lips curling back to expose yellowing teeth. Lying helplessly on the floor, Mags began to fight to stay conscious. His vision had already started to darken as the lifeblood spilled out of him. In his weakened state, Mags thought Ray looked strikingly similar to the Ray thing in his dream. Even now he wondered if indeed it had been a dream at all?

"Why?" he croaked weakly.

"Why, Mags? You stupid shit, it's about fucking money. I nearly had it all, but you fucked it up for me."

"Money, you did all this for money?"

"Yes, Mags, me and Kansky would have cleaned up. That's why Sergatov had to go. All we needed was you fucking idiots dead and we would have been rich beyond belief."

"I thought we were friends, Ray." Mags fought to get the words out.

"Was my friendship worth a few hundred quid a month? You either thought nothing of me Mags, or you were simply taking the piss."

"No, I..." Mags' voice broke as he fought to speak. Only a hoarse dryness escaped as he started to lose consciousness. Ray got up from his chair, and walked over to Mags. He slapped him hard across the face, leaving a huge red welt on his deathly pale skin.

"Don't die on me, Mags, we've still got plenty more to talk about yet."

"Hold on, old buddy, nearly there."

"I'm dying, hurry up, Darryl, please." Mark's breathing now came in shorter, desperate motions. Darryl kept an eye on the road, and another on the amount of blood now climbing through his passenger's fingers. Hammering the Calibra, Darryl drove like a lunatic through the city, reaching up to over a hundred miles an hour on the deserted roads. They reached Hills Road, and Darryl saw the signposts already for Addenbrookes hospital.

"Not far now, mate, hang on." He pushed the car hard, hitting Hills Road at one hundred and ten miles per hour. Every few seconds he glanced at Mark, and knew that if he didn't get there soon, he would be delivering a corpse. Giving his full attention back to the road, he had to brake sharply for a roundabout. The wheels locked and skidded as the car dropped speed too quickly. To his horror, Darryl saw a man crossing just before the roundabout.

"Oh shit!" he screamed, unable to slow the car any quicker. He just had time to see the man's panic, saw him try and leap to the safety of the kerb. The thump was sickening. Darryl instinctively leant back hard in his seat as the body of a man crashed over the Calibra's bonnet before hitting the windscreen. The glass shattered into a billion starred fragments, showering them with razor sharp splinters.

"Bollocks," he said, quickly jumping out to see if the man was badly hurt. Lying awkwardly across the bonnet, the broken remains didn't stir. Darryl reached for the man's arm, desperately searching for a pulse. He looked at the shattered head, now unrecognisable as that of a person, and didn't expect to find one. He let the arm fall limply, and the darkly inked tattoo of a swastika caught his eye. Darryl rolled the body over, and saw a black eagles crest emblazoned across the other arm. Neatly inked on the man's broken neck, the familiar emblem of the Nazi SS glared back at him.

"I fucking know you," Darryl said to himself.

"Darryl, I'm in shit here," Mark groaned through the shattered windscreen.

"Fuck it, I know you. Jake the biscuit's crew." Darryl seemed happy that he'd made the connection, and rolled the broken corpse off of his bonnet. The body landed with a sickening thud, headfirst onto the hard road. Darryl ran back to the driver's side, jumped in and threw the Calibra back into gear. A second later they were on their way to hospital again.

"Well there's a thing, Mark, you'll never guess who that was? It was one of Jake the biscuits weirdos. It's a fucking small world."

As the Mondeo cruised quietly down Mill Road, Andy Slater cursed himself for losing Ray Callard.

"Where the fuck did he go?" he asked, perplexed.

"You're a fucking useless cunt, Slater, you know that?" Boris snapped angrily.

"What the fuck could I do?"

"Well if you didn't drive like an elderly woman we could have caught him."

"Fucking hell, Boris, he's driving a turbo charged Jaguar, I'm driving a Ford fucking Mondeo."

"So fucking what. You let him get away you dizzy fucker."

"You want to drive?" Slater jumped on the brake pedal, sending Boris, who wasn't wearing a seat belt, flying hard into the dashboard.

"You think you can do better? You know, you really are a miserable bastard."

"I can run faster than you can drive, Slater."

"Really, well then why don't you get out and run?"

"I tell you what, the only person who's going to be getting out is you, when I knock you out."

"That's your answer to everything isn't it, violence?" Slater sat shaking his head in disgust.

"As it happens, yes. Now fucking drive, you worthless cunt."

"Where?"

"Back to base. I want to check on Mags."

"Right, but stop fucking moaning." Slater pulled off, still muttering under his breath. Boris eyed him casually, and found that despite the fact that Andy Slater was a copper, and a whining copper at that, he actually quite liked him. He had balls, Boris acknowledged that much, and respected it. He rubbed his nose, still sore from where Slater had punched him earlier. It had been a good shot, Boris admitted, and he hadn't expected it either. He nodded his head. Indeed Andy Slater had some balls, especially for a copper.

Ray Callard slapped Mags across the face again, hard enough to leave a thick red handprint.

"Wakey wakey, Magnus," he said laughing like a child. Mags could no longer speak. The life was ebbing from him like a raging river.

"The whore squealed like a cunt as I killed her, Mags. You should have been there. It was something special." Ray bared his teeth as another cruel smile broke his features.

"Oh God, Mags, if only you'd asked, I'd have given her to you. I never wanted the useless cunt anyway.

"Fuck, fu..." Mags desperately tried to speak, but he no longer had the strength.

"The kid, Mags, little cunt. He's yours you know. The bastard is yours. I should have killed that little fucker too."

Ray punted Mags hard in the ribs with his foot. He stood back and watched with pleasure as more blood pumped from the abdominal wound. He knelt down, ignoring the blood that soaked into his trousers.

"Look at me, Mags, look into my fucking eyes." Mags weakly tilted his head until he fixed his stare on Ray Callard. Bright red eyes burnt evil behind them. Mags knew the Ray thing had been no dream. It was here now, gloating as he died.

"The little cunt bastard is yours, Mags. Too bad you'll never get to see him again. Tomorrow I'll find the little fuck and gut him slowly, like a fish. He'll scream like his whore of a cunt mother." Ray bared his yellowed teeth as he spat the words out. Mags couldn't understand it. He'd killed the Ray thing, but here it was, taunting him.

"Look at me, Mags, don't die yet, you cunt." Ray slapped him again, but now Mags barely acknowledged the blow. His glazed eyes continued to stare out blankly.

"Don't die yet, I want you to suffer. Stay with me, Mags. Come on, old mate, suffer for me, another five minutes at least." Mags' body stiffened as Ray pushed the barrel of the Kalashnikov into the gaping wound. Blood squelched out as the hard metal entered the torn flesh. Mags grasped the weapon with the little strength he still possessed. Ray pushed harder, and the pain crashed through Mags like a wave, flooding his senses with indescribable pain. Now he began to wish for death, the merciful release it would bring. Instead the pain ran through him like a demon on a path of hell-bent destruction. With burning red eyes the Ray thing continued to cackle as the pain ate him away towards a slow lingering death.

Chapter Ten

He looked up and saw the sword fall. Instinctively he rolled over, hearing the thud as the vicious blade bit hard into the earth. Mags jumped to his feet, and with one deadly swing cut the cloaked figure in half. Blue streaming entrails snaked out of the severed body, hissing and bubbling as they burnt greedily into the ground. All around he saw the battle raging, amour-clad men cutting through evil eyed cloaked figures. Across the field he saw a heavily armoured soldier cutting through bodies, limbs severing and spilling evil luminous blood. Deep amongst the mass of fighting, he saw the wolf's head, fluttering in the cold wind, held aloft proudly and defiantly above the battle.

Mags swivelled the sword in his hands, readied it for the kill and ran into the battle. Now the cloaked warriors had begun to retreat, evil curved blades discarded on the battlefield as they ran. Mags delivered the sword at a fleeing figure, taking its head off with one powerful sweep. In horror, Mags watched as the headless figure ran on, oblivious. Another armoured soldier ran his sword through the headless body, this time ending the macabre flight. The soldier, a young man of no more than twenty, pulled his sword from the still twitching figure, raised it proudly and let out a victory roar.

"It's over, sir, we're winning!" he shouted defiantly. Mags looked around. The bodies of the dead littered the fields for as far as the eye could see. The cloaked army had now made a disorganised retreat up a slight rise, a small hill flanking the battlefield. Everywhere he looked Mags could see his army, swords held aloft in the spoil of victory. Two soldiers had hoisted the wolf's head banner aloft, and now waved it wildly.

Suddenly the cheers of the victorious army began to fall silent. Mags saw swords fall, their defiant gestures now silenced. The retreating cloaked army, had now stopped. Mags saw thousands of them. Each figure now seemed frozen in time, silently rooted in the ground like statues. Above them on the peak of the hill, Mags could see the proud outline of a huge dark wolf. Even from such a distance he could see the majestic shape of the mighty beast, its huge jaws hanging open in a sickening half smile, its bright red eyes surveying the scene of carnage. Quietly, appearing from the gloom five more wolves appeared out of the misty air and took up position next to the black wolf. Now Mags watched in amazement as one by one, armoured soldiers began to sink to their knees. The heavy sound of creaking armour became almost deafening as thousands upon thousands of men knelt before the majestic gathering. He followed suit, glad to be relieved of the weight of his heavy armour. Up above on the hill, the huge black wolf threw its head back and let out a long piercing howl. It started as a bellowing call, but grew and grew in its intensity. Mags began to feel his head hurting, a low muffled pain that ran wild through his head. Instinctively he covered his ears, but the howling grew to a sickening orchestra as one by one the other five wolves joined the chorus, their heads thrown back as they sang to the darkening sky.

"Fuck!" Mags screamed, clasping his hands over his ears. The pain penetrated his brain, eating into it like a hot knife. He managed to look around, and saw with no surprise that his entire army now fought wildly and with pure desperation to block the haunting noise. He saw soldiers writhing on the bloodied battlefield, hands clamped defensively over their ears in a vain attempt to shield the pain. Mags fell heavily forward, his face slamming into the muddy ground. The haunting melody continued to pick up intensity, the sound penetrating every corner of his mind. He began to scream, aware that his brain was sure to explode, madness now gripped him with its mighty grip as the crescendo heightened. Dark blood began to run from his ears, the liquid snaking through his clamped hands like a broken river. He screamed hard, unable to take the pain any longer. As he did he took in a mouthful of mud, the cold wet soil clogging his mouth. Violently he began to vomit, losing control of his body as waves of nausea took control of him. The sharp cold fingers of death began to wrap around his as he lay helplessly on the dirty battlefield. Mags knew he couldn't fight any longer, his body wracked with pain like he had never known. Death would come as a welcome release. Blackness began to cover his vision, creeping like a shroud through his mind. As the pain intensified further, Mags began to slip away, into a world of darkness where only black shadows crept across him like waves until he willingly gave into their embrace.

"In there, you silly cunt."

"Where?"

"There, what are you totally fucking stupid?" Boris tore into Slater with his usual enthusiasm, annoyed that Slater seemed unable, or incapable of finding the back road that led to the rear of the White Rooms.

"I've never been round the back before. How the fuck am I supposed to know?" Slater protested angrily.

"Use your fucking loaf, man. What the fuck does it take to get in the police force these days?"

"Piss off. I've had about enough of you and your fucking moaning." Slater could feel the rage welling inside him again. How he hated this man. Slater wasn't a fighter, never had been. But Boris the blade stirred an emotion in him, a dormant prime evil urge. As he steered the Mondeo cautiously down a dark narrow alleyway, he finally understood after years on the job, just why otherwise rational sane people were driven to acts of mindless violence. He thought back to some of the cases he had worked, murders that had shocked and sickened him. With a tinge of self shame he realised that he had been overly hard at times with suspects who had killed out of the sheer weight of pressure, nagging wives, blackmailing business partners, whatever the reason, he had judged them long before any trial had. Right now he could happily murder his passenger, no guilt, no remorse, no cares at all. The idea scared him, yet somehow it soothed him and instilled a sense of courage he doubted he had ever experienced. Without warning he stood on the brake pedal, hard. Boris once again flew forwards, crashing noisily into the windscreen. Before he could gain any composure, Slater grabbed the desert eagle from his hands. Boris' eyes widened in shock, but Slater's clenched fist caught him square in the face, sending him reeling again, this time clumsily into the foot well. Boris recovered instantly, reflexes now primed for a murderous counter attack.

"Try it!" Slater levelled the desert eagle at Boris, who saw to his amazement that the barrel now stood only two inches from his face.

"You haven't got the fucking bollocks," Boris taunted.

"Really? Think about it for a second meathead. Right now the city looks like a fucking war zone, bodies everywhere. Do you think the police are really going to pin one more on me?" Slater managed to grin as he finished.

"Anyway, do you really think too many man hours will be spent finding the killer of Boris Hunter, the famous 'Boris the blade'?" he added.

"You fucking daren't." Boris looked a little unsure of himself as he spoke, something Andy Slater wasn't long in noticing.

"You keep thinking that, Boris, then when I blow your thick head off, it will come as a nice surprise, an early Christmas present." Slater knew he had the upper hand, and revelled in his torment.

"So, the way I see it, Boris, at the moment you're fucked."

"Put the gun down, Slater. Fight me like a man," Boris said.

"Like a man? Fuck, that's a bit rich. Fight you fair and square you mean, like those skinheads back there?"

"They murdered one of my men, in cold blood. They deserved to die, Slater."

"Did they?"

"Yeah they did." Boris held Slater's eyes, seeing a powerful force behind them. Once again he raised Slater another notch in his estimation.

"Right then, get out. We'll do it man to man, fair and square. Think you can do that Boris, or will you be needing the gun?" Slater lowered the weapon, expecting Boris to begin tearing him apart with his bare hands. Instead Boris shot him a quizzical look, almost amazed at Slater's actions.

"Let's do it then," Boris said getting out of the car. A thin smile crossed his lips. He knew he was going to destroy Slater with ease. But another thought struck him, a surprising idea. Andy Slater would make a great member of the pack.

"Too bad you're a copper, Slater, too bad indeed."

The Calibra wheel spun angrily into the reception area, scattering two drunks. One had a makeshift bandage wrapped around a bloody head wound. The bandage fell off as he dived for cover amongst some parked cars. Darryl leapt from the Calibra, and hit the doors of the casualty department like a hurricane. Two nurses seated at the reception nearly fainted with fright as he came flying in, toppling an old tramp who was busy urinating against a hot drinks machine.

"I need help, quick," he panted.

"You'll have to wait in line, young man." One of the nurses, a plump overweight woman with a bad complexion spoke, barely acknowledging his presence, even though she was slightly annoyed at his dramatic entrance.

"No, I need some help now, you miserable old cunt. Now!"

"Excuse me, young man, if you can't be civil I'm afraid you'll have to leave." The plump nurse had already pushed the silent alarm button situated under the counter. Violent drunks she knew, called for the security guards.

They would be here soon to remove the abusive man. She dismissed him and went back to reading her Woman's Own magazine, where Brad and Jennifer were talking babies.

"Fucking hell, there's a man dying out there. Get me a doctor." Darryl looked at the plastic nametag pinned to the huge bloated breast of the plump nurse. He read that she was a staff nurse, and her name was Rosemary. He tried a different approach.

"Look, Rosemary, I'm sorry about that, but I need some help," he said. Rosemary didn't even look up from her magazine. Suddenly two security guards came shuffling down the corridor. The taller of the two, stood about six feet four inches and resembled a twig. His companion was much smaller, a ruddy complexion man who carried a huge swollen gut. Warily they approached him, and Darryl saw out of the corner of his eye Rosemary give them a nod.

"You have to leave, mate," the taller security guard said. Darryl read their identification badges. The fat man's name was Dave, and his taller friend was Vernon.

"Listen to me, you fucking retards, fuck off now while you still can."

"I don't like his tone one bit, Vern, do you?"

"No I don't, Dave. I'm not happy at all." Vernon threw Rosemary a quick knowing smile. Darryl wondered if he was banging her. Probably they were used to ejecting countless drunks on a Saturday night after the pubs were closed. Darryl looked through the glass foyer doors, wondering how Mark was holding up. He figured that probably he wasn't doing so well. Time was short, and Dave and big Vernon would have to find out the hard way that he wasn't your typical Saturday night drunk.

"Lads, last chance. Go away," Darryl warned. Vernon smiled, before winking cockily at the adoring Rosemary. Dave made the first move, his huge gut heaving as he clumsily lunged forward. With the grace of a cheetah, and the speed of a striking cobra, Darryl pivoted on his right leg. In an instant his left foot caught Dave square in the face. Dave was asleep long before he hit the floor. Vernon's smile evaporated. He contemplated simply running off, but knew Rosemary had him down as her knight in shining armour. As Darryl advanced on him, his bowels loosened and a thin hot stream of warmth ran down the back of his trousers. In a futile gesture he threw his hands out to push Darryl away, but like a bolt of thunder Darryl unleashed a wicked short chopping left hook. Two of Vernon's front teeth spun through the air as he fell. They landed on Rosemary's magazine, leaving a thin smear of Vernon's blood spread across the Brad and Jennifer article. Rosemary watched open-mouthed as Vernon fell like a chopped tree. Her surprise gave way to concern as she watched her knight in shining armour fall, and then only disgust as she first saw, and then smelt the foul liquid that had escaped down Vernon's trouser leg. Calmly Darryl walked back to the reception.

"Now then, Rosemary, a doctor if you will," he said. Rosemary leapt from her chair, her fat buttocks wobbled as she disappeared through a door marked 'staff only'. Within seconds she returned, ashen faced with a doctor, a small Asian man with thick glasses.

"Out here," Darryl said already heading for the foyer doors.

Boris wanted to smile as Slater circled him. What was Slater doing? Boris thought he looked like a turn of the century prizefighter with his fist held out in front of him. Lazily Boris threw out a long left jab. Slater blocked it easily, and countered with a stiff jab of his own. It missed Boris by nearly a foot. Again he curbed the urge to smile. He really didn't want to taunt Slater at all. He admired his guts and didn't want to belittle him for his lack of fighting skill. Boris threw another lazy jab, trying to put some realism into the fight. Suddenly Slater rolled under it and unleashed a shocking right uppercut. Panic alarms went off in his head as Boris knew he wouldn't be able to avoid the blow. The punch exploded under his chin, sending an orchestra of pain through his head. White lights danced in front of his eyes, and with an overwhelming sense of embarrassment, Boris crumpled backwards to the ground.

"Cunt!" he swore, shaking his head. Clumsily he climbed to his feet, aware that Slater had really come to fight. Even as brightly coloured stars danced across his vision, Boris made a mental note to raise Andy Slater another notch in his estimation. With his head clear, Boris decided to bring about an early conclusion to the fight. Slater advanced, now fuelled with confidence. Suddenly two lightening fast jabs shook his head back. Before he could even think about ducking and clearing the grogginess from his brain, a clumping right hand smashed into the side of his face. Slater fell like a limp corpse, landing awkwardly in a heap on the frozen road. Darkness washed over him like a shroud. For the moment he no longer cared about anything as his mind slipped away into a peaceful deep sleep. Boris stood back and admired his handy work, pleased at the swift execution, but also praying Slater wasn't badly hurt. Boris knew his own capabilities. Indeed he had killed men with a single punch before. He knelt down to examine his stricken opponent, and noticed the already huge swelling on the left side of his face.

"A wolf if ever there was one," he said quietly. Boris Hunter was a hard man, a feared individual. He liked things that way. Nobody took liberties with him. But he was also a fair man too, honest. He watched Slater sleeping peacefully, and secretly admired him. Before this night only one man had ever put him on the floor. That had been a mad Irishman who had gone berserk in one of their clubs. Mags and the team had been driving about in the van on that particular night when a distress call went out. They had been there in five minutes flat. Boris and Mags had gone into the club first, only to find the biggest Irishman they had ever seen bowling the doormen over like skittles.

They had tried to take the huge bastard down with a couple of bar stools, but even as they broke over his back he barely acknowledged any discomfort. The Irishman had turned round and crashed a huge right hand on Boris' chin, sending him flying over a table. Mags kicked him hard between the legs, but even he had lost his nerve when the crazy bastard had laughed back at him.

Clambering up from the floor, Boris had launched a titanic right hand that landed squarely on the Irishman's right temple. With relief he watched as the huge fellow wobbled before he finally, and thankfully slumped unconscious to the floor. It had been the best, and most desperate punch he had ever thrown. The impact had fractured the Irishman's skull, but in turn he had broken twelve bones in his right hand and spent eight weeks wearing a plaster cast. Now as he knelt over the body of Andy Slater, he realised that he held a lot of respect for the man. He willingly admitted that Slater had caught him fair and square, and dropped him on his backside. Boris wasn't a boastful person, but he did know there wouldn't be many people who would ever manage to do the same.

"Wake up Slater," he said, shaking him. "Come on, mate, wakey, wakey." Boris gave him a couple of heavy slaps, mindful of the growing swelling on his face. Andy Slater coughed heavily and began to stir. His eyes still slightly glazed, half opened. A slight groan escaped him as he tried to lift his head. He still looked dazed and confused as he peered up at Boris.

"Did I win?" he asked hopefully.

"No, it was a draw," Boris replied, helping Slater into a sitting position.

"Fuck, my head hurts," Slater said, gently rubbing the dark red bump that sat proudly on his left cheek.

"You'll live, don't worry." Boris extended his left hand, and Slater reached out and took it. In one steady movement he pulled Slater to his feet. Oddly he noticed how slight Slater was. Probably only about eleven, maybe twelve stone. Slater wasn't a big man by any means, and that only impressed Boris even more. Slater punched like a heavyweight.

Mags felt cold, deathly cold. He could no longer feel any thing below his chest, which came as a welcome relief, as the pain in his stomach had been unbelievable.

"Finish me, Ray," he said weakly.

"When I'm ready, Magnus, when I'm ready. You need to suffer a bit more yet."

"Sick man. You're a sick fucking man," Mags croaked. Flecks of blood left his mouth as he spoke. He spared a fragile laugh, coughing a dark liquid as he did so.

"What's so fucking funny?" Ray snapped, annoyed.

"You, Ray. You want me to suffer, but I can't feel a thing." Weakly Mags lifted his right hand, and extended his middle finger. A defiant grin crossed his lips. Ray Callard didn't smile. Even in death Mags was taunting him. It wouldn't do.

"Smile at this, Magnus, if you can." Ray sat the barrel of the rifle against Mags' left thigh. He squeezed the trigger and a single round exploded through Mags' femur, shattering the bone and destroying flesh and muscle as it cut a deadly path. Mags jumped violently, his back arching, his mouth fixed in a silent scream.

"Hurt, Mags?" Ray asked, now amused. A small laugh escaped him as Mags' body spasmed violently as fresh dark blood pumped madly from the fresh wound.

"Not so fucking funny now, is it?"

"You alright, Slater?" Boris asked, steadying his still groggy opponent.

"Yeah, I'm okay. What the fuck did you hit me with?"

"You did okay, Slater, for a fucking slag copper anyway." Boris threw him a smile, and was glad to see Slater return the gesture.

"Come on, let's go and have a drink."

"Good idea. I'll have a brandy," Slater said, fumbling for the car keys wedged in his trouser pocket.

"You alright to drive?" Boris asked.

"How far is it?"

"About twenty yards down the road."

"I'll manage," Slater told him, as he finally produced his keys. A loud bang shattered the quiet night. Instinctively Slater and Boris both scrambled behind the Mondeo.

"What the fuck?" Slater said, scanning the shadows of the road ahead.

"Gunfire, definitely gunfire," Boris whispered.

"Where from?"

"Fuck! Mags." Boris bolted from the safety of the Mondeo. Slater watched him sprint away, unsure of what to do.

"Boris, Boris!" he called. But Boris continued running either unaware, or not interested in Slater's call.

"Fuck it!" he swore. He walked to the driver's side of the Mondeo, and saw the desert eagle sitting on the dashboard where he had left it. He eyed the weapon, fighting the urge to pick it up and run after Boris. He couldn't do it. He was a policeman after all. Besides, he knew that the gun was responsible for recent murders, and he didn't want any part of it. A cold icy chill ran down his spine, and his mind raced as he thought of Killian. What would his boss have done? Slater thought about it briefly, and decided Killian would have phoned for back up. He definitely wouldn't have picked up the gun.

"And it cost him his life," Slater whispered.

"Oh fuck it," he said, leaning into the Mondeo. He snatched the desert eagle off of the dash, and began running up the darkened road, his lungs burning under the exertion. Andy Slater promised himself that he was going to quit smoking, one way or the other.

Boris turned the darkened corner, and found himself at the entrance of the White Rooms' car park. His blood chilled when he saw Ray Callard's Jaguar parked in the darkness. He prayed he wasn't too late. The rear fire doors were open, and the bright dance floor lights bathed the car park. Boris stopped in his tracks, fear freezing him like a statue. Through the open doors, Boris saw Ray Callard kneeling over a body. He could clearly see the darkening puddles of blood pooling on the dance floor. He knew the body was Mags'. Never before had he been so scared, or so angry. His brain became numb; confusion threaded through his mind like dark fingers. He knew at least, that Mags was already dead. But then, Mags was his greatest friend, and he was bound by a code, a law built on love and honour. The primitive urges rooted deep in his very genes took over. Fuelled by adrenaline and deep hate he began to run. Ray Callard had plenty of time, ample warning. As he toyed with what remained of Mags, heavy footfalls broke his attention. He turned quickly, eyes fixed on the figure now sprinting across the car park.

"Well I never. Boris the blade." He lined the Kalashnikov's sights calmly on Boris, carefully sighting his chest. Boris picked up speed, his massive frame building momentum as he crashed through the half open fire doors.

"Die, you motherfucker!" he screamed. Suddenly he cartwheeled through the air, his body slamming into the floor like a slab of raw meat. Unaware of the gaping hole in the right side of his chest, he vainly tried to get to his feet. Like a beaten boxer, he fell backwards, landing awkwardly on his left side.

"Oh dear God, I've waited so long for this," Ray Callard gloated, pacing menacingly towards Boris.

"Do you know, Boris, ever since I first met you I've wanted to kill you."

"Fuck yourself, Ray. You're a worthless piece of shit." Despite the pain, Boris defiantly spat the words out, blood spraying from his lips.

"Oh my! I'm gonna get off on this." Ray levelled the rifle only inches from Boris' head, let out a dry demented laugh and pulled the trigger.

O'Neil was asleep when the telephone on his desk noisily disturbed his deprived rest. He came back from deep sleep too quickly, arriving in the conscious world with a start. Groggily he clambered for the telephone, knocking over a cold cup of coffee.

"What?" he snapped angrily.

"Sir, it's Jenny McAllister in the control room.

"And?"

"A call just came in sir. Gunshots reported from the White Rooms club. Thought you'd want to know, sir."

"Get me a car ready Jenny. I'll be down in one minute." O'Neil slammed the phone down, and immediately sprang from his seat, cursing the stiffness in his lower back. He'd spent too long lately sleeping at his desk, and his tired body was now paying the grim price. O'Neil didn't honestly think things were about to get much better either. Cambridge city was rivalling down town Los Angeles for murders lately. As he bolted out of his office, the image of a nice comfortable bed seemed little more than a distant dream.

Impatiently Darryl paced back and forth, nervously waiting for some sort of news. Dave the security guard sat impassively on a chair a few feet away, a terrified look on his chubby face.

"You don't have to baby-sit me," Darryl said, throwing him a withering look.

"They told me I've got to keep an eye on you," Dave replied almost apologetically.

"I'm not gonna run amok with a machine gun, you divvy shit!"

"Please. Don't hit me." Dave shrunk back in his seat, fear escaping him like a foul scent. Darryl hesitated, realising the situation wasn't the fat guard's fault. For a second he felt ashamed. After all the fat pile of shit cowering in front of him was only doing his job, following orders from equally inept people, like Rosemary. Out of the corner of his eye, Darryl caught the now silent bloated nurse watching him.

"Fatty, what's the word on my fucking mate?" he bellowed. She sat dumbstruck with fear, her large mouth hung open. Disgustedly Darryl watched as a thin stream of saliva fell from her lips, before pooling on her magazine.

"Are you deaf as well as fucking ugly?" he asked advancing on her. She moved so fast that her cheeks rippled, the rolls of excess flesh rolling madly. Rosemary disappeared into the room behind her, the door literally crashed off its hinges as she burst through.

"Fucking fat bitch," Darryl said to himself. Laughter caught his attention, and the sight of big Dave the security guard chuckling even raised a smile on his own face.

Slater couldn't hold his bowels much longer. The fear that ran like a wild demon through his stomach threatened to explode. He turned the corner, almost falling headfirst over the low brick wall that bordered the White Rooms' car park. The loud explosive bang made him instinctively duck. Through the open doors at the rear of the White Rooms, the bright dance floor lights set a perfect vision as Boris flew through the air, a hole the size of Slater's fist spurting blood and tissue.

Initially Slater couldn't quite believe what he had seen. It couldn't be, could it? He blinked hard, hoping he would wake from this madness, and find his wife asleep next to him. He blinked again, and the horror only intensified as he saw Boris on the floor, vainly trying to get back up. Blood poured from the huge wound like a fountain. Slater felt his bowels protest again, as the icy fingers of fear clenched a vice like grip around his innards. Confusion swirled through his mind. He didn't know what his next move should be. He held the desert eagle in his right hand, a hand he saw embarrassingly that would not stop shaking. He had just seen Boris get a hole blown right through him, and Boris was invincible, wasn't he?

Slater knew that under normal circumstances Boris would be his mortal enemy, but he had spent time with him, and although he didn't for one minute condone his methods, he respected him greatly. Deep down, Slater knew that the respect was born out of something else, something he didn't care to admit.

In Boris he saw qualities he didn't possess; courage, true loyalty to his fellow man, and most of all belief in what he was doing. The last few years as a copper had driven any belief out of him. Once he had been keen, fresh and ready to take on the world. He knew those days were gone, dead.

Slater's thoughts escaped to Killian, and he realised anything he had left, any enthusiasm, any lingering belief in a cause died along with him. The menacing figure now standing over Boris, loomed clearly into view. The sight of Ray Callard came as no surprise. It merely intensified his anguish.

Slowly Callard raised the barrel of a huge weapon. Slater had no idea what type or make it was. In slow motion the gun travelled a path along Boris' stricken body, before stopping finally inches from his face. Slater knew Boris was about to die, and cursed himself hatefully for not acting, for at least doing something. The desert eagle shook madly in his hand. He knew what he should do with it, but defeat stabbed him through the heart when he admitted dejectedly that he neither had the nerve, or the conviction to use it. Under a freezing winter sky, huddled against a brick wall under the cover of darkness, Andrew Slater finally succumbed to the demons of his own shortcomings and began to cry like a child.

Ray Callard's face contorted in shock, all traces of the cruel smile evaporated as the Kalashnikov let out a single dull click. He squeezed the trigger again, this time urgently. Click! With pure disbelief he realised he was out of ammunition. Dry hoarse laughter from Boris brought a contorted hateful mask of insanity.

"Thirty rounds dickhead, thirty rounds. Made in Russia, regarded as the most reliable assault weapon in the world, deadly accurate, but it needs bullets you muppet." Boris blew a heavy stream of blood as he broke into a bellow of laughter. Ray regarded him with a twisted baleful glare. He brought the butt of the weapon down hard, and gave a satisfied grunt as he heard the loud cracking sound as Boris' ribs broke on his right side.

"Not so fucking funny now is it, you cunt?" he growled, baring his teeth. Boris curled into a ball, clutching his ribs as waves of agony crashed through him. He burst into a fit of coughing, spraying blood in all directions as his body vainly tried to reject the build up of internal bleeding.

"You fucking dumb shits never learn, do you?" Ray said, raising the rifle again. "I might be out of bullets, but you're still gonna die." As he began to bring the rifle butt down into Boris' face, movement caught his eye. Ray Callard suddenly forgot all thoughts of murder, frozen in place he stared in amazement and total disbelief as a figure burst through the open doors.

Slater shook heavily, the sobs racking his entire body. Shame cut him apart with a cruel sharp deadly blade. Boris was a dead man, and all he could do was stand and watch, hidden in the shadows. With self-loathing he made himself face the final act, forced himself to watch the closing scene on another mans life. Click! Slater wiped tears from his eyes. Click! The heavy dull echo came from the weapon Callard now held. Slater knew enough to understand what it meant. The relief hit him hard. He wouldn't have to watch Boris have his head blown into pieces. He would ring for an ambulance. That was the answer. They could save him; he was still moving. Slater began fumbling frantically inside his trouser pocket. His mobile wasn't there. Desperately he began searching his other pockets, praying he had merely misplaced it. He began to panic as he realised he had either lost it, or forgotten it.

"Fuck, fuck, fuck!" he cursed. Suddenly a sickening thud echoed from the White Rooms. Boris writhed on the floor, clutching his ribs. Ray Callard stood over him, the weapon raised over Boris' head. When death beckons it takes many forms. Boris wouldn't die at the mercy of a bullet. He would meet his end at the hands of a lunatic, bludgeoned to death without mercy, helpless as the very lifeblood drained from him. Time froze. Everything stopped, deathly still except the cold biting winters chill, whose icy finger reached and probed every corner of Andy Slater's mind. The deathly chill ran through his head, its dark voice taunting him, eating his sanity like a darkened spirit.

"Run, run for your life," it taunted.

"No, I can't," he sobbed.

"Leave him, fuck him," the voice demanded.

"He'll die. I can't leave him."

"Fuck him, he's a no good, worthless cunt."

"No!"

"Fuck him, let him die."

"NO!" Slater snapped. The conflict fell from his mind, discarded back to its dark lair as he leapt over the wall, bounding across the frozen car park. The desert eagle held out in front of him, Slater headed for the White Rooms. Exhilaration coursed through his veins, a warmth he couldn't explain, a strength he had never known. With every purposeful stride, Andy Slater began to feel a metamorphosis occurring. He was being reborn.

"No, Ray!" Slater shouted, storming into the brightness. Ray stood over

Boris, still gripped by amazement.

"Put the gun down, Ray."

"Slater, you fucking wet bastard," Ray regarded him with amusement, barely able to conceal his contempt.

"Put it down, Ray."

"Or what, Andy, or what?"

"Just drop it."

"You gonna shoot me, Andy?"

"If I have to, yeah I will."

"You haven't got the fucking balls you stupid fucking wimp," Ray laughed, dismissing Slater with a contemptuous grin.

"Fucking try me, Ray, you sick fuck."

"Listen, Andy, let's be fucking honest shall we? Without Killian you are, well basically you ain't shit. I enjoyed doing him you know, gave me a lot of fucking satisfaction. I fucking hated the wanker. I'm glad I got to kill him, I really am." Ray stretched his grin even further, making sure Slater was left in no doubt that he had indeed enjoyed taking Killian's life.

"You sick cunt, Ray, I fucking pity you, I really feel fucking sorry for you," Slater said, disgustedly.

"Don't pity me Andy, save it. Mind you, if I were you I'd say a prayer for your friends here. They fucking need all the help they can get."

"Fuck yourself, Ray. Put the gun down, I'm warning you." Slater's strength multiplied under his renewed sense of belief. Ray Callard thought for a second that something danced behind Slater's eyes, a hidden power he had never seen before. It made him uneasy. If only briefly he lost his composure.

"Last chance, Ray, last chance," Slater said, his voice strong, his eyes firm.

"Go away." Ray laughed his lunatic howl, banishing Slater to the corner of his mind. He knew he couldn't possibly pull the trigger. It was Andy Slater after all. Ray laughed again, and then began to bring the rifle butt down with deadly intention.

"Ray. NO!" Slater cried. Something from deep within summoned the strength to pull the trigger. The desert eagle kicked with intense power, spewing its deadly cargo. The round impacted high, tearing a horrific path through the air, before tearing the left side of Ray Callard's throat away. Arcs of fresh warm blood jetted through the air, pulsing indiscriminate patterns of dark blood across the dance floor. Ray recoiled, surprise the only emotion displayed across his face. He dropped the Kalashnikov, staggering wildly as his hands vainly tried to stem the hopeless and utterly unstoppable flow of blood. Silence descended as Slater watched Ray stagger wildly, the only sound the pitter patter as blood rained down onto the floor. Ray fought to speak, but his larynx now lay somewhere behind him, deposited, smashed beyond hope with other lumps of shredded flesh. Slater pulled the trigger again, and a second shell hit Ray high on the forehead. Slater looked away in revulsion as the high calibre round brought unbelievable destruction. Ray Callard's frontal lobe exploded in a cloud of smashed bone and darkened tissue. The round knew no distinction between life and death, and carried on its murderous journey, spinning madly as it destroyed every piece of brain tissue in its path. When Slater found the strength to look again, Ray Callard's body lay sprawled across the floor. His reign of terror had ended, but Slater knew his legacy had only just begun. Before him lay the still bodies of Magnus Vandersar and Boris Hunter.

"Well done, Slater," Boris croaked, his voice barely audible.

"Boris, I thought you were dead." Slater scrambled to his aid, the relief flooding over him.

"Mags, what about Mags?" Boris managed. Slater looked over at Mags, now totally still.

"I don't know, mate. Look, I've got to get you help. Shit, you've lost too much blood." The dark pool continued to spread,. Slater didn't believe any man could lose so much blood and still be alive.

"I'll get help, Boris, don't…" He paused mid-sentence, cocking his head at a familiar sound.

"Sirens. Help is on its way, Boris," Slater exclaimed.

"So are the police, Slater. Give me the gun."

"Why? I killed him, I'll tell the truth, Boris, I had no choice."

"Doesn't matter, they'll crucify you." Boris began coughing again, spitting blood in the process.

"Give me the gun," Boris said, holding out his hand. Slater grimaced at the sight of the blood-drenched hand, and once again the gravity of Boris' injuries hit him.

"The gun, Slater," Boris managed, clutching his gaping wound.

"But…" Slater began to protest, but Boris cut him off angrily.

"The gun, give me the fucking gun!"

"Boris, I can't let you take the rap for it." Slater became overwhelmed with respect. Unashamedly he let tears course down his weary face.

"Do it, Slater, think of your wife."

"I owe you, I won't forget." Slater reluctantly handed Boris the gun. Once again his hand had begun its uncontrollable shake.

"Now get the fuck out of here," Boris said. His eyes locked Slater's, and the bond of mutual respect was forged forever.

"Thanks," Slater whispered.

"Fuck off, Slater, go now," Boris replied, his own voice now hushed. Slater listened to the sound of the approaching sirens, now very close. He nodded, a final gesture to Boris. He doubted very much he'd ever see him, or Mags again. Boris mustered every last ounce of strength his frail body still held. Slowly he pulled himself up to a near sitting position. He pointed the desert eagle at Ray Callard's ruined corpse.

"Woe to the vanquished," he whispered, and emptied the last of the magazine into the dead flesh of Ray Callard's body. Slater was already running across the car park when he heard the shots ring out. He wanted to go back, compelled by something he didn't understand, something he had never really known. Loyalty. As he hurdled the brick wall and headed down the dark cold road towards his car, Slater realised why Boris had fired the weapon. Now he had powder traces etched into his hand. When the forensic teams sorted this mess out, there would be little doubt as to who finally killed Ray Callard. Boris the blade would take the fall.

Tears streamed down his cheeks as he reached his car, the biting cold freezing them to his face. As he sat behind the wheel of the Mondeo, Slater knew now what respect and loyalty meant. He should have driven off into the night, forgotten the whole episode and lived his life, in peace. As Slater stepped out once more into the freezing night, he knew he couldn't forget what had happened. Even as a procession of police vehicles sped past him, he continued to walk back to the White Rooms. A police land cruiser swept by, the passenger waved, and Slater realised he knew the man, a sergeant who had worked at Parkside for several years. He stared back blankly, declining to return the gesture. He knew now finally, that he had no affinity with these people at all. His people needed his help, and if that meant going down with a sinking ship, then so be it.

"How is he?" Darryl asked, jumping to his feet as an overly serious doctor approached.

"Well he's very poorly."

"No fucking shit, doctor. You spent seven years at medical school to tell me that?" Darryl hissed the words out, leaving the diminutive doctor no option but to hit Darryl with the hard truth.

"He's being prepped for surgery now. I can't say how this is going to turn out for him."

"What are the odds, fifty-fifty?"

"If I were your friend right now I'd be happy with fifty-fifty. His chances are not that good." The words came out as a crushing weight. Darryl swayed and thought he was going to collapse.

"Yeah, but you can save him, right?"

"Do you have a God, my friend?" the doctor asked sombrely.

"Yeah, I think I do, why?"

"Well now is a good time to pray to him."

"That bad eh?" Darryl swayed again, and felt his legs tremble.

"Listen, can I speak to him, just for a bit. Please."

"One minute, no more," the doctor said, before leading Darryl through a series of corridors. They came to a room, and Darryl read the sign above the door. 'Theatre three'. He entered, and the sanitised smell assaulted his nostrils. Several nurses were busily milling around, carrying trays of sterilised instruments. There across the room he saw Mark laid out on a trolley. He was covered with a green gown, and Darryl almost laughed at the sight because the gown didn't fit, but thought better of the idea.

"Hey, how you feeling, mate?" he asked as he approached. Mark tilted his head, and a broad smile crossed his face as he saw Darryl approaching. He tried to speak, but winced in pain.

"Doesn't matter, don't worry," Darryl said, reaching for Mark's hand. He gave it a tender squeeze and watched helplessly as Mark began to cry.

"Easy mate, come on, don't worry," he said reassuringly. "Listen, when this is over you've got to start thinking about eating salads you greedy fat fuck." Darryl patted Mark's protruding stomach gently, and felt slightly better when Mark managed a smile.

"That a boy," he said. When two nurses came with an orderly to take Mark away, Darryl gave his hand one last long lingering squeeze. From his position on the trolley, Mark spared one last frightened look, before he was wheeled away. Darryl watched him go, keeping a firm smile etched across his face until he was gone. Then Darryl let the smile disappear, and he wondered if he would ever see his friend again.

O'Neil watched as the two paramedics gently loaded Boris into the back of the ambulance. He shook his head at the sight, wishing he didn't have to keep seeing such carnage. Lately he'd seen too much, way too much. The body of Magnus Vandersar had already been taken away, with him barely clinging to a thread of life. A forensic photographer now busily took photographs of Ray Callard, or at least what remained of Ray Callard. O'Neil had seen some horrific sights over the last week, and he knew when the truth came out, Ray would be held responsible for most of them. A serving police officer, allowed to rape and murder, brutally murder while on duty. O'Neil knew his career prospects were now dead. He wondered if he would even get to keep his job after the enquiry, and he didn't doubt for a second that there would be an enquiry, a big and very public enquiry. Early retirement now seemed an attractive option. The sight of Ray Callard, almost headless, didn't fill him with horror, merely self-loathing. How had he not known? Why did he not see? Those questions would haunt him for the rest of his days, long after the enquiry had dished out its findings. Andy Slater stood watching the photographer take pictures, and O'Neil thought he looked different now, almost older. There was a look behind those eyes that he had never noticed before, a hardness, a cold baleful stare.

"Andy, are you okay?" he said, walking over. Slater turned and watched him approach, O'Neil felt a sudden chill as those eyes locked onto him, almost like a predator regarding its prey.

"Are you okay, Andy?"

"I'm fine, sir, just fine."

"Look, I owe you an apology. You were right, about Ray."

"You owe me nothing, sir. I take no satisfaction from being proved right. Look at the cost." Slater's voice trembled as he spoke.

"That's true Andy, and of course jobs will go over all this." O'Neil gave a long defeated sigh. Slater eyed him for a second, almost feeling pity. He knew O'Neil was of course referring to himself. He didn't particularly like him, but Slater understood that O'Neil wasn't to blame for anything. The police internal enquiry however would need its customary sacrificial lamb, and O'Neil was it.

"I want you to have this, sir," Slater said, handing him a small leather wallet. O'Neil took it and opened it. Inside he saw Slater's warrant card.

"What's this for?" he asked, puzzled.

"I'm out, that's it, sir."

"But why, Andy?"

"I'm sick of it all; I've had enough of this shit."

"Are you sure about this, Andy?" O'Neil asked, still shocked.

"Sir, I've never been so sure about anything in my life," Slater replied. He gave O'Neil a friendly smile, before heading through the open doors and out into the cold night. He paused halfway across the car park, before looking back at O'Neil.

"Sir, good luck," he said.

O'Neil smiled at him, still holding the warrant card in his hands numbly. Slater nodded before walking off into the night, suddenly free again for the first time in a long while.

Chapter Eleven

After the storm

Rosemary let out a long heavy sigh, her robust breasts wobbling under the exertion.

"He needs rest, stop making him laugh please," she said, her face reddening as she spoke.

"Come on, Rosemary, have a heart. He loves it, don't you mate?" Darryl patted Mark heavily on the shoulder, and suddenly the room erupted in laughter as Mark winced under a fresh wave of pain.

"You poor thing. I don't envy you one bit with friends like this lot." Rosemary managed a rare smile, finding Mark's ceaseless harassment strangely amusing. She reminded herself that for the last two weeks he had laid in his bed constantly whining, and eating. In fact she had never seen anyone eat on such a scale.

"I think it's time to leave, lads," Mags said from his position by the window. "Give us a push Darryl," he said, taking the brake off of his wheelchair. Mags winced as he moved, well aware that his miraculous recovery was still anything but complete. Darryl eased the chair forward, clumsily bumping into Mark's bed. Mags groaned, and fresh laughter echoed the small room.

"Bastards!" Mags said, forcing himself to smile.

"Thanks for coming then, lads," Mark said, already devouring an entire bowl of fruit Boris had brought in for him.

"Hurry up and get better, you lazy fucker," Boris quipped, opening the door for Mags and Darryl.

"Look after him Rosemary. Make sure he gets his share of bed baths and all that," Mags called as Darryl wheeled him out into the corridor.

"If there's a God, he'll make him better soon. He'll eat us out of food by the end of the week." Rosemary rolled her eyes as she spoke. Mags, Darryl and Boris all grinned, and really did pity the poor woman. They watched her head off along the corridor, laughing like children as her fat-laden body quivered.

"Fucking hell, she's one hell of a woman," Darryl remarked.

"Ain't she just!" Boris agreed, screwing his face up.

"Could you fuck that, Mags?" Darryl asked, grinning like a child. Mags gave him a disgusted look.

"Yeah, with a big hammer I could."

"Where to, my physically challenged friends?" Mohamed laughed as Darryl and Boris struggled to lift Mags into the back of his cab. Mohamed took extra pleasure in the fact that Boris especially was struggling, his whole upper body heavily strapped to protect his heavy wounds, and broken ribs.

"I won't always be crippled, Mo," Boris warned, throwing him a dark look.

"Oh dear," Mohamed replied, still sporting his massive grin. "You know, I've always said you guys are a walking fuck up. I still stand by that belief." Mohamed positively cracked up, shaking under the weight of his heavy laughter. When he'd finished, he turned and saw the three very unhappy men sitting in silence, their eyes focused entirely on him. Darryl passed him a crumpled piece of paper, the edges frayed and yellowed. Mohamed studied the address written on the paper before throwing it onto the empty seat beside him.

"I know that address," he said happily.

"Let's go then," Mags ordered, grimacing uncomfortably from his seat behind.

"Okey dokey, boss." Mohamed threw the cab into first gear, eyeing his side mirror as he pulled out into the heavy traffic milling past Addenbrookes hospital. He didn't see Darryl reaching over,. The first he knew was when Darryl flicked his ear sending a stinging pain reverberating through his head.

"Fuck! That hurt," Mohamed screamed, almost colliding with an oncoming ambulance. When he looked back in his rear view mirror, all he saw was three cheeky grins staring back at him.

Slater looked on in dismay. How the hell had he allowed his garden to get in such a state? Where would he start? Then a thought struck him. He didn't actually know anything about gardening.

"Bollocks to it," he said, throwing his spade onto an overgrown patch of weeds. Reaching into his jacket pocket, he produced a near empty packet of Marlboro's. Greedily he fished one out and lit it.

"I thought you were going to quit?"

"Angie, sorry honey I didn't see you there."

"I crept up on you. Here I brought you this." She passed him a steaming cup of tea. He took it readily, welcoming some relief from the biting cold.

"You're lost aren't you?" Angie wrapped her arm around his waist as she spoke.

"Yeah, I guess I am, babe," he replied, before sipping some tea.

"Are you sure you did the right thing?"

"What the police? I've got no regrets, Angie. None."

"Sure?" she said, stroking his waist.

"Positive. Time to move on, sweetheart."

"What are you going to do?" she asked, watching him intently. He took a deep draw on his cigarette, feeling the cold air as it flowed down his throat.

"Dunno, honey, but I'll tell you this much, I don't rate my chances as a gardener."

"There, you fucking muppet," Boris shouted, pointing at a row of neat terraced houses.

"I can see," Mohamed said, grinning.

"Pull over then, you dizzy fucker," Boris moaned, as Mohamed drove past the address he had been given.

"Sorry, boys," Mohamed said, with his trademark grin in place. He hit the brake hard, sending his three passengers hurtling forward. Before any threats came his way, Mohamed threw the cab into reverse. Mags groaned as pain assaulted his entire body.

"One day, Mo, I'm really going to fucking wipe that smile off your face," he said, rubbing his shoulder.

"Sorry boss," Mohamed replied, still sporting his massive grin.

Andy Slater drained his cup, relishing the sweat tea as it hit his stomach. The warm feeling lifted him momentarily, on such a cold day.

"Andy, there's someone at the front door," Angie called from the kitchen.

"Get it, will you, babe," he shouted back. Absently he reached for another cigarette, noticing with annoyance that he was almost out. From the house behind him, he heard muffled conversation. Probably her mother he thought, wishing he had another twenty cigarettes.

"Honey, you've got guests," Angie shouted from behind him. Slater drew heavily on his cigarette, blowing a cloud of smoke out into the freezing air.

"Thought you'd of quit by now, policeman." A voice behind him shouted. Slater spun round, the look of surprise on his face instantly turning to a huge grin.

"I'm not a policeman anymore, Vandersar," he said, hurrying through his overgrown garden to greet the three unexpected guests.

"Boris, Darryl. How the fuck are you?" he asked, unable to hide his pleasure. "Angie, throw the kettle on babe," he said, ushering everyone back into the kitchen.

"So how you been?" Mags asked as Darryl wheeled him up to the kitchen table.

"Bored," Slater replied, pulling himself a chair.

"So you really quit the old bill then?" Boris asked.

"Yep, sure did."

"How's it feel then?" Darryl cut in. Slater looked him in the eye, before turning his attention first to Boris and then Mags.

"Feels great. I'd had enough, you know."

"So what now then?" Mags wondered aloud, smiling politely as Angie passed him a hot mug of tea.

"Oh I dunno, I thought about gardening," Slater said with a dry smile.

"Fuck the gardening, Slater, we've come to talk business," Mags said to him.

"Oh?" Angie handed her husband a mug of tea, he took it without breaking away from the conversation.

"You saved our lives, Andy, we owe you," Boris cut in.

"No you don't. You owe me nothing."

"Yes we do," Boris replied, taking a large gulp of tea.

"We do," Mags agreed.

"I think what they're trying to say, Andy, is that, well how do I say this?" Darryl managed, looking embarrassed.

"How would you like to join us?" Mags asked finally.

"You are joking?" Slater asked, almost spilling his tea.

"No we're not joking. In fact we're deadly serious, Andy," Mags said firmly. Slater sat back in his chair, taking the idea in.

"I don't know what to say. Honestly I'm flattered, but I don't think I'm cut out for what you lads do," he said honestly. Mags smiled at him, a reassuring smile that somehow left Slater feeling slightly embarrassed.

"We don't expect you to, Andy," Boris reassured.

"We want a security consultant mate. Somebody who's good with their head, not with their fists," Mags told him.

"So I wouldn't have to be out there on the front line, you know, as a bouncer?"

"No way. Besides, Slater, you ain't good enough." Boris laughed as he spoke, playfully launching a mock punch at Slater.

"Well I'm flattered, lads, honestly I am. Tell you the truth I'd have to speak to Angie."

"No, Andy. You've got to do what you think is best," Angie said, leaning over to kiss his cheek.

"You mean you don't mind?" he asked, surprised at her response.

"I just want you to be happy again, honey, I want us to be happy again," she said.

"But…." He began, but Angie gently pressed a finger to his lips.

"Great, so that's settled then!" Boris exclaimed, holding his hand out. Slowly Slater took it, and the firm warm grip Boris gave him made his mind up.

"Well I guess then, I'm on board." Slater locked eyes with Boris, and knew his decision had been right, that with these men he had found a new direction in his life. Slater didn't know what the future held, and deep down he wondered if he really wanted to know anyway? Mags held out his hand to Slater, who took it in his own.

"Welcome to the Wolfpack, Andy," he said, fixing him with those cool piercing eyes.

"It's an honour," Slater replied, suddenly overwhelmed as the idea scrambled his mind.

"Wolfpack," he whispered. Andy Slater liked it, and no matter what his future held, right now seated here in his kitchen, for the first time in his life, he was a part of something he never before knew existed.

Epilogue

"Hello, my name is Maria Mason. I'm in charge of Jake's case.

"Hi, Magnus Vandersar. Pleased to meet you." Mags regarded Maria, admiring her beautiful little body and endless legs. He frowned at himself. Now was not the time to hit on women. Old habits died hard. Maria led him through a large wooden door, into an expansive playroom brightly lit by a huge bay window. Mags' face contorted at the sight that greeted him. Children ran everywhere, under tables, standing on chairs, everywhere he looked a hyperactive child ran riot.

"Forgive them Mr Vandersar, they're not usually like this," Maria said, smiling at his discomfort.

"You mean they're normally better than this?"

"Oh no, worse. Much worse." As Maria spoke, a small boy, probably about seven years old, leapt off of a table. Mags caught him in mid air.

"Easy superman, you'll hurt yourself," Mags said, gently placing the boy firmly on the ground. He watched amazed as the child climbed back up onto the table. This time he jumped onto a group of girls who were playing with dolls.

"Can I change my mind?" Mags asked.

"Too late," Maria chuckled. "There he is," she said pointing over to the corner of the room. Seated on an old wooden chair, his eyes fixed intently on a television mounted high up on the wall, sat a small boy. Mags felt his whole body loosen and begin to tremble. It was the most beautiful child he had ever seen, his golden curled locks a mirror of Mags' own hair. The boy sat alone, unaffected by the riot that raged all around him.

"Jake, there's someone here I want you to meet," Maria said. Slowly the child turned to face them, his innocence melting Mags' heart. Jake climbed down from the wooden chair and wandered over to them.

"Hello sir," he said, holding out his hand. Mags felt his legs twitching as he knelt down. Gently he took the tiny hand and shook it.

"Are you my daddy?" he asked, his wide blue eyes so penetrating.

"Yes, I am," Mags managed, his voice trembling madly. Emotion took hold of him. The vision of Penny shone out like a beacon from the child before him. Suddenly he could control himself no longer. His head dropped as tears gushed down his cheeks. His whole body shook as a mixture of pain and joy ran through him. Maria quietly backed away, turning her attention to the unruly superman wannabe.

"I'm sorry kid, I lost it there for a second," Mags said, desperately trying to compose himself.

"It's okay, I cry too," Jake told him.

"Big guy like you, nah I don't believe it."

"Sometimes I do, when I miss my mummy," Jake replied, his head bowed. Mags lost his battle with emotion. Pulling the child to him he hugged Jake. Every ounce of pain he had ever known disappeared as the child wrapped his arms round Mags' broad shoulders.

"I'll never let you go again," Mags whispered. Across the room, as a full-scale riot took place, Maria Mason forgot her professional duty. She stood and sobbed as a father and son were finally reunited.

Printed in the United States
22499LVS00006B/248

9 781413 714500